THE LAST DESCENDANT

BY: CLINTON MATHEW

The Last Descendant: The Hidden King

ISBN: 978-0-9990871-1-4

C Mathew Books

Contents

BOOK II

THE HIDDEN KING

Chapter 1: The Depths of Darzomil

Even though the city was engulfed by the darkness of the mountain's caverns, Darzomil was fully alive. Hordes of mountain folk rushed through the weaving dirt paths of the city. Houses, stores, schools; all were composed of the dark stone of the mountain. Traders and merchants were shouting from the front door of their stores, attempting to steer anyone they could toward their goods. The footsteps of the civilians buzzed like bees and the crying of a child couldn't be heard over the clamor of the crowd. Even though the city appeared chaotic, it was a conforming system. Within the anarchy there was order. There was no one unique in the entire city of Darzomil, no one who could separate themselves from all the others around them, save for one. A Descendant of the gods from Aithnen, trapped in the nation in the skies.

Serafine sat at a small, circular, wooden table with an empty chair across from her. The diner was a quiet one, with only one lonely man sitting in a dark corner of the room. A warm, crackling fire was enclosed within an immaculate marble fireplace. An emptied mug of ale rested in front of Serafine as she held the Shadow Stone in the palm of her hand. The light from the tabletop candle made the violet edges of the stone glisten. A sonorous whisper hissed from it. The words were indistinguishable, but it sounded like a foreboding warning. It cast a shadow over Serafine's mind, its darkness latched onto her, bound to her soft skin. The voice was a leech, stealing the life from her breath.

"That stone has been in Kordon for far too long," said an old, round man who was standing next to the empty chair. The voice of the stone faded and Serafine's mind cleared once again. She recognized the man standing before her; Wallen. As he sat down, the chair creaked from his immense weight. "Undoubtedly, that's why you brought it to me, correct?"

"Yes. The Shadow Stone was held in the foul clutches of Kalil's servants, but Cail helped me take back what is rightfully mine. Now, all I need is a path back to Aithnen so I can return the heirloom of my people."

"You were wise to come to me. I do know of a way for you to return to the Domain of Fire. Ijsbrandur marks the edge of Kordon. If you fly west of the Iron Fortress, you'll find nothing but an empty horizon, a void of endless clouds. However, to the south, there lies the Tower of the Sun. In ancient times, it was a spire that was used by the entire world as a bridge between Kordon and the other three nations. The tower was an anchor for a nation that was detached from the rest of the world.

"Kalil believed that Kordon being in the sky was evidence of divine intervention and that the rest of the world deserved nothing more than to be forced to look up to the heavens to see the Nation in the Skies. The tower was too sturdy for him to destroy, so his only option was to cut off any access to it. He burned the bridge that connected the Tower of the Sun to Ijsbrandur, and no one from the ground has entered Kordon since, save for you, of course."

Serafine nodded and said, "I flew up from Aithnen thanks to my father's crimson eagle, who is now trapped beneath the ocean of clouds. If what you say about the tower is true, then it's my only hope for a safe return to my home."

"That it is," Wallen acknowledged, looking into Serafine's blue eyes. "Since the bridge leading to the tower has been burned to ash, your only hope is through Cail's falcon."

Serafine cursed under her breath. She knew how attached Cail was to Laney. Convincing him to leave her side would be like ripping a leech from flesh. But what choice did she have? The Descendant of Aithnen left her home for hundreds of years in search of the Shadow Stone. Now that she finally had it within her grasp, she couldn't let an unconscious girl get in her way. She would steal Cail's falcon if need be.

"Your help, as always, is greatly appreciated," Serafine said as she rose to her feet, but Wallen swiftly snatched her forearm.

"Wait," Wallen said with a quiet, but firm, voice. He rose from his chair and looked at the waitress standing behind a wooden bar. "Leave us." Without hesitation, she quickly shoved the lone man out the diner's doors and hurried to the kitchen, leaving the restaurant completely empty save for Wallen and Serafine.

"What kind of authority do you have here?" Serafine asked, shooting a glance of confusion at Wallen. He wore a sly smirk on his face.

"I built this restaurant up from rubble. Nothing happens here without my knowing." Wallen walked to the center of the diner and forcefully stomped his foot into the floor. A previously indistinguishable slab of stone, not much wider than Wallen's foot, sunk beneath the ground and the fireplace immediately went dark. A low reverberation rumbled beneath their feet and the fireplace slowly descended into the ground, revealing a hidden corridor.

Wallen snatched a candle from the nearest table and said, "Come with me, there's something I must show you." Serafine nodded and Wallen led her into the corridor, guided only by the candle's faint light. The hallway was flooded with drapes of cobwebs and Serafine could hear insects and rodents crawling up and down the walls. Serafine hated insects. She would've set the entire corridor ablaze had Wallen not been with her.

They stopped suddenly and Wallen lifted his candle up to light a torch which hung from the ceiling above their head. The torch emanated a bright radiance which illuminated the cramped, circular room that Wallen had taken Serafine to. Just before them was a wooden pedestal rising about as high as Serafine's waist. On the pedestal rested a stone, but not just any stone. It was an Air Rune. Serafine was mesmerized by the rune's beauty. The onyx stone gleamed in the light of the fire and the markings, markings of the language of Dragonspeech, were as white as the clouds of the heavens.

"I don't understand," Serafine said with perplexion. "I thought Cail found all the Air Runes in Kordon."

"He did," Wallen responded. "This rune was originally hidden in Aithnen, but an ancient king, named King Lothic, gifted it to me with the wish that it would be given to the Descendant of Kordon when the right time came."

"Isn't that now? Cail did save Kordon from Kalil's reign of terror after all," Serafine argued.

"That's true, but I still fear that Cail has much to learn. What he did for the nation of Kordon is honorable and goes beyond what anyone could've expected of him, however, I fear that his sight doesn't go beyond the borders of Kordon; I don't think he can see the rest of the world. Millennia have passed since Neptil, the world within which we live, has breathed as one spirit. Petty quarrels have divided the four nations, bringing toil and hardships to everyone."

"Thanks to the Fontanians," Serafine interrupted with a bitter voice.

"That attitude is exactly why Neptil is in its deteriorated state. You've been trained from your birth to hate Fontana. The loathing hatred that your people feel toward the Fontanians is suffocating the world, draining its essence."

"To be fair, they feel just as much hostility for us as we do for them."

"Which is why we need Cail," Wallen responded as he retrieved the rune from the pedestal. "However, the quarrels between Aithnen and Fontana can wait for a later time. I wager you'll need this if you're to return to your home."

"I don't understand," Serafine said, staring at the curves and patterns drawn on the rune. "Cail can just fly me to the tower with the help of his falcon. Why does he need this Air Rune?"

"Strictly speaking, he doesn't need it, but he'll undoubtedly want it, which will give you the leverage you need. He has left Elona before so he could acquire his powers, and he'll do it again."

"I don't know. That was during a time when he was trying to discover himself. He thinks he has found all the Air Runes and now he knows he's powerful enough to take down anyone he comes across. I believe he'll be content to stay at his home in Elona with Laney, safe from danger and peril. He won't leave for a new, trivial power."

"But it's not trivial, not in the slightest," Wallen placed the rune back onto the pedestal and gazed into the darkness of the stone. Serafine could see that he was hiding a truth about the stone. It was different from the other runes that had been found throughout Kordon. After a moment of heavy silence, Wallen said, "King Lothic told me the tale I'm about to pass on to you, a tale that might convince you to take the rune.

"Shortly after the gods forged the four nations of Neptil, they also gave birth to four beings, demigods; one for each of the nations. For Conrian, the Kingdom of Light, a fierce dragon named Kaida. In the vast oceans of Fontana lived a colossal sea turtle named Tradell. Aithnen was ruled by a ferocious lion named Cosimo. Finally, the nation of Kordon was protected by a magnificent falcon named Loni. All four of the divine beings cherished life above all else, which is why they felt isolated and lonely. In the beginning, they were the only living beings on Neptil. These demigods gave birth to all the animals and races of the world that we see today. We wouldn't be standing here today if it wasn't for them.

"The four wizards of the world each created magical staves, but the demigods forged magic themselves, magic with unimaginable power. Knowing that these powers could lead to dangerous times, the demigods decided to hide each of these powers in a different nation, hence the reason why this Air Rune was in Aithnen."

"You mean to tell me that I've yet to unlock the potential of my own powers? That there is a rune hidden in the world that belongs to me?" Wallen nodded. "Where is it?"

"In Fontana," Wallen responded with an emotionless face.

Serafine cursed under her breath. Fontana would be the death of her. She had been taught to know that it was sacrilegious to even set foot on Fontanian soil. In order to obtain that which she desired, she would have to betray the teachings of her parents and go where no Aithnenian had gone for millennia. The task of realizing her fullest potential would have to wait, though. Right now, Serafine's only priority needed to be convincing Cail to help her find her way home.

"What powers will this rune unlock? What will it turn Cail into?" Serafine asked after silently pondering over what she should do.

"I don't know," Wallen said with regret. "I wish I could tell you, but the Divine Powers are abilities that have been possessed by no one other than the demigods themselves. It'll undoubtedly unlock a terrible power within Cail, which is why it's imperative that you wait until the right moment to give it to him."

"I'm not convinced that it's safe to give it to him at all," Serafine said. She reflected on the time she witnessed Cail summon a swirling cyclone that kept an entire army at bay. Everyone stood as still as statues, amazed by the prowess of the wind that dwelled within the Descendant of Kordon. To think that he could obtain magic that was even more powerful than a tornado chilled the fire within Serafine and put the fear of death into her heart. Having made her decision, she said, "No. There's far too great of a risk in giving this sacred power to him. I've seen what he's capable of. When irked, he can transform into the mightiest of warriors and it's as easy to touch him as it is the wind. If this rune possesses what you claim it does, then Cail can never be allowed to touch it."

"Serafine, eventually this rune will fall into Cail's palms," Wallen said, trying to convince Serafine. "Each of the demigods took magic from themselves and preserved it to be given to each of the Descendants. The rune sitting before us is Loni's gift to Cail. He is divinely destined to take control of this power. You must use this rune to your advantage; use it as leverage. Cail's prowess can be bent to your will if you so choose. The key to your home is before you, but you're welcome to find your own path."

Against her better judgment, Serafine snatched the rune from the pedestal and held it in her palm. It felt deceptively light, no heavier than a small pebble. Her mind was screaming for her to put the rune back in its rightful place, atop the pedestal, but her heart greatly longed for Aithnen. Hundreds of years had passed since she had known the emerald flowing fields of Edenor, the Valleys of the East, the mountainous Bodaway Volcano. She missed her family, her friends, the tastes of the fresh foods, the radiant sunrises, and the star-flooded night skies.

"I know this is a bad idea," Serafine said, staring at the Air Rune.

"It's what needs to be done," Wallen responded without hesitation.

Serafine nodded and placed the rune safely in the inside pocket of her beige cloak. From the same pocket, she retrieved the Shadow Stone and showed it to Wallen. "Did King Lothic tell you anything about this?"

"Ah, yes. The Shadow Stone," Wallen said after a moment of observation. He took the stone from Serafine's palm and held it in the light of the lantern's fire. It shined gloriously and glistened like a precious jewel. "The surface possesses alluring beauty, but darkness dwells within, as its name suggests. Just like the Air Runes harness the magic of the wind, the Shadow Stone contains dark magic; the magic bides within, waiting for anyone to release it from its cage."

"That stone was locked away in a temple for millennia, and you claim that it defiled our sacred grounds?" Serafine asked, insulted by what Wallen had told her.

"That's correct. A stone just like this was found on the island of Irda, by Kalil. That stone led to the demise of the free islands of Kordon, and this stone could bring about the fall of the democracies of Aithnen, should the stone fall into the wrong hands. With that being said, this is also the key to breaking down the barrier between Kordon and Aithnen. If you wish to have a peaceful, free world, then returning the Shadow Stone to its rightful place is your only choice."

Now that Serafine knew this stone was capable of unleashing a tyrannical king on an innocent nation, she wanted nothing to do with it. As with the Air Rune, there was an immense amount of risk in taking the Shadow Stone back to the temple. The ocean of clouds would be drained and Aithnen would feel the warmth of the sun once again, but it would be all too easy for the Shadow Stone to be stolen, leading to the rise of darkness.

"I just helped Cail to eradicate evil and malice from his home. If I take the Shadow Stone with me, it could give birth to that same malevolence. Perhaps the right choice is to destroy it," Serafine pondered aloud.

"Perhaps you're right," Wallen said. Serafine looked surprised by his remark. "However, I think the leaders of the Kingdoms of Aithnen should decide what is right." He offered the Shadow Stone back to Serafine.

She took it and placed it back in her pocket. "I agree," she said with a heavy heart. Serafine's first choice was to destroy the stone and be rid of the evil within it, but that wasn't for her to decide. She needed to respect the will of the leaders of Aithnen. "I assume that my next course of action is to find Cail?"

"Yes, but not before I show you one last thing. Follow me." Wallen snatched the lantern which was hanging from the ceiling and led Serafine out of the chamber, through the dark corridor and the diner, and into the buzzing streets of Darzomil. Serafine had to constantly evade the wild traffic of the civilians, but Wallen steadily walked through the crowd. Anyone who bumped into the rounded man bounced off him, usually forcing them to run into someone else. Serafine had to push and shove away hundreds of people so she could keep up with Wallen, who was surprisingly quick on his feet, but she trailed right behind him nonetheless. It wasn't long before Serafine realized that Wallen was leading her out of the city; the density of the crowd started to dwindle.

Once they had escaped the cramped city, they walked down a narrow dirt path, just wide enough for Serafine and Wallen to walk side by side. The path led them to a cliff, hanging over a steep drop into darkness. Serafine's stomach turned as she looked over the edge, knowing that a single misstep would lead to a death as certain as the sunrise. "Where are you taking me?" Serafine asked, looking at Wallen.

"We're about to plunge into the heart of the mountain, into the depths of Darzomil." Wallen stepped forward onto a narrow stone staircase which circled around the edge of the cliff, descending deep into the mountain. The light above them slowly faded and it didn't take long until they were solely guided by the illumination of the lantern in Wallen's hand, silence surrounded them except for the echoing clicks of their footsteps, and the air's warmth evaporated, chilling Serafine to the bone.

After several moments of descending into darkness, the staircase stopped and led them into a cave with an entrance so small that Wallen had to duck in order to enter. Serafine immediately realized that this was no ordinary cave; it was a shrine. An ocean of gold coins flooded the towering cavern and stone altars held ancient texts and glistening jewels. Serafine was nearly blinded by the immaculate gold. In the center of the cave stood a silver statue of a falcon, at least twice as large as Emey, Cail's falcon. The falcon's wings were spread out wide and its beak was open as though it was calling out to them. Serafine felt as puny as an ant in the cave, as humbled as the dirt and rubble beneath her feet.

"This is the Shrine of Loni," Wallen said as he approached the statue. He stood before the magnificent bird, staring at it in awe. The statue stared back with a terrifying glare, a scowl that could pierce through anyone's courage. "Sadly, this statue does no justice for the magnificence of Loni. He's the Father of Kordon, Protector of the Skies, King of the Clouds."

"Do the mountain folk of Darzomil know of this place?" Serafine asked, flabbergasted by the immensity of the shrine.

"Of course. Where do you think all this gold came from? The people of the city offer a small portion of their earnings in an attempt to please the spirit of Loni. They think that by doing so, their lives will be at peace."

"What do you believe?" Serafine asked without looking away from the statue's trenchant eyes.

"Who can know for sure?" Wallen responded with no small amount of wit. "The mountain folk have remained safe through all the years of Kalil's corruption, so there must be something looking out for us."

Serafine was skeptical that the spirit of a mythological creature demanded money in order to protect the civilians of Darzomil; it seemed like a scam. *Why wouldn't Loni protect all the people of Kordon? If he truly was as powerful as Wallen claims, why wouldn't he destroy Kalil himself, instead of forcing Cail to do it?* Serafine thought silently. She didn't want to offend Wallen or offer him insult, so she kept her doubts to herself. Instead, she asked, "Why did you bring me here? Isn't this something you should show to Cail?"

"I have a nagging feeling that you'll have to be the one to do that," Wallen answered with a melancholic voice. "The quest you are about to embark on, returning the Shadow Stone to your homeland, will be a tall task. It will take days, years even, and it will test your strength. As I age, the days grow shorter, speeding like a boulder tumbling down the side of a mountain. My days are numbered and, to be completely honest, I fear that my life won't survive long enough to see your return."

"Please don't say that," Serafine interrupted. The thought of Wallen's death brought tears to her eyes. "You've guided me ever since I arrived from Aithnen, two thousand years ago, and I wouldn't be where I am today without you."

"Then I have fulfilled my purpose," Wallen said with a slight smile. "Bearing that in mind, you must promise me that you'll show this shrine to Cail, should the worst come to pass for me."

"You have my word," Serafine responded. A glistening tear ran down her cheek. Wallen used a thick finger to dry her face and took her into his arms.

"There's no need to let sadness thrive. I've lived a life full of purpose, a life that helped bring peace to Kordon. Even though weakness is beginning to plague my body and bind my muscles, I know that I am strong."

Chapter 2: The Awakening

The ground was dry, brittle, and bleak. An encompassing blanket of gray veiled the sun and cast darkness on the world around Cail. Drops of water started falling from the sky and plopped onto the parched grass. The rain was cold, but Cail was unfazed by it. Wet raindrops trickled down his skin as he observed the atrocity around him. Thousands of bodies were piled on the ground, all as dead as a winter night. These weren't the bodies of warriors or soldiers, but of civilians. Men, women, and children. Not a single soul was spared, not a single body held the color of life.

Cail walked to the corpse of a woman, laying on the ground apart from the mounds of dead bodies. He could see that she was beautiful. Her skin was pale and as smooth as silk, her hair matched her dark brown eyes, and her body was gentle and slender. Cail rested the back of his hand on her cheek, which had rivers of dried blood streaming down to her neck. She felt as cold as ice and Cail could feel that any hope of life had abandoned her.

"What is this accursed land?" Cail asked himself without looking away from the woman. Never before had he witnessed an abomination such as this. He had experienced mass amounts of death in battle, but this was different. The people who lied dead before Cail wanted no part of violence, but it sought them out like a raging storm.

"The world you see is imminent," a dark voice echoed. Cail's head snapped around, looking for the source of the voice, but he saw no one other than the legion of corpses. "There's nothing you can do to stop fate. Everyone you see is destined to die." The voice clamped down on Cail's spine like a vice grip. Even though Cail could see no one, he felt an evil shadow stalking him.

"Who are you? What do you want?" Cail bellowed into the air.

"You'll have to find me if you wish to know those answers." The voice was cold, chilling Cail's bones and stripping him of his vitality. Warmth flew from Cail's body like a flock of frightened pigeons and his heart slowed, softly pulsating in his thinned chest.

"Where are you?" Cail asked softly. He felt weak, malnourished.

"Hidden."

The voice faded into the dark sky and Cail could only hear the faint howling of the wind. Even though the voice was gone, its malice remained. Cail could feel its malign aura hovering over him, haunting him like a ghost. With the help of the Air Runes, Cail had revived a powerful magic that killed an era of tyranny in Kordon, but now he could feel a new darkness rising to power.

The sun beamed through the bare window and landed on the living room wall. Gentle warmth gradually woke Cail as he started to rise from the soft sofa on which he rested. He rubbed his eyes as he tried to forget about the nightmare which was still fresh in his mind. Cail was relieved to feel warmth being restored to his blood; it cleansed his skin and cleared his mind. The darkness from his dream evaporated and the corpses disappeared.

"It's high noon and you're just now rolling off your hind end. I'll never know how you do it." Cail turned around and saw his father, Cecil, chuckling while he read a thick book in his rickety, wooden rocking chair. Every sway of the chair sent a whining creak through the hardwood floor.

"I'm sorry, dad," Cail responded as he rose to his feet. "Nights haven't treated me well lately. I've witnessed dark dreams, visions of death and decay. Destruction beyond measure."

Cecil laid his book on the table next to him, rose from his chair, and walked before his son. "Kalil and his faithful servants are dead, slain by the wind you possess in your palms. The shackles of evil have loosened and Kordon has entered a new age of freedom and peace. There should be nothing else troubling your mind."

Cail could refute none of what his father said. Elona, which had endured an age of isolation, was now a part of Kordon, the nation of islands above the clouds. Kalil's malicious reign died at the hands of his most trusted servant, Tarvaris. Cail reminisced about the battle with Tarvaris Ozean, his ancient ancestor. Even though six months had passed, the wounds were still fresh in his mind. Not only did he remember the fight against Tarvaris, but also the clash against Laney when Tarvaris' dark powers morphed her into a vicious zurak. After Cail's victory, Laney transformed back to her normal body, but remained unconscious ever since the conflict.

"If the world has been restored to perfection, then why am I still haunted by dreams of darkness?" Cail asked with a pained voice. Even though he had banished evil from the lands of Kordon, he couldn't banish it from his memory.

"I don't know, Cail. In regards to your dreams, I think you're still witnessing these horrors because your mind is still healing. Our thoughts are more fragile than we're led to believe. When one is traumatized, as you were that day in the Iron Fortress, it can take years to heal."

"I suppose you're right," Cail said, then he walked to the open window and breathed in the fresh Elona air. A cool breeze oozed into the house and brushed against his face. He saw a woman working in a nearby garden, a group of ten children playing amongst themselves, and three men engaged in a private discussion. A cheerful revelation popped into Cail's mind; everyone he saw was saved by him. Every single Elonian, including Cail's own father, was enslaved by Kalil and suffered under his tyranny, but for no longer.

"I'm beginning to grow worried about Laney," Cail said without looking away from the window.

"I must confess that I am as well. Her body rested for six long months, recovering from the malevolent assault. Her faint breath still flows through her nose, but I can't help but think that we're nursing a corpse."

Cail walked up the rickety stairs and into the bedroom where Laney was resting. He kneeled on the hard floor next to the bed and took Laney's hand in his. Her fingers were thin and as cold as frozen water. Her face was colorless and rested as still as stone. Even with all her ailments, Cail admired her beauty and gentleness. He remained by her side, praying that her eyes would open, but they stayed shut.

"I fulfilled my promise, I came back to you," Cail said, praying that Laney would hear him. He retrieved her vial from beneath his shirt. Soldir was a vial that harnessed the light of the sun and used it to shun the darkness. Cail held it firmly in his hand, running his strong fingers over its smooth grooves which flowed like rivers. A white light glistened from inside the vial, a star within glass. Cail vividly remembered the day she gave the vial to him, the day he left to find the remaining Air Runes. *I want you to take it as a promise that you'll bring it back to me,* Laney had said as she gave the vial to Cail. A small tear, as cold as a raindrop, escaped from Cail's eye and tricked down his cheek. "Please wake up so I can return your gift to you."

Then Cail heard three solid knocks coming from the front door. As he sprinted down the stairs, booming pounds echoed throughout the house. Cail yanked the door open and a tall, thin man stood on the stoop in front of Cail. The man was panting heavily, as though he had been sprinting for hours. Sweat streamed down his wrinkled forehead like a rapid river and his brown hair was cast every which way.

"Can I help you?" Cail asked, looking at the man incredulously.

The man took in a few more deep breaths in an attempt to fill his lungs with fresh air. "My name is Loran. Queen Beda sent me from the Ivory City. We're in desperate need of your help. The city has come under attack."

Cail was taken back by what Loran told him. "Attack? By zuraks?"

"I wish that were so," Loran replied. "These attackers stemmed from within the city's walls. The Blue Assassins, as they've proclaimed themselves, move as lightly as a feather, but attack as ferociously as a dragon."

"Assassins you say? Who have they killed?"

"No civilians have been laid to waste yet, however, the Blue Assassins have taken the Red Pumas as their hostages. We can't help but fear the worst."

Cail cursed under his breath. He anticipated that new enemies would rise, but not this quickly. Kordon was still healing from the venomous leech who was Kalil. Now the Blue Assassins were quickly moving on an injured nation like a vulture creeping over a dying animal. As much as it pained him, Cail saw no option other than leaving Laney to run to Cestmir's aid. Cail desperately desired to be by Laney's side when she woke from her elongated slumber, but it was imperative that Cestmir remained protected. It was a stronghold, a beacon of light for all of Kordon.

"I'll fly to Cestmir and investigate this new enemy. Feel free to stay here and rest. You must be sore from your strenuous voyage," Cail said to Loran, resting a hand on the traveler's weary shoulder.

"You are most gracious to me," Loran said with a slight bow.

Cail ran to Emey, who was resting in an open pasture. Her emerald feathers matched the flowing blades of grass that swayed in the gentle breeze. She looked at Cail, pointing her golden beak directly toward him. She sensed that Cail needed her wings, so she rose to her feet, revealing a patch of matted ground upon which she laid. Cail gracefully hopped onto her back, but just before Emey launched off the ground, Cail heard a faint voice calling out his name. He spun his head around and saw his best friend, Kadir sprinting through the tall grass toward him. Kadir leaned against Emey and gasped for fresh air. "I'm glad I found you before you left," Kadir said, looking up to Cail. "Where are you headed, anyway?"

Cail dropped down from Emey's back and said, "I was headed to Cestmir to attend to an urgent matter. Is there something you need?"

"Yes. Lydia sent me to find you. She needs to speak with you immediately."

"Can't it wait? The City of Cestmir could be in grave danger," Cail said with no small amount of impatience.

"If you leave, you may never be able to speak with her again. Lydia is dying."

Kadir barged through the front doors of Lydia's home, with Cail following closely behind him. In the far corner of the hut was a bed with a group of people, small and large, huddled around it. "Make way for Cail!" Kadir bellowed. They obeyed his command, moving so that there was an opening just wide enough for Cail to kneel down next to Lydia. Once he did, he could see she was plagued by a vicious ailment, draining the light from her eyes. Her hair was as white as snow, her skin was wrinkled and colorless, and her mouth looked as dry as a desert.

Lydia cracked a smile when she saw Cail's melancholic face. "You came to see me one last time."

"Of course I did," Cail responded, fighting to hold the burning tears in his eyes. "After all you've done for me, I couldn't leave you without saying goodbye."

Lydia let out a soft chuckle and placed her weak hand on Cail's broad chest. "Kordon is now free thanks to the gentleness in your heart. As long as you cling to your compassion, the people of this great nation will treat you well."

Cail could no longer control his emotions. A cold tear of sadness slithered down his cheek to the corner of his mouth. "Why do you have to leave?"

"Because time is calling my name. We would have nothing to live for if we never died. Don't drop too many tears, young one. I've lived a full life, a life filled with purpose and happiness. I will close my eyes so that they may open under a new sun."

She tried to pair comfort with her words, but Cail only felt pain. He didn't only feel the pain of losing Lydia, but also the pain of losing a part of who he was. Lydia enabled Cail to find the magical staff deep within the Elonian woods, she taught him of the four nations of the world, she helped him to believe that he could become the man that he was in that moment. Now that she was about to die, that part of his life would die with her. He would have to muster a new courage that she freely gave to him.

Cail could no longer hear Lydia's breaths as she stared off into oblivion. The small amount of strength that remained in her hand slowly diminished and her eyes slid shut. Lydia had passed.

Kadir laid a gentle hand on Cail's shoulder and said, "I'm sorry, Cail. She lived a good life. All we can do is take comfort in knowing that she is rid of all suffering." Despite Kadir's compassionate attempts, Cail found no refuge in his words. No comfort would be found while wounds gashed his soul. Tears were streaming down his cheeks and dropping onto his forearms. Cail dried his face and walked out of Lydia's hut without saying any more. He clung to the hope that the radiant sunlight would strip him of his pain, but it did no such thing. Sadness stuck to Cail like iron chains, constricting his breath and compressing his muscles. The agony he felt was the same he experienced when he watched Lionel, the King of the Red Pumas, die by the hands of Kalil's servants.

"Miles delivered the ill news to me," Cecil said, referring to Laney's father; he was standing just behind his distraught son. "I'm sorry you had to watch her drift away, but it's something all of us must experience at one time or another."

"This doesn't feel real," Cail said without looking at his father. "It feels as though I'm imprisoned in a dark dream. All I need to do is wake up, but I know I can't."

"I've experienced that same sentiment as well. Your mother was snatched away before my very eyes," Cecil said with a heavy heart. His words were daggers that carved into Cail's chest, cutting at his vulnerabilities. "For years, I've clung to memories of her; of our short time as a family, but I know there's nothing I can do to bring my sweet Ilona back."

"We're still a family," Cail responded as he turned around to face his father. No tears fell from Cecil's face, but his sadness was painted on his entire body, a canvas of sorrow.

"Not without your mother. She's a missing cog."

"But we're not without her," Cail said. An expression of surprise sprung onto Cecil's face. "I know you've felt her presence, just as I have. I've even seen her with my own eyes."

"You've seen her?" Cecil's voice was filled with incredulity.

"Her spirit came to me and claimed that she had been sent back by the gods to protect me on my quest." As Cail said this, tears began to stream down his father's face. Cecil had always contained his emotions and kept his composure in front of his son, but his feelings rushed out of him like a rapid river. Cail was frozen in shock by the sight of his father openly weeping in front of him. He couldn't think of what to say except for, "I'm sorry, dad."

"Don't be sorry," Cecil said as he wiped his cheeks dry and smiled at his son. "I'm happy you could finally see your mother for the beautiful woman she was."

"That she was," Cail responded. Even though Cecil's crying had ceased, Cail could still see that his father was ridden with sadness. He decided to shift the conversation away from dwelling on his passed mother, "As much as it pains me to leave Laney, I must make my way toward Cestmir. A traveler named Loran has informed me that the city has been taken from the inside."

"Yes. Laney's father offered the man his hospitality after I spoke with him. Do you need someone to go with you?"

"No. I need to move swiftly and silently. Companions traveling with me will draw far too much unwanted attention."

"As you wish. I must warn you, the Blue Assassins aren't to be taken lightly. They're lethal hunters."

"You know of them?" Cail asked.

"All I know are the ancient tales of their clan. They're a lawless bunch that originated in the Domain of Fire, Aithnen. According to legend, they were responsible for the downfall of hundreds of democracies in all four of the nations of the world. They've resided in all of the nations for years, but fled from Kordon as soon as Kalil rose to power."

"But the ocean of clouds below us blocks anyone from traveling between Kordon and Aithnen, so how did they pass through?"

"I don't know, Cail," Cecil responded with a slight hint of disappointment in his voice. "All I can do is recite stories of old. No matter what, you must exercise extreme caution. The Blue Assassins are a deceptive group, waiting to pounce on their prey."

"You have my word," Cail said as he cast a comforting smile toward his father. "Please look after Laney while I'm gone. Even with the safety of Cestmir being threatened, I hate leaving her."

Cecil placed a solacing hand on Cail's shoulder and said, "You have nothing to worry about. I'll ensure that Laney remains in good hands until she wakes." Cail nodded to his father, who smiled at Cail in return. Before Cail could turn to leave, his father said, "One last thing to keep in mind: According to the ancient legends, the Blue Assassins were known for their speed and stealth, but were easily overmatched by strength."

"They're not the only ones who are light on their feet," Cail responded with a smirk.

Chapter 3: A World of Puppets

Emey flew through the northern sky, high above the ocean of clouds beneath her. The cool air breathed new vigor into Cail's lungs. Vitality coursed through his muscles and he felt the power of the wind in his veins. All of the Air Runes in Kordon had been found, but more awaited Cail in the rest of the world. A slender, weak boy left Elona not much more than three years ago, but the magic of the Air Runes transformed him into a formidable foe, a nation's liberator.

Cestmir swelled as Emey flew closer. It was hard for Cail to believe that a place as radiant as the Ivory City could be held under siege. White towers reached as tall as mountains and gleamed in the magnificent sunlight. From a distance, the city was glorious and peaceful, like a gem resting on a pedestal. Cestmir was so appealing to the eye that Cail had to remind himself of the malicious threat that awaited him.

Emey descended as Cail guided her toward the city's entrance. She no longer needed to flap her robust wings. Instead, she held them out, allowing her aerodynamic body to gracefully glide above the clouds. With a gentle thud, Emey's golden talons landed on the white bricks of Cestmir's court, in front of a marvelous fountain with water as clear as the finest gems. When Cail hopped off his falcon, he expected to see a silent city, a city riddled with fear, but he actually saw a boisterous city. Little children were playfully splashing the fountain's water while their parents chatted amongst themselves. Civilians were busily pacing in and out of the city's streets, walking from shop to shop, buzzing like bees. Danger and peril appeared to be absent from the city.

"I don't understand," Cail said to himself, confused by the livelihood of Cestmir. The adults shot brief glances of suspicion at Cail, but then returned to their conversations.

Cail weaved through the clamoring crowd, slithering like a snake. He should have been happy to see thousands of people minding to their own business, but he couldn't cast aside his suspicions. Cestmir appeared bright and cheerful, but a hidden darkness was waiting, remaining at bay until the opportune time to pounce.

"Cailean Ozean! The Last Descendant of the gods!" a womanly voice bellowed over the noise of the crowd. Cail turned and saw an elderly woman waving to him from inside a small jewelry shop. Fine gems and jewels glistened on the shelves and gold statues stood along all the walls. As Cail approached her, she said, "I'm blessed and overjoyed to finally meet the savior of Kordon." Even though a long life wrinkled her face, her smile shined as bright as the sun.

Cail returned a gentle smile to her and said, "You are too kind."

"Happiness is painted on your face, but I can see no small amount of fear in you," the woman said, her smile fading.

Her words bit into Cail's heart like a wintry gust. He felt a strong sense of worry, as though a dagger was just about to pierce through his back. "I must confess that my mind is troubled," Cail responded with a hushed voice. "A man rushed to my home in Elona and spoke of the city being in disarray, but that doesn't appear to be the case. Is Cestmir truly safe, or am I too blind to see its peril?"

The woman stood before Cail, only rising up to his belly. She put a thin, scrawny hand on Cail's forearm and asked, "Have you eaten yet on this fine afternoon?"

Cail was taken back by her response. "You didn't answer my question."

"You should place more faith in your eyes. Cestmir is alive and well, thanks to you," the woman said with a soothing voice. Cail was perplexed by the warning given to him about Cestmir, but his heart was calmed by the light in the woman's eyes. She led Cail out of the shop and pointed across the street. "That diner, The Dancing Dragon, serves the finest meal a young boy, such as yourself, could ask for. Tell them I sent you and you'll be served well."

"Thank you," Cail said, giving the woman a slight nod. He proceeded across the street, swiftly avoiding the flooded traffic of civilians. Cail walked through the light, wooden door and was greeted by a soft curtain of warmth from a snapping fire. All of the broad, oak tables were taken, save for one in a dark corner. Cail quickly strode to the table before anyone else could steal it from him. Before a waitress could introduce herself, a cloaked man slid into the chair opposite of Cail. The man appeared to be much larger than Cail and a black hood hung over his head, veiling his face in darkness. "Can I help you?" Cail asked, surprised by the stranger's audacity.

"You're the one who needs help, coming to a broken city all alone," the man replied, his voice as deep as a drum.

"Cestmir is very jubilant for being a broken city," Cail responded, confused by the man's claims. He tried to catch a glimpse of the man's face, but all Cail could see was darkness.

"Only because they're being watched. The people who surround you, even the ones in this very restaurant, are nothing more than puppets and the Blue Assassins hold their strings. If a Cestmirian does so much as slightly drift from conformity, they'll be killed and cast aside like a dog."

"But where are the Blue Assassins? And how can they stalk over an entire city? Especially one as large and diverse as Cestmir?" Cail asked.

"The Blue Assassins have overtaken the Red Pumas and now control the chambers beneath the city; they've dismantled the protectors of Cestmir. The people of the city are terrified of the assassins because they are masters of disguise. There could be dozens of them in this restaurant as we speak." Cail looked around at all the customers, none of whom looked peculiar. "That's why the Cestmirians conform, that's why they're afraid. At any given moment, the Blue Assassins could pounce on their mistakes."

Cail leaned in and whispered to the stranger, "Cestmir is a stronghold of Kordon, a symbol of fortitude. I must reclaim it, but I know almost nothing about who I'm faced against."

The man said nothing for a moment. Cail could feel the man's invisible eyes piercing into him, carving through him like a knife. "I surmise that's your way of asking for my help?" Cail nodded in response. "Then tell me, why should I help you?"

"If the Blue Assassins have as firm of a hold on Cestmir as you say, then we must do something to help," Cail insisted in a hushed voice.

"I'm not from this city, I have no attachment to it. Why should I care?"

"If you're not a civilian, then why are you here?" Cail asked, irritated by the man's selfishness.

"I don't have to explain myself to a stranger," the man replied. Cail rolled his eyes in frustration. The man paused for a moment, as though he was trying to decide whether or not he would offer his assistance, and then he said, "If your mind is truly set on finding the Blue Assassins, then I'll point you in their direction, but I'll do no more for you."

"Fine," Cail said with a strong hint of vexation. "Where must I go?"

The hooded man leaned close to Cail and whispered, "Around the back of this diner there's a set of storm doors that will take you to a tunnel that runs beneath the city. This tunnel will lead you straight to the enemy's hiding chamber." Cail motioned a thankful nod to the man and darted out of the diner.

The rear of the building was bleak and dark. Loud chattering oozed through cracks in the walls and the ground was carpeted with a layer of dirt and dust. The storm doors were made of thick maple wood and appeared to be just wide enough for Cail to squeeze his shoulders through. He quickly glanced around him, looking to see that no one was watching him, and then he flung the storm doors open. They beat the ground with a loud bang and Cail cursed under his breath for being so careless and noisy. He swiftly descended into the black, closing the doors behind him.

Cail slowly progressed through the blinding darkness, always keeping one hand on the dirt walls of the tunnel. All sounds and sources of light abandoned Cail, leaving him in a dark void. The dirt beneath his feet was soft and he could smell the moisture in the air. A faint shriek resonated through the tunnel, a cry for help. Cail stopped in his tracks, paralyzed by fear. He remained as still as a statue, holding his breath. After several moments of silence, Cail slowly progressed until he saw a single source of light in the far distance. He was so desperate to use his eyes that he didn't care what awaited him in the light. Cail sprinted down the corridor, his feet sinking deeper into the ground with every step. He progressed through a narrow archway and into a dungeon filled with despair. Rusted iron prisons held men and women who were beaten and battered, cold chains drooped from the prisoners' wrists and ankles, and weapons and instruments of torture hung on the walls. Nightmares couldn't draw the atrocities that laid before Cail's eyes.

In the cell nearest Cail, a scraggly and malnourished man trudged toward Cail and wrapped his bony fingers around the bars that confined him. "You there," he whispered. Cail could see a mountain of fear in the man's eyes. "What are you doing here?"

"I've come to rescue all of you," Cail said with confidence as strong as steel. The prisoner's body quaked and he violently shook his head.

"No. They'll find you. They'll kill you. Get out while your limbs are free."

"Where are the Blue Assassins? They must be stopped."

"One puny boy has no hope against an army such as this. The Blue Assassins are ruthless. They offer no mercy because none was given to them." Cail leaned in closer to catch a clearer glimpse of the man. His pupils were void of hope, filled with the darkness of death. Gashes and wounds ran along his dry skin, leaving trails of dried blood. If the man had muscles at one point in his life, they had abandoned him. Cail looked around the chamber and saw dozens of prisoners staring at him with the same eyes as the man; their gaze flooded with hopelessness. Fear weighed on Cail's lungs and he struggled to breathe. He started to run through the cells, desperately trying to find an escape, but there was none. Cail was trapped within a labyrinth of prisoners, hopelessly searching for light in the dead of the night. He stopped and bent over his knees, gasping for air. Then a thick hand rested on his shoulder.

"It's a wonder they haven't found you already, with all the noise you're making." Cail stood up and saw the hooded man standing beside him, the man from the diner.

"I thought you weren't coming down here," Cail said in between deep breaths.

"I wasn't going to, but I had a nagging feeling that you would need my assistance, and I was right." Cail could see a slight smirk from beneath the man's hood. "If we are going to proceed, I need your word that you'll step as lightly as the wind and remain silent."

"Of course, but first I must know your name."

Two thick, strong, pale hands removed the black hood, revealing a boy, who looked approximately the age of Cail, standing before him. The boy had hair as radiant as the sun and eyes as blue as a clear sky. His neck was thick, but not overly bulky. He stood a full head taller than Cail, outmatching him in both height and width. "My name is Micah." He extended a pale hand toward Cail and Cail shook it. "I may not have ever lived in Cestmir, but I remember its days of glory. I remember the streets being flooded with friendly folk and gleeful children, not this world of puppets we see now."

Cail reached up to put his hand on Micah's shoulder, "If we work together, we can take down the Blue Assassins and free this city." Micah smiled with ivory teeth and led Cail onward through the dungeons. As they wove through the jail cells, Cail desperately desired to free all the prisoners, but he didn't dare to leave his guide. The corridors came to an end and they stood in a circular chamber with no doors, save for the one through which they entered. Micah stood still in the middle of the chamber and Cail approached from behind.

"I thought you knew where you were going? This is a dead end," Cail said, irritated with Micah.

"I do," Micah responded with a smirk on his face, this one more sinister. "This is only a dead end for you." Cail spun around and saw that the entrance was now blocked by dozens of men, all as large as Micah, with matching black cloaks. If these men were the Blue Assassins, then Cecil's description of them was far from accurate; Cail had no hope of overpowering any of them. None of Cail's abilities could help him escape the fact that he was grossly outnumbered. Micah's strong hands gripped onto Cail's shoulders and he said, "It would be wise to come with us without a fuss."

"You lied to me?" Cail asked through gritted teeth. He was fuming from his seething anger. "Why are you betraying the one person who can protect Kordon from the Blue Assassins?"

"Because I am a Blue Assassin. We all are," Micah said as he pointed to all the men surrounding Cail. "You fell into our trap like a mouse. To be honest, I thought it would be a little more difficult. Nonetheless, my master will be happy. Now, will you come quietly, or will I have to drag you along the way?" Cail saw no need to waste his energy fighting a futile battle, so he dejectedly surrendered.

Micah and his legion of cloaked soldiers marched Cail through the depths of the dungeons until they arrived at a place that wasn't unfamiliar to Cail; the Chamber of the Red Pumas. Thousands of men were waiting for Cail in the chamber, but instead of the Red Pumas, these men were all dressed in black cloaks. As Cail walked forth, he could feel thousands upon thousands of eyes turning toward him, casting their malice and spite at him. He was stranded in an ocean infested with bloodthirsty sharks. Micah led Cail to the throne that once belonged to Beda, but was now taken by a giant man, twice the size of Cail. The man had a rough face with dark skin, his red eyes pierced through Cail like a knife, and his broad feet were planted into the ground like trees. When Cail arrived at the throne, the man stood up and approached Cail, his shoulders rising high above Cail's head.

"I've waited a long time to meet you, Cailean Ozean, savior of Kordon," the man said with a thunderous voice. He wore a dark smirk on his face, which allowed his yellowed teeth to surface "There's a sage, not far from here, who would pay a pretty price for your head."

"Calling yourselves the Blue Assassins is a bit misleading since all of you wear black," Cail said, trying to ignore the man's attempts at intimidation. He stood as confidently as he would if he had an army with him.

The man reached into his black cloak and from his pocket, he retrieved a flower and held it in his rough, thick hand. It was an object of beauty, boasting petals that were deep blue and as soft as velvet. As the man observed the flower he said, "This flower is called The Sapphire Rose. It can only be found in the gardens of my ancestors, in the nation of Aithnen. There are two groups of people who may possess this flower: my kin and the people we kill. The reason we're called the Blue Assassins is that this flower is the only trail we leave. We're an army of shadows, with feet as light as the wind.

"For centuries, we've traveled throughout the entire world, doing our deeds for the highest bidder. A couple thousand years ago, we came to Kordon for a job, which we completed with ease, but then something happened that we did not expect. Our home, Aithnen, disappeared behind a floor of clouds, stranding us here in the nation in the sky. We sought out refuge on an island far to the west, creating a suitable settlement for our new home. For three thousand years, we lived in peace and tranquility, until a few weeks ago. The Sages of Pazia came to us, presenting an offer we simply could not refuse; the promise of our return to Aithnen."

"So, you intend to strip an entire nation of their protector just so you can acquire a free pass to your home?" Cail asked, failing in a futile attempt to pass guilt onto the man.

"Now we're on the same page," he said with no sign of remorse. The man looked down to the flower once again. "This is the final rose that I have with me, and you are my final target. I will give you the gift that you are destined for; the gift of death. Then I will drag your wretched corpse to the Sages so we can finally return to our home."

"Who do you think you are to threaten me? I saved Kordon from the suffocating grasp of a tyrant, I've attained power that was divinely gifted to me, and you have the audacity to abduct me?"

The man let out a soft chuckle, mocking Cail's arrogance. "To answer your question, my name is Barok Zilith, King of the Blue Assassins. I've lived for thousands of years, killed thousands on the battlefield and thousands more away from it. You should look around you. You're surrounded by a legion of my finest warriors, all of whom could kill you in the blink of an eye." There was no denying that Barok was right. Cail would struggle to fight off a dozen of these warriors, but battling against an entire army of them was beyond hopeless. "The Sages don't just want your corpse, but also something that you possess; the Shadow Stone." Cail shot a glance of intrigue at Barok.

Ever since Cail had gifted the Shadow Stone into the rightful hands of Serafine, he had cast it out of his mind. The Sages had stolen it from a sacred temple in Aithnen, and they intended to steal it again. Quietly, Cail said, "I don't have it."

"Excuse me?" Barok asked, glaring with burning eyes.

"I don't have the Shadow Stone. I gave it to a friend a few years ago."

"And who is this friend?" Cail could hear fierce anger rising in Barok's voice. His temper was building like a wave rising above an ocean.

"Why should I tell you?" Cail responded with a sly smirk on his face. "You're going to kill me regardless of whether or not I tell you the name of my friend, so I think I'll hang on to that tidbit of information."

Barok's face grew as red as his eyes and a sonorous growl oozed through his teeth. Despite the assassin's rage, Cail's conceited smirk remained on his face. Barok swiftly snatched Cail by the collar of his shirt and hoisted his body in the air, his feet dangling over the ground. Cail knew that Barok was no weakling, but he didn't expect the King of the Blue Assassins to be the brute he was. Fear crept back into Cail's mind and his confidence was swept away like a scent in the wind.

"Yes, you will die regardless of what you tell me, but I can make the remainder of your life unbearable if you continue to vex me," Barok growled. His thick hand clamped down on Cail's shirt and his ire possessed his entire body. "I'll ask you one last time. Who has the Shadow Stone?"

Torture and agony loomed over Cail like an oncoming storm. This storm had black clouds of death, threatening the lives of all those living beneath it. Fierce winds and pelting rain accompanied the storm, wreaking havoc on a world that was previously at peace. Fear gripped Cail and paralyzed his muscles, it froze his mind. He had encountered countless dangers and perils in his quest to kill Kalil, but this was entirely different. Cail was engulfed by the shadow of a sinister army; all alone while he stared into the dark eyes of death. It would be easy for Cail to accept his fate, to tell Barok the truth, to betray Serafine's safety, but what is easy is not always what is wise.

"I'll never tell you," Cail said with a menacing smirk. His victory was brief as Barok let out a thunderous roar and slammed Cail's back onto the rigid stone, knocking the wind out of Cail's lungs. Cail tried to recover to his feet, but his body remained as still as the stone beneath him. He gasped time and time again, desperately trying to cling to even a tiny wisp of fresh air, but there were only venomous fumes of the Blue Assassins who surrounded him. After several seconds of lying in throbbing agony, Cail rolled onto his belly and began to crawl on the cold, hard stone. Then a massive wooden club pounded onto the middle of his back, viciously plopping Cail onto the floor once again. He let out a cry of pain and tears were forced out of his eyes. The

Assassins surrounded Cail and started to kick and beat him mercilessly, fracturing his bones and gashing his flesh.

"Enough!" Barok shouted after what seemed like an eternity of punishment. Cail laid hopelessly still. Crimson blood flowed from dozens of wounds on his body and his eyes were glazed with tears of pain. The King of the Blue Assassins walked over to the battered boy before him and kneeled down by Cail's ear. Softly, he asked, "Have you had your fill of pain?"

Cail ignored the foul stench coming from Barok's breath and whispered, "You'll never beat the truth out of me." Barok rose to his feet once more without saying anything in response. He snatched the broadest club he could find and, without a word of warning, crushed the back of Cail's head with it, knocking him unconscious.

"Get this wretch out of my sight," Barok said, looking over to Micah.

"To the dungeons?" Micah asked as he reached down for Cail's arm.

"Yes. Once he wakes, his true punishment will begin."

Chapter 4: A Village Torn

Serafine expected Elona to be quiet and timid, as it always was. The village had a history of being a peaceful sanctuary, a place of comfort and healing. Ever since Serafine and Cail had killed Kalil's faithful servants, she greatly admired the simplicity of Elona. It was a place where she could find peace in her mind and throw away the worries of the world. She had never known a small, quaint community such as Elona. Serafine was raised in the glorious palace of Kye, which was the heart of the entire nation. Kye was a vast city, covering more land than a mountain. Even though beauty and glamor could be found throughout Kye, so too could peril be found. With Serafine being the daughter of the King, it was imperative for her to be protected at all times. She felt trapped, like a monkey in a cage. There were very few moments that she wasn't surrounded by guards, moments where she could enjoy her own company.

That was why Serafine loved coming to Elona; she felt free. No one knew that she was a princess in her past life, and no one would care if they did know. Her being a princess bore no weight on the lives of Elona. They accepted her for who she was; a Descendant of the gods. Elona gave her a sense of security. Even though she didn't have any protection, she knew she didn't need it.

As Serafine walked off the bridge and onto the island, she stood before a great oak tree, towering high above her. The emerald trees glimmered as radiantly as a queen's dress, swaying in the gentle breeze, the leaves whispering with every sudden gust. Serafine had spent months inside Silman's colossal mountain, searching for a way to return to Aithnen, but this tree reminded her of the preeminence of the outdoors, of the fact that everyone needed to breathe the free air. After Serafine had finished admiring the tree, she continued into the heart of Elona. The village she entered wasn't the same Elona she remembered, though. There was a raucous crowd in the center of the town, a crowd that sounded hostile and full of anger. The people's rage roared like a powerful wave crashing onto an unsuspecting beach. Some of the men brought shovels and pitchforks and all the others were waving their fists in the air. They weren't mad at each other, though. Everyone was circled around something or someone.

Serafine sprinted toward the horde of people and shoved men and women out of her way, trudging to the center of attention; a slender man who was slouched on his knees. Shame and guilt was painted on his face, just as anger was on the faces of the Elonians. He was thin, almost to the point of malnourishment, and his long, brown bangs covered his eyes. His clothes were ragged and dirty, stained by no small amount of sweat.

"What is the meaning of this?" Serafine called out to anyone willing to answer. The clamor of the crowd slowly died to a dull murmur. At first, no one dared to claim responsibility for the outrageous gathering.

"This man is guilty of murder," said a booming voice resonating from behind Serafine. She spun around and saw Cecil with a face matching the anger of the crowd. "Or at least he would've been had I gone from my home. He's nothing more than deceitful scum and he must be punished."

"I would like to hear from him before we go about dealing punishments," Serafine responded, taken back by Cecil's brash behavior. She kneeled down before the man and gently lifted his chin so she could see his face. His bangs gently slid to both sides of his head, revealing dark brown eyes filled with fear. "You should keep in mind that any lie that slips off your tongue will result in an anguishing death. Now, who are you? Why have you come here?" The man said nothing. He just blankly stared into her eyes, refusing to cooperate.

After waiting for an answer, Serafine's patience diminished. She held out her right hand and a ball of flame ignited in her palm. The man's eyes immediately homed in on the fire, but he remained silent. Serafine brought the inferno closer to the man's face, the sweltering heat summoned sweat from the pores of his skin. Just as the flames were about to touch his face, the man bellowed out, "Stop! I'll talk! Please, keep the fire away from me."

Granting the man his wish, Serafine clenched her fist, extinguishing the fire, and shoved the man to the ground. Standing over him, she said, "Speak swiftly, or I will no longer care what you have to say."

"My name is Loran—" he started to say but was interrupted by Cecil.

"Lies! That's what he said to Cail!" Cecil yelled irately.

"It's the truth, I swear!" Loran responded, his voice filled with desperation. "Loran is my name. I was sent here to convince Cail to leave Elona and go to Cestmir."

Serafine swiped down and snatched Loran by the collar of his greasy shirt. Loran whimpered in fear, intimidated by Serafine's strength. "Who sent you? What do they want with Cail?"

"I was sent by Barok, King of the Blue Assassins," Loran responded. The name shot ice into Serafine's spine, paralyzing her bones. She dropped Loran and he fell to the ground with a thud. Serafine looked as though she had seen a ghost, her face as pale as the clouds in the sky.

"You lie," Serafine whispered, hoping that she was right, but fearing that Loran had told the truth.

"No. The Blue Assassins have overtaken Cestmir and now Cail is their prisoner."

"That's not true!" Serafine shouted as she clubbed Loran across the cheek with her fist. He plopped onto the ground and grimaced in pain. "Barok died centuries ago."

"Believe that if it brings you comfort, but the truth is that he lives and now he has what he came to find: The Last Descendant," Loran said with a sinister smirk on his bloodied face.

"What does he want with Cail?" Cecil asked, interjecting himself into the interrogation.

"I don't know why he needs Cail, but the Master has been possessed by his desire to return to Aithnen. He's not the same leader he used to be. This obsession has drowned him beneath an ocean of greed. There's nothing he's not willing to do to go home, including the sacrifice of his own men. We're nothing more than his pawns."

"Yet you continue to serve him," Serafine said with disgust.

"Only so I can return to my home as well. Once I do, he'll mean nothing to me," Loran admitted. He pushed himself up to his feet and stood face to face with Serafine. "What does it matter, though? You're going to kill me, aren't you?"

"It would be the logical decision. You're a weed that could spread through green pastures. Depravity should be killed, no matter how trivial it is. Still, you could prove to be much more useful alive, rather than dead," Serafine said pondering over the choices laid before her. She looked to Cecil, seeking his counsel. He did nothing but gently shake his head, signaling for her to kill Loran. She turned her gaze back to Loran and looked deep into his brown eyes. Trust and skepticism blended and swirled inside Serafine's mind, clouding the right decision.

If he can abandon Barok, the Master of his clan, then he can just as easily abandon me. Still, he's of more use to me alive than dead. The only question is, will his use outweigh the risk of him betraying us? Serafine thought silently to herself. Having made her decision, she said, "I have found a way to return to Aithnen, but I need Cail to be kept alive in order to do so. If you pledge your fealty to me, I can promise you your home. When you arrive in Aithnen, you'll be a free man with no ties to the Blue Assassins. What do you say?"

"I'll be absolved of all the crimes committed by the Blue Assassins?"

Serafine hesitated. She knew of the obscenities to which he referred. Heinous acts had been executed by this gang of criminals. Bearing the entire situation in mind, she said, "Yes. I will see to the pardoning of all your wrongdoing if you remain loyal to me."

Without any sort of pause, Loran kneeled before Serafine and said, "You have presented to me an offer I simply can't refuse. I pledge myself to you as payment for my freedom."

"I can't allow this!" Cecil interjected. "This criminal tried to kill Laney in her sleep, and we're going to ask him to join us?" The crowd surrounding them hollered in agreement.

"Everyone, stop!" Serafine pleaded, begging the Elonians to lay their hostility to rest. "You have no idea what the Blue Assassins are capable of. I've seen them with my own eyes. If Cail went to Cestmir by himself, then he's undoubtedly captured by now. Loran is our best chance to save Cail from his imprisonment." The crowd quieted, mulling over what Serafine said.

Kadir stepped forth and said, "I'll go with you to Cestmir. Cail must be rescued, no matter the cost." Serafine was taken back by Kadir's size; he had grown taller and broader since she last saw him. His arms had nearly as much muscle as Serafine's thighs, his chest was level with the top of her head, and his neck was as stout as a tree stump. Kadir was unquestionably strong, but Serafine knew that he had never faced a formidable foe like the Blue Assassins. Nonetheless, his strength would prove to be a great asset. Serafine extended her arm and shook Kadir's hand, accepting his offer to serve. His grip strangled her palm, but she managed to hide the discomfort.

"I know Cail will offer you a great reward once we save him," Serafine said, looking into Kadir's blue eyes.

"He's my friend. I don't need a reward for helping him."

Serafine cast a smile toward Kadir. She could see the close affection that he felt for Cail, the willingness to sacrifice himself for his friend. For a moment, she was jealous of Cail; she envied the friends he had, friends who would give everything away for his safety, friends who would love him until the end of all days. Then she realized she did have a friend such as that; Cail. He was the reason she could breathe the free air; he rescued her from the shackles of Kalil's servants. It would have been painless for Cail to ignore the girl who was locked away in a high tower, to cast her out of his mind, but Cail did the selfless deed.

"Who else will join me to save Cail?" Serafine yelled to the crowd, trying to recruit anyone she could for the mission, but none stepped forth. Cowardice thrived and no one summoned the courage to say anything. Instead, everyone remained silent and then dispersed back to their homes, leaving Serafine, Cecil, Kadir, and Loran alone in the middle of the village. Serafine was dejected, disappointed by the Elonians refusal to fight for the boy who had saved them from evil. In a way, she felt as though she had witnessed betrayal.

"I would come with you, but if the Blue Assassins are anything like the legends of old, then I would be no match for them," Cecil said after everyone else had gone.

"And I would never ask you to come," Serafine responded, wearing a fake smile on her face, but they could all see her discouragement. "We'll do the best we can with what we have, just like we did against Kalil."

"As someone who has never heard of the Blue Assassins before just now, I'd like to know exactly what we're going up against," Kadir said. He used confidence to mask his fear, but Serafine could hear the trepidation in his voice.

"You're going against the most fearsome gang in all of Aithnen," Loran interrupted before Serafine could open her mouth. "Many people claim that the Blue Assassins are the criminals, but the real crime rests in what forced us into being. Aithnen is a prosperous nation, filled with riches and goods for all, yet the rich and powerful hold an infinite amount of wealth from those they deem unworthy. The democracies of the Domain of Fire were born without any flaws and protected everyone who lived within their jurisdictions. For thousands of years, Aithnen thrived as a utopian society.

"Then greed consumed the heart of one of the Four Kings, King Olizar. When he traveled through the streets and saw his constituents, he didn't see anyone who was his equal, he saw people who should be beggars instead. The greed in his heart morphed into corruption and the corruption turned into hatred. For a time, he didn't act on this hatred, for fear of being stripped of his powers.

"Having grown weary of seeing those he deemed lesser than him, King Olizar no longer ventured through his city and he isolated himself from the very people he swore to protect. Subtle was the sword that he used to slash the privileges from his citizens. One law was changed after another, feeding his greed off us like a leech. The corruption in Olizar's heart seeped into the hearts of the three other Kings and they also asserted themselves as dominant tyrants. For a while, all the Aithnenians complied, giving in to our Kings' commands, but not for long.

"Barok, like many of those around him, struggled to survive. He had to fight for food, water, shelter, the essentials of life. Being gifted with astute wisdom, Barok saw what the Kings were doing and was outraged by it. It was disgraceful, in his mind, for him to be forced to fight for survival every day of his life while his leaders sat upon mountains of riches, soaking in jewels and gold. The injustice of the Kings of Aithnen. gave birth to the Blue Assassins. We're simple liberators."

"Cail also liberated the nation of Kordon, but he didn't try to kill innocent people," Cecil protested, still feeling bitter toward Loran's actions.

"I was only acting under the orders of my Master. For reasons unbeknownst to me, he wanted Laney dead. I presume because she's close to the boy," Loran responded.

Kadir turned to Serafine, who had remained silent throughout the entirety of Loran's story, and asked, "Is what he said true? Did the Kings of Aithnen do this to their own people?"

"I wish I could say they hadn't," Serafine said softly. She refused to maintain eye contact, ashamed of the truth. "Regretfully, my father, Alban, was one of the Kings who was influenced by Olizar."

"Your own father did this and you stood idly by? You did nothing to protect your fellow citizens?" Kadir's anger began to boil in his breath.

"There was nothing I could've done!" Serafine exploded, infuriated by Kadir's accusations. "I was but a child at the time, there were no words that my father would've listened to." Despite Serafine's defense of herself, Kadir remained unsatisfied.

"Enough!" Cecil blurted out, annoyed by their bickering. "You can cast blame at each other all you want, but that won't save Cail. Serafine, come with me and I'll give you the supplies you need for the expedition. Kadir, you need to stay with Loran, I don't want him anywhere near Laney." Loran shot a furious glance at Cecil, but he paid him no mind.

Cecil led Serafine into his kitchen and started combing through the wooden pantries, searching for food. As he looked he said, "So long as Loran is with you, my mind will find no comfort. He's not to be trusted."

"You have nothing to worry about, Cecil," Serafine responded with confidence. "I'll keep my watchful eyes on him at all times."

A solid thud pounded through the ceiling, coming from the bedrooms. Cecil and Serafine remained silent for a moment, patiently listening, but there was nothing. Cecil waved his hand at Serafine, giving her the signal to follow him. They crept up the stairs, wincing at the wood creaking underneath the weight of their feet. The hallway at the top of the staircase was dark and silent and all three of the bedroom doors were left wide open. Cecil's bedroom was the closest, so they snuck through the doorway.

The bedroom remained just as Cecil had left it. Cecil's striped pajamas were neatly folded and placed on the seat of his reading chair in the far corner, his thick sheets were firmly tucked in, his plump pillows remained in their designated places, and the sunlight beamed through the open window curtains. After closely examining his bedroom, Cecil whispered, "Let's check the other rooms." Serafine nodded and followed Cecil.

Laney's room was just across the hall. Through the door was the unchanged bedroom, save for one detail. "Laney's gone!" Cecil exclaimed. He sprinted to the side of the bed, observing the messy sheets that were cast to one side. Cecil reached down and held the ivory sheet in his fingers. Then anger flared in his mind and he clenched his fist. "Loran," he growled through gritted teeth. "He followed us back to the house. This was his plan the whole time."

"That's not possible," Serafine said softly, thinking about how Loran could've accomplished this abduction. No matter the scenario she ran through her head, none of them added to the outcome of Laney being stolen. "Kadir was with him the entire time. There's no way he did this."

"Kadir was with who?" said a soft voice coming from behind. Cecil and Serafine both spun around and saw Laney standing in the doorway. She wore a white, wrinkled gown, her hair was dried and messy, and vigorous color had returned to her skin.

"Laney! You're awake!" Cecil exclaimed. Serafine looked at Laney in awe, unable to believe her eyes. Cecil ran to Laney and threw his arms around her, overjoyed that she had finally woken from months of unconsciousness. After he let go of Laney, she wore a confused look on her face. As if he could read her mind, Cecil said, "You've been trapped in a deep coma for months."

Laney's eyes ballooned and she stammered, "N-n-no. That can't be. I remember everything clearly." She placed her palm on her forehead, trying to snatch the memories from her mind. Then she recited them as the recollections were displayed in her eyes. "We were bombarded by the zuraks, and they dragged me to Kalil. For three long, excruciating years he tormented me and swung the threat of death in front of my face, but he never gave it to me. At first, I had hope that Cail would return, which offered me the strength to endure Kalil's torture, but then the days turned sour. Doubt poisoned my mind and dampened my spirit. Every cut, bruise, and scar dragged me further away from home. I began to beg for my death.

"Then Cail returned. He charged the Iron Fortress, beaming like a sun in a cloudless sky. And then…" Her words drifted off and her eyes glazed. Laney closed her eyes and rubbed her forehead, trying to hone her thoughts. She let out a grunt of frustration and then said, "That's all I can remember before waking up a few minutes ago."

"Laney, that was six months ago," Serafine said, placing a comforting hand on Laney's shoulder. Laney shot an incredulous glance at Serafine, but Serafine continued, "Tarvaris, Kalil's servant, cast a malicious, powerful spell on you. Cail freed you from the curse and saved Kordon from the tyranny of Kalil, but the spell took a toll on your body. We didn't know if you would ever wake up."

Laney's emotions stirred. She felt overwhelmed by the thought of six months of her life passing in the blink of an eye. She held out her arms and looked for any fresh wounds that Kalil had dealt her, but all she saw were faint scars, remnants of her imprisonment. Then her mind turned toward Cail, her savior. "Cail saved us all?" Laney asked. Cecil nodded in response. "Where is he? I greatly desire to see him."

"He's gone to Cestmir," Serafine responded. She carefully mulled over her next words, not wanting to trouble Laney's fragile mind. "He was told of unusual activity in the Ivory City. Kadir and I are preparing to depart to meet him there."

"I'll go with you!" Laney insisted.

"Absolutely not," Cecil interjected. "You've only just awoken. We don't know if this curse has done anything else to your body, or if it is even gone for good."

Laney cursed under her breath. Then she said, "When you find Cail please remind him of his promise. He has something that belongs to me."

Chapter 5: Buried Beneath

Cold air howled through the barred windows, freezing the grim chambers that imprisoned the captives of the Blue Assassins. Iron cells with rusted bars were stacked side by side, creating an organized array of agony. Mossy stone encompassed the prison, allowing no illumination, save for the small rectangular window near the ceiling. The cells were lifeless; jars filled with poison. Every prisoner was beaten and battered, tortured like wild animals. Some of the newest captives fervently searched for ways to escape, while seasoned prisoners didn't move, fully aware that any attempt to leave the depraved labyrinth was futile.

Every day the guards worked their way through each of the cells, mercilessly beating their prisoners. The Blue Assassins didn't pummel their captives in an attempt to gain intel or items of value, instead, they did it for pleasure. Screams of agony, pleas for salvation, and begs for mercy were all that would satisfy the Blue Assassins. Cail didn't allow his pain to surface. It was impossible to hide all the gashes and bruises he had been dealt over the past two weeks of his imprisonment, but he blanketed his fear and torment deep within his mind. No matter what the Blue Assassins did to him, he would protect Serafine with all his might. Only he knew that she had the Shadow Stone and as long as that secret was kept, Serafine's life would be sheltered.

The chamber doors flung open, sending a thunderous pound through the prison. Even though Cail couldn't see the doors from his cell, he knew what approached; he knew the guards had come to unleash their punishment on the prisoners. Cail closed his eyes, focusing his mind on creating a shelter, a refuge from all the pain he would soon endure. He heard a faint click of the first cell. Then onerous thuds beat deeply like a thunderous drum, each pound followed closely by a shrilling shriek. One by one, the guards progressed through the cells, wailing on the prisoners as though they were meat being tenderized. Cail was the last cell in the prison, so he had to hopelessly watch everyone endure their anguish.

The guards opened the door of the cell neighboring Cail's and immediately assaulted the prisoner with vicious aggression, but the prisoner didn't scream or beg for mercy; he accepted his fate. As Cail's neighbor was snapped by thick leather whips and beaten by broad wooden clubs, Cail wanted to look away, but couldn't. In an odd way, watching another person's torture prepared him for his own. It hardened his skin and closed his mind from any torment that would be thrown in his direction.

The prisoner's body collapsed onto the hard stone of the floor and the guards stood over him, each wearing a sinister grin. After admiring the pain they had administered, the guards turned toward Cail and then whispered amongst themselves. Fear shot through Cail's spine, but he refused to allow it to surface. He tried to maintain a sealed mind and a skeleton made of iron, but his trepidation outweighed his courage. All four of the guards strode from the neighboring cell to Cail's. One of them retrieved a brass key from a leather pouch hanging on his waist. With an onerous click, the door of Cail's cell swung open and the guards filed through. They all wore thick black armor, completely covered from head to toe. Their clubs were longer than Cail's legs and the whips were broader than his palm. "I'm ready," Cail said in a soft voice, succumbing to the punishment he was about to endure.

The largest of the four guards stepped forth, each footstep sending a tremor through the ground. Through yellowed teeth, he said, "We have very strict orders to take you to Barok unhurt." Cail was leaning on another day of agonizing torture, not expecting to be taken to the King of the Blue Assassins himself. Although, he was now presented with a sliver of leverage, which he fully intended to use.

"And if I refuse to come?" Cail asked, firmly standing his ground.

"Refusal is not an option," the guard snapped back.

"It is if you can't hurt me," Cail responded wearing a sly smirk on his face. The guard immediately recognized that Cail was using him as a pawn. He lunged toward Cail, trying to snatch him by his thin, ripped shirt. Cail swiftly dodged the guard and blasted him in the side with a powerful gust of wind, flinging the guard against the cell's bars. The guard slammed headfirst into the iron bars and laid still on the ground, unconscious. The three remaining guards quickly shuffled out of the cell, not afraid of Cail, but of what would become of them if they allowed Cail to escape. One of the three stood at the cell's door and growled, "You'll pay for that. Barok will make you suffer in ways you couldn't possibly imagine."

"What more could he do to me?" Cail responded, almost daring the guards to defy their King's orders and hurt him. The guard let out a menacing chuckle and then led the other two out of the prison.

After the guards were out of earshot, the man trapped in the cell next to Cail's said, "What madness is in you? Barok will unleash his fury on you!"

"How can he do that if I'm no longer caught in his trap?" Cail responded with a smirk. The prisoner said nothing in response as he cast an expression of incredulity. Cail walked over to the unconscious guard, who's body remained in his cell. "Only a fool would leave a guard with a prisoner," Cail said as he kneeled beside the limp body. He reached into the guard's pouch, ignoring the dried food crumbs, and retrieved the brass key. Proud of his cunning theft, Cail held the key in the light, admiring its rough edges. He weaved his arm through the bars of his cell and unlocked the door. For the first time in weeks, Cail had the freedom to go wherever he wanted, he had the freedom to jump, run, sit, rest, and most importantly, he was liberated from the torture he had endured.

Cail tossed the key through the bars of the neighboring cell and said to the prisoner, "Empty all the cells. There's someone I have to find, the only person who can rid this city of the Blue Assassins." That person was Beda, the girl who had taught Cail in the art of combat, the Queen of the Red Pumas. She and her army were buried somewhere deep in the dark chambers and Cestmir would never be free until they were found.

As Cail sprinted toward the prison's doors, he could hear the cells clicking open and the prisoners' clamoring grow louder. The excess of noise would undoubtedly attract the guards, so Cail had little time to spare. He darted through a towering archway which led him into a labyrinth of hallways. Each hall was dimly illuminated by a single torch perched on the side of the wall. Three options were laid before Cail, one to his left, right, and one directly in front. He had no choice but to blindly trust his instincts. He chose the right hall.

He jogged as swiftly, but also quietly, as he could. Every step sent a jolt of pain through his bones. The weeks of torture had taken their toll on his body and his muscles had weakened. Cail pressed onward nonetheless. The hallway curved like a snake, twisting and twirling, testing what little strength remained in Cail's legs. At last, Cail reached the end of the hallway and arrived in a small chamber that looked to be a cramped bedroom. It was far from luxurious. A narrow bed with a thin mattress and dull sheets was pressed into the corner, a dirt-stained wooly rug was matted in the middle of the floor, and in the corner opposite the bed, a rickety dresser stood, barely large enough to hold a few changes of clothing. Not wanting to waste more time than what was necessary, Cail quickly spun around to leave, but before he could take another step, the rug coiled around his foot and Cail plummeted to the cold, hard floor. Cail cursed at himself for being so loud and clumsy. His hands and knees burned from scraping against the stone bricks. Cail grimaced from the intense searing sensation, he felt as though he had walked straight through fire.

Cail shoved the pain aside and, in a similar fashion, pushed his body off the floor, but before he rose to his reddened knees, he noticed something peculiar beneath the bed. From where he had landed, there appeared to be another leg of the bed, but it was directly beneath the center, suggesting that it was something else. Curiosity won the battle and Cail crawled beneath the bed on the floor carpeted with dirt. In front of Cail was an iron lever, nearly rising to the bed's mattress. Cail pulled on the lever, it didn't budge. He tugged harder until it finally started to shift, grinding against the stone floor on either side of the stem. The lever snapped into place and then a low rumble reverberated from behind Cail and the floor beneath him quaked. After the room quieted, Cail laid still, frozen by the fear that someone had heard the commotion and was on their way to take Cail back to his cell of anguish. There were no approaching footsteps, though. He pushed himself from beneath the bed and when he rose to his feet, he turned around and noticed that the dresser had slid from the corner, revealing a tiny crawlspace, slightly wider than Cail's shoulders. The crawlspace was just wide enough for Cail to crawl through, but narrow enough that he wouldn't be followed.

He slithered into the hole, moving through darkness. Once his entire body was in, the dresser slid back to its original position, engulfing Cail in complete darkness. The darkness was heavy, weighing on his eyes. Cobwebs were draped along the walls and the stone bricks turned to cold, moist dirt. After progressing through the darkness, Cail heard faint voices above his head. "We've rounded up nearly all the escapees, sir," a voice said. The voice was shaky, riddled with fear. An unmistakable voice boomed in response.

"Nearly? 'Nearly' isn't good enough. 'Nearly' allows for the return of the Last Descendant! I don't want to see your face again unless you have Cail in chains. Now, get out of my sight!" After Barok's tirade ended, Cail heard shuffling footsteps above him, shortly followed by the heavy thuds of Barok's feet. *I must have found a hidden system of tunnels,* Cail thought to himself. He continued trudging through the darkness, ignoring the footsteps and clamoring above his head. Without warning, Cail's hand fell through a hole, followed by the rest of his body. His body flipped over and solid concrete smacked his back after a short fall. Throbbing paralysis froze his spine for a moment. Tall, muscular men ran to Cail's side and surrounded him as he laid motionless. Dread settled into his mind as he knew that he was about to be taken captive once again. A silhouette of one of the guards leaned over Cail's head, but this guard had slender shoulders and a thin face. Then Cail realized it wasn't the silhouette of a guard.

"As clumsy as ever. Did you learn nothing from me?" Cail let out a sigh of relief when he heard the familiar voice. Beda and her army of Red Pumas surrounded him. He was safe at last. She offered her hand and Cail accepted. Beda tugged Cail upward and launched him onto his feet and off his back. She was deceptively strong for her size and every bit as fast. Beda's appearance had changed a lot since Cail had last seen her. She had grown taller so that her eyes were level with Cail's, her brown hair had darkened, almost to a shiny shade of black, and her muscles were much more defined than ever before.

"I managed to escape only minutes ago," Cail said looking around at all the soldiers. "You've been hiding underground?"

"Temporarily," Beda responded. "I weaseled from my miserable prison a few days ago, and I've been slowly smuggling my soldiers to safety ever since. There's only three more men to free and then we'll be ready to charge the Blue Assassins. I don't know what their motive is, but I will exact my revenge. Barok will pay for what he has done to Cestmir."

"He took Cestmir so he could strike a bargain with the Sages of Pazia," Cail said. "They came from Aithnen, but they've been trapped in Kordon for centuries. The Blue Assassins were promised a safe return to their home if they delivered my corpse and the Shadow Stone to the Sages."

"If you're still alive, I'm assuming Barok doesn't have the stone?"

"That's right. The Shadow Stone is held safely in Serafine's hands, although I don't know where she is now. She could be anywhere in Kordon, assuming she hasn't returned to Aithnen already," Cail said. Then he paused for a moment, allowing Beda to ponder over what he told her. "Is Barok really so powerful that he could overcome the Red Pumas?"

"He needed the perfect storm, and he got it," Beda answered. She proceeded to say, "Months had passed since our victory, months of recovery and replenishment. Cestmir could breathe the free air once again, thanks to you. The Blue Assassins slowly seeped into the city, appearing as innocent and guiltless as a tourist. They seamlessly molded in with the rest of the civilians, perfectly camouflaging as natives. I was blind and blissful; I never expected the city to be hit so soon, especially after we had just freed Kordon from the malicious tyrant.

"The Blue Assassins waited until all their warriors had trickled into Cestmir, then they attacked at night. I was awoken from my slumber by shrilling screams of agony. Cries for help echoed throughout the black sky, I can still hear those voices; they're ghosts that haunt my sleepless nights. By the time I was ready to rally my soldiers, they had already taken us as hostages. I had no choice but to go into hiding. While Barok's guards searched the White Castle, I attempted to free some of my soldiers, but the Blue Assassins are much swifter than I. They found me and, until a few days ago, tormented me in a wretched prison."

Silence fell over the room. Cail could see the pain in the eyes of the Red Pumas, he could see the city being seized by Barok's army. He could hear the screams of helpless men, women, and children. He could smell the smoke of homes and stores caught ablaze by the cruel mercenaries. He felt the blistering heat of the fire; it pierced through his skin. Without realizing it, Cail had clenched his fist as his anger flared. The atrocities committed by the Blue Assassins were unforgivable.

"What can we do now?" Cail asked, desperately wanting to exact revenge.

"Three of our strongest generals are still imprisoned. They're tightly protected by a legion of guards, so using force to break them out would be nigh impossible," Beda answered, sorting through their options.

"We'll have to use stealth, then?" Cail proposed.

"I would say so," Beda answered. She rubbed her thin chin, lost in her own pondering. "I think the wisest choice would be for you and me to go alone and free the generals ourselves. A large crowd would draw far too much attention—" Beda was interrupted by grunts echoing through the cramped tunnel that Cail had crawled through. The Red Pumas moved swiftly to form a defensive wall protecting Cail and Beda. They drew their pointed, glistening swords and tall shields, bracing for whatever escaped the tunnel. Beda stood on her toes so she could peer over her soldiers' shoulders. No one dared to say a word or let out a heavy breath. Cail decided not to spend any energy trying to see over the wall of soldiers. A man escaped from the narrow tunnel and Beda hollered, "Halt!" She wasn't yelling that command at the mysterious person, but at her soldiers.

Beda weaved in between the Red Pumas and Cail followed closely behind her. Standing in front of the army was Kadir. His clothes were powdered with dirt and his hair was dry and brittle. Soon after, Serafine emerged from the tunnel and rose to her feet. Seeing two of his best friends filled Cail's heart with overwhelming joy. "How did you find us?" Cail asked. He couldn't help but let a smile crawl onto his face.

"Quite by accident, to tell the truth," Serafine responded, walking toward Cail. Her long, brown hair was tied into a tail, seemingly untouched by the dirt in the tunnel, her eyes possessed a piercing focus, like a tiger staring down its prey. "We managed to slither through the castle unseen. It appears that the will of fate has brought us all together once again."

"Fate, you say?" Beda repeated. A clever smile emerged and confidence radiated from her face. She turned to Kadir and asked, "Kadir, would you like to be the commander of a great army?"

He was taken back by the question. Leading an army as powerful as the Red Pumas was a dream he always fantasized, but he never imagined that the opportunity would present itself to him. Stuttering, he said, "Y-y-yes. But what army? The Red Pumas belong to you."

"True. However, Cail, Serafine, and I are going to find a few prisoners. That means you're going to be in complete control of the Red Pumas while I'm gone. Do you think you can handle that?" Kadir swiftly, and quite clumsily, saluted Beda, almost smacking his hand against her forehead. Satisfied with Kadir's acceptance, Beda turned to Cail and Serafine and said, "Let's move. There's no time to lose."

Traversing deeper into the castle also meant traversing deeper into darkness. Guards heavily monitored all the chambers, especially those holding prisoners. The trio didn't want to risk being caught while freeing random civilians; their sole focus was on the generals. Beda led Cail and Serafine through the murky dungeons of the castle, slithering as briskly and silently as a shadow. She found a corridor that was impassable for the Blue Assassins, being the broad men that they were, but was just wide enough for them to squeeze through. The corridor curved back and forth until it led them to a steep ledge. It overlooked a massive dungeon flooded with rectangular, iron prison cells. Cail's heart sunk when he saw the hundreds, if not thousands, of Blue Assassins walking throughout the dungeon, clamoring amongst themselves. They were a pack of wolves, ready to pierce their teeth into whatever came before them. The very sight of them sent chills down Cail's spine. All too well he remembered the weeks of torture he endured, he remembered the clubs bruising his skin.

He looked at Beda and whispered, "Now what do we do?"

She remained silent, closely looking over the guards like a hawk searching for a branch to land on. The expression of incredulity on her face told Cail that she didn't imagine that there would be this many Blue Assassins guarding her generals. With a hushed voice, she said, "We need a distraction to draw them away from the cells. We're going to need Kadir and my soldiers to do that."

"What do you want us to do?" Serafine asked.

"Wait here. I'll bring a small group of the Red Pumas along to create a diversion. Once we do so, you two need to move swiftly in order to free the generals. Then we can all retreat and prepare to take the Blue Assassins down once and for all."

"Have you completely lost your mind?" Serafine interjected, nearly shouting so that all the Blue Assassins could hear her. "You truly expect to elude these murderers like a rabbit running from a fox?"

"I think you underestimate the speed of some of my fastest men," Beda responded with a sly smile. And with that, she darted off, running in the same direction they had come from, vanishing into the darkness. Serafine plopped onto the ground, with her legs crossed, and cursed under her breath.

Cail stayed silent for a moment, waiting for Serafine to calm down, and then he asked, "Why did you go back to Elona? I thought you were going to go home."

"That's true," she responded with a poised voice. "However, I need you to return to Aithnen." Then she continued to tell Cail everything that Wallen had told her. She told him about the power of the Shadow Stone, the four demigods, even the danger of the Blue Assassins. However, she decided to keep the Air Rune hidden until she absolutely needed it. "You and Emey are a paramount part of uniting Neptil once again."

"I don't know, Serafine," Cail responded with a raspy whisper. "Being home over the last few months brought peace and contentment back into my heart. My body has replenished, my bones have healed, my thirst has been quenched. I came here to try to be the hero once more, but I was overpowered by the Blue Assassins. They throttled and beat me, brought me within an inch of my life on several occasions. The last couple of weeks have shown me that maybe I'm not destined to do this anymore."

"That's nonsense!" Serafine answered as quietly as she could. "You're a descendant of the gods, the protector of Kordon, the Master of the Wind. You're simply going to throw all that away because you're afraid of a formidable foe?"

"This isn't just about the Blue Assassins, it's about everyone who will turn against me and try to hurt the ones I love. My father was nearly killed by the zuraks, they imprisoned the entire village, and Laney is still unconscious thanks to Tarvaris' curse."

"No, she isn't. She awoke just before Kadir and I left Elona. She's alive and well now," Serafine revealed, hoping to calm Cail's emotions, but it only made them worse.

"What? When were you planning on telling me this?" Cail asked, angered by the fact that he had been kept in the dark.

"When it became necessary to do so, as it just has. I don't intend to sound insensitive, but she's a simple girl, someone whose life carries no weight in the fight between good and evil. You, on the other hand, are much more important to your people. You're a beacon of hope. The good people of Kordon look to you as a symbol of optimism. You're a sign that justice is divinely destined to prevail in this country."

Cail didn't know how to respond to Serafine's beautiful articulation of what he embodied. He didn't even know that he embodied anything. Ever since he had returned to Elona, Cail had become so enveloped in his worries for Laney that he had lost track of everything he accomplished, all he had become. Cail had evolved from the scrawny young Lord of Elona into an unmatched power in Kordon. Almost unmatched, in truth. The Sages of Pazia remained a menace to him. Doing whatever they could to manipulate fate, to stop Cail from rising to power. Only in their death would Cail find safety. Until Cail brought the Sages to their demise, they would only continue to harass him, to barrage him with endless villains until Kordon was theirs. Kalil and the Blue Assassins both rose to power by the work of the Sages. How much more would the nation of Kordon suffer before the Sages paid for what they've done? How many more innocent lives would be endangered by this atrocity? How much pain would Laney have to endure before she could rest with a peaceful mind? Destroying the Sages was the only way to protect her from danger.

"Serafine, I'm ready to—" Cail's words were cut off when she put a hand in his face. Serafine hung over the edge of the cliff they were perched upon and watched the Blue Assassins below them. They clamored amongst themselves, hooting and hollering like mindless baboons. The sea of soldiers parted in the middle and two guards strode through, dragging a prisoner, a slender girl, through the crowd. The inmate's screams and pleas for help were muffled by a thick cloth wrapped around her mouth. Cail looked more closely and noticed that it was Laney! He nearly let out a yelp when he saw her, but somehow managed to hold back the noise.

"Poor soul," Serafine said with a gentle whisper, not looking away from the scene.

Anger took over Cail's mind. He snatched Serafine's shirt by the collar and said, "You let her come with you?"

"Of course not!" Serafine insisted, almost insulted by Cail's accusation. "We're not stupid. She must have snuck away after we left."

Dread sunk into Cail's heart and his stomach felt as heavy as iron. He desperately wanted to jump down from the cliff and kill every last one of the guards, but he knew that any attempt to do so would be folly. The guards threw Laney into her cell, slamming the iron door shut in her face. From the distance, it didn't appear Laney had been beaten too badly, but time was of the essence. All they could do was wait and hope that the Red Pumas would come in the nick of time.

Chapter 6: Liberation

Nearly two hours had passed since Laney was trapped in her cell. It was agony for Cail, having to watch Laney from afar. Every draining second carved into Cail's skin, piercing his bones. Dozens of Blue Assassins stood guard, ensuring that no one would stealthily snatch her from their grasp. The black cloaks of the guards were shadows of death swarming around Laney, leaving her in the wake of imminent danger. As desperately as Cail wanted to take on the Blue Assassins by himself, he knew it would only end in him being locked up as well. Patience, as painful as it was, was the only answer.

A sonorous pound resonated throughout the chamber. Cail and Serafine looked at each other, as though to ask if the sound was real or a figment of their imagination. The Blue Assassins silenced as well and everyone waited in burdened quietude for another sound. Shrill screams of pain echoed off the walls, coming from a corridor just below Cail and Serafine. The screams didn't belong to prisoners, but to guards. The moment to strike had finally come. Slowly, the Blue Assassins started filing into the corridor, cautiously approaching the disturbance.

Serafine grabbed Cail's shoulder and whispered into his ear, "The generals are over there." She pointed off to the distance. Cail's heart sunk when he saw that it was in the opposite direction of Laney's cell. "We need to move down this ledge and release them without being seen. After that, we'll lead them back here and regroup with the Red Pumas."

"You get the generals, I'll free Laney," Cail insisted.

"Not a chance," Serafine asserted. Anger was seeping from her whispers. "I need you to release the generals. We cannot defeat the Blue Assassins alone; we need the strength of the Red Pumas. Laney must wait until the city is free." Cail possessed half a mind to protest further, but he knew it would do no good. Serafine was just as stubborn as he was and far more aggressive. She led him down a dirt ramp that wound around the wall of the chamber and took them to the floor of the prison. The cells surrounding them were empty and there were very few guards remaining. Serafine swiftly strode with soft footsteps through the prison, peeking around every corner to ensure they weren't being watched. Cail followed closely behind, concentrating all his focus on moving as silently as Serafine. Then something tugged on his body, something he couldn't control. Serafine maintained her quiet movement, soundlessly running in a straight line, but Cail drifted to left. It didn't take long for him to part from Serafine, and when she realized he had gone, she couldn't call out to find him without alerting the remaining guards.

Cail had no idea where his body was taking him, or why it had betrayed Serafine; all he knew was he had to follow. He was taken by the wind, a servant to his master. Turning this way and that, his feet pounded against the ground, clouds of dirt puffing around his feet with every step. By sheer luck, there happened to be no guards near Cail, or else he would have been captured immediately. Then he stopped. In the jail cell just before Cail was someone he so desperately wished to see, but not in this prison; Laney. She was sitting in the corner of the cell, paying no attention to the world around her. Every day for six months, Cail had laid his eyes upon Laney's smooth, resting face, but now she was alive and breathing. The color of life had returned to her skin and her hair beamed like the sun. Her bright eyes were vigorous and beautiful. Cail saw a new person.

Once Laney saw Cail standing just outside of the cell, she jumped to her feet, ran to the bars of her cell, and whispered, "Cail! You're safe! I was so worried about you, I couldn't help but come here."

Cail froze, not knowing what to say. Part of his mind wanted his frustration to flow through his body and out his mouth. After all, why not? He had saved her from the clutches of a malicious, cruel, and evil emperor, and then, as soon as she recovered from her coma lasting six months, she ran back into a seized city, owned by murderers and criminals. Her actions were careless and imbecilic, but he couldn't bring himself to scold her. The sight of Laney brought happiness into his heart, happiness that calmed his exasperation. Cail didn't care that Laney had put herself in harm's way, he only cared about her being with him at that moment.

"Don't worry. I'll find a way to get you out of there," Cail managed to say after stumbling over silence. He looked on the ground, hoping to find some sort of object he could use to pick the cell's lock, but there was nothing, save for dirt and pebbles. Then Cail heard a pair of heavy footsteps approaching. The reverberations were too deep to belong to Serafine; undoubtedly, the footsteps belonged to guards. Not wanting to lose any spare time, Cail swiftly darted around the cell neighboring Laney's and hid behind the bars. The guard that approached was a brute, too stupid to observe the surrounding environment and see that the Last Descendant was only a few meters away.

"Hey, you! Come over here!" Laney called out to the guard, trying to keep him distracted. The guard approached, each of his steps sent a wave of vibration through the floor. Cail noticed that this guard was larger than most of the others. His shoulders were broader, his belly was rounder, and he towered taller. The hood of his black cloak masked his face, but the annoyance in his breath could be felt. Laney seemed to be unfazed by the guard and she asked, "How much longer am I going to be stuck in here?"

"You'll be summoned once the Master is ready for you," the guard growled with a thunderous voice. Laney carried on a vexing conversation with him as Cail started to creep around the corner of the cell and toward the guard. Then he felt a rock hit against his foot. The rock skidded across the floor, each bounce bringing it closer to the guard. Cail was tempted to dive for the rock, but knew that the guard would undoubtedly hear him if he did so. He closed his eyes, praying to the gods that the rock would stop, or miss the guard entirely; he cursed himself for being so carelessly clumsy. Then he heard a pang resonate off the guard's iron shin guard. Silence fell upon the conversation between Laney and the guard. Cail had no time to freeze, no time to think. He only had time to act.

Almost subconsciously, Cail thrust his arms and blasted the guard in his side with a violent stream of white wind. The guard toppled over and slammed into the ground, shaking the dirt below him. Moving with unmatched speed, Cail sprinted to the stunned foe and snatched his sword from its sheath. It took both hands to hold the bulky blade. Cail lifted it over his head and then slammed the point of the sword into the guard's chest. A shrill cry of pain pierced Cail's ears and ricocheted against the walls of the chamber. Shortly after, a few faint voices conversed in the distance; Cail assumed they were guards beginning their search for the source of the scream for help.

"Cail! Hurry and take his key! It won't be long before the guards find us," Laney said with an urgent voice, pointing at the fallen foe. Cail frantically dug through each of the guard's pockets. He could hear heavy footsteps beating like the drums of war. They were ominous, foreboding. The echoes rung louder and Cail's lungs stiffened. Then he found the key. It was in a pocket hidden by the sword's sheath. Only one key was in the pocket; presumably, a key that unlocked all the cells. Wasting no time, Cail slid the key into the slot and twisted it. A perfect fit. The cell door opened with a clang. Laney snatched Cail's thick forearm and dragged him along as she sprinted away. She had no idea which direction to run in, she only knew they needed to run away from the legion of oncoming guards. Her plan seemed to be working. The clamor of the Blue Assassins was disintegrating and pounding footsteps morphed into soft raindrops.

A thick hand snatched the collar of Cail's shirt and pulled him and Laney to the ground. Cail hit his head on the rough ground and his vision was blurred. Four silhouettes stood over him, four entities as dark as shadows. Cail cursed under his breath for being so slow, for being captured by the Blue Assassins. "Will you quit lying around?" One of the voices said with no small amount of irritation. It was at that moment Cail realized he wasn't captured by the guards. His vision came back and he saw Serafine, along with three large men, the generals, standing above him.

The generals were rough figures. Cail quickly saw why it was so important to find them. They were giants; towering well over three meters tall, their shoulders were stout foundations, their biceps had pulsing veins, and their legs were immovable tree stumps. As Cail and Laney quickly rose to their feet, Serafine said, "You're lucky we found you before the guards did. Now, follow me. Our escape isn't far from here." Without any sort of fuss, Cail and Laney followed Serafine and the generals out of the chamber and into another cramped crawlspace. The tunnel led them back to the cave in which the Red Pumas were hiding, but Beda and her small battalion were still missing.

Once they all climbed out of the crawlspace, Serafine's boiling temper took over. "Have you completely lost your mind? Your shenanigans could've gotten all of us killed! The objective was to get the generals and get out, not run around freeing whoever you wanted."

"I'm sorry, I don't know what came over me. One moment, I was right behind you, and then before I could stop myself, I was in front of Laney's cell," Cail explained, but it brought no satisfaction to Serafine. She angrily snorted and stomped away for a moment.

After Serafine had calmed down, she returned to Cail and Laney and asked, "What happened? Just as I released the generals, I heard a dreadful cry echoing through the air."

"I had to improvise," Cail responded. "I tried to sneak up behind one of the guards, but it backfired and I had to kill him swiftly."

"And it's a good thing you did, too," said a voice coming from behind them. Cail immediately recognized it as being Beda's voice. She, along with about twenty of her soldiers, walked into the cave. "The Blue Assassins had nearly closed in on us when they heard the scream, then they quickly ran off to find you. I'm happy to see you all made it back in one piece."

"No thanks to Cail," Serafine said, still feeling bitter toward Cail's recklessness.

"Calm down, Serafine. We're all here safely. Besides, if Cail wouldn't have killed that guard, we would've been captured by now."

Still disgruntled, Serafine asked, "We have the generals now and that means all the Red Pumas are safely in this cave. What do we do now?"

"Now it's time to take back our city," Beda said.

A volcano of rage exploded as Barok was delivered the ill news. At one time, he had all the Red Pumas pinned in his prisons. Now, there were none. They were all free and their whereabouts were unknown. For all he knew, the Red Pumas could've reclaimed the city outside the White Castle. "Is there a single soldier among you who isn't completely incompetent?" Barok bellowed. His voice blared like two boulders crashing into one another, cracking the rough surfaces. He was accompanied by his four generals, all of whom remained silent in their shame. Seeing that his generals weren't going to answer to their mounting failures, Barok said, "Get out of my sight." Without hesitation, they all darted away, fearful that if they didn't, Barok would take their lives.

Barok was alone, left to his thoughts. He scowled as his anger still clouded his mind. Nearly two thousand years of hardship and suffering had brought him to that moment, and it was being thwarted by the very boy he needed to capture. Cail was turning into a pest, a menace. The boy was a plague that was killing the body of Barok's dreams of returning to Aithnen. He knew there was no option other than to find Cail and kill him.

The towering doors of the throne room swung open and Loran ran through, his feet clapping on the marble floor and the flames of the torches swaying as he sprinted past. "My Lord!" he bellowed as he approached Barok. "My Lord, I bring good news to you. I know where the Red Pumas and the Last Descendant are hiding."

Barok cast a glance of intrigue at his soldier who had just returned from his venture to Elona. "Is that so?"

"Yes, my Lord," Loran said in between deep inhalations. "I've tricked them into believing that I would betray you in exchange for my freedom. I've sent everyone to prepare for an ambush, we just await you, sir. There's no time to lose. They're preparing to wage war on us."

Barok walked closer to Loran and placed his hands on Loran's thin shoulders. "You've done well, my brother. Once this is over and we are free to return to our home, you'll be rewarded handsomely," Barok said with a wide smile. Hope had been restored. Loran, the deceiver, had delivered his enemy as easily as a freshly baked pie. "Take me to them."

Loran obeyed his Master's commands. He led Barok out of the throne room, past all the hopeless and beaten prisoners, deep into the dark tunnels below to castle, and stopped in a massive cavern. The cave had over a dozen holes along the jagged, charcoal walls. There was no illumination, save for a giant burning mound, rising twice as high as Barok, on the other side of the cave, although Loran and Barok were too far away to tell exactly what was burning. Despite the blazing inferno, the air surrounding them was cold; chilled like the wind of a wintry night.

"Where is everyone?" Barok asked impatiently.

"They'll come," Loran responded with intentional vagueness.

Perfectly on cue, soldiers filed out of the cavern's hole, sprinting from the darkness. A legion of hooded black cloaks approached their master, ready to defend their king. Barok's army stood before him, eagerly awaiting their orders.

"My brothers," Barok called out with a booming voice, "the Red Pumas have proved to be a formidable foe, but thanks to Loran, they will no longer stand in the way of our return to Aithnen!" He expected a cheer or battle cry, instead, they stood in silence.

"You're right, the Red Pumas are a formidable foe," said a voice coming from a dark hood in front of Barok, the voice of a man he didn't recognize. The mysterious soldier removed his hood and instead of seeing the face of one of the Blue Assassins, Barok saw the face of his enemy, the face of the Last Descendant. With a sly grin on his face, Cail said, "You look surprised to see us."

Barok turned to Loran, who was standing a great distance away from his former leader, and asked, "This is what you've chosen? What makes their freedom greater than mine?"

"I wasn't just offered freedom, I was promised a new life," Loran responded. His words were a cold knife that dug deep into Barok's skin, as traitorous words usually do. They're a smooth blade that slides through flesh and slowly carves into the heart, it steals whatever breath remains in the lungs. Barok couldn't believe what he was hearing. None of his men had ever betrayed him, none of them ever had a reason to. He wasn't just their leader, he was their brother.

The realization of the inevitable glazed his eyes with tears. He turned to Loran and said, "We were so close to accomplishing our goal. We've toiled for centuries. Why would you do this to me now?"

"I suppose I've grown weary of living a life filled with bloodshed. The guilt of all the people we've killed has weighed on my mind for years. Serafine, the Descendant of our great nation, has opened a door for me to make amends. To answer your question, I'm doing this because you lack the remorse necessary to do what's right."

Barok's sadness caught fire and burst into rage. With a deep, growling voice, he said, "Loran, you will pay for your egregious betrayal; your lies will bring your death." Barok snatched Loran by the neck and lifted him off his feet. The massive hand of the fallen King of the Blue Assassins encompassed Loran's thin throat as Loran started gasping for breath.

All the Red Pumas swiftly drew their swords in response, moving as a singular unit. A legion of glistening blades was now pointed at Barok, ready to strike if he didn't let go. Even though death was waiting on his doorsteps, he didn't want to endure any pain that wasn't necessary, so he released Loran from his grasp. Loran plopped onto his back and started wheezing and coughing, trying with all his might to reclaim control over his lungs.

Cail stepped forward, still with a blade in hand, and said, "I believe the time has come for you to join your followers." It was at this moment that Barok realized what was being burnt in the towering mound across the empty cavern, or rather who was being burnt; the Blue Assassins. Barok didn't beg for his life, he knew it would do no good. The Red Pumas had taken back their city and his fate was sealed. His fiery red eyes locked with Cail's. Barok reached into his black cloak and retrieved a small item from his hidden pocket. The army of Red Pumas tensed and started moving forward to come to Cail's defense, but Cail held a hand up, halting them in their tracks. Cail could see that Barok wasn't drawing a weapon, but something else. Barok removed his hand from beneath his cloak and in his thick, dark fingers he held the last Sapphire Rose. It was a magnificent flower, with petals as blue as an ocean. Barok gave it to Cail, a gesture that was typically done to the victims he had killed.

"I have now given you your death," Barok said with a sinister grin. Cail's confidence morphed into confusion. Barok was outnumbered by the hundreds of Red Pumas, his legion of assassins was now a burning pile of ash, and he had been betrayed by one of his own. Even so, he had the audacity to claim that he was about to kill Cail?

"You're mad," Cail said in a hushed voice.

"No. I just see what's hidden from your view."

"Which is?"

"Your killer. The person who will betray you is in this city. Honestly, it's quite embarrassing that you can't see through her tainted skin, you can't deduce what's going to happen. She's seen the success that you've become and envy will begin to fuel her hatred. You must watch your every move if you wish to remain alive."

Without a will of his own, Cail swung his fist across Barok's broad face. A thin stream of blood leaked from the corner of his mouth, but otherwise, he seemed unfazed by Cail's uncontrolled aggression. "Where is she?" Cail growled, but to no avail. Barok wasn't intimidated. He simply looked back at Cail with yellow teeth protruding from his malicious smile.

"Undoubtedly, you intend to kill me, so why should I tell you anything?" Barok asked.

"You can die quickly by the blade, or slowly in flames," Cail threatened, hoping to scare the information out of Barok.

The confident smirk left Barok's face as fear crept into his mind. He was tempted to give in to Cail's demands, to spare himself the agonizing pain of fire. With a hushed voice, he said, "I will tell you one thing: she doesn't know she'll betray you, not yet. Oh, she's done it before. She's convinced herself that those days are left in the past, but I've seen the truth. Her betrayal will be reborn."

"You still haven't told me who she is," Cail said with an unmoving voice.

"And I never will."

"As you wish," Cail said with a cold voice. Then he turned to the Red Pumas and said, "Barok, the King of the Blue Assassins, has chosen death by fire. Throw him into the inferno." The soldiers obeyed his commands, snatching Barok by the arms and dragging him across the floor of the cave.

"The Blue Assassins were only the beginning!" Barok bellowed as he was taken away. "Your traitor will always follow you!" There was nothing that Barok could say that would affect Cail. He didn't care about the empty threats from an enemy about to be slain.

The Red Pumas tossed Barok into the flames like a log chopped from a tree. His shrill screams filled the cave and reverberated off the walls. The wails of agony continued for just a moment longer, and then they died, just as he did. Cestmir was free once again. Cail looked toward Serafine and noticed her gaze had not yet left the cracking inferno. Her eyes were lifeless, unblinking, flooded with fear. "What's wrong?" Cail asked.

She broke off her stare and said with a shaky voice, "Nothing. I just have old memories of them, of what they've done."

"That's what they shall remain; nothing more than memories," Cail said, trying to comfort Serafine's fear, but he sensed that it did nothing to help.

"Cail, there is something I need to ask of you, something of paramount importance," Serafine said. "As I mentioned to you earlier, the Tower of the Sun is my only remaining path to Aithnen, but it can't be reached by foot. If I'm to return to my father's kingdom, I'll need your help."

Cail's mind immediately turned to Laney, who was now waiting in the city. She had just woken from months of unconsciousness, and telling her that he was leaving again seemed unbearable. He would pull a dozen blades out of his skin rather than leave her side again. He also remembered the Sages and their constant barrage of enemies they were sending to kill him, to reclaim the Shadow Stone. "I can't leave," Cail said, regret filled his voice. "At least not until the Sages of Pazia have been dealt with. They must pay for what they've done to the Ivory City. They must pay with their lives."

"And how do you plan on killing them?" Serafine asked. Cail could hear irritation and anger rising in her voice. "They're nothing like you and me. The Sages are mystical beings. We cannot kill them with fists or swords."

"How do we kill them?" Cail asked.

"I don't know, but my father could tell you. Please, you must come with me to Aithnen," Serafine pleaded. She was beginning to grow desperate in her attempts to sway Cail's mind. The Air Rune weighed down the pocket of her robe, reminding her of the leverage she possessed, though she didn't want to use it so soon.

Even though it pained him, Cail said, "Very well. I'll go with you. It appears I have no other choice." Then he looked at Loran and whispered into Serafine's ear, "What should we do about him?"

"Leave him to me. You need to rest for the upcoming journey." Cail nodded in agreement and left the cave, making his way toward the beaming sunlight in the city. Serafine waved to a couple nearby soldiers and they followed her as she walked toward Loran. She said to him, "Your deeds today haven't gone unnoticed. With that being said, it's time for you to go to your cell." She motioned her hand, signaling for the soldiers to take Loran into custody.

He immediately protested, "You said you would free me of my transgressions!"

"And I will when the time is right. Once the barrier between Aithnen and Kordon has been broken, you'll be free to return to your home, but until then, you're not to be trusted." Serafine turned to the soldiers and coldly said, "Take him away."

The soldiers dragged Loran, as he kicked and flailed, out of the cave. Serafine was proud of herself. Not for freeing the entire city of Cestmir, but for finding a way to sway Cail's mind, to manipulate him, to bend him to her will, and she didn't even need to mention the Air Rune. She decided that it would be best to keep it hidden from view, should she need it in the future. There was no need to let her mind be troubled by the Air Rune. For right now, she could focus on her return to Aithnen.

Chapter 7: Kye's Corruption

Cestmir had been free from the suffocating clutches of the Blue Assassins for three days. The citizens were no longer tormented by the threat of a legion of murderers watching their every move. A busy buzz had returned to the city as shops reopened, schools were filled, and vitality had been restored to the streets. As he walked with Kadir through the main roads of Cestmir, Cail took joy in seeing the wind of life breathed back into the Ivory City.

"You really intend to leave Kordon?" Kadir asked as they strolled through the streets.

"Serafine needs my help, and I intend to give it to her," Cail responded. His words were flooded with contrition. He so desperately wanted to return to Elona with Laney, to talk to her, to sit with her, to be in her presence.

Cail stopped a short distance away from the fountain by the city's gates. Laney was standing by herself in front of the fountain, deeply gazing into the clear water. A cool breeze summoned tiny ripples on the surface; otherwise, the fountain's water was serene. She hadn't noticed Cail and Kadir's arrival, so Kadir whispered to Cail, "Have you told her?"

"Not yet," Cail whispered back. "I haven't had the heart to."

"You will though, won't you?"

"Yes. I suppose there will be no better time than now." Kadir nodded and headed back into the city as Cail approached Laney. As he walked toward her, his mind froze. He had been consciously awaiting this moment for months, and now that it was finally upon him, he had no idea what to say, no idea what to do. Then she did exactly what Cail wished she hadn't, she did what he was unprepared for. She turned around. Cail had so many things he could say to her. He could tell her that he was thrilled that she was awake, he could scold her for coming to Cestmir and endangering her own life, or he could tell her that he loved her. With everything that he could say, he was unable to say anything at all.

Her pale eyes were glazed with tears like a winter morning's frost. Without saying anything, she flung herself into Cail's arms, hugging him so tightly that it nearly squeezed the breath out of his lungs. With one side of her face pressed against Cail's chest, she said, "I know I shouldn't have come here, I know it was reckless, but I couldn't help myself. It felt like the gods brought me here."

"You don't need to apologize," Cail responded. He couldn't bring himself to be angry with her. "You're safe now. That's all that matters." Laney let go of Cail and cast a bright smile at him, a smile he had not seen in a long time, a smile he had almost forgotten.

"You're right," she said lightheartedly. "We're both safe and now we can return to Elona." Silence fell on Cail as he dreaded what he was about to tell her. The quietude was contagious and spread to Laney like a disease. She sensed what Cail was about to say, but her mind refused to accept the truth. "You are coming home, aren't you?"

The words rested on his tongue, clinging to it like an iron chain. He managed to loosen the bond. "I can't. Serafine needs me to help her return to her home, and I need her to help keep you, and everyone else in Kordon, safe. Evil will continue to peek its ugly head if I don't do this."

"I won't let you go, Cail!" Laney protested, distressed by Cail's plan of action. "Not after all Kalil put this nation through. Kordon needs you."

"If I don't go with Serafine, enemies far worse than Kalil and Barok will surface and invade Kordon."

"Cail, please don't go," Laney pleaded. Her voice shook. Cail could see she was on the verge of breaking into tears.

"This is something I must do," Cail responded, sternly standing his ground. "Nothing is going to sway my mind. I have to do whatever it takes to stop the Sages of Pazia, to protect Kordon."

Laney ran away, sobbing. Cail wanted to run after her, but he knew it would do no good. Nothing could change her mind and nothing could change his. He plopped onto the fountain, sitting on the smooth, ivory marble. Cail dipped his fingers into the cool water and gently waved his hand around. The water grooved around his fingers, creating a soft current. His ears were soothed by the trickling sound. For just a moment, he had forgotten all about Laney, about the stress he was under, about the weight placed on his shoulders. Their first meeting wasn't anything like he expected it to be. A glorious reunion filled with happiness and cheer was what he had envisioned in his mind, but the reality was much different. In a way, he felt betrayed. Cail had fought valiantly to save Laney and bring her home, he stood by her side every day, waiting for her to wake up, he kept the faith that she would wake up one day. Now, she couldn't respect his wishes, she couldn't see what he was trying to do, she couldn't see that he was trying to protect her. He lost control of his anger and pounded his fist into the water. Cold drops splashed onto his face and cooled his temper. With a sweep of his hand, Cail wiped the water off his face and onto his shirt. He looked up and noticed Serafine looking at him with a sly grin.

"That tends to happen when you try to punch water," Serafine said with a gentle laugh. She sat down beside Cail. "Things didn't go over smoothly with Laney, I take it?"

"You were listening?" Cail asked.

"Not intentionally. She wasn't exactly whispering," Serafine responded. Cail's face reddened. He was embarrassed that his argument with Laney could be heard by anyone. "You don't need to worry about her. She'll come around in time."

"I'm not so sure. She seemed upset," Cail said, his voice plagued with sadness.

"Trust me. She cares about you. Eventually, she'll see you're trying to do the right thing." Serafine rose to her feet and then turned toward Cail. "We have more pressing matters to attend to."

Cail nodded and stood as well. Serafine walked away, wanting Cail to follow her, but before he did, he stared in the direction that Laney stormed off. The guilt of making her cry shrouded his mind. Part of Cail wanted to run after her, to ask for forgiveness, and to stay with her. It would be easier than what he was about to do. *Staying with Laney would solve nothing.* Cail thought to himself, and he was right. The Sages of Pazia had empowered Kalil and Barok, enemies he could overcome. How long would it take the Sages to find an enemy who was stronger than Cail? What if they could find an enemy who was powerful enough to trap Kordon in the next age of darkness? Would the immediate satisfaction of being by Laney's side outweigh the agony that would soon follow? No. Cail knew he was making the right decision, and Laney would simply have to accept that.

"Are you coming or not?" Serafine yelled after realizing Cail was standing idly by the fountain. Cail snapped to his senses and darted to Serafine. Then they left Cestmir on Emey's back, embarking on their newest venture to the Tower of the Sun.

"How could he do this to me?" Laney blurted out as she plopped onto a thickly cushioned sofa. Kadir and Beda, each sitting in their own luxurious chairs, said nothing during Laney's outburst of emotion. On the brink of tears, she continued, "With Cail having saved Kordon, I thought he would come home and live a peaceful life. We could return to the days where there wasn't a world outside of Elona."

"Laney, those days ended when Cail found the staff in the forest," Kadir interjected, rising from his chair. "Cail isn't the same boy that you and I remember. He's a warrior, a protector. Hiding in his home and pretending the rest of the world doesn't exist would bring his demise. If he hides, the world will find him."

"What am I supposed to do, then?" Laney asked. She felt hopeless. Ever since she had gone with Cail into Elona's forest, he had changed. Cail wasn't the same friend she had grown up knowing. He felt distant from her now, but not for the reasons she expected. While it's true that he was leaving, that wasn't the reason she could feel a barrier between them. It was something hidden, something buried beneath the surface. There was no limit to what she would give to have him back.

"Cail risked his life for all of Kordon when he set out to kill Kalil," Beda said, breaking her silence. "He sacrificed his own comfort and safety so he could cement the safety of us all. In the same way, we can all do what we can to help Cail. He needs us just as much we need him." Shame drenched Laney and drowned her selfishness. Cail had given up so much: his home, his family, his friends. What had Laney given back to him? Nothing except for impatience. She wanted to do something to help Cail, anything. What, though? She would be nothing but a crutch, a trap that Cail's villains could use against him.

"I suppose you're right," Laney said to Beda. "With Elona being safe now, I was hoping that Cail would come home and things would go back to normal."

"Cail's world is bigger than Elona now, Laney. I would love to have him at home as much as you would, but that's something he simply cannot do right now," Kadir answered. Laney said nothing in response. Even though she didn't want to admit it, she knew Kadir was right. Cail had left, he needed to leave, and there would be no telling when he would return. For the first time, she feared that Cail would never return, that he had been killed by his life. Kadir could see through Laney's silence; it told him everything he needed to know. Still, he needed to hear it confirmed. He asked, "Laney, do you love Cail?"

Laney was taken back by the question. She was floored that Kadir would ask her such a question. She answered, "Love is a complicated word."

That wasn't the answer Kadir was expecting. He didn't even know how to respond to it. He knew the truth, he knew that her feelings weren't as complicated as what she had just claimed.

As Emey sailed over the ocean of clouds, her feathers soaked in the warm sunlight. The bright, yellow ball of sunlight looked over Emey like a father looking over his child, offering serenity and peace of mind. Cail peered over the top of Emey's head and looked out to the immense world of clouds surrounding him. Serafine, being too afraid to look beyond Emey's wings, tightly clung to Cail and kept her eyes closed like a bolted door. Cold air massaged Cail's face and he could feel the pressure evaporating from his bones. He felt weightless, unattached to the world around him. For a moment, Cail felt like he was the one who was flying, not Emey. They had to land on several islands on the way, Emey wasn't accustomed to the additional weight of a second person. The sun was sitting on the horizon by the time they reached the coast of Ijsbrandur. With their source of light waning, Cail decided it would be best to rest for the night. Before they did, he observed the land around him. The last time he was on the island, it was home to a foul race of monsters, the zuraks. They had all been killed off along with their leader, Kalil. Visions of the great battle between the zuraks and the

Kordonians flashed into Cail's mind. A plethora of brave men were lost that day, but not in vain; they had paved the way for Kordon to be a free nation, and free it was. The gruesome memories faded when Cail saw the state of the land. Once, Ijsbrandur was a desolate wasteland. Now, the ground was recovering. The dirt, which had been as course as the head of a hammer, was soft and moist, thin emerald blades were beginning to poke through the ground, and the foulness of the air had dissipated. Kalil's evil had truly died; life was victorious.

"I'm glad we came here," Cail said to Serafine. She returned an expression that displayed confusion. "I didn't realize how badly Kalil had suffocated this island. With his death, there is new life."

Serafine walked toward Cail and said to him, "You should be proud. The gods picked the right person to protect the Nation of the Skies." The compliment carried immense weight. Serafine wasn't one to pass out niceties with ease, so Cail knew that what he had accomplished was special.

Cail sat on the soft dirt, leaning his back against Emey's side. "You know quite a lot about my nation, but I know almost nothing about yours. What should I expect in Aithnen?"

"To be honest, it's hard for me to say. A couple thousand years have passed since I left my home, since the Sages stole the Shadow Stone." Serafine retrieved the violet rock from her pocket and held it in the palm of her hand. The surface glistened in the dusk sunlight, shining like a fine gem. "I'm just happy I was able to leave Aithnen before the ocean of clouds covered our land, or else you would never know of the land of fire." Cail was glad as well. He couldn't imagine living in a world that was trapped beneath a wall of clouds. Some of the people in Aithnen had never seen the sun, had never even known what the sun was.

"How old are you?" Cail asked, amazed that she had been in Kordon ever since Kalil's rise to power.

"I'm just shy of three thousand years old," Serafine answered. Cail was baffled by her claim; she didn't look any older than he was at twenty years old. "The people living in Aithnen look the same as the people you know here in Kordon. The Ignacians, as we're properly called, were gifted with prolonged lives. Some of our ancient kings lived to be over ten thousand years old. Every race of the world has a different gift."

"What is the gift that was given to the Dragonfolk?" Cail asked, wanting to learn more about his people.

"How should I know? Kordon isn't my home," Serafine snapped back with a short temper. Her attitude was as hot as the fire she could summon in her palms. "Aithnen is a vast land, nothing like Kordon. There are no islands or open skies to fly over; it's an extensive continent with an array of environments."

Cail tried to imagine a world with an all-encompassing mass of land, but he couldn't. No matter where his adventures in Kordon had taken him, he had always been surrounded by the clouds. He couldn't envision a world where there was nothing but land surrounding him, land as far as the eye could see. In a way, it felt constricted. Kordon was a free nation, with open skies surrounding all the inhabitants. Emey could take him to wherever his heart desired. She could fly through the clouds like a fish swimming in the ocean. Then Cail remembered his childhood, the time when all he knew was the island of Elona. There were no other islands surrounding him, just an infinite universe of clouds.

"If the Tower of the Sun will take us to Aithnen, then why haven't more Aithnenians come to Kordon?" Cail asked.

"Because a lot of Aithnenians don't even know about the tower, and those who do know can't enter it. You see, the Tower of the Sun will take us down into the Bodaway Volcano. The volcano is a vicious place, threatening death to those who are weak. Lava and fire fill the volcano like water fills a lake. Only those who possess control over the element of fire can transcend the jagged paths, which is why I can lead us through. Once we've made it out of the mountain, we'll be awaited by the Ash Plateaus, a grueling trek through treacherous cliffs that extend far beyond the volcano's reach. It will be a three-day venture if fate treats us well. That will take us to my home, Kye. The city of Kye could be a nation on its own. Sadly, it's a divided city; split amongst the rich and the poor. Those who hold the wealth care very little for the less fortunate citizens and they possess all the power over those who could strip them of their wealth."

"How is that possible?" Cail asked, outraged by the injustice in Kye. "Is there no way to talk sense into them, to teach them to care for their brothers and sisters, to show them the joys of compassion?"

"I'm afraid not," Serafine answered, saddened by the truth of it all. "The wealthy citizens of Kye find contentment and happiness in their riches, not in helping the poor. This frightens me. With the growth of the divide between the affluent and the impoverished, so grows the animosity between the two groups. When I left Kye, the city had yet to reach a state of hostility, but I fear that unless things change, that fate could become inevitable. The two sides are destined to clash."

"Clash? Do you mean the city will be at war with itself?" Cail asked. Serafine only responded with a silent nod. "We have to do something! The city can't be allowed to descend into chaos. Surely there's something that can be done. Your father is the King, isn't he?"

"Yes, he is, but his powers are limited. You see, Aithnen was no stranger to tyrannies in its ancient history. Cruel kings who preyed on their citizens. Because of this, the Kings of the four cities of Aithnen were stripped of many of their powers. Now, officials, who are elected by select groups of citizens, pass the laws of the land, which is why the rich have so much control; they control those who control the laws. Even though I don't like this situation any more than you do, it isn't our top priority," Serafine said, looking at the rock in her hand. The sun's light had nearly vanished, so the Shadow Stone wasn't shining as brightly as before. "Deep in the heart of the city, there's a temple that was home to this stone. We must return it to its rightful place if Kordon and Aithnen are to be united once again." Cail knew of the temple. He had seen it before. Not in real life, but in a dream. Caldir had taken Cail there and showed him the truth about the Shadow Stone; the truth that the Sages of Pazia had stolen it from Aithnen to curse the Domain of Fire, to trap them beneath a ceiling of clouds.

"If our upcoming expedition is anything like you say it is, we better get some rest for the night," Cail said after a moment of sitting silently in his thoughts. Serafine agreed and she rested her head on the small bag she had packed for the journey.

Cail laid his head back against Emey's soft side and slowly drifted into peaceful sleep. His rest was peaceful only for a short while, though. From the darkness of his unconsciousness, Cail was taken to a dream not unfamiliar to him, the dream containing thousands of corpses lying on the ground. They weren't the same people he had seen before, though. New faces laid before him. More people who had suffered, more people who had endured pain and agony, more people who had died. Then Cail saw the silhouette of someone who was not dead standing in the distance. This person had the build of a man, a tall, strong one at that. As Cail approached, he realized that the person wasn't a man at all, but the shadow of one; a dark outline of a treacherous warrior.

"You did well to save Cestmir," the shadow said, Cail could feel the cold cruelty oozing from his voice. His words bit into Cail's skin like the fangs of a snake, spreading poison and fear into his mind.

Piecing together the puzzle in his mind, Cail said, "You unleashed the Blue Assassins on the Ivory City."

"Very good," the shadow replied, letting out a menacing chuckle.

"But, why? What do you have against Cestmir?" Cail inquired.

"It wasn't Cestmir that I wanted, but you. I wanted you to see what I'm capable of, and now I've seen what you can do."

"Then you should now see I'm no one to trifle with," Cail said, trying to intimidate his unrecognizable opponent.

"Be careful, Cail," the shadow said, then he strode even closer to Cail. He was a towering man, his chest level with the top of Cail's head. "You shouldn't make enemies when you could make friends. I think you could help me and I could help you."

"You can help me?" Cail repeated, skeptical of the claim. The same being who was responsible for the imprisonment of thousands of citizens of

Cestmir was supposed to deliver on an empty promise? Despite his skepticism, Cail decided to hear what the shadow had to say. "What can you possibly do to help me?"

"Kye will welcome Serafine back with open arms; she is the King's daughter, after all. You, on the other hand, are an outsider, an alien to Aithnen. The Ignacians can easily sense when a foreigner is amongst them, and they are less than hospitable, to say the least. I can offer you protection as you travel through the streets of Kye."

"In exchange for what?" Cail asked, knowing there must be a catch.

"All I ask is that you aid me in the quest to rid Kye of all the corruption dwelling within. For too long, the less fortunate have suffered to the blessed. The time has come for justice to be served. That is what you want, isn't it?" Cail couldn't deny that he was tempted by the shadow's offer. He did want there to be justice in Kye, he wanted to be a beacon of hope for all people, he wanted to end the corruption. Still, Cail remembered the suffering that the shadow had thrust upon the Cestmirians. Where was the justice in that?

"After everything you did to the innocent lives in Cestmir, there's nothing you can tell me that I can trust," Cail responded, staring into the dark face of the shadowed man. "You could just be using me to take the riches from the wealthy and give them to you; to do your own selfish bidding."

"Yes, I suppose I could," the shadow acknowledged. Then he said, "However, once you see the state that Kye is in, it will be evident that I'm telling the truth." Cail said nothing in response. He had a nagging fear that the man was right, that Kye was a much darker and crueler city than Cail had ever imagined. Perhaps it was possible that Cail would need protection, but at what cost? What would he have to do to prove his loyalty to this mysterious being? The shadow said to Cail, "Your venture to Kye will be a tenebrous and tumultuous one. You'll have plenty of time to ponder over what I've offered to you. I want you to see the corruption of Kye for yourself. While you're walking through the city streets, I want to you to think about the repression that has been instilled there and how easy it would be to reverse it if you simply trusted me. When the time is right, I will find you. Make sure you choose wisely."

"Who are you?" Cail asked, desperate to see the identity of this ghastly figure.

"You will come to know me as The Hidden King. The tale behind that name will have to wait for a later time, though. Find me in the streets of Kye, once your eyes have been opened to the city's depravities."

The Hidden King's voice faded and the world around Cail darkened until he could no longer see his own hands. Cail could only hear the thoughts inside his own head, thoughts volleying back and forth about what the right decision was. In the blinding darkness, he could find no illumination.

Chapter 8: Fall Into Fire

The sun peeked over the clouds and brought a new day. It would be Cail's final day in Kordon, for a time that is. Orange light filled the sky and the ground was still damp from the cold night. Cail's eyes were heavy, but he couldn't bring himself to find any more sleep. He wanted to forget the dream from the night before, but it felt nothing like a dream; it felt all too real. Haunting eyes followed Cail, watching his every move. Cail looked all around, but the only person in sight was Serafine, who was still sound asleep. As the morning dragged on, Cail was left to ponder over his thoughts. Fears lurked into his mind, fears of the dangers that awaited him in Kye. Perhaps he should listen to the Hidden King, perhaps he needed the protection in a foreign land.

"No," Cail said to himself. What protection did he have when he left Elona for the first time? What protection did he have when he ventured across the islands of Kordon? What protection did he have against Kalil and Tarvaris? None. And he would need none now.

"No, what?" Serafine asked. Cail hadn't heard her wake. She rubbed her darkened eyes as she rose from the ground.

"It's nothing," Cail lied. He feared what Serafine would think if she knew his mind was being bent by nothing more than a dream. Wanting to change the subject, he asked, "Are you ready?"

"This is the day I've been waiting on for centuries. Of course, I'm ready."

Cail gathered his small number of personal belongings and asked, "Where do we go from here? I'm assuming Wallen gave you specific directions?"

"None more specific than to fly due south of Ijsbrandur. I have a feeling the Tower of the Sun will be hard to miss." Serafine's response made Cail feel uneasy. He had no idea what the tower would look like, how far away it would be, if there would be any islands along the way, or if they'd even be able to find the Tower of the Sun at all. Serafine sensed Cail's nerves, so she said, "Wallen wouldn't suggest this as an option if he didn't think Emey was strong enough to take us there." Her words brought little comfort to Cail's troubled mind. He looked up to Emey, who was now standing tall above him. Undoubtedly, she was a strong creature. Each of her wings was as long as Cail's entire body, her chest was a solid wooden barrel, and thick muscles flowed underneath her feathers like invisible rivers. Cail knew Serafine was right; Emey was strong enough to do this. He just hated testing Emey's limits.

The time had come for their departure, but Cail's feet remained planted to the ground. In the same way that it was difficult to leave Elona for the first time, it was also hard for Cail to leave Kordon. With every passing day, the world around him was expanding. Perhaps there were no limits to its immensity, no borders to where he could not go, no way to know when to stop. All he knew was that this wasn't the time to stop. Serafine needed him in the same way he needed her to bring light into the darkness of Kalil's tyranny. With that thought, the selfish bonds he had with Kordon unlocked. He was free to hop onto Emey's back, to leave Kordon's soil for the last time. Serafine followed suit and wrapped her arms tightly around Cail's stomach. Emey bent her legs and then launched into the air, beginning their trek through the southern sky. The wind howled in Cail's ears as Emey flew with great velocity. It didn't take long for Ijsbrandur to disappear. They were accompanied by nothing more than the beaming sun and a vast ocean of clouds beneath them. The emptiness of the world around them was dizzying and disorienting. Had it not been for the sun, they surely would've lost their sense of direction. After a couple hours of flying, Cail's mind began to play tricks on him. He would see objects on the edge of the horizon, but they were never anything other than hallucinations. To his pleasant surprise, Emey showed no signs of fatigue or struggle. Still, Cail knew her strength wouldn't endure for eternity.

He turned his head around to Serafine and shouted to overcome the deafening noise of the wind, "We need to turn back! If Emey's strength fails, we both die!" Serafine didn't respond. She directed Cail's gaze forward. He saw another object in the distance, but this was no hallucination. A dark cylinder rose through the clouds and up toward the empty sky, high above Emey. She began her ascent, flapping her wings more fiercely than she had before. What was once a small cylinder turned into a massive tower, a colossal piece of architecture. The bricks were as black as onyx and didn't have a single chip. The Tower of the Sun was pristine. Emey spotted a balcony extending from the top of the tower. She darted through the air directly toward it. Cail could sense her strides becoming more laborious, making him glad that they had finally arrived at the Tower of the Sun. With one last thrust of her wings, Emey rose to the balcony and landed just before the entrance to the tower. The balcony was made of the same onyx bricks that the rest of the tower was and it led to a small wooden door with a burning torch perched on both sides of it. After hopping down, Serafine quickly made her way for the door, but Cail stood with Emey, not wanting to leave his loyal companion.

As he stroked Emey's emerald feathers, he said to her, "You've been by my side for my entire life, ever since I was born. You need to fly home." Emey locked eyes with Cail. Her bright, yellow irises latched onto him, holding him in his place. She wanted Cail to stay as much as he didn't want to leave her.

"You'll see Cail again," Serafine said to Emey, approaching the magnificent bird. Serafine cautiously placed her hand on Emey's neck, not wanting to scare the falcon. Emey jolted her neck back at first, but Cail calmed her so that Serafine could stroke her feathers. "We'll clear the skies and then you'll be reunited with Cail." Even though Emey didn't respond, she understood the promise that Serafine had made. Emey turned around and launched into the sky, flying to the north. Cail watched as she faded into the horizon, saddened by her departure. Serafine put a consoling hand on his shoulder and said, "Don't worry about her, Cail. She'll find her way home."

Cail found no solace but realized there was nothing he could do about it now. He and Serafine had but one choice; descend to Aithnen. They each grabbed one of the torches that was mounted near the entrance and then Cail opened the small door leading into the tower. The tower was dark, like the corridor of a cave. A thin staircase spun around the wall of the cylindrical tower and descended into darkness. "We better get started. The volcano is a long way down," Serafine said, then she led the way down the steps. A couple hours passed and the only sound was the clapping of their footsteps echoing off the Tower's walls. In a way, the silence was restorative. Cail was left to his thoughts, sorting through the stressors that troubled his mind. Part of his mind worried about Laney. She seemed irate that he had left her so soon and didn't know if that anger would pass by the time he returned, or if her anger would ever come to pass. Another part of his mind worried about Kordon. There was no telling what kind of enemies would arise while he was gone. Kordon's only defense rested in Beda and her army.

Without looking back, Serafine said, "You're awfully quiet."

"I have a lot on my mind," Cail responded. There was still one question he needed to have answered. "Why is the Tower of the Sun guarded by the volcano? Is it so bad to tear down the barriers between Kordon and Aithnen?"

"It's hard to say. This tower was built by the gods, so they must've had a good reason for where they placed it," Serafine responded. Cail saw no reason why there needed to be shields dividing the four nations of Neptil. A world with open boundaries could lead to one unified world, a utopian paradise. Serafine continued by saying, "There's something you must know about the Bodaway Volcano. It's a cavernous volcano filled with thin walkways, jagged cliffs, and imminent danger. However, another threat is hidden there; the Kazrads. They're a race of mountain folk who possess half our height, but twice our strength. Although they're not very cunning it will be important to watch our tongues. Making an enemy out of the Kazrads will lead us to certain death."

"They dwell within the volcano?" Cail asked, amazed that anyone could live in such conditions.

"Yes. They mine riches and jewels from the volcano's rocks, which they're very jealous of. If you value your life, you'll keep your hands to yourself and leave the talking to me." Cail couldn't imagine how a people as undersized as the Kazrads could cause any trouble, but he decided not to test Serafine's patience.

After walking in silence for a while longer, Cail noticed that the air started to change. His breaths were more laborious, a foul stench of smoke rose through the tower, and the air grew warmer as they descended. By the time they reached the floor of the tower, Cail was already beginning to sweat, but Serafine seemed unfazed by the extreme environment. She led Cail through an archway, which rose just a little higher than his head, and they entered the massive chamber of the Bodaway Volcano. A broad pillar of black smoke rose from beneath them, ascending through the crater, the cavern was illuminated by the glowing red lava beneath, and thin dirt paths weaved throughout the entire volcano, creating an intricate labyrinth. Cail was speechless. He could easily see why no one could traverse through the volcano and enter the Tower of the sun.

"Only the Kazrads can thrive in an environment like this," Serafine said as she looked for the correct path to take. "We can't afford to linger here. If we do, we'll pay with our lives." Cail nodded in agreement and followed Serafine after she had chosen a nearby walkway. She walked on the narrow path with ease, but Cail had to hold out his arms to maintain his balance. He stopped in the middle of the walkway and looked down. Leagues beneath him was a vast lake of lava snarling at Cail like a hungry shark. Cail's stomach turned and the cave started to spin. His body began to teeter back and forth, bringing him within inches of falling over the edge. Then he closed his eyes and forgot about the fall into fire. Even though his eyes were closed, he could see. The mountain stood still and he felt dizzy no longer. Keeping the core of his body tight, Cail took one step after another, cautiously striding toward a solid cliff. Once he felt firm land under his feet, he opened his eyes and saw Serafine standing before him, waiting impatiently.

She led Cail onward, traversing across a series of walkways and descending down steep cliffs. The heat intensified and the lava's scorching radiance glowed like the sun. Cail was now profusely sweating and his muscles were beginning to pulsate and cramp. Despite his pain and ache, Cail managed to keep up with Serafine's frantic pace. She didn't stop until they stood just before the lake of lava. Instead of still water, liquid fire jumped into the air and roared like a lion. The heat was sweltering, almost to the point of boiling Cail's skin.

"This is our last hurdle," Serafine said to Cail. There was one arched path leading over the lava to the other side, where there was an opening in the wall of the volcano; an escape to clean air. Cail noticed one caveat, though. There was a gap in the middle of the walkway. The gap stretched much farther than he could jump. It was an invitation to an excruciating death.

"Is there no other way?" Cail asked, afraid of a fatal misstep.

"What other way do you need? If we cross this last bridge, then we leave this volcano with our lives. That's more than anyone in Aithnen can say."

"I can't make that jump. We need to find another path," Cail insisted.

"Do you trust me?" Serafine asked. Cail was taken back by the question. He didn't know what his trust in her had to do with his inability to cross the walkway. However, he did know his physical limitations and jumping over this sizable gap was beyond them. Serafine locked her fiery eyes with Cail's, awaiting his response.

"Yes," Cail answered. "I trust you."

"Then I need you to follow me," Serafine insisted. "I've led you this far into the volcano, I won't let you fall now." Cail couldn't deny that Serafine had proved to be trustworthy. She had done so much for him throughout his quest to free Kordon. She could've betrayed him at any point, so there was no reason why she would do so now.

"I can't cross the gap," Cail reiterated. "It's too far for me to jump."

"You forget that I control fire," Serafine responded with a smirk, then she turned proceeded onto the walkway.

Cail wasn't sure what she meant by what she said, but decided to place his faith in her. He stepped onto the walkway, standing just over the bed of scalding lava. Closing his eyes did nothing; he was too close to the fire, he was in the belly of the beast. His steps were shaky and full of fear. Invisible iron chains were wrapped around his shoulders, trying to drag him down to his death, but he would not fall. With a new strength in his step, Cail pushed forward until he caught up with Serafine. The aperture was so wide that flying was the only possible way to cross.

Instead of trying to jump, Serafine held out both her hands toward the lava. A sonorous rumble shook the entire volcano and the lava slowly started swirling. Then a dark circle formed in the lake, a circle directly beneath the crevice. Serafine lifted her hands into the air and the dark circle rose from the lava and became a cylindrical pillar of solid rock. It ascended until it was level with the walkway, and then the rumbling of the volcano silenced.

"How?" Cail asked, amazed by Serafine's mastery over fire.

"I'm much older than you, so I've had plenty of time to hone my skills," Serafine responded, then she used the new stepping stone to skip across to the other side. Despite the shorter distance that Cail had to traverse, the sight of the growling lava still made his stomach turn.

"Will you hurry up?" Serafine called out to him. Cail didn't say anything in response, partially because his nerves were cramping his lungs. He took a couple steps back and then launched himself over the lava with a running start. As his body hung in the air, he felt a wave of liberation hit his body, the same liberation he always felt when he rode on Emey's back. Cail felt unattached from the ground beneath him. There were no chains dragging him down, no weights tied around his ankles. In that moment, he was one with the wind.

Cail refocused his mind on the pillar he had launched himself toward. His feet successfully landed on the pillar, but he used too much strength in his jump and his feet slipped on the rock. With only a split second to spare, Cail snatched onto an indentation on the pillar just before his body plummeted into the scorching lava. With a burst of strength, Cail pulled himself away from the fire and onto the pillar. Then he leaped over the crevice once more and landed safely on the other end of the walkway.

"You should stop relying so heavily on luck. Eventually, it will stop smiling on you," Serafine said with no small amount of condescension. She led Cail off the walkway, but when they made it to solid ground, she froze. Serafine was paralyzed by what stood before her; a fully armored line of Kazrads. Even though they were every bit as short as Serafine had described, perhaps even shorter, Cail could tell they were a force to be reckoned with. A thick, full beard was mounted on each of their faces, their massive muscles were protected by impenetrable iron plates, and fierce glances shot out of their dark eyes like streaking arrows.

"What do we do now?" Cail whispered to Serafine, but she gave no response. Fear was tattooed on her face.

One of the Kazrad soldiers stepped forth and barked, "Who dares to trespass onto our land?" Serafine remained silent and frozen. Cail had never seen her act like this before. Clearly, she knew something about the Kazrads that Cail didn't. There was a terror hidden beneath the surface.

Cail knew that saying nothing would only raise the Kazrads' suspicions even more, so he said, "My name is Cailean and my friend is Serafine. I'm accompanying her on her quest to return to her home in Kye."

"You've descended from the Tower?" the Kazrad asked with intrigue. Cail nodded in response. "Well, now. That is interesting. Wait here for a moment." The Kazrad retreated to his comrades and they whispered amongst themselves. Their discussion lasted for several minutes, leaving Cail and Serafine to stand in awkward silence. Finally, the Kazrad returned to Cail and said, "We have direct orders to kill anyone who crosses that bridge and tries to enter Aithnen."

"Kill us?" Cail repeated, appalled. "Why?"

"Because our Lord knows there's only one person who can cross it; the Descendant of Kordon. That is who you are, aren't you?"

"Yes, but that still doesn't explain why I should be killed," Cail argued.

"And I would tell you if I could," the Kazrad responded. "Lord Arul, our leader, isn't the same Kazrad that we swore to protect. His body is healthy and strong, but I fear that his mind has been poisoned; a paranoia that lives inside him is consuming his thoughts. There's one thing you must know about us: we're not soldiers, we're miners. If it were up to us, we'd be digging for riches beneath the volcano."

"What are you talking about?" Serafine interjected, yelling at the Kazrad. "My father told me of the horrors that your people would do to intruders: torture, slavery, punishment."

"And your father is?" the Kazrad asked.

"One of the Four Kings, the King of Kye," Serafine responded.

"Now I see," the Kazrad responded, realizing who Serafine truly was. "If that's what your father truly believes, then he is wrong. We're not the brutal savages that your father says we are. You see, the Kazrad soldiers used to be nothing more than guardians, protectors of our home in the volcano, but now, our Lord is asking us to be killers. There's a fine line between what we used to be and what we are now. It's weighed on all our minds for years, which is why we're not going to kill you, but you must promise us one thing."

"Yes, of course. Anything," Cail responded, relieved that they wouldn't have to put up a fight against the brutish might of the Kazrads.

"You must promise to never come to the volcano again. If our Lord discovers that we let you pass through unscathed, we will know no end to his wrath. Our deaths will be slow and painful."

Serafine put her hand on the Kazrad's shoulder and said, "You've shown us an incomparable amount of mercy. You'll never see us in the volcano again."

A bright smile shone from the Kazrad's stern face, something that Cail didn't believe to be possible. "I assume you intend to return to Kye?" the Kazrad asked. Serafine nodded in response. "I'll warn you, there's been a lot of dark rumors stemming from that city. Rumors of an internal war."

"Yes, I know the people of the city are frustrated," Serafine responded. "Which is one of the reasons why we're desperate to return."

"The people are beyond frustrated. Animosity floods Kye much like lava floods this volcano. Injustice has thrived for too long, and the offended party is hungry for retribution. Kye is no longer safe."

"Safe or not, Kye is my home. There is no alternative for me," Serafine asserted. Her confidence was restored and she no longer feared the Kazrads.

"Fair enough. The next step of your venture is through there," the Kazrad said, pointing toward the opening in the volcano's cave. "Hopefully the Ash Plateaus will offer you as much mercy as we did."

Without saying anything more, Cail and Serafine proceeded past the Kazrads and out of the Bodaway Volcano. Cail inhaled the Aithnen air for the first time; it was cool, but also dry. The sky hovering over them was unlike the one to which Cail was accustomed; a gray blanket enveloped the land, casting dull darkness everywhere. The Ash Plateaus were aptly named. A thick layer of gray ash covered the cliffs that surrounded the volcano for miles beyond what could be seen.

"We should rest here for the night. A long trek awaits us in the morning," Serafine said as she set her belongings on the ground.

"How can you tell it is nighttime?" Cail asked, observing the bleak sky.

"There are subtle differences between the night sky and that of the day. You forget that I lived here for nearly a thousand years before leaving for

Kordon. We can tell the time of day." Cail plopped onto the ground as well. The thick layer of ash was surprisingly comfortable. It felt as though the entire ground was a firm mattress. He scooped some into his palm. The ashes were weightless and as soft as snow. They were so soft that they could've been packed into a pillow and easily mistaken for feathers. Cail brushed the ashes from his palm and looked up at the sky once again. He had only been exposed to this world for a few moments and he felt trapped. The thick layer of clouds felt like a bag that was tied over his head, holding in his breaths. It was at this moment that he realized just how much he depended on the sun's light and the open skies of Kordon. How blessed he had been, but also how blind, blind to the suffering of the natives of this land. For centuries, the Aithnenians had been forced to breathe the same air time and time again while the Kordonians enjoyed the luxury of fresh breath. Cail dreaded the upcoming days, knowing that he would be forced to breathe in recycled fumes. While Cail was lost in his thoughts, Serafine had laid down and fallen asleep, or at least pretended to be. With her back turned toward Cail, she reached into the pocket of her tunic and fingered the Air Rune that she kept hidden from view. In a way, she felt empathy toward Cail. She knew that she would want to possess her strongest power if it was inches away from her. However, that was all the more reason to keep the Air Rune hidden. She had yet to discover her true potential, so why should Cail find his?

Serafine closed her eyes and imagined a world in which the Air Rune was given to Cail. The sky was flooded with whips of lightning, clouds as black as the night, and thunderous storms. Tornadoes tore through Aithnen's cities, thrashing the innocent people living within. The storm swallowed the Bodaway Volcano, consuming the immovable mountain of fire. It was a twirling cone of death, destroying anything that dared to stand in its path. Serafine stood at the foot of the volcano. Her hair violently whipped in the wind and her clothes were pressed against her body. It took all her strength just to stay mounted on the ground. She looked at the top of the tornado and saw Cail flying above the destruction. He wasn't the same person she knew, though. His hazels eyes were now blank; white voids that were corrupting his mind. "Who are you?" Serafine bellowed at Cail, but he only responded with a sinister smirk. Then the tornado roared even louder and slowly engulfed Serafine, trapping her in its squalls.

Serafine gasped as she woke from her nightmarish vision. It was now the middle of the night and Cail was sound asleep. The world around her was no longer in chaos; it was calm and serene. She felt the Air Rune in her hand and held it out in front of her. She knew that with this power, he could bend the entire world to his will. Serafine darted away from Cail and toward a nearby cliff. Leagues below her, there was a broad river with jagged rocks protruding from the surface of the water. She lifted her arm to cast the Air Rune away, but then she halted. There was a wall in her mind, a barrier preventing her from throwing the rune. No matter how hard she tried, her fingers remained tightly gripped around the stone. She quietly growled, angry at herself for being so weak. The vision replayed itself in her mind once more. She saw the black clouds, the innocents dying, the engulfed volcano. Then she saw Cail's malicious smirk.

"No!" she bellowed into the night, then she flung the Air Rune from her grasp. It plummeted into darkness and then a faint splash echoed through the canyon. She had rid the world of the tyrant that Cail would become. Serafine had protected Cail from himself.

Chapter 9: A Warning From the Dead

When Cail opened his eyes, he was in a place that he didn't expect; Lydia's house. Not only was he there, but Lydia was sitting just before him. She looked nothing like the last time he had seen her; she was alive and vigorous. Youth was spread over her skin like a soothing lotion, her hair was now thick and brown, and her arms and legs were toned.

"Lydia?" Cail asked incredulously. He couldn't believe what he was seeing.

"Yes, it's me, Cail," she responded. There was one last thing he noticed about her: she wasn't blind! Instead of having glazed eyes, they were a glistening shade of emerald, shining in the light of the nearby candle. Cail could tell she wasn't blind because of the focus of her eyes; they latched onto Cail, in the same way she would hold on to his hand if he was dangling over the edge of a cliff.

"Am I back in Elona?" Cail asked, still bewildered.

"You'd like to be, wouldn't you?" Lydia asked with a gentle smile on her face. "No, you're not in Elona. Right now, you're fast asleep just outside the Bodaway Volcano. However, I've brought you here to discuss a vision you revealed to me quite some time ago. You remember it, don't you?" The vision immediately sprung into his mind, a vision of a tree interacting with the four different elements of the world: a cloud, a ring of light, a ring of water, and fire. The fire burned brightly in his mind, he could still feel the scalding warmth from the tree in his vision being engulfed in flames. That fire was much more vicious and intimidating than the lava of the volcano. It was the kind of heat that pushes a body backward, cutting through skin like a sharpened sword.

"Yes, I remember the dream," Cail answered. "What of it?"

"You didn't listen to my interpretation very well, as it seems. Don't you remember the raging fire that engulfed the tree, the symbol of your life? If you're not careful, Aithnen will bring a painful death to you."

"It was just a dream," Cail said with a softened voice. He wanted to believe what he said, but he knew the truth that was in Lydia's words.

"If that was just a dream, then why did you come to me for answers?" she inquired, but Cail said nothing in response. "You've already felt the effects of Aithnen's environment. It will only worsen the longer you remain."

"But Serafine has the Shadow Stone. Once we return it to its rightful place, Kordon and Aithnen will share the same sky," Cail argued.

"Even so, the dangers of Aithnen will continue to weigh heavily on your body. Kye is much more perilous than Serafine knows. As we speak, the folks of the corrupt city are gathering arms in preparation for a rebellion."

"I'll survive," Cail insisted, determined to make his way into the city.

"Cail, there are others who can help you destroy the Sages of Pazia. Please don't go into Kye," Lydia pleaded, but Cail had no room in his mind for such thoughts. He had set out to accompany Serafine to Kye, and he would do just that. No amount of danger was going to sway his mind.

"I've come this far. Turning back isn't an option, at least not until the Shadow Stone has been returned."

"As you wish," Lydia said, although her voice was filled with discontent. "After that, you must leave Aithnen, or else it will consume you."

Cail didn't understand why Lydia was persistently trying to convince him to return to Elona, but he had a different question that needed to be answered. "You seem to have a vast knowledge regarding ancient legends. What do you know of the Hidden King?"

Lydia's eyes widened as though she had seen a ghost appear just before her eyes. "How do you know that name?"

"I asked you a question first," Cail said without hesitation.

Lydia scowled at Cail, and then she said, "The Hidden King is dead; he has been for millennia. A menace is what he was, so it would do you well to put him out of your mind."

Cail was unsatisfied with her answer. He knew Lydia was hiding crucial information from him. The only way to discover the necessary truths was to keep pushing. "The Hidden King can't be dead. He came to me in a dream, even claimed that he was responsible for the imprisonment of Cestmir. Lydia, I must know who, or what, he is."

For a moment, Lydia pondered over Cail's plea. It was blatantly obvious that she knew a lot about the Hidden King. All that was left to decide is whether she would tell Cail. She rose from her chair and as she walked toward Cail, she said, "I won't tell you anything about the Hidden King." Cail's spirits sunk with her announcement. Then Lydia spoke again, "However, I will show you." She reached out her right palm and gently placed it on Cail's forehead. A white light immediately blinded him and then the light slowly dimmed. Cail was no longer in Lydia's house, but now he was in a magnificent throne room. Radiant sunlight beamed through the stained-glass windows, brilliant ivory marble created a strong foundation underneath Cail's feet, and colorful flags were draped on the walls. At the front of the throne room was a large man, not in the stomach but in his muscles, pacing back and forth in front of the golden throne. On the man's head was a crown embedded with shining gems and jewels and a red cloak made of velvet gracefully hung from his shoulders like a curtain.

"Sire! Your prisoner has arrived!" a voice called out from the other end of the throne room. Cail spun around and saw two guards, completely covered in iron armor, escorting a large man toward the King. The man was tall and broad. His hair was black and messy, his skin was dark, and his eyes wore the expression of a hunter, someone who had killed before and would surely kill again. The guards marched past, not acknowledging Cail's presence, or perhaps they couldn't know he was there.

"Claeg," the King said, acknowledging his newest prisoner. "I've waited far too long for you to be dragged into my castle. Your poisonous words and acts have been spewed across all of Aithnen. Many of our most loyal leaders have fallen prey to your insidious agenda."

"And what agenda is that?" Claeg scowled back to the King.

"The agenda of defiance," the King responded. As he spoke, he strode back and forth before his prisoner. "The Four Kings have grown weary of your rebellion. We demand respect, order, and obedience. You have become a fish that has strayed from the ocean. You were ambitious, but in your ambition, you've wandered into a world you cannot live, a world which has no room for revolt. Thousands of people have grown restless. Our cities are no longer safe. Now that you're in my suffocating grasp, you must answer for your depravities." Claeg didn't answer with words. Instead, he responded by spitting in the King's face. The King concealed his anger while he wiped the saliva from his forehead. The guards were shocked when they saw their King wear a smile on his face. "You can cast any insult you want at me, it won't change the punishment that will be brought down on you."

"In the same way, no threat will change what I've done," Claeg responded with a sinister grin. "I've planted a weed in Aithnen. No matter how many times you pluck it from the soil, it will grow again. Your citizens have grown weary of the oppression that you've allowed to descend onto them! They—" Claeg was cut off when the King whacked Claeg's right cheek with the back of his hand. A red imprint of the King's massive ring immediately swelled onto Claeg's thick face. The King's face was just as red, though. He was fuming; anger poured from his glare like light from the sun.

"How dare you try to pin the suffering of Aithnenians on me! I've only ever served my people, cared for them as though they were my own children."

"Then why did they fly to me so easily? Why were they so eager to betray the ones who looked after them? Perhaps it's because you weren't looking after them at all. Kill me if you wish, but what I've done will not end with my death. There will be others like me; people who will see you for who you are. Never forget, this is just the beginning."

The King opened his mouth to respond, but Cail heard nothing. Instead, Cail was blinded by white light once again. Once the light dimmed, he was in the comfort of Lydia's home once again. She was still standing before him with her palm softly pressed against his forehead. Once she saw that Cail had come to his senses, she returned to her seat, folded her hands on her lap, and stared into Cail's eyes. He had so many questions about what he had just witnessed, but he didn't know where to start. Instead, Lydia spoke before he could.

"Claeg was tortured and killed by the King of Kye, who is Serafine's father, for his crimes."

"Why does that matter? Why should I care about an ancient criminal?"

"Because his spirit still endures. Claeg is the Hidden King. He spent his entire life defying the powers that be. Thousands upon thousands of lives were spent because of his rebellions. Now, his spirit corrupts weak minds, trying to bring down the Kingdoms that have stood tall for millennia."

Cail rose from his chair and paced back and forth, pondering over what Lydia just said. It pained him to admit that his mind was weak. The Hidden King had easily corrupted his thoughts and bent his beliefs. Or was Lydia the one who was trying to manipulate him? Perhaps she couldn't see what Cail was trying to accomplish. All he wanted was a world without borders, nations without corruption, people without suffering. Isn't that what the Hidden King wanted as well? The Kingdom of Kye was no stranger to affliction. No matter what it took, he needed to eradicate Kye of its corruption, even if it meant continuing the work of the Hidden King.

"Was he a king? How did Claeg earn his title?" Cail asked.

"He wasn't a crowned king, but many people viewed him as one. Anyone who possesses the power to overthrow cities will be feared like a king. The memory I showed you was the first time his enemies ever laid eyes on him. Claeg moved like a shadow through Kye, unseen even in the light of day. He was a ghost who had yet to die."

"How is it that you know so much about Claeg and the Kingdom of Kye?" Cail asked as he returned to his chair. "You lived in Elona for your entire life, yet you know so much about a foreign land."

"Since my death, the gods have illuminated me, opened my eyes. I've seen things that are far beyond your comprehension. The things I've shown you are only the surface of what has been shown to me."

"Tell me!" Cail eagerly insisted. "I want to know everything!"

"I'm sure you do," Lydia said with a soft chuckle. "The world will offer plenty for you to see as you venture throughout the vast nations. You'll encounter different races, beasts, and lands. I will leave it up to you to witness the wonders of Neptil." Cail was discouraged by what Lydia said. Ever since he was born, he had a curious mind. He wanted to discover the hidden gems of the world surrounding him. Cail wanted to unlock the mysteries of the world, to live his entire life with the knowledge that no one else possessed. "Before you return to your body, there's something you must know, something about Serafine. She's not who you think she is."

"I know exactly who she is," Cail said with a strong wave of defiance. "She's the fierce leader of Aithnen and she's my friend. There have been plenty of opportunities for her to betray me, yet she has proudly stood by my side. She helped me find the Air Runes in the Sacred Realm, she fought valiantly by my side as I sought to overthrow the zurak army, she even helped to free Cestmir from the clutches of the Blue Assassins. Serafine has gone above and beyond what a friend should be expected to do."

"Has she, though? Have you ever pondered over why she would do these things for you?" Lydia asked, deeply gazing into Cail's eyes.

"Because she's my friend," Cail responded without hesitation.

"You're not seeing it, Cail!" Lydia shouted as she pounded her thin fist on the arm of her chair. Cail was shocked; he didn't think that she was capable of being angered. She rose to her feet and strode to the fireplace. As she stared at the luminescent flames, she said, "Blindness plagued my entire life, but even then, I could see more clearly than you do now. Serafine is using you, Cail. You're nothing more to her than a mean to an end. She desperately sought to return to Aithnen long before you met her, long before she was captured by Kalil. Tell me, what do you think will happen once she's home? Will she still be a great friend to you, like she has in the past?" Cail hadn't considered that possibility. For a moment, Cail felt stupid and gullible. Serafine had used him for her own personal gain and he was far too blind to see it. His mind felt tired and stretched. Serafine, Lydia, the Hidden King; they were all tugging his consciousness in different directions and he didn't know which way to go.

"If Serafine is as unreliable as you say, what should I do, then?" Cail asked.

Lydia turned around and as she walked toward Cail, she said, "You must leave Aithnen as soon as the skies are cleared. Remember your vision of the burning tree, remember the scalding fire, remember that Aithnen is a perilous place for you." As Lydia spoke her final words, the room surrounding Cail dimmed. The warmth of the fire faded and darkness enveloped Cail.

The next time he opened his eyes, he was lying at the foot of the Bodaway Volcano. It was still the middle of the night. The air was cool and chilled his skin, Serafine was fast asleep with her back pointed toward Cail, and a soft howl echoed through the air. All of his drowsiness had left his body, so he sat upright, gazing into the darkness. Cail pondered over the upcoming decisions he would have to make; he would have to decide whether he wanted to accept the Hidden King's offer or not, he would have to decide whether Serafine could be trusted or whether she was traitor, he would have to decide whether or not to return to Elona when the opportunity arose. All the choices paved a forked road with no map, they left him in a world with no sun, no sense of time or direction, they left him deserted in the middle of an ocean with nothing but towering waves around him. He didn't know which way to turn.

Cail rose to his feet and walked to a nearby cliff. The ground was cold and hard and small pebbles crunched beneath his footsteps. His heavily scuffed shoes hung over the drop-off which descended all the way down to a river. A faint whisper of the water reverberated off the canyon's walls. Cail sat down on the edge of the cliff and hung his feet loosely over the gap. He closed his eyes and listened to the water. The rushing rapids of the river soothed his ears and cleared his mind. For the first time in months, he could sort through his thoughts and see clearly.

Lydia had ordered him to steer clear of Serafine, and Aithnen for that matter, simply because of a vision he had. Cail had no reason to turn his back on Serafine; in fact, he would be a traitor if he did. Even if Serafine did do all those things so she could get home, isn't that what anyone would do? Cail knew that if he had been barred from his home for centuries, he would do whatever it took to find a way back. That didn't make Serafine his enemy. If he wanted to unite Kordon and Aithnen, then this is something he would have to do. There was the matter of the Hidden King, though. Cail had witnessed a lowly criminal brought before a king, but what exactly was his crime? In a corrupt city, even the most righteous folk can be wrongly sentenced as convicts. Thwarting the prevalent immoralities of Kye could possibly mean devoting himself to the Hidden King. Cail might have to defy the law of Aithnen. He decided that that would be a decision to make after seeing the state of Kye. Resolving these issues in Cail's mind caused his eyes to fall heavy. A wave a weariness oozed over his body and his muscles grew weak. He returned from the cliff and dozed off until the morning.

Chapter 10: Poisonous Fumes

The morning sun rose swiftly and Cail was yanked out of his peaceful state of hibernation when Serafine shook his shoulders. "Time to get up!" she shouted as she abruptly woke Cail. "We need to utilize as much daylight as we can. The days are much shorter in Aithnen than they are in Kordon." Cail melodramatically groaned as he pushed himself off the ground. The night seemed like nothing more than the blink of an eye, but Serafine allowed him no time to loiter; she was unusually anxious to start their venture for the day.

"What's the hurry?" Cail asked, annoyed by her impatience.

"We're about to enter a vast land of dangerous cliffs, jagged paths, and carnivorous beasts. The journey through the Ash Plateaus is no less than two days, and that's only if we're lucky. If we're to have any hope of traversing through unscathed, we need to move as swiftly as we can." Cail made no objection to Serafine as he gathered his belongings: a small bag which was just big enough to hold a few changes of clothes, some fruits and vegetables, and a small hunting knife. Even though he packed as lightly as he could, the extra weight strained his sore muscles with unpleasant heat. Serafine led the way but stopped upon arriving at the beginning of a narrow stone path. She faced Cail and said, "This is the Road of Purity. It will safely lead us all the way through the Ash Plateaus if we manage to remain on it. There's something you should know about the path we're about to take: the air is poisonous. A wall of smog envelops the Road of Purity and those who part from the path are seldom ever found. You see, the air of the Ash Plateaus doesn't attack your lungs, it attacks your mind. Only a handful of travelers were ever saved after leaving the path and they all claimed to see nightmarish hallucinations, visions of their deepest, darkest fears; some even said they saw traumatic memories play out before their very eyes. The Plateaus are alive; they feed off the weak-minded. Undoubtedly there will be traps trying to lure you away from the Road of Purity. No matter what you see or hear, you must promise that you'll stay with me. I can make no promise to save you, should you fail."

"I promise I'll remain by your side," Cail said without hesitation. There were dozens of experiences that popped into his mind that wouldn't be in anyone else's worst nightmares, experiences he wanted to cast out of his mind forever. Serafine was satisfied with Cail's answer, so she led him onto the Road of Purity, which steeply descended down the side of a cliff. Serafine and Cail were surrounded by a slew of plateaus; cliffs on top of each other, beside each other, chaotically stacked like berries in a bowl. The path descended further until the adventurers were enveloped by walls of stone. A thin layer of smog hovered over the ash-covered ground on both sides of the path. The smog was transparent, like a white cloud, but did not touch the road. In front of Cail and Serafine was a pass with a towering mountain on both sides; the trench was dark and there was no telling what awaited them. Serafine waved her hand, motioning for Cail to follow her. Haunting silence hovered over them like the smog hovering over the ground. Even though the path remained bare, the surrounding smog thickened and grew darker. The plateaus disappeared as the smog grew denser and it wasn't long before Serafine and Cail were trapped between two towering walls of smog, which were as dark as smoke.

A howl echoed through the air, a howl of a beast unknown to Cail. It was a ghastly echo, a warning for intruders to turn away. "What was that?" Cail asked, terrified of any predators that could be hunting them.

"Firewolves," Serafine responded without looking back to Cail. "Another reason to stay on the path. They're vicious hunters with red fur and razor teeth. They won't leave the smog, though. Some claim that they were born from within the poisonous fumes." The howls continued as they proceeded, each one blaring louder; the wolves were getting closer. To Cail's surprise, Serafine abruptly stopped, dropped her bag to the ground, and sat in the middle of the path. "We've made good progress for today. Get plenty of rest tonight. Another long trek awaits us tomorrow morning."

"It's the end of the day?" Cail asked. He knew they had been traveling for a long while, but without the sun, Cail had absolutely no sense of time. It turned out that Serafine was right; only a few minutes had passed before the light started to gradually dim. Just like a hand covering a candle, the veiled sunlight faded until it was too dark to do anything but wait for the morning. The night was so dark that Cail couldn't distinguish between reality and his dreams. He closed his heavy eyes and his mind drifted into the heavy darkness. His body felt weightless, as though he were flying through the open air. The invisible world surrounding Cail had lost its grasp on his joints and he was free to go as he pleased. Joy and glee warmed his heart as he floated through the darkness. Then he felt a noose catch onto his ankle and begin to tug his body down to the ground. Cail struggled with all his strength, but he couldn't break free from the bond. His back slammed onto the cold ground and then a circle of torches ignited around him, providing illumination in the thick of the night.

"You've had time to think. I want an answer," a sonorous voice boomed from beyond the flames. Cail pushed himself up from the dusty ground and found that he was standing before a man with a familiar body figure. The man was a giant with broad shoulders. He was covered from head to toe in impenetrable steel armor, a matching helmet veiled his face, and a massive sword was sheathed and attached to his thick leather belt. Even though Cail couldn't see the man's face, he didn't need to. He knew that he was standing in the presence of the Hidden King.

"I want to wait until I have seen Kye. The state of the city will determine whether I need your help or not," Cail insisted.

"By that point, it will be too late for you to make a decision. Kye is filled with hostility, which is what you will be met with. I can't protect you if I don't have your trust." Cail was beginning to grow weary of that word: trust. It was suffocating him, drowning him beneath an ocean of expectations. He was being expected to blindly follow what everyone was doing and unquestionably believe what everyone was telling him. It stripped him of his power, of his control over what was happening in the world.

"Serafine said the same thing to me, that I should trust her. The only difference is that she has earned my loyalty. She helped me in my quest to overthrow Kalil. You, on the other hand, have shown me no such evidence that I can trust you. You've asked for loyalty before you've given any to me."

A deep growl rumbled from beneath the helmet of the Hidden King. The steel armor grinded as he clenched his fist. "Know this: Serafine, the Descendant of Aithnen, is the last person you should trust. She's the reason I'm dead, she's the reason corruption has been allowed to endure."

"But Serafine left Aithnen years before you were killed," Cail argued.

"That's true. However, she was still responsible for my capture. In order to see the entire truth, we must travel into the past." The blanket of darkness lifted and Cail was now standing by himself in a small hut. There were no windows, save for a small circular hole which was barely larger than Cail's head. The walls were rounded, making a dome, and made of brimstone. The ground was made of rough and solid lumps of sand that pushed into the arches of his Cail's feet. Other than a curtain draped over the front entrance and a thick wool carpet on the floor, there was absolutely nothing in the hut. Cail could hear fast footsteps swiftly approaching and he wanted to run through the curtain, but he knew that no matter what he did, he would surely be spotted. The curtain lifted and in walked two people Cail knew very well: Claeg, the Hidden King, and Serafine, the Descendant of Aithnen. Cail quickly realized that he was part of another memory, he was as visible as the wind. Serafine looked no different than she did in the present, even though this memory took place no less than a couple thousand years beforehand.

"I trust that the conversation with your father went exactly as we had planned?" Claeg asked.

"Surprisingly, yes it did," Serafine responded.

"Good, very good. You've done your part for the rebellion, now I will do mine. I'll assemble the strongest legion I can and they'll march upon the meeting of the Four Kings." Claeg and Serafine froze in place, paralyzed by time. Cail cautiously approached and stood beside them, patiently waiting for them to move, but they remained as still as stone statues. He waved his hand in front of Serafine's blank stare, but she didn't move an inch.

Cail's heart stopped when he heard a voice from behind say, "They can't see you." Claeg was sitting on the carpet with his legs crossed. He was no longer covered in armor. Instead, he wore a brown tunic with green leggings, his black hair was neatly combed, and his blue eyes gently gazed into Cail's. "Come sit with me, there is much for you to learn." Cail did so without hesitation. Even with the carpet being as thick as it was, jagged rocks still poked Cail's thighs. "For centuries, this hut was my home. Only my closest friends knew where I lived, and none of them betrayed me, or so I thought. Serafine and I didn't cross paths until about ten years before she would leave for Kordon. She came to me claiming that she was frustrated by her father's greed and that his reign as King of Kye needed to come a close.

"Naturally, I was skeptical and suspected this to be a trap. Over time, she proved her loyalty to me by leaking valuable intel; discussions which were only meant for the ears of royalty. She told me what the Four Kings of Aithnen argued about, what they agreed upon, what laws they planned to thrust on their citizens. I used this intel as fuel for frustration; every poor decision made by our King was a catalyst for rebellion."

"What happened when you tried to invade upon the meeting of the Four Kings?" Cail asked, remembering the conversation he had just watched. "Were you successful?"

"Unfortunately, we were not. My greatest warriors went into a trap and were captured by the enemy, which also began the fall of everything I had worked so valiantly to create. This occurred just days before Serafine left for Kordon on her quest and I've never seen her since; she's hidden behind a wall of cowardice, pretending that I no longer exist."

"If you can enter my mind and haunt my dreams, then why can't you find her?" Cail asked, annoyed that the Hidden King was stalking him like a shadow.

"I don't know. There's a barrier I can't break through, which tells me that my suspicions are true; that she betrayed me to her father." Cail sat in silence for a moment as he pondered over what he had been told. He saw a lake with several rivers feeding into it; he didn't know where the rivers came from, where the rivers had gone, or even what was in their waters. All he knew was that they ended in the lake, they ended in the present. Cail didn't know what to believe. He simply couldn't ignore all the sacrifices that Serafine had made for him, all the battles she had fought by his side. On the other hand, there was also the matter of what he had just witnessed. Serafine had previously told Cail that she never heard of the Hidden King, yet she was one of his closest allies.

"Why would she lie about knowing you? What does she have to hide?" Cail asked, breaking the silence.

"Lie? What exactly did she say?" Claeg asked in return.

"She claimed that she knew nothing of the Hidden King, but that her father might. It was odd, though. I could see the fear in her eyes, as though a snarling wolf was standing just before her."

"It was the fear of facing me once again, the realization that her consequences were following her," Claeg said. Bitterness and anger were rooted in his voice, plagued by haunting memories of Serafine's betrayal. "Ever since she betrayed the rebellion, she has kept a lot of secrets. Only she knows what she wants. I, on the other hand, have been completely transparent. You know my past, you know what I'm doing, and you know what I hope to accomplish. So, only one question remains: will you join me?"

Cail lost his breath; his mind was torn in two. While it was true that Serafine had lied about knowing Claeg, that didn't necessarily translate into becoming Cail's enemy. Perhaps there was an explanation for her dishonesty, a complication that intricately involved many lives.

"I'm sorry, Claeg. I can't turn my back on Serafine. She has sacrificed so much for me, she has been nothing short of a loyal friend."

"Cail, this is the last time we will speak before you enter the city. Kye is a battlefield. Every day, innocents are killed, families are torn apart, fire is spread like a plague. If you don't pledge yourself to me now, I can't promise that you'll have another opportunity."

"That's a chance I'm willing to take," Cail asserted with confidence. He wanted to be the same friend that Serafine was to him.

Claeg let out a sigh of disappointment and then rose to his feet. "If there's no way to convince you otherwise, then I believe the time has come for you to return to your journey." Weariness struck Cail as though he had inhaled poisonous fumes. No matter how hard he tried, his eyes were too heavy to keep open and Cail gradually drifted into darkness. The next time he opened his eyes, Serafine was standing over him, gently nudging his side with her foot. The thick darkness of the night had faded away and Cail could finally see the world around him, although it was as bleak as the day before.

"The morning greets us and so does our next day of travel," Serafine said with a smile as warm as the sunlight. Cail rubbed his heavy eyes and slowly sat upright on the cold dirt road. Once he had cast his drowsiness aside, Cail noticed that she was peculiarly giddy. He cast a confused glance and Serafine answered him as though she had read his mind. "If all goes well today, we should enter the Kingdom of Kye, and shortly after, the barrier between Aithnen and Kordon will dissipate." Serafine waited for a response from Cail, but he just sat silently in place. "You haven't said a word, is something wrong?" Cail's mind was so locked in his conversation with Claeg that he had hardly paid any mind to what Serafine had said.

"I know the truth," Cail replied, breaking his sullen silence. "I've seen the truth about you and the Hidden King."

"I don't know what you're talking about," Serafine sternly asserted.

"Don't lie to me. Claeg showed me what really happened; I saw you conspiring with him to take down your father's reign."

"I would never do such a thing to my father!" Serafine blurted out with an eruption of anger. She paused for a brief moment and allowed her rage to simmer. "I'll admit, it's true that I gave confidential information to Claeg, but it wasn't so that I could allow chaos to seep into my father's empire. Claeg was a treasure coveted by the Four Kings for centuries. No matter the Kings' efforts to capture the outlaw, the Hidden King lived up to his title and slipped through their fingers time and time again. As a last resort, my father approached me and asked me to rebel against him, or at least to appear to. He knew this was the only way to catch Claeg, and he was right. It took years of capturing and interrogating the Hidden King's loyalists, but my father's persistence was closely followed by success. Claeg was killed for his atrocities against Kye."

"And yet, he has approached me in several of my dreams. His body is dead, but his spirit endures. How can this be?" Cail asked.

"I don't know. I've never heard of anyone persevering through death. Regardless of whether he is alive or dead, Claeg can only do as much harm as what you allow. Cast his lies and deception aside; he only intends to use you." For reasons unbeknownst to Cail, he felt burning anger in his heart. He remembered that she was the one who lied about knowing Claeg, but for what reason? Why was she ashamed of her past? "If you're done asking questions, we should travel onward. I fully intend to reach the city by nightfall." Cail did have a plethora of questions burning in his mind but decided to set them aside until a later time. Several days had passed since he had rested in a comfortable bed and he was willing to do whatever was necessary to heal his aching body.

The Road of Purity was a daunting trail. A rough, jagged path wove back and forth and legions of carnivorous beasts awaited inside the walls of dark smog. It was impossible to see through the barriers that surrounded them, but Cail could feel hungry eyes glaring at him, carving into his will to survive. Seconds felt like minutes, minutes like hours, and hours like days. Serafine stopped for nothing. If Cail paused to rest his feet, she left him behind, expecting him to sprint to catch up. Her determination was as fortified as an iron castle and nothing would come between her and the Kingdom of Kye. Much to their dismay, the light of day started to dwindle like grains of sand slipping down an hourglass. As the world darkened, Serafine sprinted faster, forcing Cail to push forward with all his might. Then, without warning, Serafine stopped in her tracks and Cail nearly crashed into her. It was so dark that he didn't even notice that the walls of smog had dissipated. They stood upon the edge of a cliff that hung over a vast desert, an ocean of sand. The desert wasn't bare, though. A city of beige buildings awaited on the horizon, inviting Cail and Serafine. Serafine couldn't help but wear a proud grin on her face.

"I've waited two thousand years for this moment, Cail, and I'm sure my people have anxiously awaited my return. I am their only hope of seeing the sun again, their only hope to breathe in fresh air. For too long, the Sages of Pazia cursed the Aithnenians to breathe in the same poisonous fumes, for too long, they have been blanketed by a veil of clouds. Tonight, we will rest. Tomorrow, Kordon and Aithnen will form one body, they will breathe the same air," Serafine said without looking away from the Kingdom of Kye. Specks of light were glistening, creating an array of small stars throughout the city. Cail had completely forgotten about the alleged hostility and animosity and admired the serenity of the city from afar.

"Is Kye anything like you remember? Do you even remember what it was like?" Cail asked with a soft voice.

"No amount of time could make me forget my home. I remember the sand sinking beneath my feet, I remember the warm aromas, I remember the brilliant marble of my father's palace and now, you'll experience it as well."

Chapter 11: History in the Dust

As Cail trudged through the shifting sand of the desert, he reminisced about his venture through the desert of Pazia. Visions of his tumultuous struggles flashed through his mind. He remembered the piercing howls of the sandstorm, he remembered the thrashing gusts that beat against his body, and he remembered the grains of sand pelting his skin. Cail could feel the strength draining from his muscles, the memories feasted off his vitality. Even though there was no such storm surrounding him now, he could still feel the fear it had instilled in him. Pazia had poisoned his mind and seized his courage.

"Kye is a vast city," Serafine said, breaking their silence as they gradually approached their destination. "The city is much larger than Cestmir and much less inviting. No matter what happens, I need you to stay by my side. Kye is much too dangerous of a city for us to separate."

"If Kye is as dangerous as you say it is, then why are fighting so diligently to return?" Cail asked. He truly didn't see the point of having a hostile home.

"Because Kye is a part of who I am. If you're dealt a cut on your arm, do you kill your entire body? No! You acknowledge that you have that pain in your life and do everything you can to allow it to heal. In the same way, I acknowledge that Kye is a broken and injured city; our people are suffering, pain and crime are on the rise, children are starving and homeless. Along with the suffering comes the hope of redemption. While you dream of a world without borders, I often envision a city without pain, without turmoil; a city that's ready to rebuild its trust in one another." Cail was shocked by the affection Serafine felt toward her home. He had never heard her speak as passionately about anything before that moment. Elona had a tight grasp on his heart, though. There was nothing that Cail wouldn't do for his home and the people most dear to him. Serafine reached into her pocket and retrieved the Shadow Stone. Then she said, "This is the first step to our recovery. The people of Kye will see the return of the Shadow Stone as an omen; a sign that good fortune is soon to follow. Hope and anticipation will flow like a river. The Shadow Stone is an echo that will catalyze an avalanche."

At long last, Cail and Serafine reached the borders of Kye. Dirt roads neatly organized the houses and buildings into rectangular arrays. Every building matched the color of the tan desert. Cables hung overhead with laundry hanging to dry. With the day coming to a close, the streets were nearly empty, save for a few wanderers making their way back to their homes. Even though no eyes could be seen, Cail could feel that his movements were being watched. As they progressed further into the city, more of the natives emerged from their doors to get a glance at the two travelers. Whispers buzzed through the air; rumors about who they were and the audacity they possessed. Cail could feel their hostility; part of his mind wanted to reach out to Claeg for help, but he knew it was too late. Serafine seemed unfazed by all the quiet clamor. She proceeded forward as though she was walking through the glistening hallway of a castle.

"Before we see my father, there is a short errand that we must attend to," Serafine whispered to Cail. Then she turned toward a small shop squeezed between two homes. There were no windows on the outer walls of the shop and a small wooden sign hung next to the door. "Hidden Gems" was painted on the sign in a beige colored paint that matched the rest of the shop. The door creaked as Serafine pushed it into the store and Cail couldn't believe his eyes. Glass shelves were planted on all four of the walls, with each shelf holding dozens of priceless artifacts, some of which looked ancient. He saw statuettes of gold, silver coins, thick, dusty books, and magnificent swords. The rest of the room was flooded with golden statues wearing glistening iron armor.

"My goodness," said a soft voice from the behind the clutter of the store. A small woman emerged from behind the statues and slowly walked toward Cail and Serafine. Her bright eyes twinkled on her wrinkled face, her smile was warm and inviting in the same way as a radiant sunrise, and time had robbed her hair of its color. "I've seen many surprises throughout my numerous days, but I never expected to see the return of Serafine, the Daughter of Fire. I hope good fortune has returned as well?"

"It has," Serafine answered with a broad smile, she was relieved to see the old woman. "I succeeded in reclaiming the Shadow Stone and now our people can soak in the sunlight once more.

"Splendid! The gods certainly chose wisely when they ordained you to be the Descendant of Aithnen," the woman exclaimed, overjoyed by the news. Then she turned to Cail and asked, "Now, who is this young man?"

"Another Descendant chosen by the gods," Serafine answered. "This is Cailean Ozean, the Descendant of Kordon, Protector of the Skies. Cail, I introduce you to Bethil. She's a longtime acquaintance of my father." Cail expected Bethil to extend a hand of greeting, but she only extended a suspicious glance deep into his eyes, as though he was a bandit.

"Kordon, you say? Even before the blanket of clouds covered our nation, an era had passed since any of the Dragonfolk stepped onto our soil. The air in the high skies fed them arrogance and selfishness. They took great pride in knowing that they lived high above everyone else," Bethil said.

Before Cail could protest, Serafine interjected, saying, "If that's true, then Cail is nothing like them. He's proven himself to be a great warrior and an even greater friend. Dark forces would still bind my limbs if it wasn't for Cail." The complement flooded Cail's mind with guilt. He was ashamed to have ever questioned Serafine's loyalty to him, for she had just displayed it.

"Well, I suppose we all should be thankful for that," Bethil said. Her stern face lightened and she extended her hand for Cail to shake, which he did. After Bethil pulled her bony hand away from Cail, she said, "I think a reward is in order. With you being from Kordon, I believe I have something that might be of interest to you." She led Cail to a dark corner of the shop that was barely illuminated by a flickering candle. Bethil knelt to the bottom row of the bookshelf and retrieved a thick notebook which was slightly larger than Cail's hand. She blew on the cover of the notebook and a cloud of dust flew into the air. Handing the book to Cail, she said, "This book was acquired by my great-grandfather and has remained in this store ever since. Within these pages lies many secrets and hidden treasures of Kordon; ancient legends that no living Kordonian knows about. I think this book will mean more to you than it does to me. I'll leave you to begin your reading. I have something I must discuss with Serafine." Bethil waved her hand, motioning Serafine to follow her. Cail held the book in his hands, frozen in shock. The answers to some of Kordon's greatest mysteries and riddles now rested within his fingers. He opened his mouth to thank Bethil, but she and Serafine had already fled through the back door of the store, which was covered by a purple drape.

A thin layer of dust remained on the cover of the notebook, so Cail wiped it clean with his thumb, revealing the title, which read, "The Chronicles of Kordon" Cail opened the cover and flipped through the dried pages. The paper was stiff and brittle and the ink was faded, but still readable. Although, one page caught his eyes.

The Lost Skies

There are many wonders found throughout Kordon, but none are more magnificent than the city of Amani. In ages past, the city housed the royalty of the Nation in the Sky. It was a utopian paradise; sickness and hunger were strangers to the Amanians, every citizen had a strong house made of golden walls, and an impenetrable army of soldiers guarded the King's Castle. Amani was a Kingdom too powerful to fail, or so everyone thought. After centuries of peace and prosperity, an ill day approached that would forever change the entire nation of Kordon. This day appeared to be no different than all the rest. The sun beamed upon the Golden City, much like it had for the millions of days that had come before, but it would shine on the city no longer. At the same time that the sun had risen over the horizon, so also did a legion of Dragonfolk riding on the backs of their fierce dragons.

The city was met with an ambush of scalding fire and piercing roars of the dragons. The Amanians were outmatched and outnumbered. Genocide and slaughter were on full display as this ruthless clan of Dragonfolk rebelled against their own people. Even though the wanton attack seemed to be a hateful assault on the Amanians, the Dragonfolk held no regard for the people of the city, for their eyes were on another prize: The Gleaming Globe. This coveted treasure was the heart of the city, revered by the Amanians as a direct connection to their gods. Pure white light emanated from this polished orb and the flawless *surface of the Gleaming Globe was untouched, for the Amanians also feared the light. However, there was one man, from the invading Dragonfolk, who didn't fear it. Instead, he wanted nothing more than to claim the light as his own, he wanted nothing more than to rule Amani.*

Durai was his name and he led this legion of Dragonfolk and Dragons to conquer, and conquer he would. The Dragonfolk tore through the city; slicing through flesh with their swords, setting fire to houses and stores, ruining the unsuspecting lives of the Amanians. Then their eyes turned toward the castle. A golden fortress looked over all of Amani with an encompassing moat as wide as a river. Towers rose from the castle like mountains, the glass-stained windows gleamed in the sunlight, and giant flags of all colors flapped in the light breeze. The dragons glided over the moat and landed just before the castle's doors. The Dragonfolk dismounted and charged into the marble halls, slaying anyone who stood in their path. They pushed through to the throne room where the King awaited with his army. The Amanian soldiers fought with all their might, but they were simply no match for the Dragonfolk. A proud army was laid low and not a single soldier of the invaders was harmed. The King of Amani stood upon his throne with a slain legion of soldiers at his feet. He was defeated. Durai mercilessly beheaded the King and the Dragonfolk claimed the castle as their own. Amani was no more.

Immediately after his victory, Durai did what none of the Amanians ever dared to do: he took the Gleaming Globe into his hands. It became a part of him, it embedded itself in his skin, it gave him power beyond what he ever imagined. Durai discovered he could alter the world around him. He created a Kingdom exactly to his liking, he created his own paradise. The wonderful part was that he did so at no expense to his brethren. Everyone flourished in this utopia. The Dragonfolk and their esteemed dragons lived in harmony.

From that day forth, the Dragonfolk wanted nothing to do with the rest of Kordon. They had laid waste to Amani and created Conrian, the Kingdom of Light. Over time, the Conrians grew prideful and jealous of their new home and deemed themselves as the only ones worthy to set foot in their glorious kingdom. Other Kordonians migrated into the Golden City, which infuriated Durai. He believed that becoming the King of a new nation was a sign of divine intervention, and thus, Conrian was a holy land, only to be inhabited by those deemed worthy by the King. Using the power of the Gleaming Globe, Durai parted Conrian from the rest of the world, creating the Lost Skies. Thousands of ambitious explorers attempted to brave the empty void, but none ever returned.

"Are you enjoying your new book?" Cail looked up and saw Bethil just before him once again with Serafine standing just behind her. He hadn't even heard them enter the room.

"It's astounding," Cail said as he closed the covers and carefully placed it into his bag on his back. "Who wrote it? Are all the stories written in here true?"

"It's hard to say whether they're true or not," Bethil said with a soft chuckle. "The only way you'll ever know is if you search for the answers yourself. Seeing is believing, after all. What story were you reading, anyway?"

"It was the story titled, 'The Lost Skies,'" Cail responded.

"Ah, yes," Bethil nodded, remembering it vividly in her mind. "That is a fascinating tale. Conrian is one of Neptil's greatest mysteries. The piece in this book is probably the clearest explanation you'll find about the Kingdom of Light. To my knowledge, no one in the other three nations has ever ventured there since the city was hidden."

"That's ridiculous," Cail scoffed with skepticism. "If this city even exists, there's no way it could simply disappear. There must be some way to find it."

"Your home was hidden from the rest of Kordon for centuries, was it not?" Serafine asked. Cail couldn't muster an argument in retort. She was right, Elona was the only world Cail ever knew throughout his childhood. What if there were children just like him in Conrian? What if they were living in ignorance? What if they also dreamed of finding a world unlike anything they had ever imagined? He remembered standing on the coast of Elona with Laney, dreaming of a world beyond his own.

"That's enough chatter about the book," Bethil said, changing the subject. "The hour is late and darkness will be descending upon the city within a few moments. I have two spare bedrooms the two of you can use for the night." She led Cail and Serafine into a dark hallway and they climbed up a winding wooden staircase that creaked with every step. At the top of the staircase was a narrow hallway with three doors; a bedroom for everyone. Bethil pointed to the one on the right and said, "Cail, that will be your room. Make yourself feel at home."

The bedroom was small, but also cozy. There was enough space for an attenuated bed and a wobbly nightstand, but not much else. Cail dropped his bag on the floor and plopped onto the bed. The mattress was far more soothing than Cail's eyes had led him to believe. His body sunk into the fabric and he lost his mind in relaxation. Cail's thoughts drifted far away from the room that his body was in. Immediately, he could see Laney again.

She was in her bedroom, sitting at her small, wooden desk, writing in a notebook. *What is she writing?* Cail thought to himself. His aura drifted closer to her and he peered over her shoulders. Laney was writing furiously on the parchment, her quill scratching the paper. Then she stopped and sat back in her chair. A soft sigh escaped from her breath, as though she had just sprinted all the way across Elona. Cail started reading the paper, expecting to find words of affection or encouragement, but his eyes saw something quite different. Frustration and vexation were mapped in her notebook. Angry words were aggressively sketched on the paper, pointed words that could carve through flesh. Then Cail saw something even worse written on the page: his name. He was the root of all her anger. Tribulation and rage were alive and well in Laney's mind, and it thrived just as Cail did. Laney put her face in her palms as she started to cry. He had watched her endure the physical suffering of Tarvaris' curse, but being forced to see her emotional pain was unbearable. His heart was broken for her. Finding some way to relieve these burdens off Laney's mind would be the only redemption for Cail, but there was no way to do so. Hot tears burned his eyes as well, so he shut them. The tears cooled as they trickled down his cheeks and rolled off his chin. When Cail opened his eyes, he had returned to the guest room he was sleeping in. The room was now illuminated by a thin, flickering candle sitting on his nightstand, presumably left behind by Bethil. *It was all just a dream.* Cail thought to himself, but then he could still feel the moist trails made from his tears. Everything still felt so real. His emotions endured, trapping him in binds of sadness.

Cail's heart pounded far too rapidly for him to fall back to sleep, so he reached into his bag, retrieved the notebook and began reading another excerpt. This one was much different than the first, being more of an observational piece, rather than a delve into history.

Interactions

I'm one of the lucky explorers who could understand the inner workings of Conrian before it was closed off from the rest of the world. Doing this with all four of the nations of Neptil has been my lifelong mission, and now I can share my findings and observations with you, the reader. A good starting point, in my humble opinion, would be to take an in-depth glance at all four of the nations and delve into the reasonings of each of their actions. Only then can we begin to understand the functions of the world, the interactions of all that is.

We shall begin with my native nation, Kordon. There are a large number of peculiarities in regards to the Kordonians. I should know, after all. Self-reliance is a virtue amongst my people. We know how to support ourselves in a multitude of ways: building our own houses, growing our own food, pushing through our own adversities. Every family takes great pride in their own sovereignty. In a similar fashion, each island of Kordon is its own principal state. There are no Kings or Queens, no supreme leaders, no dictators. The only sources of authority are the Lords of the islands, and even they have limited powers. I think Overseer would be a better title than Lord. In truth, the Lords have no absolute authority. They don't create laws, they don't enforce laws, they aren't even appointed by their own people. The Lords of Kordon are figures of leadership who take charge of their islands in times of imminent peril. In a way, organized anarchy reigns supreme in Kordon.

Aithnen is considerably different than the Nation in the Skies. Four Kings rule over the Domain of Fire. Contrary to what the citizens are led to believe, the power isn't invested in the Kings, but in the officials who are handpicked. These esteemed individuals control everything that happens in Aithnen and they answer to no one. There is one thing extremely odd about these legislatures: no one knows they exist. I only discovered the truth by breaking into one of the castles and eavesdropping on the King of Kye himself. It appears that the Four Kings have been deceiving their citizens for centuries. During my visit to Aithnen, I told this revelation to dozens of folks of all backgrounds and upbringings, and they all laughed in my face, claiming that the accusations were ludicrous. No matter what I said, they couldn't be convinced. Their brains were stiffly manipulated into believing the lie that the Kings possess all the power.

Fontana was my most dangerous trek. The entire nation is enveloped by the raging seas with waves rising as high as mountains and storms strong enough to lift bodies off the ground. Despite the extreme environment, the People of the Sea fully embrace their home. They love the ocean and, in my opinion, they draw power from it. I've never seen a race so ruthlessly strong and stout while at the same time being unquestionably brilliant. A strong race must be led by a strong leader. I was shocked to discover that the leader of Fontana, called the Supreme Chancellor by the natives, isn't divinely ordained by the gods, but instead is chosen by his or her own people. Fortunately, my visit to Fontana came at a time just before this selection took place. One could sense a great deal of anxiety and anticipation in the environment. There was no shortage of frustration and discontent. A large number of Fontanians argued and bickered amongst themselves about what the correct choice was, but, also, I could still sense a respectful bond with each other. The fluidity of the process was quite intriguing.

Conrian is a rare nation. Their King possesses unlimited power over his people, but I never sensed any kind of angst. Durai's authority gave his brethren a sense of security, perhaps a false sense. He was revered as a demigod; Durai's reign was worshipped and exalted, everyone would do anything they possibly could to please him, and he lived a life of relaxation and luxury in his castle. Despite the unity between King Durai and his people, I still feel a nagging anxiety in my heart. I can't help but feel as though there's a darkness crawling beneath the surface, just as maggots thrive beneath a log.

Cail heard three knocks on his bedroom door. He quickly snapped the notebook shut and stuffed it into his bag. After clumsily stumbling off the bed, Cail opened the door to find Serafine on the other side. To Cail's surprise, she showed no signs of having just woken from sleep. Her hair was neatly tied into a tail that reached down her back and energetic color was on her skin. Quietly, she said, "Hurry and gather your belongings. The morning has arrived and I want to depart before Bethil wakes." Cail looked at Serafine's eyes more closely and saw that they were glazed, as though she had been crying. Before he could ask what was wrong, Serafine had already turned around and made her way down the hallway.

Chapter 12: An Ailing Palace

Serafine didn't speak a word as they proceeded into the city of Kye. The hour was still early enough that there was no one out and about, no wandering eyes were awake to spy on them. No expression or color was painted on Serafine's face. Gloom and despair oozed from her body like a poison, infesting Cail's mind. He could feel her darkness, her depression. It weighed on his heart like iron chains and cramped his stomach. He couldn't imagine what had upset her so badly, though. Cail sorted through the previous day's events, trying to think of anything he could've done to vex her, but nothing came to mind. Then, one particular moment stuck out in his mind.

"Yesterday, after Bethil gave the notebook to me, she took you into a separate room for a conversation. What did she say?" Cail asked.

"That was a private discussion," Serafine said with an emotionless voice.

"And you've been on edge ever since having it."

Serafine let out a deep sigh and then said, "My father is dying. Bethil told me that he's been the victim of a cruel illness for decades and it has slowly drained him of his livelihood. She doesn't think it will take him much longer to move into the next life." Cail didn't know how to respond. His mother had passed away when he was just an infant, so he had no memories of her. Watching a parent die before his eyes seemed unbearable. Yet, it was what Serafine was being forced to endure. There was nothing she could do to stop it, nothing she could do to reverse what was about to transpire.

"I'm so sorry," Cail said with melancholy. "I wish there was something I could do to cure him."

"I know you do," Serafine responded with a gentle smile, but it didn't last. The pain of losing her father suppressed any happiness she clung to. "He's ruled over Kye for an era, establishing a foundational reputation. Still, I fear what is to become of this city. Rebellion has spread like a plague for years and it will only grow worse unless a suitable heir is found for my father."

"The throne won't pass on to you?" Cail asked.

"Not automatically," Serafine responded. "I was my father's only child. When a King has no sons, the other three Kings must unanimously decide who inherits the city. They're a stubborn bunch, stuck in the ways of old. I can't imagine that they would elect to make me Queen."

"I think they should. You would offer compassion to your allies and terror to your enemies." Cail spoke the truth. He had witnessed firsthand what she was capable of. Given the opportunity, there was no telling what she could accomplish.

Cail couldn't express how thankful he was that Serafine had accompanied him through the city. It was a labyrinth of beige buildings, a forest of urbanization. Serafine knew the cracks in the city like she knew the cracks on her palm. As the morning grew later, nosy folks started to leave their homes and their curious eyes locked onto Cail and Serafine. Cail could sense that they knew who he was, they knew he was an outsider, they knew he wasn't an Aithnenian. Their stares were hostile, silent threats ordering him to leave their city, but he would do no such thing. He was vehemently determined to return the Shadow Stone back to its rightful place.

Serafine and Cail reached the end of the maze of buildings and arrived at Serafine's home: The Castle of Kye. It was a magnificent guardian towering over the city. Flawless ivory walls reached into the sky with navy spires as sharp as spears. A tall fence with iron, spiked posts surrounded the castle, rising as high as trees. Two stout guards protected the castle's gates. Their faces were as blank as a starless night, their chests were blocks of iron, and they each held spears that could pierce through bricks.

Serafine confidently strode toward the guards and once they saw her, disbelief crawled into their eyes. The two guards glanced at each other as if to ask if they were truly seeing the same thing. Serafine said, "Yes, it's true. I have returned to my father's palace." The guards immediately fell to their knees and bowed before Serafine, praising her like they would a god.

"You haven't arrived a moment too soon!" said one of the guards. His voice was slightly muffled from his face pointing to the ground. He lifted his head and continued, "Your father, he's unwell. A vicious ailment has chained him to his bed and rumors of his demise are beginning to circulate throughout the city. The people of Kye are growing restless. They view the death of the King in parallel to the death of his kingdom."

"If you allow us to pass, I can promise you that my father's kingdom will endure, even if he does not." The guards rose to their feet and opened the gates with a powerful clang. An ear-piercing screech sounded as the gate's doors swung open. Cail and Serafine entered by themselves into a vast courtyard. An emerald shrubbery awaited them, creating a maze. To Cail's surprise, Serafine's memories didn't struggle in the least bit. She knew exactly which turns to take and which to avoid. After dissecting through the maze, they arrived at the front doors of the castle. Towering brown doors stood before them, doors made of wood as thick as tree bark. Serafine pushed them open with all the might in her body and the wood slowly grinded against the concrete floor.

A colossal hallway awaited Cail and Serafine. Ivory bricks molded together to assemble tall walls which curved into a matching ceiling. White pillars stood in a straight line beside both sides of a maroon velvet carpet. Unique, complex carvings were engraved in the pillars. The carvings reminded Cail of powerful rivers flowing through grassy plains. To Cail's surprise, the hallway was bare and silent. They stood alone, quietly admiring the immensity of the hall.

"Where is everyone?" Cail asked, turning toward Serafine.

"I have no idea," she responded. "The castle never used to be guarded by an iron fence and citizens could come and go as they pleased. For reasons unbeknownst to me, my father has holed himself away from the people he promised to watch over. These halls used to be filled with jubilant citizens of Kye, and now they're flooded with silence. That must change."

Serafine proceeded forward and Cail closely followed. The clapping of their footsteps beat against Cail's ears until he heard the relieving sound of clamor coming from the neighboring room. The carpet led them through an archway, which curved just above their heads, and Cail and Serafine walked into a gathering hall filled with hundreds of people talking amongst themselves. Dozens of long, wooden tables were neatly filed throughout the hall, each filled with people who were talking, eating, or silently sitting. Vibrant banners were mounted on the walls, hanging from the ceiling all the way to just above the marble floor. "Serafine has returned!" someone called out from the middle of the room. Every voice immediately hushed and Cail could feel time halt. For a split second, he forgot how to breathe. Hundreds of eyes were locked on him and Serafine. Every face held the same expression, but Cail could feel the emotions from them. Some were in disbelief that the protector of their nation had finally returned from a venture that had lasted centuries, others were angry that she had the audacity to return at all, and others were relieved to see that she was alive and well. Despite the large array of feelings and opinions, no one uttered a word, no one dared to crack through the silence.

"Yes, it's truly me. I've returned with that which I set out to find. Please, someone, tell me where I can find my father," Serafine commanded.

"Bless my eyes, it really is you," said a woman who rose from a nearby table. Cail could immediately see that she was no ordinary woman. She had an appearance that was more mature than Serafine, but her skin was still dark and fair, matching Serafine's. Her green eyes glistened in the castle's light and her auburn hair was neatly tied into a bun. Serafine immediately darted toward the woman and flung herself into the woman's arms. They hugged each other and ignored everyone else during their heartwarming embrace.

After letting go of Serafine, the woman asked, "Aren't you going to introduce me to your new friend?"

"Of course. Cail, this is my mother, the Queen of Kye, Ina." Wanting to offer a proper amount of respect, Cail gently bowed his head before the Queen. "Cail is the Descendant of Kordon and the reason I've come home."

"Then it is I who should be paying respect," Ina said. Then she gently took Cail's right hand into both of hers and said, "I can't express how grateful my husband and I are to see Serafine home safely."

"Bethil told me of father's illness," Serafine interjected. All traces of happiness faded from her mother's face.

"I don't think it would be wise to discuss this matter for everyone to hear," Ina whispered into Serafine's ear. She led Cail and Serafine through an archway on the other side of the hall and through a series of dimly illuminated hallways. They stopped in front of a wooden door and then Ina said, "I'm sorry, Cail. I must ask you to remain here. There are some family matters that must be discussed." Cail nodded and Serafine and her mother entered through the door. Cail sat on the hard cement and closed his eyes; rest was hard to come by and he needed to seize any opportunity he could find. Then he heard a giggle. Cail's eyes snapped open and he saw a young boy, who looked no older than ten years of age, standing before him. Startled, Cail jumped to his feet.

"Once everyone knows, you'll be as good as gone," said the boy. He wore a sinister smile. Some hidden evil had seized his mind.

"I don't understand," Cail responded. "Once everyone knows what?"

"That you don't belong. The folk around here don't like outsiders. It'll start with the whispers. People will notice your quirks: the way you move, the way you talk, the way you treat everyone around you. After the whispers..." the boy's voice trailed off like an echo.

"Cail, what are you doing?" Serafine asked. She was now standing in the doorway. Cail turned his view toward her and then back to the boy again, but the boy had vanished. A faint whisper of the boy's giggle reverberated against Cail's mind. Cail stammered, knowing Serafine wouldn't believe a word of what he said. "My father is ready for you."

"Already?" Cail asked.

"What are you talking about? My mother and I were in there for at least an hour talking to my father," Serafine responded. Cail was taken back by what she said. He had no explanation for the rapid passage of time. Serafine asked, "Cail, are you alright?"

"Yes, I'm fine," Cail lied, trying to hide his insanity. "I just dozed off and had an odd dream." Cail rose to his feet and followed Serafine into the bedroom. It was a lustrous room filled with the riches of a king. A diamond-studded chandelier hung from the ceiling, a bronze coat hanger stood next to the door, and a magnificent oak dresser was pressed into the corner. Fine china was mounted on the walls, each with its own elegant design. A tea table stood in the middle of the room with four small wooden chairs surrounding it. Behind the table sat the bed, a fortress of comfort with a thick, plump mattress. Underneath the warm covers rested the King of Kye; he appeared to be a shadow of a glorious king. His sleek hair and thick beard were as white as snow, black circles were painted around his eyes, and his skin was yellow thanks to his ailment. The King looked miserable.

"Don't be shy, boy. Come closer," the King said waving his hand, motioning for Cail to approach him. At first, Cail was reluctant, but he gradually proceeded closer to the King. Once Cail was beside the bed, the King took Cail's hand and said, "I regret that you must see me like this, but I have no say in the matter. My daughter, Serafine, told me of all you've done for her. My Kingdom is forever indebted to you. Ah, but I forget my manners. My name is King Alban." The King wore a smile on his face, but Cail could still see his pain. He turned his gaze toward Ina and Serafine and said, "Leave us for a moment. I must speak with Cail in private." Without protest or hesitation, they swiftly departed from the room. Once the door was shut, the smile on the King's face faded. "My sickness isn't contagious, yet it has bled onto the people over whom I rule. The rebels of Kye are growing bolder. Every day, they gain new followers, they gather more muscle that's used to defile this city. Because of this, the other three Kings are looking to push forward with their plans to replace me, even before my inevitable death. Until recently, I was reluctant, but now I see that it must be done. The city of Kye is just as sick as her King. As much as I've loved being the King of Kye for all these years, I can no longer deny the imminent fact that the time for transition has come."

"It's very honorable that you have reached this realization all on your own," Cail said after a brief pause. "However, I don't understand why you've decided to tell me this."

"I'm telling you this because in three days, there will be a meeting amongst the Four Kings in the city of Taurim. Obviously, I'm in no condition to travel, so I want you to go as my ambassador and represent the city of Kye."

Cail couldn't say anything immediately; he was too shocked by the King's request. "I-I don't know what to say," Cail stammered. "I'm greatly honored that you see me as being worthy of this responsibility."

"You wouldn't be standing before me in this moment if you didn't possess strength, wisdom, and determination," King Alban said. A gentle smile peeked through his beard, through his pain. "Serafine will remain here to provide a more forceful watch over the city. With your help, order will be restored to Kye once more."

"I won't let you down," Cail said, smiling as he placed an assuring hand on the thick shoulder of the King.

"There is one last thing," the King said. Then he rolled onto his left side and reached into the drawer of his nightstand. From it, he retrieved a small roll of parchment tied together by a thin, maroon strip of velvet ribbon. The King turned onto his back again and handed the parchment to Cail. "This is proof that you are who you'll claim to be. The Kings are expecting you, but they'll demand that you present them with this parchment, but you must not open it before the appropriate time."

Cail took the roll and stored it away. "What's my next course of action?"

"You can come in now!" the King bellowed to Serafine. Obeying his command, Serafine immediately entered the King's bedroom. "I've given my daughter instructions to take you to a stable not far from the castle so you can be given a horse for your upcoming venture. That should allow you to reach Taurim within a day of your departure."

"That's very gracious of you," Cail said with a bow. Then he followed Serafine out of the bedroom. The walls of the hallways were covered with decorative candles and paintings of ancient royalty. Each of the portraits stared into Cail's eyes with a cold glare that froze his spine. It was a helpless feeling, as though he had been dropped into an icy lake. For a reason unbeknownst to him, he had a nagging feeling that the castle was haunted, that it wasn't mere coincidence that King Alban was dying, that there was a malevolent force draining him of his life. *Don't be ridiculous, Cail.* he thought to himself. Cail shook the paranoia from his mind and asked, "What should I expect in Taurim?"

"A much warmer greeting than you were given here," Serafine answered with a saddened voice. "Kye is a shadow of its former self. I remember a jubilant city that was the heart of Aithnen. When the rest of our nation struggled, they looked to us for guidance, and we would give it to them. Not only are we unable to offer guidance, but we're the ones who need it." The suffering of oppression was all too fresh in Cail's mind as well. Kalil's tyranny was a malicious plague that poisoned Kordon for centuries, it was a suffocating ocean of constraint, it was a mountain of fear that blocked the light of the sun.

"What can I do to help?" Cail asked.

"You can do what my father asked of you. Kye needs a leader with a strong, forceful hand. If we have a king who is gritty and unbreakable, then a new hope will be restored to the city. While you're gone, I will work on breaking into the intricate vines of the rebellion. The revolt against my father must be directly addressed. Everyone involved must be held accountable."

"And what of the Shadow Stone?"

"I will take care of that," Serafine responded. "The temple to which it belongs is beneath the city, in the Buried Temple. Right now, you just need to focus on the meeting of the Four Kings." Her answer flustered Cail's mind. The Shadow Stone was the sole reason for his departure from Aithnen, and now he was leaving its fate in Serafine's hands while he traveled leagues away. A part of his mind wanted to abandon the promise he made to the king and lift the curse of the Shadow Stone himself. It would certainly be easier to do that. His better judgment was screaming in his mind, begging him to stay in Kye, but it was too late. Cail had already made his promise to the King and he refused to be known as a breaker of oaths.

Once outside of the castle, Serafine led Cail through the shrubbery one last time and then they parted through the front gates. They proceeded down a grim alley with dark shadows and cool air. Cail was relieved when he saw the stable at the end of the alley. It was a raucous den of animals. There were horses, cows, sheep, pigs, chickens, and even a few rabbits. The horses were all magnificently beautiful, but one stood out from all the rest. Its beady, black eyes were focused on Cail, unflinching. There wasn't a sign of fat on the horse's body, just pure muscle. The tail had dark brown hair which matched its mane.

"What are you two doing?" a voice shouted from behind the clamoring animals. A bald, old man with a hunched back emerged and walked toward Cail and Serafine with a heavy limp in his step. His eyes shot out a sharp gaze, trying to intimidate them.

"I have an order from King Alban," Serafine responded and then she handed a dry piece of parchment to the man. He growled as he snatched it from her grasp. His eyes bounced back and forth as he skimmed over the page. Seeing that the man was unsatisfied with what he just read, Serafine said, "The King has promised a generous payment for compliance."

"And if I don't comply?" he scowled back at her.

"If you don't comply, you will wish you had," she responded. "An angry king is beyond anything I can control. You'd have to face his wrath yourself."

The man muttered something inaudible under his breath, probably some profane curse. Then he said, "Fine, go on then. I'll be waiting for my reward."

"And the map?" Serafine asked.

"Go fetch it for yourself," the man responded, pointing to a table behind all his animals. Then he limped away through a dark door. Serafine immediately strode to the table, snatched the map, and brought it back to Cail.

"This will be your guide to Taurim. You'll be traveling due west of here." Cail took the map from her and looked over the aged paper. Kye truly was the heart of Aithnen; Serafine's home was in the middle of the diamond-shaped nation. On the map, there was a curved trail that proceeded to the west; it looked to be a dangerous venture. Along the trail, there was a forest, a mountainous range, and a lone tower in the shape of a spire. Serafine could sense Cail's dread, so she said, "There's no need to fret. The road ahead of you will be much more kind than the Ash Plateaus."

"That's easy for you to say," Cail responded with no small amount of skepticism. To the south of Kye he saw the Bodaway Volcano, and to the east he saw something more peculiar. "There's an ocean to the east?"

"Ah, yes," Serafine answered. "That's the Endless Sea. Legends say that Fontana is deep in the heart of that ocean, but no one has ventured there for millennia. My people greatly fear the Domain of Water."

"Why? What grudge does your nation hold?"

"It's no grudge!" she asserted with an outburst of anger. "If you heard half the stories I've been told, you would see the Fontanians for who they truly were. You would see their cruelty and selfishness."

"And how do you know they aren't just stories?" Cail asked.

"I don't need to explain myself to you," Serafine responded with a cold tone of voice. Cail could hear the bitterness in her words, but he didn't understand where it was coming from and why she was directing it at him. He had a half mind to push for a justification, but he decided otherwise. Without saying anything else, Cail jumped onto the horse that had caught his eyes. Once he was safely mounted on the horse's back, he gave the reins a light whip. The horse galloped out of the stable and Serafine proceeded back toward her father's castle.

Chapter 13: A World Apart

When Laney opened her eyes, she found herself sitting on a cold floor of cement. The mysterious chamber was dark and silent; illuminated only by a single torch lodged in an iron stand. *Where am I?* she thought to herself. She tried to remember anything from before the present moment, but her mind was clouded. There was no recollection of what she was doing, where she came from, or even who she was with. Confusion morphed into frustration which then evolved into fear. She was afraid of never being able to remember anything ever again. What if she never remembered why she was in her present situation? What if no one remembered her? Then, in her moment of mental freefall, her mind clung to the edge of the cliff and pulled her body onto solid ground. Laney wasn't alone on the cliff, she saw Cail standing before her, but something was wrong. He couldn't see her. They were separated by an invisible veil, a barrier between her reality and his. The anger and bitterness she felt for Cail rekindled. Her mind was still soured by Cail's departure, by his betrayal.

His body became transparent, like a ghost, and then he faded into the darkness. Laney's mind returned to the dark chamber within which her body was contained. She heard a sonorous click of an opening door from behind her and then two voices: a man's and a woman's. "I trust our plan is proceeding without any setbacks?" the man asked. Laney didn't recognize the man once he had stepped into the flickering light of the torch. He was tall, round, and had a full head of thick, white hair that matched a bushy beard. However, Laney did know who the woman was: Serafine. Even though Laney was standing directly in the light of the fire, they paid no mind to her. They either didn't know she was there, or they couldn't see her.

"Yes, father," Serafine answered in a monotone voice. "Cail rode to the Wilderness in the West. He should arrive within two morning's time."

"Excellent," the King responded. A sinister smirk crept onto his face, an expression of malice and deceit. "He'll be greeted by an army of my strongest knights, and there he will meet his demise."

"So, the time to return the Shadow Stone has finally come?" Serafine asked.

"Not quite, my dear," the King responded, placing his muscular hand on her shoulder. "We must be patient for just a short while longer. Once my knights have returned, they will bring the Last Descendant to our feet, and then we will slay him. Only then can we break down the divide between Aithnen and Kordon. As long as the Last Descendant lives, so do the Dragonfolk." Serafine remained silent after her father's words. Her silence was the silence of guilt. In her heart, she knew that what she was about to do would surely end Cail's life, but there was no other choice, not for her. Serafine knew that in order to fulfill the destiny that her father had saved for her, she would need to execute this betrayal. Still, her silence forced her father's mind to grow suspicious. "You seem less than enthused," the King said with his back turned to his daughter.

"N-no," she stuttered, unsuccessfully trying to convince her father. "I just wish Cail didn't have to die."

"I know," the King responded with a softened tone. "But, this is part of the process. For you to become what you've dreamt of, Cail must die. So, what do you want more? Do you want the all the power you're capable of, or do you want Cail to live?"

"I want power," Serafine responded with a growl. Her voice was riddled with malicious venom. A vicious predator was conceived in that moment. Serafine, the Descendant of Aithnen, had become consumed by something far more powerful than any magic in Neptil. She was possessed by greed.

Laney felt her shoulders being shaken by a strong force. It was at that moment that she realized she had awakened from a dream. She was lying on her bed with Kadir standing over her with his hands on her shoulders. Cold drops of sweat were rolling down her forehead, her skin was chilled, and she was desperately gasping for air. "Thank the gods you're awake," Kadir said with a sigh of relief. Laney was still too shocked by her dream. Her eyes remained glazed as her mind was locked on the revelation. Cail was in mortal danger. Immediately, all the anger and bitterness in her body evaporated and she felt an overwhelming sense of fear; fear that she would never see Cail again.

"What are you doing in my room?" she asked, coming back to her senses.

"Laney, no one has heard from you all day. It's the middle of the afternoon. Dozens of us were looking for you throughout the entire village. I came up here as a last resort, which I'm glad I did. You look awful. Are you feeling okay?" Laney immediately shot off her bed and looked into the mirror on her desk. She realized Kadir was right. Her skin was as pale as a cloud, her hair was moistened by the layer of sweat on her forehead, and she looked famished.

"The dream I was having was about Cail. However, it didn't feel like a dream; it felt like I had traveled to see him, like I was in another world."

"Traveled?" Kadir repeated. "Traveled to Aithnen, you mean?"

"Yes. This felt like a perverted reality, but I can't shake the feeling that," Laney's voice faded off for a moment. She was afraid of the words that sprung into her mind. The words wouldn't dissipate, though. They whispered in her head, reverberated against the inner walls of her skull. Finally, she said them. "Cail's life is in danger. He's been betrayed."

"What?" Kadir asked, flabbergasted by Laney's claim.

"I saw Serafine and her father conspiring against Cail. They sent him blindly into a trap. For some reason, they need him killed before they can return the Shadow Stone to its rightful place."

"You're sure of all this?"

"As surely as I see you in this moment, I saw Serafine and her father plotting Cail's demise," Laney said, morbidly afraid that they would succeed.

"I'm sorry, I still don't understand. If all this is true, and Serafine has, in fact, turned her back on Cail, why would she wait until now to do so? She fought a war beside Cail, our war. This all seems too farfetched to believe."

"It was all just a means to an end. Ever since Cail freed her from the Servant's tower, her mind has been bent upon returning to her homeland. It's been her obsession, her compulsion, her fierce addiction." Laney didn't have very many memories of Serafine, but she cursed herself for allowing the Descendant of Aithnen to come anywhere near Cail. "I can't believe I was so blind, so gullible. I didn't have the wits to see what was just before my eyes."

"No one ever does," Kadir said, trying to ease Laney's guilt. "A liar's strike is an agonizing puncture to reality. You see past events in a new light, a light you never wanted to see. At times, you wish you would've been kept in the darkness. It's simpler if you are. There's less pain, less heartache." Laney knew he was right. If Cail had stayed in Elona and left Serafine to find her own way, there would be no need to fear for his safety.

Laney imagined this fantasy in her head. She woke up to a pleasantly cool morning with the bright sunlight peeking over the ocean of clouds. The village of Elona was back to what it used to be before Kalil and Tarvaris unleashed their chaos upon the Dragonfolk. Then she imagined herself lying in a field of grass just outside the village. The emerald blades had grown just enough to provide her with a firm mattress of support, but not too much to where it scratched against her smooth skin. She heard footsteps approaching from above her head, but she didn't need to look, she knew who it was. Without saying a word, Cail laid in the grass next to her. They didn't look at each other, though. Their gaze was fixated on the empty, blue sky above them. With every second of silence, Laney's heart pounded harder. This was the moment she had been waiting for. After years of dreaming, she would finally have the opportunity to say to Cail, "I love you."

"You do?" Kadir asked. A hot wave of embarrassment flooded Laney's mind and red lava poured onto her cheeks. She had allowed her imagination to completely consume her body and she had accidentally said those three fateful words, words that were only meant for Cail's ears.

"I do what?" Laney asked, trying to play dumb.

"You just said that you love me," Kadir responded. An expression of confusion and dubiety was planted on his face. Then his daze disappeared. Kadir had discovered the truth. "You love Cail, don't you?"

Laney paused. She didn't know what to say. Kadir was one of her best friends and he knew her as well as anyone else did, yet it was so grueling to admit the truth. Why, though? Why was her tongue frozen and paralyzed? What fear had gripped her mind and rendered her to be so cowardly? Surely, it was the fear of Cail being killed; the fear that she would never have the opportunity to tell the truth to Cail's face. While that fear was prevalent in her mind, it wasn't what was holding onto her words. Truthfully, there was a far greater fear that suppressed any courage she might possess; the fear that Cail didn't feel the same way about her. Such a rejection would crush her soul, it would deflate her spirit. Laney didn't know how she could respond to a defeat such as that. What choice would she have, though? The next day would come regardless of Cail's answer. The sun would still rise and set, the people of the world would go about their usual business, and the breeze would still breathe life into her lungs. In this moment, Laney reached a conclusion she had never seen before: Cail was not her existence. She still loved him with a boundless affection, but she would no longer allow her love for him to be her weakness. It was her strength.

Liberation was the prevailing emotion she felt. She was no longer bound by the anxiety of waiting, day after day, for Cail to return and give her his answer. She could go to Cail and give him hers. This feeling of freedom allowed her to say what she'd been wanting to say, to say the truth.

"Yes," she answered Kadir's question. "I do love Cail. That's why I'm so worried about him. I care about him and he means the world to me."

"I understand that, but we can't go running off to another world just because of a dream. For all we know, he could be safe in Aithnen with Serafine," Kadir argued. He was right, which frustrated Laney even more. There was no way for her to know that Cail's life was truly in danger.

"How will we ever know, though? We're a world apart from Cail. If his life truly is in danger, we're his only hope. Isn't Cail worth traveling to another world?" Serafine asked, pleaded. Kadir had no answer. His silence told Laney everything she needed to know. There was no changing his mind. Kadir viewed a venture to Aithnen as a futile effort, a worthless hassle.

"I'm sorry, Laney," he responded, refusing to remove his blank stare from the floor. "If you want to go to Aithnen, there's nothing I will do to stop you. However, you must see that this mission is suicidal. Whatever happens to Cail is beyond our control; his life is in the hands of the gods."

Nearly on the verge of tears, Laney burst through her bedroom door, down the rickety stairs and out of her father's house. Kadir didn't pursue after Laney, he saw no point in doing so. Laney sprinted through the dirt roads of the village, paying no mind to the townsfolk who shot suspicious glances at her. She continued to run, hoping that her steps would cast away her emotions, but they did no such thing. Finally, she stopped and stood on the coast of Elona with her toes hanging over the edge of the island. Throughout her entire life, she stood in the exact spot as she was standing in the present moment. That spot had always soothed her mind, calmed her emotions, cleared her thoughts. Although, this time was different. A violent hurricane was thrashing about in her head, wreaking havoc upon every source of serenity. It was an uncontrollable cyclone; this storm couldn't be stopped and anything that came in its path was feebly thrown aside.

"It wasn't just a dream," said a calm voice from behind. Laney spun around but saw no one standing anywhere near her. She rubbed her eyes, expecting to see someone, but she was alone. Just before she looked away, the silhouette of a man appeared before her. The silhouette gradually solidified until it became the man himself; he was an older gentleman wearing a gray cloak and a matching pointed hat. A bushy, white beard was on his face, gray hair flowed down past his shoulders, and a thick, wooden staff was grasped by his bony hand. Laney opened her mouth to call for help, but the man held up a finger, telling her to keep quiet. "No one, except for you, will see me."

"So, now I'm delusional?" Laney asked.

"Not exactly," the man chuckled. "I'm not a figment of your imagination. In life, I guided Cail through the challenges that were cast upon him by Kalil. Eventually, I died by Cail's hand, although the dark magic that possessed me left him no choice. He did what he needed to do, he did what I would've done if our roles were reversed. The reason I stand before you today is to say that I have also seen the same vision you have. Serafine's betrayal is despicable and selfish. Unfortunately, Cail is as blind as we are. The King has fooled Cail into believing that he is honoring the Kingdom of Kye. Little does he know that he's walking directly into a deathtrap. Even with Cail being a Descendant of the gods, he's no match for the legion that awaits him."

Like a flame abruptly ignites, Laney suddenly realized who was standing before her. "You're Caldir!" she exclaimed, nearly loud enough to be heard from the village. The wizard gave a slight nod in response. Laney had heard the villagers tell a slew of fables about Caldir, none of which she wholeheartedly believed. "I really do want to help Cail, but I have no means to do so. He's a world away from me. I fear that I would have the same fate as before; the fate of being taken as a captive of Cail's nemesis."

"Which is why you must convince Kadir to go with you. Alone, you will be captured by the King's army of knights, but when you're paired with Kadir, the two of you can save your best friend," Caldir responded. Laney cursed under her breath. She knew that Kadir would never agree to come with her, not after their most recent discussion. He didn't even believe that Laney's dream was real, and now she was supposed to convince him that the ghost of a wizard confirmed her vision to be true? Not a chance. She'd more likely succeed in saving Cail on her own than she would in convincing Kadir of the truth. Caldir interrupted her silence by asking, "What do you say?"

"I say that even if I could convince Kadir to come with me, we wouldn't be able to go. We have no way of knowing what direction to take." On cue, a faint screech resonated through the air. Laney and Caldir both recognized the familiar call immediately; it was the call of a falcon, Cail's falcon. Emey glided through the air, occasionally flapping her wings to give her a boost of speed. Her emerald feathers elegantly waved in the wind like the field of grass upon which Laney stood. Just before landing on Elona, Emey let out one last screech, this one much louder than the first. Her wings accelerated as she descended to the ground, sending out gusts that lashed upon the blades of grass. With a sonorous thud, her talons mounted firmly on the ground.

"It appears that you've found your ticket to Aithnen," Caldir said with a light chuckle. Then the wizard turned to Laney and, with a somber expression on his face, he said, "If you ever wish to see Cail again, you know what you must do. Your life depended on him, and now, his life depends on you."

Laney walked over to Emey and gently stroked her feathers. As she listened to Emey's purrs, she pondered over the daunting task that stood before her. Undoubtedly, an expedition to Aithnen would be a perilous adventure. She knew her life would be threatened, but she also knew it would be worth it. Waiting in Elona and praying that her vision was nothing more than a dream would be a betrayal in itself. Cail had sacrificed so much not only for Laney, but for all the Kordonians. Only because of him, they could all live their lives without the shadow of tyranny looming over them. Laney saw no choice other than to risk everything she had, even her own life, to save Cail.

"How can I convince Kadir?" Laney asked as she turned around, but the wizard was gone. "How can I convince Kadir?" she repeated with a soft whisper.

Chapter 14: Beasts of the Wood

Raine, the name Cail decided to give to his newly acquired horse, trotted on the sandy trail which led through the desert. To Cail's surprise, Raine didn't struggle in the slightest while pushing forward. Even though the hour of the evening was late, the heat was still sweltering. Cail's dried tongue craved for water, or for any kind of nourishment.

Something on the horizon awaited Cail, something he least expected to see. A wall of emerald trees sat just beyond the edge of the desert. They stood as firm as the Iron Fortress of Ijsbrandur. While Cail was happy to leave the scorching heat of the desert, he couldn't shove aside a nagging paranoia about the forest before him. It seemed too good to be true. Surely, he must have been hallucinating the safe haven from the heat. Although, as he approached, he realized the tall forest was real, indeed. Raine stopped just before the border of the trees, perfectly content with remaining in the light of day. Cail hopped off the horse's back and landed on damp grass. He had never seen such a contrast in environments before. The arid air of the desert had snatched all the saliva from his mouth, and now, the humidity of the forest clamped down upon his lungs, restricting his breathing. He could feel the moisture on his skin.

Every step through the forest was arduous. Vines and roots weaved in and out of the ground, obstructing Cail's footing. Light was scarce and a heavy mist clouded the air. Trips and falls were inevitable. Cail's arms and legs were burned and scratched from all the abrupt tumbles. There was no sign of a paved trail, but it didn't matter; Cail only needed to keep pushing westward to his destination. Despite his isolation in the forest, Cail heard plenty of activity all around him: the rustling of small critters in thick patches of grass, the calls of owls ricocheting off the bark of the trees, the faint roars of terrible beasts. The wood was undoubtedly alive; Cail could only hope that it wasn't perilous. Even though there was little light to begin with, it was quickly beginning to fade and Cail was forced to end his trek for the night. He dropped his pack onto the ground and tried to find a soft patch of dirt to lay on. The ground was moist, yet lumps of dirt and tree roots still pushed into his back. He closed his eyes and settled into the darkness, left to listen to the sounds of the forest. All the noise was a constant reminder that he was not alone; the following day would show whether that was good or bad.

The morning came far too swiftly for Cail. He was only able to enjoy a very light sleep and the lids of his eyes were still leaden, but Cail knew he had to push onward. The light of the morning lifted the thick haze and Cail could see his path more clearly, but the air was still damp and humid. It wasn't until about an hour into his venture that he realized something very different: the forest was silent. He had not heard a single animal stirring about for the entire morning. With no sound, the forest was eerie and ghastly.

There was absolutely no sign of the ocean of wood coming to an end. Every tree looked identical to the next, there was no sun to guide his direction, and there was no sound other than leaves and grass crunching beneath his feet. After walking for the entire morning, Cail found an empty patch of dirt and decided to rest his aching body. He groaned as his muscles throbbed and the scratches on his skin burned. The expedition had proven to be much more tumultuous than Serafine had made it out to be, but Cail remained blind to her treachery. Serafine hid behind the wall of Cail's trust, a wall that Cail wouldn't bust through on his own volition. He wholeheartedly believed her to be his friend and ally. After all, why wouldn't he? She fought by his side as he tried to free Kordon from Kalil's suffocating darkness and she even rescued him from the clutches of the Blue Assassins. She had proved her loyalty and Cail had no reason not to trust her.

A twig snapped from behind the trees. Cail quickly twisted his head around and silently scanned the area, but he saw nothing. Then he heard more footsteps lightly padding the ground around him. Cail was surrounded. He jumped to his feet and tried to plot a course of escape, but it seemed futile. From the trees emerged burning eyes, eyes Cail had seen once before. Snarls rumbled as a pack of gigantic wolves approached from all directions. Ivory blades protruded from their mouths and crimson eyes glared at their prey. Cail's heart stopped, for he was certain that the end of his life was nigh. These wolves looked exactly like the one he faced in the dungeons of Beda's temple. Battling one of these massive beasts was a challenge in itself, but he was no match for dozens of them at one time.

The largest wolf of them all stood just before Cail, standing tall enough on his four feet to look straight into Cail's eyes. "Who dares to intrude into our wood?" the wolf growled. Cail was shocked the beast could commune in a comprehensible language. He was so paralyzed by fear that he had forgotten how to speak.

"M-m-my name is Cail," he finally stuttered. "I mean none of you any harm. I'm just passing through on my way to Taurim."

"Taurim, you say?" the wolf repeated with a deep, thunderous voice. Cail nodded his head nervously, praying that he didn't upset the vicious predators. "Many years have passed since travelers have gone to or from that tainted city."

"Tainted?" Cail asked.

"You heard correctly. A vicious war ravaged that city beyond salvation. Thousands of innocent lives were slain. Taurim was deprived of its riches, stripped of its beauty, robbed of its vitality. Now, the only thing that thrives there is death."

"That can't be," Cail retorted. "King Alban has tasked me with the responsibility of attending a meeting amongst the Four Kings. They're to decide the fate of Kye's future. How can that be if Taurim is dead?"

"I'll let you discover that for yourself," the wolf said. A sinister grin exposed his terrifying teeth that were capable of tearing Cail's body to shreds. "I'll strike a bargain with you. You can pass through this forest and go to Taurim, but you must retrieve something from that accursed city if you wish to return to Kye. In Taurim, a terrible beast stands guard over the death-ridden land. He is a foul creature made of darkness and decay. None can live while he does. I need you to bring me his head. If you try to pass through the forest again without doing so, I won't stop my brethren from ripping your flesh with our piercing claws."

The thought of being tortured and tormented by the pack of massive wolves sent chills down Cail's spine. "Why do you care about this beast so much? What did he do to you?"

"Nothing," the wolf responded plainly. "Although we're not the most innocent creatures, we are just. The acts of this beast are unspeakable. He has laid waste to a city that was home to thousands of beautiful families. We want nothing more than for that atrocity to answer for his crimes." Cail couldn't begin to imagine what acts were so heinous that would make a pack of wolves hate the committer of the crime. He could see the detestation in their eyes; they loathed the beast. Cail sensed that it wasn't just the crime that the wolves hated, but he decided against pushing the predators for more information.

"How much farther must I trudge through this forest?" Cail asked.

"Not much. The foot of the Hazel Mountains is no more than an hour away from here. A word of caution: those mountains are not for the faint of heart. Some of the strongest Aithnenians have met their doom there. Now, leave our sight before I change my mind." Terrified of what would happen if he stayed, Cail sprinted away, trying his best to ignore the snarls hurled at him by some of the other wolves. Just before he was clear of the pack, the lead wolf called out to Cail.

"Wait!" Cail stopped dead in his tracks, knowing that it would be useless to continue running. As the wolf slowly approached, he said, "You're displaying a mountain of loyalty to King Alban for running this errand. Why?"

"It's not the King I'm loyal to, but Serafine."

The wolf scoffed, as though what Cail had said was supposed to be a joke. Then he said, "If Serafine's the one who has your trust, then you don't know the first thing about the Princess of Kye."

"Why does no one else trust her?" Cail shouted in frustration. He was beginning to believe that something was being hidden from his view. Still, he couldn't ignore everything Serafine had sacrificed for him.

"Others have also told you to be wary of her, haven't they?" the wolf asked. Cail gave no response other than a slight nod of his head. Then, as

Clinton Mathew

though the wolf had gained a glimpse into Cail's mind, the beast said, "The Hidden King has been weighing on your mind, hasn't he?" Cail didn't know how to respond. He had never even known about wolves being in the forest until a few moments ago, and now they knew one of his deepest secrets.

"I've never told anyone about that," Cail responded with a soft voice.

"Maybe not with words, but you just told me with your eyes," the wolf responded. It's not hard to see a mind that's troubled and manipulated. Your eyes are always weary, desperate for any sort of refuge. You see, a harassed mind is like a long winter. At first, it's subtle; the nights gradually grow colder and longer, the trees and plants begin to wither, there's no more food to reap. You might think that that's the worst of it, but it's only the beginning. Frozen storms plummet and pound your mind and blizzards bury your conscience."

"But the winter is followed by spring, right?" Cail asked with hope.

"Only if you can endure," the wolf answered. "The Hidden King will test your limits. He needs to know if you're strong enough to overcome Serafine's lies, deceit, and treachery."

"Serafine is not a liar!" Cail screamed at the wolf. Not the wisest decision, he realized. Yelling at the leader of a pack of wolves that had him surrounded would normally lead to an inevitable death, but they all stood still. "Everyone has made these claims and accusations, but have shown no evidence. However, what I have seen is that Serafine was there for me when I needed her the most. My nation was strangled by an evil dictator and she did everything I needed her to, without question or hesitation."

"That was very noble of her," the wolf said with cynicism, mocking what Cail had just said. "Well, none of this matters to me. Your life is the one in danger, as it will be if you fail to do what I have asked."

Cail had half a mind to laugh at the wolf. He knew there was no beast in Taurim for him to slay. For whatever reason, the wolf was trying to scare Cail and keep him away from the forest, but Cail's mind couldn't be fooled so easily. Nevertheless, Cail decided to keep any remaining comments to himself; it was best not to anger predators such as these. He pressed onward through the forest. His trek was much easier and far less painful than the day before. In a way, Cail was sad to leave the forest. With the haze lifted, the beasts behind him, and the light of a new day, Cail could absorb the beauty and immensity of the world around him.

Just as the wolf had promised, Cail was greeted by a slew of towering mountains that stood just outside of the forest. The ground wore a thin blanket of snow, the wind howled just like the wolves, and Cail's skin started to chill. He retrieved a brown cloak from his pack which offered little protection from the frigid air. Luckily, there was a trail that snaked through the terrain, but it was painfully obvious it wouldn't be a light stroll. Suddenly, Cail was struck by a haunting revelation: he feared that he could die in these mountains. Isolation, loneliness, and imminent danger were his only companions. They were plastered onto his skin and clothes like dried mud. For the first time since Cail was imprisoned by the Blue Assassins, he was left to venture the world on his own. He felt exposed, vulnerable, and at the mercy of forces much larger than himself. While all that was true, it did give him time to ponder over everything without the distractions of outside voices.

All the voices were starting to budge their way into his mind. They were all telling him to turn his back on Serafine, to see what he was too gullible to see, to make her answer for her betrayal. However, he didn't know that Serafine had, in fact, betrayed him. Still, she had only a few allies and an army of enemies. That had to speak for something, didn't it? It was impossible for Cail to tell.

Then his thoughts turned to Laney. Until that moment, Cail had succeeded in separating his feelings of guilt and shame from his focus, but as soon as he saw her face in his mind, his face flushed. Humiliation squeezed his thoughts, pressed upon his lungs, and clouded his mind. *I was skating on a thin layer of ice before. Surely, she must hate me now.* Cail thought to himself. Just the idea of Laney detesting Cail was enough to drive him mad. She was the one person he wanted to look at him with pride, and his actions had driven her away.

On the other hand, was it truly Cail's fault? He didn't ask for any of the trials he had been forced to face. He had not asked to save all of Kordon from a dark reign of terror, he had not asked to escort Serafine to another world, he had not asked to travel to the frozen mountains on his way to Taurim. All those things had been asked of him. Cail was being courageous, valiant, and selfless. Yet, Serafine couldn't see that. She could only see two roads to take: the one upon which she stood and the one Cail had chosen. There was no justification, no context, no explanation. Redemption would only be found once Cail had returned to Elona, but he was a world away, trudging through a frozen tundra.

The trail was encompassed by snow-covered stone. Heavy flakes whipped against his face and watered his bare eyes. Every step dug deeper into the snow until his shins were covered. Cail was ill-prepared for this daunting venture. His cloak was warm enough to fend off frostbite, but the cold still chilled him to the bone. There was no way to tell what the time of day was; a thick, bleak blanket loomed over Cail's head, blocking the sun. The elements were brutal and impartial, unleashing their fury on any who dared to challenge them. Just as the frigid wind swirled around the icy mountains, so did Cail's emotions thrash about inside his mind. Most notably, the fear of his imminent demise strangled his courage. He had never faced a hostile environment like this on his own. The only instance that came to mind was the Desert of Pazia, but even then, he was accompanied by Emey. Along with the fear followed sadness. However, Cail couldn't precisely point to what was making him feel this dejection. Perhaps it was the idea that he could die and never be found, becoming a lost memory, or maybe it was the possibility that he would never have another chance to look upon Laney's radiant, gleaming, beautiful face again, or, worst of all, perhaps his sadness stemmed from thinking that he would never return to the warmth of his own home. In that moment, Cail realized the wolf was right; the cruel cold was seizing control of his mind. He knew these horrible thoughts needed to stay leagues away from his mind, but they were as persistent as whispers from the mouths of his closest friends.

The piercing snow and howling gusts will hold power over me for no longer. Cail thought to himself. In unison, his mind and fists clenched, barricading his body from the cold and cocooning his skin in a fortress of warmth. Then, he said, "I'm the Last Descendant. The wind bows to me." Cail raised two open palms into the air. He no longer felt the brumal squalls or the pelting snow, his mind was far too fortified. One last time, Cail closed his fists and all fell silent. The cold still thrived, but the snowfall had ceased, as had the gales. Now, he didn't just feel warmth, he felt power. The same power that rushed through his veins when he found the Air Runes warmed his blood in the heart of the frigid mountains. His warmth transformed into power, and his power transformed into confidence. For the first time since entering the mountainous terrain, he believed he could overcome any trial laid before him, he believed in his own capabilities. Cail commanded the wind, and the wind obeyed.

Chapter 15: Following Shadows

The walk back to her home was the most unpleasant she had had in centuries. As soon as Cail rode away on his horse, Serafine knew exactly what she had done: she had sent Cail to his death. He was unquestionably strong, but no one could master the journey to Taurim on their own. The desert was too dry, the woods were too hostile, the mountains were too cold and slippery, and then there was the Tower. Until that moment, the Tower had completely slipped her mind. Even if Cail did manage to survive the wild, Serafine surely knew the Tower would spell his doom. She had only braved the Tower a few times in her entire life. It was a rite of passage for all Aithnenian royalty; it wasn't entirely uncommon for the weaker souls to fail its life-consuming tests. Urban legends were passed down over millennia, rumors which would help prepare the challengers. Cail, on the other hand, was hopelessly blind to the perils that awaited him, his mind was filled with blissful ignorance. In the Tower, windowless walls reflected all light, creating a rectangular prison of darkness and suffering. Besides the winding staircase descending into the dark, there was nothing in the Tower save for three chambers, each containing a test for the poor soul who dared to brave the perils. A sinister magic contained within the Tower's walls gave birth to the most excruciating fears of the challenger, forcing them to either overcome or to die.

Serafine tried with all her might to be heartless and without shame. After all, it was what her father demanded. King Alban was quickly approaching the end of his life, but there was still one last deed he could accomplish: he could cement his daughter as the unquestioned leader of not just Kye or Aithnen, but of Neptil. Ruling the world was a burning desire that her self-righteousness had kept buried for far too long. She was ready to embrace what she was fully capable of becoming: The First Empress of Neptil. However, one bit of frustration remained; her father would tell her nothing of how she would become unstoppable. She tried to find any hints of her father's plans in a recollection of the conversation from a few hours beforehand:

Serafine was standing just outside her father's bedroom door, joined by Cail and her mother, Ina. "I'm sorry, Cail. I must ask you to remain here. There are some family matters that must be discussed," her mother said. Cail nodded and then Serafine followed her mother into the bedroom. Serafine nearly started to weep when she first laid eyes on her father, partially because she was so happy to see him after centuries of isolation from home, and partially because she could see the crushing illness that was killing his body.

"My Serry," King Alban said with a spent voice. His words broke in and out due to the ineptitude of his lungs.

"Father," Serafine said softly. Then she sprinted across the room and flung her body into his arms. She was overcome with the joy of feeling her father's embrace and could no longer hold back her burning tears. Everything felt so surreal; returning to Kye and feeling the warmth of her father. It nurtured her heart and soothed her mind. Serafine pushed herself off the bed and asked, "You look awful. Who did this to you?"

"Claeg," the King growled. "We tortured and punished his body, broke his bones like twigs, ripped his flesh like paper. I was determined to fully display my wrath for his betrayal to the Kingdom, but he possessed something far more powerful than his muscles. A dark magic dwelled within his skin. Just before his body perished, he cast a malicious curse not only on me, but on Aithnen."

"And it truly worked?" Serafine asked with an incredulous scoff.

"I laughed at him as well," Alban responded. "We all did. Even though there was arrogant humor in my eyes, a fiery rage burned in his. Fearful of what he would do should he escape, I cut off his head. For a number of years, life went on as it always had. Mornings turned to evening and back to morning again, the seasons cycled between scorching summers and frigid winters, and the stability of Aithnen remained intact.

"That is, until one night during which I ventured just beyond the city's borders to gaze at the vast desert that stretched all the way to the horizon. As you and your mother know, it's always been one of my favorite places to think and ponder over troubling conundrums in my mind. Although, this night was very different; I was greeted by something I didn't expect. Ghastly whispers hissed from the thick ocean of sand. The words were indiscernible, but I sensed they were calling out to me, trying to lure me to my death. Then, as clearly as I see you now, I saw a pair of large footprints, much larger than my own, mold in the sand only a few paces in front of me, but there was nobody to which the prints belonged. There was no one that I could see, but I felt the presence of the apparition standing before me. It was filled with darkness, hate, and abhorrence. I could feel its fierce desire to take my life.

"Running faster than I ever had since my adolescence, I fled from the fiend. The locals cast no small number of suspicious glances at me, but I cared not. Returning to my castle and burrowing myself into this safe bed was all that remained in my mind. If any words were thrown at me, my mind must have reflected them.

"After successfully avoiding any further contact with society, I returned to this very room, fully prepared to barricade myself within the warm, thick sheets of my bed. However, to my dismay, there was no warmth to be found. The room was as cold as a bitter gust in the dead of a wintry night. It carved through my skin and bit down on my bones. It was at that moment that I knew I wasn't alone. The same whispers started once again, only louder. Then, I saw him; the silhouette of the loathsome traitor I killed years beforehand stood by that window." Alban pointed to the only window in the entire bedroom. "He didn't say anything, and he didn't need to. I knew he had come back from the grave."

"Impossible," Serafine said softly, not wanting to believe the tale.

"Your father speaks the truth," Serafine's mother asserted with a stern voice. "I've seen the ghost myself. Many have who dwell within the castle."

"Why didn't you try to leave, then?" Serafine asked.

"We did," the King responded. "As you know, the road to Taurim is far too dangerous and Ithril lies too close to the wretched Fontanians, so our only hope rested in the Northern City, Kazimo. At first, they were exceptionally generous with their hospitality, but the spirit of Claeg followed us like tar on the bottoms of our shoes. His ruin plagued Kazimo and, shortly after, we were banned to face our own fate. With nowhere else to go, we returned to our homes. Ever since that fateful night, the curse has eaten away at my health and started the deterioration of this proud nation."

Serafine couldn't believe what she was hearing. Centuries had passed and years of diligent fighting had led her back to her home, only to find it to be haunted by a ghost from the past. "Surely, there must be a way to break this curse?"

"That's my girl," the King said with a newborn smile on his face. "There is, but the only one who stands in our way is the one who came here with you."

"Cail?" Serafine asked. Her father gave a grim nod. "I'm so sorry. I shouldn't have brought him here."

"My dearest daughter," the King said, softly placing his muscular, course hand on Serafine's smooth cheek. "You have nothing to apologize for. As a matter of fact, bringing the boy to Aithnen plays very well into our hands. He knows nothing of the path to Taurim, does he?" Serafine shook her head. "Good. That's exactly where we will send him. Once he's out of our way, nothing can stop you from becoming what you were born to be."

Serafine was filled with so much excitement, she didn't know how to respond. Everything was falling into place, like stars aligning during a night of profound destiny. Yet, she couldn't neglect the fact that her rise to power would come at Cail's expense. "Does he really have to die?" Serafine asked her father.

"You know the answer to that."

She wished she didn't. Ever since that moment, even as she walked through the quiet streets of Kye, she searched for any hope of Cail's life being spared. Neptil could greatly benefit from his strength and kindness. Perhaps he would prevail in the end. After all, why not? He is the Descendant of

Kordon, the boy who overthrew Kalil and his faithful Servants. If Cail did survive through all the dangers of his upcoming expedition, Serafine decided that would prove to be a worthy test. She knew her father was just being paranoid about Cail, she could become the Empress of the World without losing her friend.

After returning to the castle, Serafine's empty stomach overruled the rest of her body, so she treated herself to a scrumptious meal prepared by the finest chef in the castle. A thick, succulent slab of roasted hog meat sat on her plate, along with grilled vegetables of all colors and a vast assortment of ripe fruit. The array of flavors massaged her taste buds and her muscles kindled a doused flame that had been extinguished due to her arduous trek.

As Serafine savagely tore through her meal, her mother, Ina, joined her at the reflective table of marble. "You did it, then?" Ina asked. Serafine let out a soft grunt in response and nodded her head. Her mother continued, "I must admit, you've always been your father's daughter. You're determined, strong-willed, and ruthless. He would never struggle with matters such as this. I think that's a large part of what has made him such a great King. One of his most well-kept secrets, which he only told me, was that he never let even the smallest feelings of affection and love interfere with what he envisioned for himself. Tell me, Serafine. Do you let love interfere?"

The question slammed into Serafine's chest like an iron hammer. She immediately dropped her spotless fork, which was stabbed through an emerald leaf of lettuce. Thinking quickly, she replied, "I don't love Cail."

"You know what I mean," her mother responded.

"He's not my friend," Serafine lied, partially wishing it were the truth. "He needed my help to save his home, and I needed his help to return to mine. There's nothing more to be said about Cail and me."

"You fought a war with someone who isn't your friend?" her mother asked. Ina's words were filled with well-deserved skepticism. "Listen, your father is dying and he's doing everything he can to ensure that Aithnen's future lies in sure hands, but there are ways of doing so without betraying your closest allies. As it stands, Cail will die in Taurim. He's no match for the knights who await his arrival. They are the best of Alban's warriors. However, it's not too late to go save your friend, to prevent the bloodshed."

"But it is too late," Serafine asserted. "Cail left a couple hours ago."

"Hours which you could easily make up. Even after all the years you've been gone, you still know Aithnen better than him." Though Serafine didn't want to admit it, her mother was right. The final hour hadn't ended quite yet. If Serafine chose to, she could easily ride to the west and track Cail down, but that would be the lesser of two challenges. Then, she would have to explain herself and confess her betrayal to Cail. Serafine wasn't sure she could do the second bit. Betraying someone is so much simpler than apologizing for it.

"No," Serafine said after reaching her decision. "What's done is done. If Father says that Cail stands in the way of my reign, then I trust his plan."

Evidently upset by her daughter's answer, Ina shot up from her chair and stormed away from the table. However, before she left the dining room, she said to Serafine, "Everything isn't as discrete as your father portrays it to be. We each have a path that life takes us on. Your father would like to think that all the paths are separate from one another and everyone needs to tend to their own road, but that couldn't be farther from the truth. Paths intersect, twist, and turn, creating an intricate labyrinth of experiences. Cail's road has merged with your own and the two of you are now sharing the same lessons that the gods must teach you. While it's true that you tend to the road you're on, the same can be said about Cail. As of right now, you're traveling down a road with a close and loyal friend. Don't let that change." With that said, Ina marched off into the nearby corridor, leaving Serafine to ponder over her advice.

Serafine was baffled by how adamantly her mother was trying to convince her to save Cail from the perils of his fool's errand. If Cail really did die during his expedition, why did her mother care? Why was Ina toiling so much to save Cail's life? Unless there was something that Serafine's mother saw in him, something that rested beneath the surface of his young skin. *What if there is some magical force keeping him alive? What if he's impossible to kill? If Cail does survive what awaits him, he will surely find me and kill me.* Serafine thought silently as she stirred the few remains of her meal. *No. That can't be it. My paranoia is getting the best of me. He's always depended on everyone around him to overcome his obstacles. It won't take him long to fall into the darkness of death.*

Growing weary of seeing the same chunks of cooled vegetables on her plate, Serafine rose from the table and decided to walk through the corridors of the castle. None of the torches in the hallways were illuminated, so she ignited a small flame in the palm of her hand to direct her through the darkness of the evening. The small fire wasn't enough to overcome the damp coolness of the castle, though. It was colder than she ever remembered it being, especially for an eve in the heart of summer. The cool air pulled up what little body hair Serafine had and then the unthinkable happened; she could see her breath in front of her. There were only a few nights throughout the entire winter in which one's breath could be seen, but never during the summer. Serafine had no explanation for the coldness she was feeling.

A soft giggle echoed throughout the hall, ricocheting off the walls.

Serafine spun around, but there was no one behind her. She carefully watched for a moment longer and then turned to keep walking forward, but she saw someone she never dreamed she'd see so soon: Cail. His silhouette stood in the distance, blocking the turn into the neighboring corridor. "It can't be," Serafine whispered, stunned by what she was seeing. She stood still, staring at the shadow she so desperately wished would disappear forever.

Neither of them moved, locked in a standstill. Then, Serafine yelled out, "What are you doing here? What do you want?"

The shadow's shoulders bounced as the shrill giggle filled the hallway once again. Then Cail ran away; he darted off to the next corridor and Serafine swiftly followed him. She trailed behind just close enough to see where the shadow was running. Serafine made one last turn around the corner of an intersection and saw that the silhouette had halted just outside of a door in the middle of the hallway. The shadow was nothing more than a black outline of Cail's body, but she could feel it staring directly at her. Malice and cruelty poured out of its invisible gaze, crushing any source of light and happiness in her heart. Instead of a giggle, a deep, sinister chuckle pounded Serafine's eardrums. Then, the apparition floated a few inches off the marble floor and drifted through the door. Serafine's heart sunk once she realized what was on the other side of the wall: her father's bedroom. The ghost was going to kill King Alban! As an act of desperation to save her father, Serafine frantically sprinted and burst through the door.

"What in the name of Aithnen do you think you're doing?" King Alban shouted. His body nearly hopped off the bed from the fright. Serafine ignored her startled father and thoroughly inspected the entire room; she looked under his bed, behind the curtains, and in the closet, which was nearly as large as the bedroom, but there was no sign of the apparition. Having had enough of the intrusion, Alban said, "Serafine! Tell me what has gotten into your maddened mind this instance."

"It's nothing," Serafine lied. The fiction was intended to convince herself, not her father.

"Nothing made you break down my bedroom door and frantically look through every crevice of my belongings?" her father asked with a skeptical tone.

"No. Well, I mean," Serafine's voice trailed off. She didn't know how to explain what she had just seen to her father, she couldn't even explain it to herself. "I saw Cail," she bluntly said.

"I know you did. I asked you to fetch a horse for him."

"No, that's not what I meant," Serafine responded. "I gave Cail a horse and returned to the castle. Then, shortly after I ate my supper, I saw his ghost in the castle. I followed it throughout a number of hallways until it led me here."

"I see," the King said. He stroked his thick, bushy beard as he pondered over what she had told him. "Unfortunately, I've been no stranger to eerie sightings in the castle, and I can't make them stop. It's excruciating, having your home turned into a prison, and it doesn't matter where my home is. No matter where I go, I still feel Claeg's piercing glare, I hear the venomous whispers." Serafine knew exactly what her father spoke of. She could still hear the shrill giggles that haunted the dark corridors, she could feel the frigid air, she could still see her own breath that clouded her vision.

"How can I make it stop?" Serafine asked, desperate to free her father and herself from Claeg's curse. "There must be a way."

"There is. I recently discovered a new truth that will give us the upper hand over Claeg, but I need you to trust my plan."

"No!" Serafine yelled at her father and then pounded her fist on the edge of his bed. Alban's eyes widened, shocked that his daughter had commanded him in the manner that she did. "I need to know what you have planned for me. You're very sick and if you pass before Claeg is defeated, I'll never be free from the suffocating chains of this curse."

"Fair enough," her father responded with placid words. Serafine partially expected her father to be enraged by her outburst, but she was pleasantly surprised by his tranquility. "In the early years after I was originally haunted by Claeg, long before my ailments forced me to become bedridden, I dug through the oldest archives in the ancient library of this castle. I spent entire days, from the early light of the morning until the darkness of the evening, searching for any clue that could help me break the vex. I read of an ancient domain, called The Shadow. According to the ancient texts, any spirit that clings to our natural world is trapped in that dark realm until either their deeds are done, or their spirit is killed."

"And you think that's where we'll find Claeg?" Serafine asked.

"It has to be," King Alban responded. "I only have a slight hunch of how to get there, but you must solve the rest of the puzzle. In the text, it said that The Shadow could only be reached by the touch of Darzomil's precious treasure. I'm assuming that means you must mine the mountain."

"No," Serafine answered. She knew exactly what the riddle referred to. She saw the answer as clearly as she saw her father lying in his bed. In her mind, she could see the chamber of gold coins that Wallen had led her to, and then there was the statue of Loni, the demigod of Kordon. That ancient statue was the key to Aithnen's salvation. "I've stood inches away from our freedom, but didn't have the wisdom to see it."

"You didn't have the knowledge," her father interjected. "There's no way you could've known about this hushed secret. All you can do now is return to the mountain and kill the filth that haunts us when the time is right."

"When the time is right?" Serafine repeated. "The time is now. I need to return the Shadow Stone to its temple so we can be freed of the immense veil lurking over our heads."

"Patience, my daughter. We must wait until my knights have returned with Cail as their prisoner. He cannot be allowed any escape to his home. Until he's dead, it's much safer to leave the divide between our two worlds as is."

"Why are you so worried about Cail, anyways? If I'm going to be as powerful as you claim I will, what could he possibly do to stop it?"

Those questions did anger the King. Serafine's father glared at her, his burning gaze carving through her eyes. "Have I taught you nothing?" His words were sharp, like a honed dagger that stabbed through her stomach. "Cail will be hit and his world will be spinning while he lies helplessly on the ground. When your enemy is wounded and unsure of what to do, a brief moment of pause is no different than surrender. You must deliver the killing strike. Will you promise me you'll do that? When Cail is returned to us, bound in chains and on his knees, begging for mercy, will you do what needs to be done? Do you promise to kill Cail?"

Serafine didn't say anything, she couldn't. Tricking him into traveling through the perilous wilderness on his own was hard enough on her conscience, but to have to kill him? She knew that would never leave her mind. There was one choice of loyalty to make: her father or her friend.

Chapter 16: The Conqueror

Smoldering twigs snapped in the cold of the morning as Cail woke from his thin slumber. A small, dim cavern, which was no larger than a bedroom, protected him from the harsh, wintry storm in the night. The warmth of Cail's modest fire was gone, but so was the danger of the frigid gusts. He had seized the wind, calmed the sharp snow, and found warm shelter. Cail realized a harsh truth as he rose from the jagged floor of the cave: The wilderness wouldn't be easily intimidated by the Last Descendant. The mountains would strike again, this time with paramount authority. Cail needed to escape the towering glaciers, or else he would be swallowed by nature and forced to face his doom.

Eager to embrace the new day, Cail snatched his pack, which he had used as a poor replacement for a pillow, and threw it onto his back. The air still chilled bare flesh, but it wasn't as cruel as the night before. His footprints were covered by a new layer of snow, but it wasn't untouched. A single trail of a stranger's footprints led to and from the entrance of the cave. Cail wasn't alone, and, more frighteningly, he had been visited during the night. Despite this unsettling discovery, Cail now had a guide through the mountains, assuming, of course, that this mysterious wanderer knew the right path to take.

Cail's venture through the terrain was quiet and serene. With a calm sky over his head, he no longer needed to fear the perils of nature; for the time being, he was safe from harm. Cail retrieved the map from his pack to view his progress since his departure from Kye. He was certain he would reach the edge of the mountains by the day's end, which left only one last landmark before his arrival to Taurim: The Tower. It struck Cail as an odd location for such a structure. There was no city surrounding it, and, according to the map, Taurim was leagues away from it.

A faint howl whispered from behind Cail and then he saw a terrible horror. Reaching all the way from the trail up to the clouds in the sky was a thick, white wall of snow. Another storm was swiftly approaching, but this time, Cail wouldn't survive its wrath. He had no choice but to flee. Cail knew his moments would be numbered; he just wished he had a few more to spare. The snow crunched as he sprinted along the trail, desperately trying to outrun the furious storm. Cail didn't dare to look back, but he could hear the storm bellowing louder with every passing second. The wind had remained quiet and still throughout the entirety of the morning, but it was beginning to stir.

A sign of hope appeared before Cail's eyes; The Tower stood just beyond the border of the mountains, calling out to Cail, offering him refuge and protection. The sight of his salvation gave him the energy to run all the more fervently. As he approached, the Tower continued to grow until it was apparent that this was no ordinary tower; the girth of the colossal pillar dwarfed the mountains. It was a mammoth among mice. The trail led straight to the entrance of the tower, with no way around it. Oddly enough, Cail could see the top of the Tower; it only rose to a height that was about twice as tall as Cail, but it descended deep into the ground like a well. It was impossible to tell how far below the mountains the Tower would take him. The black stone walls stood out like a thorn on a rose. In a world of white snow, it was impossible to miss the Tower.

Cail was nearing his destination, but flakes were beginning to drop around him; it wouldn't take long for the storm to engulf him. Growing from a gentle whisper, the wind was now a deafening roar, a ferocious beast ready to pounce on its prey. Every step spent more of Cail's strength, more of his will, more of his determination. His muscles were a resource, one that was slowly draining. Vigor could no longer be found, it could only be used until his hand was wrapped around the knob of the Tower's door. Even though it was approaching and the wooden door grew larger, Cail felt like he was hopelessly chasing an uncatchable dream.

Just as the snow started to mound on the tops his shoulders, Cail reached for the bronze doorknob, which was painfully cold, and twisted it as he shoved on the door. As quickly as he entered, he slammed the door shut. The howling of the wind was still thunderous, despite being protected by a solid wall of stone, and firm thuds beat against the door.

As he leaned his head against the cold wood, Cail took in a deep breath; it was the first time he could relax since he began his frantic sprint. He could feel the warm massage of a fire from behind him. A short, empty room greeted Cail, illuminated only by a fireplace on the cement floor. The logs were fresh and the fire had yet to bite into wood and tear apart the shards. *I must be catching up to the wanderer.* Cail thought to himself. "Hello?" he called into the darkness, but he could hear nothing beside the cracking whips of the fire. A thin log was protruding from the fireplace, so Cail took the untouched wood into his hand and used the light to survey the room around him. There was nothing on the floor, nothing on the walls, nothing that could lead him out of the homogenous room. He was enveloped by the Tower's black stone. Cail's bones were still frozen from his close encounter with the blizzard, so he sat by the fireplace and soaked in its warmth. Weakness latched onto his muscles and trapped his vitality, but the fire was melting it away.

A slight tremor pounded in the floor. Cail jumped to his feet in alarm, paranoid that the ground beneath his feet would give and he would tumble to his inevitable death. However, the ground remained still and firm and Cail anxiously waited in a stiff silence. The ground rumbled again, but this time it was louder and Cail could feel the floor start to quake. Then, only a few paces away from him, some of the stone bricks in the floor started to descend and they gradually formed a staircase, descending into darkness. There was no way of telling where this new path led, but it certainly was more alluring than venturing into the perilous blizzard just outside the Tower's door. Cail took wary and cautious steps down the stairs, and the fireplace's emanation slowly dwindled, leaving the light of Cail's makeshift torch as his only source of guidance.

As soon as his feet landed on solid ground, the staircase behind him ascended, stranding Cail in the newly discovered chamber. The room was pitch black, empty, and painfully silent. Cail felt as though he had just walked into a beast's den and he was about to face his death. There was no escape from this dungeon and whatever challenges it presented, he would have to embrace and overcome on his own.

Just on the edge of the light's circumference was a wooden altar with a single scroll sitting on top. Cail untied the scroll and held his torch closer to the dried parchment. It read:

> "Entrance is acceptance of these tests.
> Embrace your three fears; assert your dominance.
> Become the Conqueror."

When Cail looked up from the parchment, he was no longer in the dark chamber of the Tower, but in a place he remembered all too well, in a place he hoped he would never have to return: The Iron Fortress of Ijsbrandur. Everything was exactly as he remembered it. He smelled the cold iron of the floors and walls, he felt the curse of death that plagued the entire island of Ijsbrandur. He was standing on the very same platform upon which he battled his ancestor, Tarvaris Ozean, to the death. Then Cail saw something he didn't believe, he *couldn't* believe. A familiar man stood before him, a man Cail had stood before one other time. Cail recognized the crimson eyes and matching hair, the black armor, the deathly pale skin, and the brutal sword. Kalil, the slain dictator of Kordon, stood before Cail once again.

"Impossible," Cail whispered. "I must be dreaming."

"Wrong," Kalil said. A menacing smirk revealed pointed, yellow teeth. "The magic of the Tower has awoken me, resurrected me from my death, given me a second chance to fulfill my destiny. Fortune smiled upon you when my despicable servant betrayed me. I was robbed of my opportunity to prove, once and for all, that I'm the rightful ruler of Kordon!"

"But Tarvaris killed you!" Cail yelled in disbelief. "You can't be alive. I saw him kill you with my own eyes." Cail thought he was going insane, seeing a dead man stand just before him. He wasn't just terrified of Kalil, which he undoubtedly was, but he was afraid of everything Kalil represented. This menace had rained terror upon Kordon for centuries, no, millennia. Innocent lives needlessly suffered, great cities were reduced to rubble, aesthetic islands were plagued by his curses. He had laid waste to a beautiful nation that belonged to the Dragonfolk, and now, that ruinous threat had been revived.

"And yet, here I am," Kalil chuckled. "The Tower has acknowledged what is true: The fate of Kordon is yet to be decided." Using his free hand, Kalil retrieved a second sword, equally as massive as the first, from a sheath attached to his belt and tossed the blade so that it landed at Cail's feet. As Cail bent down to pick up the sword, Kalil said, "I stand in the way of your path to Taurim, and you stand in the way of my path to the restoration of my supremacy. I may be your first test, but you are my last."

With one swift movement, Kalil charged and violently swung his sword at Cail's head. A piercing clang sounded as Cail blocked the assault. Kalil asserted his aggression with ease, launching one swipe of the sword after another, but Cail managed to defend himself. Hunger and fury possessed the Dark Lord, giving him unmatched speed and strength. Tarvaris was a trivial challenge compared to his master. It took all of Cail's strength and wits to keep up with Kalil, to block all the killing blows.

Kalil roared with one last powerful swing. Cail blocked the attack, but it was so robust that it sent Cail's sword flying from his grasp and he fell onto his back, leaving him entirely exposed. Kalil lifted his sword above his head, preparing for the final strike, preparing to kill the Last Descendant. Just as the sword started to lower, Cail sent a blast of wind from his palms into Kalil's chest. Kalil flew through the air and landed on the other side of the platform. He snarled as he slowly pushed himself to his feet, angered by Cail's parry.

Cail summoned a bow and arrow made of white wind and flung one arrow after another toward his revived foe, but Kalil was too quick, dodging the shots with ease. The evil dictator responded by shooting a beam of darkness from his palms. Cail was struck in his chest and the force knocked him onto his back. He could feel a couple of his ribs were battered and possibly cracked. The dark magic had slammed into him like an iron hammer. Cail fought through the pain, though. He conjured spheres of air and threw them at Kalil. They flew much faster than the arrows and Kalil was barraged by the balls of air.

The volleying battle ensued with the two warriors delivering blows back and forth. Darkness fought against wind and wind against darkness. They were evenly matched in strength, matched in skill, matched in speed; the determining factor would be willpower. Cail's mind was strong, but it was beginning to bend and break. Every hit that crashed into Cail's body took its toll and loosened his resolve. Whereas, Kalil seemed unfazed by Cail's assault. The Dark Lord was seemingly made of the same iron as his fortress. Cail was beginning to grow desperate. His foe was trudging through the exhausting battle and Cail wasn't sure how much longer he would survive.

Kalil fired another beam of darkness, but Cail nimbly dodged it and blasted him in the side with another squall. His foe's body flung across the platform and his head slammed against the metallic floor. A limp man laid in front of Cail, a beaten body that was desperately trying to get up. The opportunity to kill his sworn enemy, to pass the first test, was just before him. Cail walked closer to Kalil, who was now lying flat on his back and whimpering moans sounded from his throat. Vulnerability had paralyzed Kalil for the moment, but it wouldn't take long for him to recover; the window of opportunity was narrow. Cail lifted Kalil's sword from the ground; it was as tall as his legs, but surprisingly light to hold. As Cail hoisted the sword over his head, Kalil weakly chuckled.

"If you think that killing me will end your troubles, you're sadly mistaken," Kalil said with a hoarse whisper. The battle had, in fact, claimed his life, or was about to. "There are plenty of others like me, more than you can imagine. People who are willing to do whatever it takes to claim power for their own. There are hordes of people like me, and not enough of people like you."

"You're wrong," Cail said, breathing heavily. He was still trying to reclaim his breath from the taxing fight. "You forced a lot of good and innocent folks into hiding, but I will give them the hope of a new day."

Kalil cackled again, as though Cail had told a hysterical joke, and then wheezed and coughed. After he regained his breath, he said, "You truly believe that? I've never even touched Kye, and the city is almost ready to fall apart."

"What are you talking about?" Cail asked.

"You've walked straight into the heart of the city, and yet, you didn't have wisdom to see it."

"See what?" Cail yelled, infuriated by Kalil's vagueness.

"To see the King's corruption! He's had his own civilians begging on their knees for centuries, pleading for him to show mercy, but he has none. King Alban only has selfishness. His throne is all that matters to him, even as his curse chews at his bones. The King is nothing more than a dying man, which is why he's doing everything he can to ensure Serafine is set to be the first immortal Empress."

"Immortal?" Cail repeated.

"Has he not told you?" Kalil chuckled, knowing very well that Cail had never heard of any of this. "I told you, the King is a deceiver, a liar, a betrayer. That's why he sent you to Taurim. There's no meeting amongst the Kings. As a matter of fact, there are no more Kings, only remnants of them. He's sent you to your death. You survived the wilderness, you may even survive the trials of the Tower, but you'll never overcome the atrocity that awaits you."

"No. King Alban wouldn't do that to me."

"You'll see. A terrible beast is waiting in Taurim, a beast born to do one thing: Kill the Last Descendant."

"No!" Cail bellowed and then he slammed the sword through Kalil's chest. The blade cut through the heart of the enemy like a knife seamlessly glides through softened butter. Kalil had no more air for speaking, but neither did Cail. He didn't mean to kill Kalil, at least not yet. It just happened as instinctively as breathing. Cail did it almost subconsciously; it frightened him, in a way. He wasn't frightened by what he just did, but by what he could do, by what could happen in the future. What if this happened again? What if this happened while he was around Laney? Would he kill her as well?

Kalil breathed his last breath and then Cail retrieved the sword from the cold corpse. The world around Cail darkened until he couldn't even see his hands in front of his face. Cail had no idea where he was, but he knew he was at the Iron Fortress no longer. The ground beneath Cail's feet had softened and the air was no longer polluted with the foul stench of death. Then, it dawned on him: Cail had returned to the Tower, he had passed the first test. If facing Kalil was only the first challenge, he was petrified of what was to come. Part of Cail wanted to turn back, find an exit, and return to the mountains. That was exactly what the Tower wanted, though. It wanted him to cower away from the obstacles laid before him, it wanted Cail to be defeated by his fears.

At first, Cail thought the Tower was simply manipulating his mind and perverting the real world into a harsh nightmare, but, even as he stood in the Tower, he still held Kalil's sword in his hand. He had truly traveled to the Iron Fortress, fought against Kalil, and slayed the resuscitated menace. It was a truly terrifying thought, to know that the Tower not only made Cail experience his worst fears, but brought them back to life.

From the darkness, a soft light emanated in the distance. Cail cautiously approached, unable to see the ground beneath his feet. A torch was burning in the pitch black and next to it was another tied up scroll, identical to the first, sitting on a wooden altar. Cail untied the scroll and read:

"A challenge from the grave has been passed.
Now, you must endure a test from the past.
Become the Conqueror."

When Cail looked away from the parchment, he discovered that he had been transported to a familiar setting once again. He was now sitting on a thin rug that had been rolled out on a solid floor of gray concrete. The bland walls that towered over his head were impossible to be mistaken. He was in the Temple of the Lake, where he had first met Beda, the Queen of the Red Pumas. Fond memories of his days in the temple flushed through Cail's mind, flowing like a river. He remembered being the scrawny, naïve boy who had only just left his home for the very first time. This temple had taught him so much: how to defend himself, how to grow stronger, day after day, how to assert his dominance over his enemies. Everything that Cail had become was thanks to Beda, his first and most valuable mentor.

"The Tower has finally sent you here," said a voice from behind Cail. Even though Cail immediately spun his head around, he didn't need to; he knew exactly who was standing behind him. Beda was smiling at Cail, as though she had long expected his arrival. Curiously enough, she was not the decorated Queen that he had last seen. Instead, she looked almost as humble as she had when she first promised to become his mentor. Somehow, the Tower had taken Cail back in time. "You look surprised to see me."

"I am," Cail answered as he pushed himself to his feet. "To be honest, my mind is spinning right now. I'm being tossed back and forth between Aithnen and memories of my past.

"Actually, you've never left Aithnen or the Tower."

"What are you talking about?" Cail bellowed in frustration. "I'm standing here with you, in your temple."

"No. You have it all wrong, Cail," Beda laughed. He felt idiotic, as though he couldn't see something that was dangling right in front of his eyes. "The Tower isn't a place, it's a magical being. It possesses the power to transform and mold the world contained within its walls. The Tower looked into your mind, into your memories, and into your weaknesses. That's what these tests are modeled from: your vulnerabilities."

"So, are you saying that none of this real?" Cail asked, perplexed.

"Have you listened to nothing I just said?" Beda blurted out, annoyed by Cail's question. "These tests are very real. They will lead you to your death if you don't take them seriously. The Tower has specifically designed each of these challenges so that you can't leave them until you've overcome one of your hidden weaknesses. For your first test, you needed to face Kalil on your own, since Tarvaris took care of him for you."

"And what do I need to accomplish here?" Cail asked.

"Years ago, I forced you to endure grueling and demanding exercises until I could tell you were ready to take the next step in your adventure. When you first walked into my temple, you were a weak boy who knew nothing of the outside world. All the islands of Kordon were strangers to you, mysterious domains waiting for you to discover them. You've grown wiser in your knowledge of the world, but no wiser in the intricacies of the lives around you."

"I don't understand what you mean," Cail interrupted.

"Then hold your tongue and I'll tell you!" Beda shot back, irritated by Cail's abrasive interjection. "After freeing Kordon from the imprisonment of terror, you returned to your home and remained by Laney's side, through every day and night, firmly clinging to the hope that she would wake from her coma. Then, Loran appeared on your doorstep, claiming that he was a victim of Cestmir's abduction, when he was a cog in the malicious machine the entire time. Yet, you didn't have the foresight to see it."

"How could I have? I was trying to do the right thing. Besides, he ended up helping us take down Barok after all," Cail argued, but to no avail.

"Only because you bribed him with freedom. When he returns to his home in Aithnen, a murderer and a criminal will be set free. The point I'm trying to make is that the possibility of a trap never crossed your mind," Beda responded calmly. Cail could think of no way to respond. He vividly remembered the miserable days he spent trapped in that dreadful prison, he remembered being starved and dehydrated, sometimes going days without food or water, he remembered being beaten, sometimes within an inch of his life, leaving his bones bruised and battered. Cail felt embarrassed; he could've avoided weeks of pain and suffering if he would've paid heed to what was in front of his eyes. "Cail, you're the Last Descendant, the protector of Kordon. Your people need you, but unless you begin to see the world with more clarity, the Dragonfolk will have no one to come to their defense in times of distress."

"I-I'm sorry," Cail hoarsely whispered, holding back his emotions.

"Being sorry won't stop you from being killed. You must open your eyes." Cail was angry at himself for being so reckless and impetuous. Continuing with their conversation, Beda said, "That brings us to your current trek. Do you still believe it to be wise to enter Taurim?" Beda was beginning to open Cail's eyes. He could see the dangers that had remained invisible to him, like a storm hiding behind a thick wall of fog. Death was following him like a shadow, stalking him like a vulture. The King of Kye truly had sent Cail on a fool's errand, a mission with one purpose and one purpose only: To kill the Last Descendant. "You failed to learn from your mistakes with the Blue Assassins. Now, King Alban is using you like a puppet until he gets what he wants."

"Serafine was stranded in a foreign land. What else was I supposed to do?" Cail asked, trying to justify his actions.

"And she is home now. So, tell me, why are you still offering yourself as a free servant to the King of Kye?" Beda asked. Cail had no answer for her. While it was true that Serafine was Cail's friend and she had helped him save Kordon, she had done so because she needed to return to Aithnen. A question popped into Cail's mind, a question that he never dreamed he would ask, but it was a question that needed to be answered: Would Serafine offer herself freely to Cail? He wanted to say yes, in fact, he almost did. Then he heard another whisper, a whisper of doubt. For the first time, Cail didn't see Serafine as a friend, he couldn't. However, he didn't necessarily see her as an enemy either. He didn't know what Serafine was, he didn't know who she was.

"I don't know," Cail said, answering Beda's question. Uncertainty softened his voice and glazed his eyes. This revelation bent and twisted his mind, it made him question a lot of what he had previously known, or thought, to be true.

"I'll ask you one more time," Serafine said gently after giving Cail a moment of silence to ponder over his thoughts. "Do you still believe it to be wise to enter Taurim?"

"No. I can't go to Taurim."

"You can't, but you must," Beda responded. "The mountains have lured you into their trap and now you have but one path to take. A beast awaits you in the dead city, a beast much more ferocious than any you've ever faced."

"Did Serafine know?" Cail asked. Anger was beginning to swell in his voice. He suspected that he had been betrayed, although he still clung to the hope that Serafine was ignorant. "Did she know she was sending me to face my death? Or was she duped by her father as well?"

"I've answered all that the Tower commanded me to. Your task was to see what you never had before, and the time has come for your third and final test." The world around Cail dimmed, Beda's Temple was fading away into darkness. Cail's greatest mentor was vanishing, and there was nothing he could do to take hold of her and stay by her side. After all the light was gone, Cail heard Beda's voice one last time, "Become the Conqueror."

"Beda? Where are you?" Cail yelled into the dark, but there was no answer. She was gone and he was alone. He was only accompanied by painful blindness. The Tower truly was attacking his weakest vulnerabilities. Every step was a futile one, since there was no source of light anywhere, so Cail just plopped onto the hard ground. He nearly let out a yelp when he landed on a sharp mound. For the time being, Cail was helplessly lost in the darkness. The whispers of doubt crept back into his mind, telling him that Serafine wasn't to be trusted. Cail closed his eyes and tried to throw away those thoughts. They weren't true, they couldn't be true. Serafine was his friend, and he was her friend. *This is exactly what the Tower wants, it wants me to turn on my friends. It's trying to exploit my weaknesses to break down my mind.*

"Hello, Cail," said a familiar, sonorous voice. Cail opened his eyes and saw a cloaked man standing before him with a burning torch in one hand and a scroll in the other. He immediately recognized the man as Claeg. "You've done well with my tests, so far."

"Your tests?" Cail repeated, pushing himself to his feet. "You're the one who's doing this to me? You're the one who's tormenting my body and mind?"

"Tormenting? Cail, I'm freeing you from your restrictions, from what bars you away from your truest potential. You've mastered the art of combat against your strongest enemy, you've seen your mistakes for what they truly are, and now, you are ready for your final test."

"Which is?" Cail asked. Claeg didn't say anything in response. Instead, he simply held out the last scroll. Cail snatched it from Claeg's grasp, untied the parchment, and read the final three lines:

"The lies of the past become the truths of the present.
Witness what only a handful know.
Become the Conqueror."

"Lies of the past? Lies about what?" Cail asked after rolling up the scroll.

"This test," Claeg said, ignoring Cail's question as though he never heard it, "is a test of acceptance. You are about to see some harsh truths. The powerful hands in Aithnen have worked for centuries to keep these events buried beneath the surface. Whether you pass or fail this final test depends on whether you can accept what I'm about to show you."

"And how do I know you're the one who isn't lying? This could all be a fabrication designed to make me turn against Serafine," Cail argued.

"I'll begin by showing events that have already come to pass," Claeg responded, trying to convince Cail of his sincerity. "First, we venture to the island of Silman and into Darzomil, the city beneath the mountain, where we'll see a gift of leverage. Now, take my cloak, and we'll be off." Claeg held out his arm, the one which was still holding the torch, motioning for Cail to take hold. Cail cautiously reached out, terrified of what was about to happen. As soon as he clutched the dry cloth, the darkness rushed away and a flood of colors surrounded them. Cail could feel his body being yanked at an unimaginable speed, nearly knocking all the air from his lungs. Then, without warning, they both came to a halt inside of a small, dimly lit chamber, but they weren't alone. Serafine and Wallen were talking to each other, but no sound came out of their mouths. Claeg said to Cail, "We're in the first memory I will show you today. Just before Serafine saved you from the firm clutches of the Blue Assassins, she came to Darzomil to find another way home, which she did."

Cail looked at Serafine and Wallen as they conversed, but then he noticed something far more shocking: An Air Rune sitting upon a pedestal. "Wallen had another Air Rune?" Cail asked, turning to Claeg.

"He did. Wallen was charged with the task of guarding this Air Rune until the right moment. You see, that rune isn't like the others you've found, it contains the climax of your powers. It's the key to unlocking your fullest potential." Cail couldn't possibly imagine what sorcery would be unlocked by finding this rune.

As Wallen talked, his voice drifted away from silence and grew louder until Cail could plainly hear what he was saying. Pointing to the rune, Wallen said to Serafine, "Strictly speaking, he doesn't need it, but he'll undoubtedly want it, which will give you the leverage you need. He has left Elona before so he could acquire his powers, and he'll do it again." Serafine said something in response, but the sounds of her voice faded before Cail could hear exactly what she said.

"She took the rune from Wallen," Claeg said. Cail looked to the Hidden King, but his hooded head remained facing toward Wallen and Serafine. "From this moment forward, possibly before then, you were nothing more than a stepping stone to her. She would make this decision over and over again if she needed to. Despite what you may think, she's not your friend."

"You're wrong," Cail said calmly. He was confident in what he believed, certain that this couldn't have happened. Serafine wouldn't return to Aithnen at his expense, Cail convinced himself. For some unknown reason, Claeg was conjuring these falsities to turn Cail against his friend. "This isn't the Serafine I know. You're just showing me a perversion of reality. I wasn't here to see this, so you could easily be showing me a lie."

"That I could," Claeg admitted. "You will soon see that this did, in fact happen, and the proof was just before you the entire time. Even though you weren't present for this memory, it was important for you to see it. The memory we just watched will lead us to a night you'll remember very well." Claeg held up his arm and Cail took his cloak into his hand once more. Just as before, Cail's body was violently tugged through a whirling array of color until they arrived at a dark scenery. The sky was bleak and gray, threatening to cover all the land in the cold darkness of night, the ground was made of rough, jagged stone which matched a wolf's fur coat, and the air was foul, ridden with thick fumes that grinded every moist throat. As soon as the flurry of lights faded, Cail knew exactly where Claeg had taken him: Bodaway Volcano. Then, he saw Serafine and himself sitting on the cold ground just outside of the volcano's entrance, just as they had a few days ago, when they first arrived in Aithnen.

This cannot be. Although, I do remember this night, the night we had traversed through the scalding volcano. If Claeg is telling the truth, then I'm a much larger fool than I ever imagined, and, worst of all, Serafine is everything he says she is. Cail thought silently.

"You do recall this evening, do you not?" Claeg asked. Cail didn't dare look into Claeg's black hood, but he could still feel the piercing gaze of the Hidden King. He didn't say anything in response, but Cail's silence served well enough as an answer.

Cail could faintly hear Serafine's voice in the distance. "We should rest here for the night. A long trek awaits us in the morning."

"How can you tell it is nighttime?" the Cail's past-self asked. Cail distinctly remembered having this conversation before they settled down to rest for the evening.

"Why have you brought me to this moment in the past?" Cail asked, turning toward Claeg. "I was shown a vision in sleep during this night, but nothing else happened. It was an uneventful evening."

"From your vantage point it was, but not from Serafine's," Claeg said as he pointed toward her. Serafine and Cail started moving much more swiftly, as though time itself was being propelled into action.

The rest of the evening played out exactly as he remembered it, which was troubling to Cail. That meant it was entirely possible that Serafine had taken the Air Rune from Wallen, she had intended to fall back on it as a source of leverage over Cail, and, worst of all, Serafine had, in fact, willingly cast her friendship with Cail aside so she could return to her home. Doubt had only whispered in Cail's mind, but now, it turned into a dull murmur. It rumbled like the precursors of a vicious storm, it reeked of rain and moisture before a downpour, it was the echo that catalyzed an avalanche.

Their movements slowed and now Cail and Serafine were asleep in the dead of the night, but Serafine was restless. She tossed and turned in her sleep. Cail could hear her murmur his name, not because she wanted his help, but because she feared him. In the same way Cail was terrified of Kalil, so was Serafine of Cail. She squirmed in her agony, begging for an escape from the torment, but there was none. All she could do was remain on the ground with her eyes shut until she had fully endured the atrocious nightmare.

"I don't remember her flailing in her sleep like this," Cail said to Claeg. He wanted to run to Serafine and shake her out of her dream, but this was nothing more than a glimpse into the past, he wasn't a part of the real world.

"You were exhausted from your long trek through the volcano. Why would you wake up for anything?" Claeg asked. That bit was true. Cail remembered how weary he was that night; his muscles ached and begged for rest, his skin reeked of the smell of smoke, and his eyelids were as leaden as iron. "The dream she's having changed the entire course of both of your lives. From this moment forward, you were no longer a stepping stone, you became her enemy."

Cail's feet nearly left the rigid ground when he heard Serafine scream into the black of the night. Deep breaths moved in and out of her mouth, as though she had been sprinting for hours. She quickly glanced at her companion to make sure he was still asleep, then she reached into her pocket and withdrew the Air Rune she had received from Wallen. Cail couldn't believe his eyes. Everything he had refused to believe was true and all the excuses he had conjured to justify his loyalty to Serafine were lies. Her head turned around and she surveyed the entire region with a shade of guilt in her eyes. She was a burglar who had escaped the store, but was afraid that at any moment, she would be caught.

"I don't care if it is leverage," Cail heard Serafine say. "Cail must never possess power of this magnitude." Serafine rose to her feet and strode toward a cliff which overlooked a broad, powerful river.

"What is she doing?" Cail asked, but Claeg said nothing in response, he kept his gaze fixated on Serafine. "Claeg, tell me what she's doing." Cail's demand was met with silence. Cail stepped to chase after Serafine, but Claeg put a cold hand on Cail's chest, holding him in his place. There was nothing left to do but watch the event unfold before his eyes. Serafine stood on the edge of the cliff, looking at the Air Rune in her hand. She stood still, frozen by her indecisiveness, and then she cast the rune into the river. "Serafine! No!" Cail screamed, but he wouldn't be heard. He was nothing more than a shadow.

Cail collapsed to his knees, grieved by the betrayal he just witnessed. Then, just as a flame snags a tree branch and erupts into a blistering inferno, rage flared inside of his mind and reddened his cheeks. He wasn't angry at Serafine, though. Cail was infuriated by his blindness. At no point in time had he even suspected that Serafine would commit such an atrocious act of treachery, as a matter of fact, he came to her defense when people had made wild accusations against her, although the claims weren't so farfetched anymore. He wanted to know exactly what she saw, what it was that had corrupted her mind and forced her to betray Cail.

"Come, Cail," Claeg said plainly, as though he entirely disregarded the state of rage that Cail was in. "We have one more memory to visit." Cail, who was still on his hands and knees with his face looking at the colorless ground, didn't want to move. He didn't want to let go of the pain he was feeling. Serafine had willingly gifted him with this suffering and Cail wanted nothing more than to give it back to her. Despite his grudge, there was nothing Cail could do except follow Claeg and pass the final test of the Tower.

The final memory wasn't a memory at all, it was a dream. It was a vision he had had just before he embarked on his venture to find all the Air Runes. An oak tree, with a thick trunk and sturdy branches wearing emerald leaves, stood before Cail. It was *his* tree, the tree that contained his livelihood and would remain robust and extant as long as Cail did. This dream was a memory that was trapped deep inside Cail's mind, so how did Claeg know about it?

"Only one other person knew about this dream, but she's dead now. How did you know about the tree? What are you?" Cail asked, partially amazed and partially terrified of Claeg's arcane abilities.

"Let's stick to the matter at hand," Claeg said, casting Cail's questions aside. "The tree you see now isn't the same as the one you saw in your dream, is it?" Cail took a closer look and noticed that it was different. In particular, the bark was discolored and withering. Instead of an oak brown, the bark was gray and it looked as brittle as a pencil.

"What's wrong with it?" Cail asked.

"It's dying," Claeg answered with a grim voice. "You have been reckless with your body, you've trusted people you shouldn't, you've endured needless suffering and torture. Every time you do, your tree grows weaker. Lydia once told you that the domain of fire would spell your doom. You should've heeded her warning. If you stay much longer, you will die. You must leave."

"How?" Cail asked. "I'm trapped beneath a thick veil of clouds, everyone in Aithnen is."

"Which is why you must take the Shadow Stone back from Serafine's grasp. You've survived a journey that was meant to kill you, which gives you an advantage over Serafine and King Alban. They won't be expecting a dead man to take the Shadow Stone from them."

"How can I get back to Kye, though? I barely survived the wilderness the first time. If I challenge it again, it will surely claim my life."

"Follow the road ahead of you to Taurim and find me in the dead city. From there, I will show you the way back to Kye." As Claeg's voice faded, so did his body and Cail was left alone in the Tower. He looked back to the tree, but it was no longer there; a red door stood in its place, a red door with a brass doorknob. Cail had mastered the Tower's tests. He became the Conqueror.

Chapter 17: Whispering Waters

When Cail entered the Tower, he was being chased by ferocious winds and a monstrous blizzard. However, when he departed, he was greeted by refreshingly clear air. It was a world alien to anything he had ever seen. An ocean of green marshes, brown swamps, and glistening wetlands stood between Cail and Taurim. He could feel the thick moisture in the air, creating a wet coat on his skin and weathered clothes. The marshes were calm and serene; soft caws resonated from the horizon, the wind had completely disappeared, and the entire region laid before him to see. Yet, Cail couldn't help but sense that something was wrong, something hidden from his view. An invisible haze hovered over the ground and stood on the waters, an indescribable aura watched over the land, waiting for any daring, or idiotic, souls to venture through the watery terrain.

Cail was immediately reminded of an incident when he was a child, ten years old, to be exact. His father had always warned him of the dangers of Elona's neighboring forest, but with Cail being the adventurous spirit that he was, it was always hard to resist. Still, he didn't want to have to face his father's wrath, so Cail cast aside the temptations.

One day was different, however. Laney and Kadir were preoccupied with their own families, and Cail's father was busy attending to the pressing needs of the Elonians, so Cail decided to stroll through the village and soak in the warm, radiant sunlight. It was the type of day that would give anyone the inspiration to write an eloquent sonnet, or a day which would be perfect for sitting by the coast of Elona and admiring the vast ocean of clouds. Nothing could possibly go wrong on a day such as that, or so one might think.

Normally, Cail would sit on the edge of Elona's cliff, with his feet dangling over the clouds, not heeding to the possibility that he could easily fall to his death. However, this day was far from normal, although Cail was blissfully unaware of that fact beforehand. Instead of going to the coast and delighting in the snow-white clouds, he decided to venture to the Western Gate, the only barrier between the village and its forewarned forest. Cail had no intentions of entering said forest, he just wanted to soak in its sensations. He wanted to the see the emerald leaves and uncut grass, he wanted to smell the aromas of the vines and bark, he wanted to taste the moisture in the air. However, one thing he could never do is touch. No matter how badly he craved to do so, he couldn't step into the forest and touch the trees, touch the plants, touch the grass. Although, he didn't understand why. It was just a forest, after all.

Cail stood on the eastern side of the West Gate, his head barely reached over the top of the wooden gate since he had yet to fully delve into his growth spurt. Even though he still stood within Elona's borders, it was all too easy to jump over the gate and run into the feared forest. At least, it would've been easy except for one thing: Cail would be defying his father's orders. That was much more grueling than climbing over a gate of any height. Entering the forest would also mean facing his father's disappointment. *There will be no disappointment if he doesn't know,* said a voice in Cail's head. *The forest isn't as dangerous as he makes it out to be. Just going a few trees in won't hurt. It'll be a nice escape from the cramped village.*

As tempted as Cail was, he still couldn't bring himself to remove his feet from the ground, to take that first step, to climb over the barrier that kept him in Elona. Instead, he turned around to walk back to his home.

"He'll never know," said a voice from the forest. It was a raspy voice, but an oddly inviting one nonetheless. Cail immediately spun around and looked through the trees in the forest, but there was no one in sight.

"Hello?" Cail called out, but there was no answer. Without a second thought or hesitation, Cail climbed over the gate, desperately wanting to know who had called out to him. His father's warnings never crossed his mind until he was already deeply engulfed by the dark forest.

The trees stood like stone towers, watching his every move, the leaves cast away all the sun's light, leaving the ground in eerie darkness, and a ghastly layer of haze floated just about the crisp dirt, slightly obstructing his view. Cail stood alone in the forest for the first time in his life. At first, he convinced himself that it wasn't so bad after all, that the fear of the forest was nothing more than a production of mass hysteria. However, as the seconds waned, a malicious curse crept into Cail's mind, a curse that also clung to the forest. Shadows lurked from behind the surrounding trees, inching closer and closer, feeding off Cail's anguish. Cail's breath was escaping him, his heart was pounding in his chest, and his vision was beginning to blur.

A thick hand landed on Cail's shoulder from behind. He spun around and saw his father standing inches away from him. Mysteriously, the creeping shadows had disappeared upon Cecil's arrival. Cail's father didn't say anything, but he didn't need to, his eyes said everything; they said that Cail was about to face Cecil's disappointment.

As Cail looked upon the vastness of the marshes, he could feel the same shadows lurking through the waters. The worst part was knowing he couldn't explain his feeling of discontent. He felt as though he was a ten-year-old boy trapped in the forest again. In the same way that the mysterious voice had lured him into the trees, Serafine and her father had lured him into this trek through the wilderness, a folly mission specifically designed to kill Cail. He was beginning to believe it might. The arduous journey was taking its toll on his body and his mind. The elements were stretching his skin, bruising his bones, constricting his breath. He was beginning to feel the same effects that his tree was: he was inching closer to his death. It became all too apparent that time was of the essence.

Cail pushed through the marshes, where solid paths were scarce. The permeable ground sunk beneath every step, as though a drowning monsoon had just passed over the land. It didn't take long for water to seep into his shoes and freeze his feet. The ponds, swamps, and marshes all had muddied water, a far cry from any of the glistening lakes he had visited. Cail craved a break from the taxing trek, but he knew he'd be sitting in water, soaking mud into his clothes, so he trudged forward. It came as no surprise to Cail that there was no sign of life in the wetlands. The environment was harsh and ruthless, with a scarce amount of opportunities for shelter or food.

Then he heard the croak of a frog, the first sound he had heard since leaving the Tower. Cail looked around for the tiny creature, but it was nowhere to be found. It croaked again, this time louder. Even though Cail couldn't find the frog, he took solace in knowing he wasn't alone.

"Who are you?" said a sonorous, but also quiet, voice. The voice came from Cail's feet, where a tiny frog, no larger than Cail's palm, was sitting in the grass. The frog's skin was painted with a vast array of colors: red, blue, green, yellow, purple. Its head was turned upward and black, beady eyes stared into Cail's. At first, Cail didn't say anything in response, he thought his mind was deceiving him. Then, the frog spoke again, "Are you deaf? I asked who you are?"

"M-my name is Cail," he stuttered, shocked that he was conversing with a frog. "You can talk?"

"Of course I can talk!" the frog said as though Cail's question was obscenely ridiculous. "All the animals in Aithnen can talk. I don't know what kind of world you come from where animals don't say a word."

"I come from Kordon," Cail answered plainly.

"Kordon?" the frog repeated. "Never heard of it. It must be a bleak world if there are no animals to talk to." Cail wanted to argue in defense of his home, but he saw no point. The frog asked, "What brings you to the Whispering Waters?"

"The Whispering Waters?" Cail asked.

"Yes, that's where you are. You've never heard of this place?" the frog asked, Cail shook his head in response. "Poor soul. You're here without even knowing what you've walked into. Why are you here?"

"To be perfectly honest, I don't know anymore," Cail responded. His words were plagued with sadness and dejection. Part of the reason he was so happy to hear the frog's croaks was because he was so alone on his expedition through the marshes. He was betrayed, isolated, and forgotten. "I was sent along this path in hopes of completing a favor, but I walked into a trap."

"King Alban sent you, no doubt?" the frog asked.

"You know him?" Cail responded, surprised by the frog's question.

"I wish I didn't. However, he, along with his wretched daughter, is at the heart of my worst memories, he's the reason I live in this miserable swamp."

"What happened?" Cail asked, alarmed by the frog's scorn.

"Centuries ago, I wasn't a frog, but a man; a highly esteemed man at that. My name was Omar and I was the closest friend of the Descendant of Kordon, we knew each other since we were both little boys."

"Boys?" Cail repeated, stricken by Omar's claim. "But that can't be. Serafine is the Descendant of Aithnen, there can be only Descendant."

"Serafine? The Descendant of Aithnen?" Omar laughed hysterically as though he had heard a joke. "If she's our protector, then Aithnen truly is doomed."

"I don't understand. I've seen her possess dominion over fire. She has more control over it than I do over the wind. How can this be?"

"Will you let me finish my tale?" Omar croaked, irritated by Cail's brusqueness. "As I said, the Descendant of Kordon, Mishal, and I were childhood friends and we remained close all the way until I was cursed to live out my life as an amphibian."

"And what happened to Mishal?" Cail asked.

"I can't be certain. If I had to guess, I would say he's been imprisoned in Kye's castle all this time."

"You're sure he's not dead?"

"Yes, I'm certain. If he was, Serafine wouldn't have any of her powers. You see, the magic granted to the Descendant only lives as long as the Descendant does. I'm not sure how, but Serafine and her father found a way to steal Mishal's magic from him, but they need to keep him alive, or else Serafine will be no different than any other Aithnenian."

"I don't understand why she's doing this," Cail said aloud, partially to Omar and partially to himself. Even though the evidence of her treachery was laid before him like a map, he only wanted to remember the friend he had made. It didn't seem possible for her to stoop down to this low of a person. Yet, if she had truly taken the magic away from the chosen Descendant, there was no telling what atrocities she could commit. He could no longer deny that she was a force to be reckoned with, he could no longer deny that she had become his enemy. "What could possess a person to do this heinous act?"

"Power," Omar said without hesitation. "Kye has been owned by her family for millennia, and Kye has been, by far, the most powerful city in Aithnen as well. Their thirst for control will never be quenched. The Descendants bow to no rulers and abide by no laws outside of their own morality, which is exactly why King Alban and Serafine sought to claim the magic for themselves: They can't live with the knowing that there's someone in the world who doesn't answer to them. Power is a crippling ailment. It gives you the illusion of empowerment, but in truth, you're just a puppet being manipulated by strings. Alban and Serafine think they can control the entire world, but they can't even control their own minds."

Even though Cail resented Serafine and her father, even though they had remorselessly betrayed him and threw him to the wilderness to die, even after all they had done and planned to do, Cail pitied them. Yes, their acts were atrocious and they were fully capable of destructing thousands of innocent lives, but they were victims of a malicious possession. Cail was unsure when Alban had lost control over his mind, but he knew, without a shadow of a doubt, that Serafine's dream seized her free will and controlled her body. He had never realized how corrosively poisonous it was to relentlessly pursue more power. It became their addiction, it swallowed their minds, and it imprisoned their compassion for others. Cail wasn't entirely convinced that the innocent lives being sacrificed had even crossed their minds, or if they could. Still, whether their harmful ambitions were a result of choice or possession, Cail knew they had to be stopped, they needed to answer for their heinous acts.

"I need to go to Taurim," Cail said to Omar. The frog's eyes widened, as though Cail had just confessed to committing the same atrocities performed by Serafine and her father, but Cail ignored Omar's startled expression. "There is someone I must meet, someone who can help me protect the rest of the world from Serafine's rise to power."

"Who are you?" Omar asked, amazed by Cail's audacity to think he could challenge someone as powerful as Serafine.

"Will you show me the way, or not?" Cail asked, ignoring Omar's question.

"Yes, yes, of course," Omar responded. The frog hopped along, and Cail followed him through the marshes. Cail was fortunate to have met his tiny companion, for he knew a score of different shortcuts and secrets which hastened their trek through the wetlands. Omar said nothing to Cail, and Cail said nothing to Omar; they firmly clung to the task at hand. The day had swiftly progressed into the heart of the afternoon by the time they reached the border of the Whispering Waters. The ground dried and strength returned to Cail's footing. A rolling hill of parched grass descended from the marshes and led to the city of Taurim; it truly was a dead city. The buildings were colorless and rotting, as though they had remained untouched for centuries, the streets were silent and empty, another symptom of death and decay, and the grass on the hill abruptly halted at Taurim's border, leaving an island of bleak, lifeless dirt upon which the city stood. "It's not too late to turn back. A monstrous beast sleeps within the city. You're certain you want to enter?" Omar asked.

"I must. Kye's only hope of salvation rests in the one who awaits me."

"As you wish," Omar said. Cail could tell that the frog knew nothing of the Last Descendant's resolve. "However, I must know who you are. No one has ever dared to challenge the rulers of Kye. They've successfully instilled fear in all of us for millennia. I must know who broke the dam and allowed the floods of freedom to seamlessly flow."

Omar had already displayed his ignorance regarding Kordon, the nation in the sky, so Cail conjured a new name, a name that would be universally recognized, an unmistakable name that would speak for itself. "When Aithnen becomes a free world and Mishal's powers are returned to him, you can tell everyone you know that you met the one who challenged the source of corruption. You can tell everyone that you met the Conqueror."

Chapter 18: Rebellion

"I crave the sun," Serafine said aloud as she laid in bed, pondering over her intricate thoughts. She couldn't help but reminisce on the scores of years she had spent in Kordon searching for the Shadow Stone. It wasn't Kordon that she missed, but what Kordon was gifted over the rest of the world. Every day, the Dragonfolk soaked their skin in all the stolen sunlight; they hid from everyone else like a burglar hides his riches. Burglary was the perfect description of their crime. There was absolutely no justification that could explain why they deserved to breathe the free air while the rest of the world suffocated. "They will know the suffering of my people. The Dragonfolk must be brought low," Serafine said with a quiet, shaking rage. Her resentment quickly evolved into disdain; the Dragonfolk had done nothing to deserve their esteemed treatment.

King Alban stood, or rather laid, in the way. He had delivered explicit directions to his daughter that their plans couldn't move forward until the King's trusted knights had returned to Kye with Cail being dragged along, either as their hostage or as a corpse. The more she pondered over her father's demand, the more ridiculous it seemed. Three days had passed since Cail's departure and he was surely dead by now, assuming that he hadn't yet fallen into the knights' hands already. The Last Descendant was alone in the wilderness with no hope of survival; surely there would be no better time to break down the barrier between Aithnen and the nation she had grown to despise.

The tool that would allow her to do so was hidden in the drawer of her thin nightstand. She pulled the rickety drawer open and withdrew the Shadow Stone. It was an alluring stone with deceptive power. Every time she held the stone, or even looked at it, she became hopelessly paralyzed by its beauty. It was far too easy to become a victim of its entrancement, to fall prey to the powerful magic contained within. The range of the Shadow Stone's sorcery was unknown to the Aithnenians, but one thing was for certain: the survival of the Domain of Fire irrefutably depended on its return to the temple.

The Buried Temple, which was aptly named, was the resting grounds for the Shadow Stone. In fact, legends were passed down that the temple was built by the gods themselves to provide a sanctuary for this robust source of magic. The temple was heavily guarded and rested deep beneath the city of Kye. It was strictly forbidden for anyone, save for royalty, of course, to enter the grounds, as an act of protecting the purity of the Buried Temple.

Three light knocks tapped on Serafine's bedroom door. "Serafine?" her mother called from the other side. "Your father would like to speak with you if you have a moment to spare." At first, Serafine meant to place the Shadow

Stone back in her nightstand, but for reasons she couldn't explain, she decided to slide it into the pocket of her cloak. In a way, it felt like the Shadow Stone was begging her to take it, like it was calling out to Serafine, like it wanted to return to the Buried Temple. Serafine would be rebelling against her father's wishes, though. She would be risking everything she had worked so hard for, she would be risking her path to supremacy, just for another glimpse of the sun. *Would it truly be a risk, though?* Serafine thought silently. Surely, Cail had no hope of surviving in the vicious wilderness. His body would wither, rot, and decay. Then, once his mind had caved and the drumming of his heart had ceased, he would be found by a beast of the wild and he'd be eaten by flesh-craving teeth.

"Serafine?" her mother called through the door once more.

"Yes, yes! I'm coming!" Serafine yelled, trying to quiet her mother's impatience. She reached into her pocket once more to retrieve the Shadow Stone and return it to her nightstand, but as soon as her smooth fingers touched the polished surface of the stone, the stone touched her mind.

It massaged her worries and relieved her strained thoughts. Instead of seeing the act of betraying her own father, she saw the coming of an age. Serafine looked through a window that showed a world over which she ruled with unquestionable authority. Families, cities, armies, and kingdoms all bowed before her and obeyed her every command. There was no need for the other Descendants, there was no threat to her imminent and immortal reign.

Serafine removed her touch from the Shadow Stone, but the vision remained in her mind. The glimpse into the future was everything she ever dreamed of, it gave her the hope of knowing that the centuries of toiling in Kordon, searching for the Shadow Stone, was worth the reward that was in store for her.

As Serafine walked into her father's room, King Alban said, "Good morning, my dear. I trust that your body has been on the mend over the course of these past few days?"

"Yes, it has," Serafine answered with a bright smile. "My muscles are regaining a strength and robustness I haven't known for centuries. Coming home was exactly what I needed."

"That's good to hear," the King said with a hearty chuckle. "Be sure to get all the rest you need now because in a few days, I expect my knights to return with their captive, be he dead or alive. The time for action isn't very far away. In the same way that a hurricane rams into an island and rips away the roots of palm trees, so too will your rise to power tear away the prevailing leaders of this world. We won't even need to keep Mishal alive at that point. You see, once the path to The Shadow has been paved, you must bring Claeg back to me. Not only does he hold our nation hostage under his curse, but he also holds the key to your immortality. There is something he knows that we don't, something that we must learn. Bring him back to me, and we will make him talk."

"I promise, father, it will be done," Serafine assured King Alban.

He put his thick, but pale, hand on her cheek. "I know it's difficult waiting in anxiety; I eagerly await Cail's arrival through the towering doors of our castle. His death will bring about Aithnen's life. You will finally have the indestructible empire that you've always fantasized about. We just need to protect the Shadow Stone for a short while longer until Cail's life has ended."

The glorious vision of Serafine's rise to power slowly drifted away like a long-forgotten dream as she saw her father's joy on his face. His happiness stemmed from the fact that she had trusted his plan. King Alban was beatific that his daughter believed in his beliefs, obeyed his commands, and was ready to ascend to authority in the way that he had intended. Serafine, on the other hand, was stricken by guilt. The Shadow Stone being in her pocket was proof that her mind had been purchased by the temptations, the whispers telling her she could give in to her deepest desire, telling her she could betray her father.

"I-I have to go," Serafine said. She could feel burning tears preparing to burst out of her eyes, tears that were brought on by the shame of what she planned to do, what the Shadow Stone was forcing her to do.

"Serafine, what's wrong?" her father asked. The King's glee had quickly turned into concern as he vividly saw his daughter's distress painted on her face. Serafine darted out of the bedroom before her father could say anything else and then she sprinted through the hallways until her paralyzing emotions forced her to stop. She pressed her back against the stone wall and let the tears of guilt run down her cheeks like rushing rivers.

Before this point, confliction was a stranger to her mind, but she could feel her mind being pulled and stretched like a rope. The temptations were far louder than whispers, they were echoes reverberating against the walls inside her head, they were shouting at her. The guilt of betraying her father's commands was at war with the indomitable desire to gain as much power as possible. There was one vision that distinguished itself from the rest, though. It was a vision that she had seen only a few nights ago, but it completely changed the way she viewed Cail. Serafine could still see him tearing apart her nation and ravaging her home.

Although Cail and Serafine's relationship was a short one, Serafine had learned a lot about her companion. He had a pure heart, a selfless mind, and an undying desire to protect the ones he loved. Cail was a gentle soul, and yet, Serafine's vision had seized her mind and forced her to accept the truth that Cail wasn't to be trusted. Serafine acknowledged that her father was right about one thing: Cail's potential was far beyond anything they could imagine. The threat of Cail's powers turned the dull murmurs of the Shadow Stone's temptations into a deafening roar. There was but one choice for Serafine: she needed to return it to the temple, she needed to defy her own father in order to save her people from a fully-realized Descendant of Kordon.

With her mind fully committed to her bright future, Serafine left the castle and entered the streets of Kye. Centuries ago, when she left Aithnen on her quest to find the Shadow Stone, the townspeople of Kye were beginning to grow weary of her father. Serafine often heard the discontent grumbles of those who remembered the golden days of the kingdom. They would complain about having a king who no longer cared about the common folk, complain about struggling to live off the amount of food, or lack thereof, they had, complain about the cruel punishments delivered to those who challenged the unquestioned crown of Kye. On several occasions, Serafine had half a mind to confront these audacious accusers and defend her father, but to do so would be to walk into the den of lions. In the castle, Serafine was protected and stood upon a mighty pedestal, but in the city, she was grossly outnumbered. She loved Kye, but she also acknowledged that it could very well be a hostile battleground. As she left the safety of her father's castle, she could feel angry and bitter eyes glaring at her from all the surrounding doors and windows. They watched her like hawks, waiting for their moment to swoop down and snatch their prey, but that moment would have to wait. Nearly everyone was lingering in their hostility, but for reasons Serafine couldn't explain, they didn't act upon it.

Deep in the heart of the city there was a small hut, with brimstone walls and arched windows, that looked identical to all the surrounding buildings, but Serafine knew it to be the entrance to the Buried Temple. A thin curtain hung over the entrance into the hut, a withering piece of fabric that occasionally flapped in the random gusts that blew out of the west.

Serafine slouched her back to enter through the short doorway and two burly guards, covered head to toe in impenetrable armor and wielding swords as tall as their thick, muscular legs, stood inside the cramped hut. To a pair of ignorant eyes, it would seem that there was nothing to protect in the hut; the beige walls were completely bare, save for a couple of windows, and nothing of value was in the entire room.

"Princess Serafine," one of the guards said as he bowed before her, the other guard followed suit. "What brings you this deep into the city?"

"Gentlemen," Serafine responded with a swift curtsy of her own. "I have great need to enter the temple."

"Is that so?" the guard asked, appearing surprised by her request. "We have strict orders from your father not to allow anyone into the Sacred Grounds, save for the King, of course."

"True, but he had no choice but to send me," Serafine answered, quickly trying to conjure a lie. "The King is bedridden thanks to his crippling illness, and since I possess the blood of royalty, he elected to send me."

"To do what?"

"That's strictly the business of the King and myself."

The guard thrust the point of his sword into the dirt upon which he stood and sternly said, "If you wish to have entry into the Buried Temple, then you better make it our business as well. Now, why has King Alban sent you here?"

Serafine silently cursed beneath her breath; her father had certainly picked the right men to guard the temple. However, there was one last option she could try. "The nation of Aithnen is under threat against a powerful Kordonian who has slipped through the seal dividing both worlds. There's a prisoner deep within the temple's walls who possesses the answer to Aithnen's salvation. I must speak with him."

"A threat from Kordon, you say? We truly are in dark times," the guard said. It appeared that the guard believed Serafine's fabrication, which did have some elements of the truth contained within. After pondering over the risks for a brief moment, the guard said, "I'm sorry, Serafine, but we can't grant you access to the Buried Temple unless we see proof that your father, in fact, sent you."

"I implore of you, please let me into the temple. There's no time to lose!" Serafine begged.

"If I may be so bold as to interject," the other guard said, "but perhaps we should let her in. She is royalty, after all, and if the King truly has sent his daughter here, we will face his ruthless wrath if we deny her entry."

The first guard stood in silence, taking that point deeply into consideration. Then he said, "It goes against my better judgment, but I suppose you're right. We should obey the orders of our King." The guard turned on his heels and used the point of his sword to swipe away a thick rug that was lying on the floor behind them, revealing a wooden trapdoor on the ground. He bent down and swung the door open with a loud creak. The guard turned back toward Serafine and asked, "You know the way to the prisoner, I presume?"

Serafine nodded in response and then proceeded toward the revealed trapdoor. As she passed the guards, she partially expected them to violently snatch her by the arms and take her away as their prisoner, but they did no such thing. A wooden, rickety ladder dropped from the narrow opening in the ground down into the darkness. The steps of the ladder bent and whined as Serafine descended into her blindness. There was no light and no sound; Serafine only experienced what she could feel on her skin. She felt dry dirt beneath her feet when she reached the bottom of the ladder. Serafine held out her hand and ignited a small flame in her palm, creating a dim source of light to guide her through the temple's dark corridors.

The moist scent of Kye's underground temple instantly retrieved suppressed memories from Serafine's childhood. Those memories were hidden away in the back of her mind for good reason; they were recollections she wasn't particularly fond of. She loved her father, but something in the

Buried Temple brought out his worst side. There was something foul in the underground fumes that summoned his aggression. One memory in particular stood out worst of all: The day they had imprisoned the Descendant of Aithnen in the Buried Temple.

"Today is the dawning of a new age," Serafine's father said to her. "The people of Kye have spoken and they've fully displayed their loyalty to our family's throne." King Alban was a much younger man in Serafine's memory, a much healthier man. He was a man filled from head to toe with exuberance, he possessed the confidence and energy of a king entering the prime of his reign. At the time of this memory, Serafine was an ignorant young princess, a girl far too wrapped up in the luxuries of being a daughter of a powerful king.

"A new age?" the young Serafine repeated.

"That's right. Today, you will know unparalleled potential, you will know the powers of the gods. Come with me, my daughter." They had been standing in a dark corridor of the Buried Temple, then King Alban led his daughter through an iron door and they arrived in a cramped chamber with a floor, ceiling, and walls all made of solid, dried dirt. In the confined prison, there was one lonely captive on his knees, with rusted chains holding his hands behind his back. The prisoner's head was bent toward the ground, hiding his face, but Serafine knew exactly who he was; he was a boy that her father despised. She recognized the jet-black hair, she recognized the muscular limbs, she recognized the pale skin. Mishal, the Descendant of Aithnen, had become King Alban's prisoner. A closer glance at Mishal's body revealed the effects of excruciating and merciless punishment and torture. Black and blue bruises were painted on his skin, paired with dozens of gashes and cuts that were sealed shut by dried blood. It was hard to look at Mishal, but Serafine didn't dare to look away, or else she would face her father's wrath.

"I don't understand," Serafine said, looking up to her father's expressionless face. "Why did you do this to him?"

"I didn't. Our own people did," King Alban responded with a plain tone in his voice. "Ignorant minds will tell you that the Four Descendants were sent into the world to protect the nations from falling into the hands of evil, but I have shown the benighted people the truth: The Descendants are a tool for the gods to bend us into their rigid system of conformity. The Descendants are nothing like us, Serafine. They do nothing to contribute to any of the nations. While they sit upon an immense mountain of power, we're left to suffer.

"Instead of leaving power in the hands of an alien to our race, that power will rest in Aithnen's future, your future."

That day had forever changed Serafine's life and the lives of those throughout all of Aithnen. Even though she had acquired unparalleled power, it didn't come without suffering. It wasn't her own pain that haunted Serafine the most, but Mishal's. The true Descendant of Aithnen had endured excruciating pain and torture as a punishment. A punishment for what, though? Mishal, much like Cail, hadn't asked for the powers he was given, they had come to him by means of divine intervention. This is what plagued Serafine's mind the most, the fact that Mishal had done nothing to deserve such cruel hardships. Still, it was necessary for Serafine to be the person she had become. A young boy's pain was a price she, along with her father, was willing to pay.

Nonetheless, the guilt of his punishment pressed back into Serafine's mind. She hadn't entered the Buried Temple since that fateful day when she stole Mishal's powers and claimed them for herself, and now, as she walked through the last corridor leading to Mishal's cell, Serafine felt all the same sensations of the temple as though she had only left a few minutes ago.

The Buried Temple held no other prisoners; Mishal was the only one who would be trapped beneath the city, leaving his legacy to rot and fade like a ghost. His body would live on for centuries and millennia, but slowly, he would morph into a forgotten remnant of what could've been. The Aithnenians who had witnessed Mishal's rise to power had passed away and no one alive in the present dared to whisper the legends of the former Descendant of Aithnen, or else they would face the fury and wrath of King Alban.

"Now, there's a face I haven't seen for an age," said a sonorous voice from the black shadows behind the rusted, iron bars of the cell. Serafine approached as close to the bars as her courage dared, but the light of the fire in her hands couldn't reach the back of the cell. The captive hid in the shadows.

"Come into the light," Serafine commanded. "I want to see your face."

"And if I refuse? What more can be done to me?" the voice shot back. "I've been stripped of my powers; my destiny has been removed. Millennia ago, I was brought into Neptil to be the divinely ordained protector of Aithnen, and now, I've been reduced to a prisoner waiting to die. Tell me, Serafine. What can you and your accursed father do to me that hasn't already been done?"

Serafine should've retorted in a fiery rage, either because of Mishal's impudence or because of his insults thrown at the King of Kye, but no words came to her mouth. Pity clouded her thoughts and doubt crept into her mind. For the first time, she wondered if all her power was worth the price of Mishal's anguish. Those insecurities spread through mind like a poison flowing through veins, infecting the body, crushing the will to fight on. *It must be worth it. My father has sacrificed so many years and so much effort to ensure my rise to power. To quit now would be to insult my family's throne.* Serafine thought to herself. She had removed the poison from her veins, she had found the will to live.

"I told you to step into the light," Serafine demanded once again.

Without any further words of protest, Mishal did as Serafine instructed and she was struck by what she saw. Mishal was unrecognizable, a shadow of the former Descendant of Aithnen. His skin was so pale that he appeared to be the ghost of himself. Instead of having a full head of black hair, his hair was as white as a blizzard's snow and he wore a thick beard of matching color. Mishal's muscles had completely diminished into thin rails and his skin was painted with cracks and discoloration. Serafine stood in shock; she couldn't believe that this was truly Mishal. He truly was waiting for his death.

"How do you enjoy the warmth of my fire?" Mishal asked as he wrapped his thin fingers around the cold bars of his cell. "Even though I haven't felt it in centuries, I remember the comfort of fire very well. It's revitalizing; the kindling gives you unmatched vigor. You must be careful, though. Vigor is a slippery slope to aggression. That's the thing that's funny about fire. You think you're fully in control, and that might even be the case, but it only takes one slip of the finger to send the world around you into a destructive explosion. At that point, you can't stop the monster you've created. You can't stop it from hurting the ones you care about." A sinister smirk crept onto Mishal's face. Then, he asked, "Have you hurt someone you care about?"

Mishal had successfully injected poison into Serafine's mind once again. This time, the insecurities of her own strengths plagued her confidence. She did feel total control over her powers, but how much control did she truly have? Hundreds of years had passed without a slipup, but she knew Mishal was right; it would only take that one time.

"Why do you care about who I hurt?" Serafine asked, trying to cast aside any weakness from within. "You're nothing more than a humbled prisoner. You were a stepping stone, paving the way for me to claim my immortal empire."

"Immortal?" Mishal scoffed. "You're nothing of the sort. The powers of fire will only live for as long as I do. Without my divine gift, my body is withering away and soon I will die, as will your 'immortality.'"

"That's where you're wrong," Serafine shot back. "My father has found a way for me to keep my powers, ensuring my imminent rise."

"That's ridiculous," Mishal laughed at her ludicrous claim. "You can't contend with the will of the gods. Either my powers will return to me, or they will diminish once I have met the long-awaited death I've yearned for since being thrown into this wretched pit. Your tyrannical empire may begin, but it will never endure."

"I suppose we'll have to see about that. However, for right now, I've come back to the temple to return something my people have long awaited," Serafine said. Then she reached into the pocket of her cloak and retrieved the

Shadow Stone. Mishal's weary eyes widened, as though he had seen a ghost walk right in front of him.

"You found the Shadow Stone? How is this possible?"

"I think it's safe to say that the gods chose the wrong Aithnenian to protect the Domain of Fire," Serafine said with an arrogant smirk on her face. "I clearly have much more resolve than you since you've been trapped in a cell while I found the key to my nation's salvation."

"You're wrong!" Mishal shouted in frustration as he beat his fist against his confining bars. "The tide will turn and you will fall!"

Serafine ignored Mishal as he continued to yell threats of her demise and she proceeded into the neighboring chamber, the chamber to which the Shadow Stone belonged. It was an arena illuminated by dozens of torches that had been burning for centuries and would emanate for centuries more. There were a number of different antiques and ancient artifacts stored in the chamber, folklore of the nation of Aithnen, but Serafine didn't possess the faintest care for any of them. Her focus remained on the empty wooden pedestal in the center of the chamber. As she slowly approached the pedestal, Serafine could feel the power of the Shadow Stone coursing through her hand. Its dark aura clung to her hand, squeezing it like a viper. Serafine needed to release the Shadow Stone to save her people, but she didn't want to; she wanted to discover the stone's secrets, she wanted to dive into its intricate and mysterious magic.

She stood before the pedestal with the Shadow Stone still latched to her hand. Memories of Kordon's radiant sunlight flashed through her mind, but she still couldn't feel its warmth, she couldn't feel its life. The heat from the fire within her body wasn't the same; sunlight and fire were two completely different forms of torridity. Fire was a tool. Serafine could use it to strike down her foes, light a darkened path, breakdown obstructing barriers. Sunlight couldn't be harnessed, though. It wasn't a tool, it was a resource. Much like food or water, the sun was a vital part of everyone's life. Without the sunlight, Aithnen was starving, everyone was craving the sun's salvation.

Without a will of her own, her hand reached over the pedestal and she dropped the Shadow Stone. The stone hit the wood and halted without another bounce. Serafine stood as still as the stone she had just dropped. She closed her eyes and listened for anything, but there was silence. There was nothing save for the darkness contained within her eyelids. Then, as though a small fire had kindled just before her, Serafine felt a gentle wave of warmth massage her skin and light seeped through her eyelids like water through a crack. Serafine opened her eyes and was nearly blinded by a ray of sunlight blasting through a crevice in the ceiling of the chamber.

The warmth of life soaked into Serafine's skin once again and she felt her vitality coursing through her veins. All of Aithnen was seeing the sunlight that beamed into Serafine's eyes and they were absorbing the same heat. More importantly, the barrier between Aithnen and Kordon had been dismantled and her path to immortality laid just before her.

Chapter 19: Moving Forward

The sun was beginning to descend and it had almost met the ocean of clouds in the horizon. Ever since her conversation with Caldir's apparition, Laney had remained by the coast of Elona with Emey sitting by her side. Laney had half a mind to hop onto Emey's back and fly toward the Tower of the Sun, to leave her world behind, and to find Cail before it was too late. However, she knew it would be to no avail. No success would follow her unless she had Kadir to accompany her on this ambitious quest.

"I'm sorry I upset you earlier." Laney turned her head around and saw Kadir standing right behind her. Before Laney could rise to her feet, Kadir plopped onto the ground next to her and said, "I want to help Cail, I really do. I just don't see the same opportunity you do."

"Would you help him if you did?" Laney asked with sharp words, angered by Kadir's insistence to remain withdrawn in the safety of his own home while Cail was threatened by the imminent dangers of the unknown world. "Kordon was as mysterious to Cail as Aithnen is to us, and yet, he sacrificed his comfort and safety to keep everyone safe. Why can't we do the same for him?"

Kadir had no response for Laney's challenge. He silently sat still, like a boulder resting beneath a layer of snow. His face was impossible to decipher. Whether he was irritated that his devotion to Cail was being questioned, or whether he felt nothing at all and was simply waiting for Laney to break the silence, Laney did not know. Then, Kadir ended the quietude and asked, "What do you propose we do, then?"

Laney's tongue froze for a second, surprised that she had finally convinced Kadir. "We need to follow Cail's course to Aithnen, but we haven't the slightest idea where Serafine led him. Although, I suspect Cail's father might know the best direction to take."

"That's true, however, Cecil might try to stop us from pursuing Cail."

"Why?" Laney asked.

"Since Cail's gone, Cecil is once again tasked with the duties of the Lord of Elona. It's his responsibility to protect the lives on this island. He'll see a rescue mission as being reckless, which I can't disagree with. Cecil will do everything he can to stop us." Laney hadn't considered that possibility, although, she instantly knew Kadir was right.

"We may be Cail's only hope, so we must do whatever it takes to find him."

"Please, come in," Cecil said with a smile after Laney had tapped the freshly painted door of his home. Laney and Kadir walked into the kitchen of the Ozean home and sat in thin, wooden chairs at the dining table, which was completely covered with plates, cups, and silverware that had been removed from the open cupboards. "Pardon my mess, I've been doing some cleaning."

"No need to apologize," Kadir responded, minding his manners.

"I've had some extra time on my hands, with Cail being gone, so I've decided to tidy my home. It's been years since I've done so. You know, you never realize what kind of mess you've created until you begin to clean it up."

"We don't think you have a dirty home," Laney said with a bright smile.

"Nor did I, but here we are, nonetheless," Cecil responded as he wiped a layer of dust from a drawer. "What brings the two of you here today?"

"Kadir and myself were talking about Cail earlier, and we were wondering if he said when he would return?" Laney asked. Out of the corner of her eye, Laney saw Kadir's neck stiffen and his eyes widened. Clearly, he was wanting to be subtler in their conversation.

"It's hard to say," Cecil answered, seemingly unsuspecting of Laney's question. "I must confess, my mind worries more with every passing day. I know that his quest to Aithnen isn't a simple stroll by any stretch of the imagination, but my heart tells me we should've seen some sign of his return by now, something to tell us that they successfully accomplished what they set out to do. Perhaps I sound paranoid, but I can't help but worry about my son."

"You don't sound paranoid," Kadir said, trying to reassure Cecil. "We're worried about him as well. That's actually why we were talking about him. We both have nagging warnings in our hearts."

"And hence, that's why you came here. You want to follow him to Aithnen and ensure his safety, don't you?" Laney and Kadir remained silent, with mouths slightly opened. They were flabbergasted that Cecil had guessed their motive so easily, he had read them like a book.

"H-how did you know?" Laney stuttered, not bothering to deny Cecil's claim.

"Eyes say much more than words ever will. If you look close enough, you can see the treachery in the eyes of a liar, you can see the trepidation in the eyes of a coward, and you can see the aggression in the eyes of a hunter. Laney, I've seen many emotions in your eyes throughout your life, especially when you've been near Cail. Affection, sadness, and joy have filled your eyes, but now, I see the same eyes he had when he first left Elona; I see the fierce desire to leave your home for a larger purpose."

"I've seen visions, not of Cail, but of Serafine," Laney said with a hushed voice. "Her and her father are planning to betray Cail to his death. I don't know exactly what their endgame is, but all I know is that Cail is in danger.

Kadir thinks my vision is nothing more than a dream, but my heart tells me it's real."

"If you trust no one else, you must always trust your heart," Cecil said as he placed a supportive hand on Laney's shoulder. "I've received word that Serafine was going to take him to the Tower of the Sun, which is just south of Ijsbrandur. Like I said, the trek is arduous, but at this point, it's necessary."

"Ijsbrandur?" Kadir repeated, dreading a journey to the other side of Kordon. "Surely, there must be a shorter path to take?"

"I'm afraid not, Kadir. Emey will help accelerate your venture, but it's a long journey no matter how you go. Also, the two of you must promise that you'll wait until the middle of the night to leave. The village folk will never let me hear the end of it if I allow you two to go chasing after Cail."

"Waiting until tonight may be too late," Laney argued.

"Laney, please. You must do this for me," Cecil insisted. As much as she wanted to leave that second, she agreed to Cecil's command.

There were three thunderous pounds on the door. "Cecil!" a voice called from the outside. Three more aggressive pounds followed the voice. Cecil dropped the rag he was cleaning the kitchen with and sprinted to the door.

After swinging the door open, he exclaimed, "Take it easy on my door! I just painted it yesterday." Laney peered around Cecil's round body and saw Alden, the bookkeeper of Elona, standing in the doorway.

"Never mind your door, you fool. There's something far more important for you to see. Follow me!" Alden insisted and then he sprinted away as quickly as his aging bones would allow him, with Cecil trailing closely behind. Curiosity got the best of Laney, so she and Kadir sprinted away as well. They all darted through the lively streets of the village, ignoring the sharp glances that were cast their way. It became apparent where Alden was taking them: To the coast of Elona. Why, though? *What could there possibly be to see?* Laney thought silently.

It wasn't what they saw, but what they didn't see that astonished everyone. No one could believe their eyes. No one could say anything except for Laney who whispered, "It's gone." Referring to the ocean of clouds that had surrounded Elona for thousands of years. There were no more clouds beneath the islands of Kordon, there was solid land. The world beneath Kordon was filled with a vast array of colors. Emerald fields, auburn mountains and plateaus, an ivory tundra, and a sapphire sea rested on the edge of the horizon. There was such a gargantuan drop from Kordon to Aithnen. Emey was still the only hope of arriving to the Domain of Fire.

"Cail did it, he really did it," Cecil said with a proud smile. Then Cecil and Alden began walking toward the village as they discussed the new discovery, their voices trailing in the distance.

"You see? We had absolutely nothing to worry about. Cail always comes through in the end," Kadir said to Laney, patting her on the back with his thick palm.

"I don't know," Laney said without removing her eyes from the newly uncovered world beneath her home. Even though she could plainly see the world Cail had entered, her nagging paranoia still lurked in her mind. Laney couldn't forget the vision of Serafine and her father, she couldn't forget the treachery they had planned. "Something doesn't feel quite right. I think we should still go to Aithnen."

"Are you insane? There's no way of knowing what kinds of danger lurk down there. Cail did what he set out to do, and that's good enough for me."

"Well, how is Cail supposed to return home if he doesn't have Emey?"

"He was able to go there without her, so I'm sure he'll find a way back," Kadir answered coldly, no longer wanting to argue. "I'm not leaving Elona, and that's all I have to say about that." Before Laney could respond, Kadir stormed away, obviously annoyed by Laney's insistence. Her mind was screaming within the walls of her skull, telling her to hop onto Emey's back and fly down to Aithnen, but she remembered her promise to Cecil. It would have to wait until the evening.

Laney spent the rest of the day laying on her mattress, blankly staring at the ceiling above her head, ignoring the faint clamor of the village outside of her bedroom walls. Nothing existed outside of the realm of her thoughts. They were entirely encompassing. Cecil's words reverberated in her head. "I see the fierce desire to leave your home for a larger purpose." Cail had already found the higher purpose he had sought after: To fulfill the responsibility of being the Last Descendant. But what was Laney's higher purpose? What had the gods sent her to this world to be?

In the same way that a lamp illuminates a dark, concealed closet, the answer to her questions emanated in her mind. The answer rested in the past. Her mind traveled to a time that was much simpler. The world was smaller, in fact, the entire world existed on the island of Elona. Cail, Laney, and Kadir were enjoying the jubilations of the Wave Days in the waning moments before Cail would be crowned the Lord of Elona.

Laney missed those moments; the moments she spent with her two closest friends, not having a care about the world around her. Until she was laying alone on her bed, she hadn't realized how important those moments were. The memories relieved the pressure of life's intricate conflicts. In Laney's mind, they were all together, blissfully unaware of the darkness that thrived in the outside world. At that time, in Elona, there was no evil, there was no malice, and, most importantly, there was no betrayal. The present was so different, though. Kadir was safe and sound on Elona, just like Laney, and yet, Laney couldn't help but feel as though he was as distant as Cail. Laney felt like Kadir had died and a shadow of himself had possessed his body. She no longer knew the man who, during a time that seemed to be a distant remnant in the past, was one of her two closest friends.

The memory tugged Laney's mind and took her to the moment where she was sitting on Lydia's rug. The blind fortuneteller was sitting before Laney with a gentle smile on her face. Cail and Kadir were standing just a few feet away, but something wasn't quite right. Their expressions, along with the bodies of everyone who surrounded her, remained still. She was frozen in time.

"You remember this moment, don't you?" Laney immediately recognized the voice. She looked at Lydia and she finally blinked. The deceased fortuneteller was speaking to her.

"But you're dead," Laney said in disbelief. "How is this possible?"

"Thank you for the reminder," Lydia chuckled. "Yes, my body is no more, but my spirit is fully alive. I heard your questions, your yearnings. Do you still want to know what your purpose is?"

"Yes, more than anything," Laney answered.

"Silly girl," Lydia said as she gently shook her head. "You desperately crave profound answers, and yet, I've already given them to you."

"You've done no such thing," Laney protested. "I would remember something as paramount as that."

Lydia ignored Laney's protestation and repeated a riddle she had said long before Cail had ever become the Last Descendant.

"You will be a beacon to all worlds,
a ray of hope, showing the path.
Your emanation, love, and compassion
They will be unparalleled."

The riddle slammed into Laney's chest and snatched the breath from her lungs. Indeed, she had forgotten all about Lydia's riddle. She felt so embarrassed for doing so, as though she couldn't find a trinket that was sitting in front of her face.

"Do you remember now?" Lydia asked after a moment of silence.

"I do," Laney answered. In the blink of an eye, Laney's mind had teleported from that distant memory to the present. Laney sat up on her bed and she pondered over the riddle and what it could mean for her destiny. Of all the words in the foreshadowing of her potential, there was one word amongst them all that stabbed into her mind like a thorn: hope. She would be a ray of hope. That was exactly what she could be for Cail; the single ray of hope in a dark void of despair. Although Cail didn't realize it yet, his life depended on Laney, his life depended on her hope.

Chapter 20: The Beast of Taurim

The dirt crunched beneath every step. It was the only sound Cail could hear in the hauntingly empty city. Taurim was nothing more than a city of ghosts, a remnant of what it once was. If the crumbling bricks were restored and the vines and mold were torn down, a beautiful city would be reborn. Even though Cail could only experience Taurim's corpse, he imagined the vibrant days of the Kingdom's past. Bakeries warmed the air with alluring aromas, the laughter of children playing in the streets tickled Cail's eardrums, and the sun's beaming rays breathed life into the streets. Cail was glimpsing deep into Taurim's past, long before he was born, long before the Shadow Stone was ever stolen by the Sages of Pazia. In a way, it reminded him of his own home. Elona boasted a similar vitality. He felt as though he was visiting a paradise, a city of refuge and safety. For a split moment, he felt secure from all the dangers in the world.

For all the jubilance Cail could feel around him, there was one thistle among the horde of roses. A young girl, not far into her years of adolescence, sat alone in the dark shadows of an alley. While everyone was vigorous and bursting with energy, the girl's face was dull and lifeless. Her bleak eyes stared into an empty abyss, as though she was waiting for death to find her, her body was railed, deprived of meals for days, if not weeks, and her pale skin was spotted with black dirt. Cail felt sympathetic for the girl; it was blatantly obvious that she had no home. By no fault of her own, she lived in the hostile streets, dreaming of a night's escape from the frigid air. Cail wanted nothing more than to reach out to her, to grant her safety. He wanted to wrap an arm around her thin, malnourished shoulders and comfort her, promise her that brighter days were ahead, but he could do no such thing. Just like the rest of the city Cail was seeing inside his head, the girl was nothing more than a faded memory. Still, Cail felt the same sadness as though her life depended on a simple act of generosity.

Cail's mind drifted back to reality and the sensations and emotions of the city had died, just like its people. In that moment, Cail saw the remainder of Taurim's history, he saw the tragedy. At the same time, Cail understood why Taurim was dead, why it was a failed city; it all traced back to that girl, or rather, what she represented. She was hopelessly anchored to her isolation in the streets. Although, she was only hopeless because no one would offer her the hope of a better life, and that was the heart of Taurim's demise. As gradually as the sun sets into the cold night, more people like the girl lost their homes, doomed to die in the streets. And yet, no one had a heart to help these people, no one had a heart to halt the suffering.

Wanting to find Claeg as quickly as he could, Cail progressed through the city. The pavement beneath his feet was cracked and jagged, forcing him to work for every step. Cail filed through blocks of abandoned houses, tall and small, crumbling beneath the weight of time. Windows were painted with dirt and dust, doors were broken and rotten, and the walls were being eaten by an invisible poison. This same poison feasted on the entire city, an omen showing the death of the land.

All the streets led to the same spot in the heart of the city: The Castle of Taurim. In its time, it was an eloquent castle. Ivory bricks gleamed in the sunlight, spotless windows glistened, and tall, bronze doors led into a towering corridor made of marble. In present time, however, the castle was a shadow of its former self. It was as haunting as a tomb. Cail swore he could hear the whispers of the dead hissing through the air. He was convinced that this castle was the beast's hiding place, it was the perfect place to take refuge.

The inside corridor was ghastly and dark and Cail's feet clapped against the marble floor. Paintings of ancient Kings and Queens hung on the walls, stalking Cail like an eagle. The castle reeked of the foul stench of death and the air was as cold as a wintry night. Adjacent to the corridor was a breathtaking ballroom. A chandelier riddled with radiant diamonds hung from the ceiling which towered five stories above Cail's head. A broad staircase made of ivory stone circled around the walls of the oval shaped ballroom, rising all the way to the top, leading to dozens of doors which would branch out to deeper parts of the castle. Magnificent murals were painted on the stone walls portraying a valiant battle from an age long past. A battalion of Aithnen's finest soldiers were brawling through a legion of monsters who didn't look much different than the zuraks who haunted Kordon for so long. Behind the dark monsters stood a vile creature which frightened Cail, despite the fact it was a still painting. The creature stood like a man, but it was something entirely different. In a dark claw, it held a broad sword with a maroon blade, black armor protected its entire body, its piercing eyes matched the hue of the blade of the sword, and a black crown was placed upon its head. "What kind of demon is this?" Cail asked aloud.

"He's not a demon, he's a king." Cail turned around and saw Claeg standing behind him, who kept his eyes glued to the painting of this ancient horror. "At least, he was a king. In the earlier years of his life, Malgor was a generous leader who led the city of Taurim into an age of prosperity. However, as you can clearly see, his fate took a wicked turn."

"And now?" Cail asked.

"Now, he is the Beast of Taurim. Malgor fell victim to the lies of a great deceiver, in the same way you did. King Alban's words spewed poison into Malgor's ears and corrupted his mind. Alban morphed a proud, young king into the monster you see in this painting."

"But how?" Cail asked incredulously. "I now understand that Alban is a deceptive man, but how can his words alone turn a king into a fiend?"

"Words have no limits, nor do ideas. Words lead to the creation of ideas and ideas lead to what we say and do. An army can slaughter entire nations, cities can be torn down and built again, lives can be taken, all by the power of one person's words. Cail, you must never underestimate the prowess behind someone's words, especially someone as deceitful as King Alban."

Cail gazed deeply into Malgor's eyes once again. The crimson eyes ensnared Cail's mind and he could feel the depravity in the painting. Malice and cruelty oozed from the mural. Cail envisioned the same vice Kalil had dumped onto Kordon for centuries. Though it was still hard to conceive that a monster such as this had spawned from words, Cail remembered the story of Kalil and how he rose to power. Centuries ago, Kalil was nothing more than a humble farmer who was content with reaping produce from the ground until a fateful day when evil opened a new door, it presented a new opportunity. Forces of good and evil have a special way of doing that, of expanding the realm of possibility.

"I assume Malgor is the beast who dwells in this castle?" Cail asked.

"He was. You'd already be dead if he was still alive, though."

"He's dead?"

"In a manner of speaking, yes. His corpse rests deep in the dungeons of this castle, however, his spirit still thrives in the same realm as mine, The Shadow. I don't know how his life ended, perhaps he was simply struck down by the curse of time, but I do know that finding Malgor's spirit is King Alban's endgame. He wants Serafine to use Malgor's dark prowess to ensure that her reign over the entire world is eternal. You must do anything within your power to ensure that potential is never realized."

"How did this all start?" Cail whispered. He intended to keep the words to himself, but Claeg still heard him.

"What do you mean? How did what start?" Claeg asked.

"All of this. Going all the way back to Serafine betraying Mishal. What possesses someone to do such a thing? To ruin a life in the name of acquiring more power? I don't understand how Serafine could do something like this."

"I wish I had the answer," Claeg said with a solemn voice. "I've often wondered the same thing. To what avail are one's actions? There's no joy to be found in the acquisition of power if it's at the expense of everyone around you. However, it's not our duty to see life through the lens of darkness." Claeg's spirit turned toward Cail and grabbed him by the shoulders. "Cail, you must prevent Serafine from finding Malgor's spirit at all costs."

"The only way to do so would be to find his spirit myself," Cail said.

"Right, you are," Claeg responded. "You must come to the Shadow. That way, we'll finally be able to meet in person."

"I'll need help. There's no one in the entire nation of Aithnen who will give it to me, though."

"I can think of one person," Claeg said, cracking a smirk on his broad chin.

"Mishal?" Cail asked. Claeg nodded. "I haven't the faintest idea of where to find him, though."

"It's good fortune, then, because I do. King Alban has him locked away in the Buried Temple, the same place that's home to the Shadow Stone. I will give you a way to return to Kye, but you must move as swiftly as the wind and as silently as a shadow. The King's army will pounce on you the second they see you. You're as wanted as their worst criminals."

"Assuming I do succeed in finding Mishal, what will I do after that?"

"Then, you must return to Darzomil. There's a shrine beneath the city that will lead you to the Shadow," Claeg answered.

"Darzomil?" Cail repeated in anguish. "It'll take me weeks to trek all the way into that mountain!"

"Cail, under no circumstance can Serafine be allowed to enter the Shadow. If she does, the entire world as we know it will perish. Either you must find a way to win the race against Serafine, or we'll all be doomed to our deaths."

Cail could already feel the weight of time hanging from his shoulders, dragging his body closer to the ground. It was an anchor, a crutch. He knew that with every passing second, his mind would worry about the possibility of falling further behind Serafine's pace, something he knew he couldn't afford to do. In an instant, time transformed from being an omniscient entity to being a scarce resource. It was suffocating, in its own way. Much like a diver whose lungs are being filled with water where air should thrive, so too was time stripping Cail of his life. He knew there was no time to panic, though. All that was needed was swift, precise action.

"You said you know of a way to return to Kye, correct?" Cail asked. Claeg nodded in response. "Good. Take me there, then I can steal the Shadow Stone, thus paving a shorter route back to Kordon."

"That's what I like to hear," Claeg said with a wide smile. "Follow me. The time has come for you to return to Kye."

Cail trailed closely behind Claeg as they progressed up the ballroom's winding staircase. When Cail arrived to Malgor's painting, his body froze. His limbs were paralyzed by the fiend's malignant aura. It was as though Malgor's spirit was in the ballroom with them, stalking them, waiting for the opportune moment to pounce upon his prey. Cail took one more glance into Malgor's piercing eyes and then he started sprinting up the stairs; Claeg hadn't bothered to wait. When they had reached the top of the staircase, Claeg stopped just before a cracked wooden door which wasn't much taller than Cail.

"Even though this door appears to lead into nothing more than a dirty closet, it's actually the only barrier standing between us and an accursed shrine. Inside, you'll find a vast assortment of glimmering gems and alluring jewels, but don't be deceived. They're a dark stash of blood money, bought by the lives of innocent men and women. You must swear that no matter how much you're tempted, you won't touch anything other than what I tell you to."

"Yes, I swear," Cail promised with the utmost sincerity.

Satisfied with the pledge, Claeg led Cail through the door. The shrine was foreign to anything Cail had ever seen in his entire life. Mounds of gold towered over Cail's head, with some piles rising as high as the ceiling. Rubies, emeralds, diamonds, and other precious rocks were scattered throughout the shrine. A rainbow beamed across the entire room, smiling directly at Cail, inviting him with open arms. Almost subconsciously, he accepted the invitation. Without thinking, Cail's legs carried his body away from the door and closer to the border of the exquisite treasure. In a matter of seconds, he was standing before a small pile of gold, only standing as tall as his knees. Cail was immediately ensnared by the treasure, perpetually imprisoned by its immaculate glimmer. The gold made him feel warm, especially in his heart. Cail felt as though the sun was rising over Elona, warming his home after a mild night. He felt as though a soft loaf of bread was baking in the oven, filling the kitchen's air with a soothing aroma. He felt as though Laney was standing before him and he could feel the heat of her body reaching out to him.

Then, as suddenly as light turns into darkness, the heat dissipated and Cail was left to witness the past, to witness the truth of the shrine's treasure. Cail found himself in a bedroom, a king's bedroom. The king was standing by a window with long, flowing drapes tied to both sides, allowing him to overlook the city of Taurim. Malgor stood only a few paces away from Cail, admiring his magnificent city. He had a charming and prepossessing face with blue eyes that glistened in the moonlight, his brown hair flowed like a gentle river, and his chin was pointed and strong. The young man who stood before Cail was a noble king, nothing like the demon of the painting.

"You asked to see me, King Malgor?" Cail spun around and saw a younger remnant of Serafine's father standing in the doorway. His belly wasn't so round, his hair wasn't so white, and his skin wasn't so pale.

"King Alban," Malgor said with a bright smile. Then he strode across the bedroom and the two kings embraced each other with a strong hug. "I'm fortunate to have the luxury of a wise king's guidance in a time of need."

"You're too kind," Alban chuckled as he clapped his palms on Malgor's shoulders. "What guidance do you seek?"

"When I assumed the crown, this city was in disarray. Thousands upon thousands of outcasts came crawling before my doors, humbled by the cruelties of the world, and I answered their call. Over the years, I did everything I possibly could to ensure prosperity for everyone. Miraculously, I was successful and the entire city reaped generous rewards. Regions of the city were rebuilt and renovated, a roof was firmly placed over every family's head, and not a single child was left to face starvation. Taurim was reborn.

"It didn't come at no cost, though. My personal riches have suffered. Slowly, the people have taken what was rightfully mine. I suppose, in a way, I feel as though I've given my entire crown away. I'm seeking your guidance because my mind is torn. I don't want my own people to suffer, but also, my own wealth is dwindling. After all, what good is a king when he has nothing buried beneath his name?"

"You're far too harsh on yourself," Alban said with a comforting voice. "You've sacrificed much more than any king should ever be asked to give. The people of Taurim owe their lives and allegiance to you, and I suggest it's time for them to pay their dues."

In the blink of an eye, Cail transported back into the castle's shrine, where he was standing in front of the small pile of gold. Its hypnotic power had slipped away, for Cail could see the malevolence beneath its allurement. "It didn't take very long for Alban to slither into Malgor's mind. Once the temptation of greed was planted, it sprouted like a weed. Taurim, a city which was once saved by Malgor, fell into darkness."

"And this gold? What's the significance of it?" Cail asked.

"This gold was taken from the hands of those who needed it most. King Malgor ruthlessly snatched this precious, scarce currency from starving families and hoarded it in this very room. That's why the gold is cursed: It possessed the King to turn against his own people. If you lay a finger on it, I fear you'll betray the ones you love the most."

Cail couldn't fathom the possibility of being tempted to betray Laney or his father. He was wholeheartedly convinced that no price could ever match the love he felt for them. Still, greed had succeeded in lowering one of the great Kings of Aithnen. Malgor, a noble man who had sacrificed his own fortune for the sake of his people, was easily corrupted by greed and descended into darkness. If he could fall, then surely, Cail could as well.

"That's enough talk about the past for now. Follow me." Cail did as Claeg commanded and the Hidden King led Cail through the shrine until they approached a ladder made of frayed rope which rose all the way to a cellar door in the ceiling. Claeg said, "Through that door is a portal which will take you to my old home in Kye. From there, you must find the Buried Temple and free Mishal. The enemy thinks you're still lost in the wilderness; don't give them reason to think otherwise. Find me in the Shadow. Until then, I'm afraid we must part ways." Claeg's body faded away until he vanished completely, leaving Cail all alone in the dungeon. The shrine's treasure reached out to Cail one last time, tempting him to immerse himself in the ocean of gems, but his mind wouldn't be swayed. There was no time for him to lose, he could lose no more steps in the race to the Shadow.

Chapter 21: The King's Guests

"Your father eagerly awaits you," said a deep, sonorous voice that startled Serafine. She was greeted not only by the two guards who kept a close eye on the Buried Temple, but by the King's entire army. The legion of soldiers stood as still as statues, waiting for the Descendant of Aithnen, or so they thought she was. After it was apparent that no words would slip from Serafine's tongue, the guard said, "Unless you intend on fighting us all, I suggest you come quietly."

"Very well," Serafine conceded. Then she followed the guards without another word. The world around her offered many distractions: The open sky with the golden sun beaming on the top of her head, the unified clanking of the army's footsteps, or the dull whispers of the townspeople who were conjuring the worst rumors. However, one dreadful thought remained plastered in Serafine's mind: The thought of what her father was about to do. There were no words to describe how angry he would be, no words to describe how truly mortified she was of facing his rage and, worst of all, there was no hope of escaping her punishment.

"Do you have any idea what you've just done?" King Alban's voice was shaking with fury, but he prevented himself from screaming. Serafine, who was standing at the foot of her father's bed, didn't know what to say to justify her defiance. Serafine's mother did nothing except stand next to her husband, too afraid to mutter beneath her breath. The King continued, "Centuries of planning and devotion have gone into what we've dreamt of accomplishing, and now, it's been completely undone!"

"That's not even remotely true!" Serafine blurted out without a will of her own. She stood still in shock, amazed that she had spoken out against her father.

"Is that so?" Alban asked.

"Yes," Serafine asserted with confidence. "Cail has no means by which he can defeat us. He's trapped in the wilderness where he has no hope of salvation, no hope of stopping me from reaching the Shadow."

King Alban remained silent for a moment longer, firmly staring into Serafine's eyes. Then, he let out a soft sigh and said, "I suppose you're right. Although the time has come more swiftly than I would've liked, I can't deny the fulfillment of your destiny. The time has come for you to venture to the Shadow."

"Claeg, the traitor of Kye, will haunt us no longer," Serafine said.

"Yes. Along with that, there's one more task to complete in the Shadow, one last obstacle that's blocking your immortality. You remember Malgor, the

Demon King of Taurim?" Serafine nodded in response. "His spirit is locked away deep in the Shadow, hidden from the light. You must find it and consume his power. Only then can you realize your truest potential."

"But father, Malgor tore apart his entire city. Do you really think that the same darkness should be allowed to thrive within me?" Serafine protested.

"Serafine, how badly do you want to be the ruler of the world?"

"I want it more than anything else!" she shot back.

"Then you must trust me on this. It's too easy for anyone to take a look at Malgor's life and view him as evil and fiendish, but I was there to see his struggles, to see his conflicted mind, to see the sacrifices he needed to make. You see my dear, sometimes others must suffer for the most noble to survive."

Serafine was taken back by what her father had just said. She understood that Cail meant nothing to her father because Cail was a foreigner to Aithnen's lands, but disregarding his own people was an entirely different matter. Throughout her entire life, Serafine had witnessed several examples of her father giving as little as he could to the peasants and muckrakers of his city, but he had never abandoned them completely. All she could see was a horde of dirty faces, disappointed by another leader who would betray their hopes and dreams. Serafine wanted to defiantly protest, to protect the innocent lives of Kye from their deranged King, but then she remembered the centuries spent in Kordon. Toil and hardship had been no stranger to her there. And what struggle did everyone know while she was trapped in a foreign land? Nothing. They sat safe and sound in their homes, praying for good fortune to come like a cool breeze during a blistering afternoon in the summer. They knew nothing of her hardships and she would know nothing of their sorrow.

"You're right, father," Serafine said after a brief moment's pause. "The people of Kye must suffer for the moment so my empire can thrive in the future." Ina's eyes widened, clearly shocked by the words that had slithered from Serafine's mouth.

Without warning, a guard burst through the bedroom door, heavily panting as though he had been running for hours. In between deep breaths, he said, "My apologies for the intrusion, my King, but I bring urgent news. A group of guards captured intruders who had made their way into the city. The guards claimed they saw them fly from the sky, claimed they captured a boy and a girl flying on an emerald falcon. The guards have taken the boy and girl into custody, but no one could tame the winged beast. It got away."

"Laney," Serafine whispered, but the King heard her.

"You know these intruders, Serafine?" King Alban asked.

"Yes. Their names are Laney and Kadir, friends of Cail's. Undoubtedly, they've come in search of him."

King Alban cursed beneath his breath, still upset that his daughter had undercut his plans. "This was exactly what I wanted to avoid. If we don't move quickly, more people will come searching for Cail." Then he said to the guard, "Bring the intruders to me. I'd like to have a word with them." The guard saluted his King and darted out the door.

"Care to tell me what your plan is?" Serafine asked.

"You'll soon see. They're about to play right into our hands," the King answered with a proud smirk. Serafine said no more and the family of nobles waited in silence for the prisoners. After a few quiet moments, faint footsteps were heard from the adjacent hallway and then the guard shoved Laney and Kadir, whose hands were firmly shackled, into the King's bedroom. They both looked fatigued and exhausted, as though they had endured an expedition lasting weeks on end. With a booming voice, the King said, "Intrusion is a severe offense in the proud city of Kye. If you wish to have any hope of avoiding the dark, cramped dungeons of this ancient castle, you better reveal your intentions of your impudent arrival."

Without hesitation, Laney said, "We've come searching for our friend Cailean." She looked toward Serafine. "This is your father I presume?"

Serafine opened her mouth to respond, but her father raised his hand, silencing her. He said, "Yes, I'm her father, the King of Kye. Cail is no longer here. I've been plagued with illness for years and he promised to be my representative in a meeting amongst the Four Kings of Aithnen. Until he returns, there's nothing any of us can do to find him."

"Nothing?" Kadir repeated with rage. "Why don't you tell us where he is? We could find him ourselves!"

"Because, Kadir, thanks to your disregard of our respected laws, you two are my prisoners now. As such, you'll live out your days in the dungeons."

"But that's not fair!" Laney blurted out. "We didn't know it was illegal!"

"Your ignorance is irrelevant," the King said coldly. "By the letter of the law, the two of you are criminals, and for that, you must be punished." King Alban waved the back of his hand, signaling for the guards to take the prisoners away. Laney and Kadir squirmed and struggled, but it was to no avail; they were no match for the strength of the King's soldiers. After they were out of sight, King Alban said to Serafine, "Those two are hiding the falcon somewhere. That bird is Cail's only chance of beating you to the Shadow. We must find it by any means necessary. Later tonight, you need to go into the dungeons and find out where they hid the falcon."

"Consider it done," Serafine promised. Her father returned a grin of satisfaction.

Serafine spent the remainder of the afternoon alone in her bedroom, pondering over the events to come, over what she was about to become. Like a tear in a muscle that shoots nagging pain through a limb, her mind continually reminded her of the people she would hurt, the people she would kill. Children were crawling through mind, searching for a trace of mercy, but there was none to be found. *Mercy is for the weak hearted,* her father had always said, *it is nothing more than an opportunity for the lesser folk, the pawns, to prey upon those who deserve the riches, those who have worked so diligently for everything they have.* She reminded herself of her disposal of Mishal and of Cail, how easily they had fallen to her deceit. "I've done it before, and I'll do it again," she said to herself. This time, she would use the entire city as a stepping stone.

Three soft knocks tapped on Serafine's door. "Yes?" Serafine called out. The door creaked open and Ina, Serafine's mother, walked through. Her skin was pale, as though she had been visited by a ghost. Something, or someone, had frightened her to her brim. She quietly shut the door behind her.

"This has to stop," Ina said firmly.

"What does?" Serafine asked.

"Everything your father has planned: Your venture to the Shadow, you consuming Malgor's spirit, the empire and the pain it'll inflict on everyone. It must come to an end. The idea of this all-powerful Empress, it's not who you truly are, Serafine. You're only becoming who your father envisions you should be, not what will truly make you happy. Is total dominion worth the cost of all the lives that will be cast aside?"

That question had been haunting Serafine's mind the entire afternoon. She had mastered the art of manipulating the closest people around her, just like her father. Mishal, Cail, Laney, Kadir, everyone who cared for her were nothing more than pawns. Is that truly what she was destined to do? Was she born to be a conjurer of deceit?

"I don't know if it's worth the cost. I don't know if this is truly what I want. All I know is I have no choice but to push forward," Serafine responded, keeping her eyes pointed toward her feet which were dangling off the side of her bed.

"That's not true at all," her mother responded. "Your father has manipulated and controlled a lot of powerful people in his life, he's corrupted a lot of minds. However, he doesn't yet possess your will or heart. The path you take will be the path you choose."

Serafine said nothing in response, for she knew her mother was right, but she didn't have the courage to admit it. The thought of being responsible for the deaths of her own brethren was eating away at her sanity, corroding it like a violent acid. Finally, she asked, "Why haven't you said anything to dad? Why haven't you defended me?"

"Your father's love and affection for me is gone, replaced by his mind's obsessive compulsion to create your everlasting empire. He's lost his sanity, lost his resolve, and, worst of all, he's lost his compassion. Now, why haven't I defended you? Even though I am the Queen, the King has ultimate authority over everyone. I fear that if I speak out against him, I'll be the next victim to be locked away in those forsaken dungeons. No one is safe from him."

"So, what can we do?" Serafine asked.

Ina remained silent for a moment, pondering over their options. Then, she said, "You need to find the falcon and fly far away from here. Go live in Darzomil until your father's time has passed. Only then would it be safe for you to return."

Serafine dreaded the thought of being trapped in Kordon once again, but it was, unquestionably, the best option. "As much as it pains me to be away from you once again, I think it's the right thing to do," Serafine said.

"I do as well," Ina said with a bright smile. Then, for the first time in centuries, she hugged her daughter as tightly as she could. Serafine held on, as though it was the last time she would feel the warmth of her mother's body.

Serafine always hated going into the dungeons of the castle. The air was plagued by the foul stench of the prisoners, damp moisture crawled on her skin, and faint screams of pain and agony could be heard howling from tortured victims. The dungeons were an accursed pit of misery in Kye. Disbelieving eyes locked onto Serafine as she passed each cell. Prisoners looked at the Princess of Kye with incredulity, wondering why a noble had ventured down into the depths of the city. The guards directed Serafine through the intertwining corridors until she arrived at the cell belonging to Laney and Kadir.

"You have a lot of nerve coming down here," Kadir said after seeing Serafine's face. "We should've seen you for the traitor you are. There's not even a meeting amongst the Kings, is there? And Cail doesn't even know he's being lied to by one of his closest allies, does he?"

Serafine ignored Kadir's accusations and said, "I've come here because I want to help Cail." Kadir and Laney both scoffed at Serafine. "Please, listen to me. Cail is headed toward a trap and I won't save him in time if I travel on foot, but I could if I fly through the air."

"And you expect us to hand Emey over to you while we remained locked away?" Laney protested.

"Unfortunately, I can do nothing to free you without Cail, and I can't save Cail without Emey. I beg of you, tell me where to find Emey, it's our only chance to rescue Cail," Serafine pleaded. Laney and Kadir stood in silence, weighing their options, of which there were few. Kadir looked over to Laney and she nodded back to him.

"It goes against my better judgement, but I suppose we have no other choice," Kadir said with a heavy sigh. "There's a forest to the west of this city, you'll find her there. I don't care how you do it, but just ensure Cail's safety."

"Thank you. You made the right choice," Serafine said. Then she whispered something to the guard standing next to her and darted out of the dungeons.

After Serafine was out of earshot range, Laney asked, "Do you think she's telling the truth?"

"I was hoping you would know," Kadir responded. "I do know that we're of no use to Cail in here."

"I'm sorry," Laney said, nearly in tears. "It's my fault that we're trapped in here. If I would've listened to you and been more patient, we wouldn't be imprisoned right now."

"Laney, you can't blame yourself. You saw a tiny window of opportunity to save Cail and took a chance. It's what anybody would've done. We all do crazy things for the people we love." Kadir's comforting words brought a light smile to Laney's face. Although they were trapped in a cell, deep beneath Kye's castle, and although their home was leagues away, and although Cail's life was still in danger, Laney's heart still felt warm. In that moment, she realized there was one thing, and one thing only, that would pull them both through this struggle: hope. Her heart feasted on the hope and it nourished her body.

While the King's guards scurried to tell him the news, Serafine made her way out of the city and ventured to the desert in the west to find Emey. Perhaps the sun's blistering heat began playing tricks on her mind, but she was convinced she heard voices ringing inside her mind, tugging her conscience this way and that. "Your mother is right. Too many people would suffer, too many people would die. Malgor's powers should remain hidden in the Shadow," one of the voices said, trying to convince her to stay away from the Shadow. Then, another voice, much louder and more ominous, spoke to her. "If you don't find this power, Cail will. He craves the acquisition of power and dominance just as much as you do. He knows you and your father betrayed him. How long do you think you'll escape his wrath if he consumes Malgor's darkness?"

"No," Serafine said aloud, shaking her head. "I know Cail. He wouldn't do something like that. He would only try to stop me from entering the Shadow."

"You're only fooling yourself," the dark voice said, beating against her skull like an ocean's waves. "You think you know him, but a new persona will be revealed when he comes face to face with this ancient spirit. Cail will have no control over it; his mind will succumb to the temptation." Serafine didn't want to believe what she was hearing, but she couldn't cast aside the doubt that the voice was cementing in her heart. Despite her mother's wishes, there was but one choice for Serafine: She must go to the Shadow, she must claim Malgor's powers before Cail could.

Chapter 22: Weightless

Cail climbed up the shrine's ladder and through the portal. The ladder led him into the room of a dark hut with a rounded ceiling. He coughed from inhaling the dirt and dust that polluted the air in the hut. It seemed as though the room had remained untouched for centuries. Thick cobwebs hung from the walls like curtains, portraits and paintings were discolored and faded, and the furniture was torn. On a tiny wooden table was a rusted dagger, not much longer than Cail's hand. Knowing that it would serve him better than nothing, he took the dagger and hung it from his belt.

Through the front door of the hut was a village of identical huts. They all rose just a little higher than Cail's head. Then, Cail noticed something that should've screamed at him like Emey's screech: The open sky was blue. He rubbed his eyes, unbelieving of what he saw. "Serafine returned the Shadow Stone," Cail said to himself. This left the door wide open for his return to Kordon, or at least it would've if he had Emey with him. Then, a horrible thought struck his mind: *Perhaps Serafine had already entered the Shadow.* It wasn't beyond the realm of possibilities. If it was true, there was no time to lose.

The village appeared to be deserted. It was silent; so quiet that Cail wondered if there was anyone alive at all. His question was answered when a voice called to him from afar. "Hello!" Cail spun his head around and saw an elderly man hobbling toward him. The man had white, dry hair that reached down to his shoulders and a thick beard that matched in hue. Once the old man arrived, he said, "My name's Edgar. It's a pleasure to meet you, son." Then he extended a bony hand for Cail to shake.

"My name's Cail," he said with a gentle smile, accepting Edgar's welcome.

"What's a young chap such as yourself doing in this rundown town?"

"To be perfectly honest, I've lost my way. I'm trying to get back to Kye."

The man grunted, obviously having a poor taste from the city's reputation. "I don't know why anyone would want to go there. That city is on the verge of war, it's been crumbling for years and it's about to break."

"You're not the first one to say that," Cail responded.

"And I doubt I'll be the last, but that's enough grim talk for now," Edgar said, brightening his face once again. "You look famished. Follow me and the villagers will treat you to a proper meal." Cail opened his mouth to protest, but his empty stomach growled, and he accepted Edgar's generous offer. As Edgar hobbled along, he said, "You have impeccable timing, Cail. We're preparing for the Feast of Friends, which is aptly named. The King has heavily taxed us and stolen much of what we used to have, but every year, all the people of the village gather together and conjure a wonderful meal for everyone. During this time, we come to appreciate what we do have and we set aside our frustrations."

"That's very noble of you," Cail said with a gentle smile. As they approached the feast, the warm scent of freshly roasted pork filled the air. In a way that didn't seem possible, Cail grew hungrier. Weeks had passed since his last full meal and the severity of his fatigue had become all too apparent. Jubilant clamor rang in his ears and for the first time since his arrival, Cail didn't feel leagues away from home, he didn't feel like a foreigner. In a way, he was reminded of Elona. Hundreds, if not thousands, of villagers sat at dozens of long, wooden tables over a stretch of land. In the center of the land was a massive, circular table that held a vast assortment of appetizers, entrees, and desserts. "This is amazing," Cail said in awe.

Edgar ignored Cail's comment and shouted, "Hello, everyone! This is Cail and he's come to join in on our festivities. Let's give him a warm welcome!" All the villagers raised their glasses and mugs in unison as a way of accepting him into their clan and then they all returned to their meals and conversations. Edgar turned to Cail and said, "Please, help yourself to whatever you'd like."

Cail couldn't believe all the food that laid before him. He filled his plate with thick portions of pork, fresh fruit and cooked vegetables, as well as a slice of flawlessly fluffy cake. As Cail ate, he could feel his muscles absorbing the energy and nutrients, as though he was breathing in the winds of Kordon once again.

"So, what brings you to our humble village, my lad?" Edgar asked after giving Cail a chance to work through his plate of food.

Cail finished his mouthful of food and then answered, "Honestly, it's a long story that I'd rather not get into. In short, there's someone in Kye I need to find and take with me."

"Who is it? Maybe we can help you," Edgar responded, trying to pry information out of Cail's mind.

"I can't tell you who it is, but I can tell you I need to find the Buried Temple, but I haven't the slightest idea of where to look," Cail said.

Edgar's eyes widened, shocked by Cail's answered. He leaned closer to Cail and whispered, "You're looking for Mishal, aren't you?"

Cail was taken aback. He felt as though Edgar had read his thoughts and knew exactly of all his intentions. Cail didn't know how to respond other than to ask, "How do you know that name?"

"I was going to ask you the same question," Edgar responded with a hushed voice. "A long time ago, Mishal was taken away from all of us, but the heartache struck me the worst, like a dagger slowly piercing through one's skin. I was the one who loved him more than anyone could. Mishal is my son."

"Your son is the Descendant of Kordon?" Cail asked, bewildered.

"Ah, but that title has been stripped from him, hasn't it? The witch and her fiendish father stole it from him, like a thief who steals gems and jewels. They're treacherous, Serafine and her father. Their words are berries with toxins and poison flooded throughout its juices. The gullible partake of their comforting words and gracious manners, but they only want to take advantage of those who will allow them."

"I know," Cail responded, sharing in Edgar's disgust and angst toward Serafine and King Alban. "That's why I must find your son. I need his help to take down the existing regime. With Mishal's help, I can ensure that no one is ever hurt by their deceit again."

"It's folly," Edgar said, shaking his head in disapproval. "Their family has suffocated the entire nation of Aithnen for centuries. A young boy such as yourself can possess no hope against their prowess and might."

"I'm not just a simple boy," Cail interjected with mysterious confidence. "I can save your son, I can save Aithnen. You have no idea what I'm capable of." Cail had no idea where this courage and mettle had come from, but it felt invigorating and organic. He felt as though he could barge through the castle's doors and take down the King with his bare hands, even though that was far from the truth. What was true, however, was that all of his struggles and all of his obstacles had built his strength and although he possessed the speed and agility of the wind, he had learned of the tenacity of fire. Cail leaned in closer and said, "Please Edgar, the entire world will be in grave danger if I can't find Mishal. All of our lives depend on him."

For a long moment, Edgar sat silently, pondering over what Cail had told him. He rubbed his thick beard and his eyes became glazed. Finally, he said, "It goes against my better judgment, but I'll help you. In return, you must promise to bring my son home. I only wish to see him one last time."

"Of course," Cail vowed without hesitation.

"Very well, then. Follow me and I'll take you to where you need to go," Edgar whispered to Cail. As the old man led Cail out of the village, he said to Cail, "Many people view the Buried Temple as a sacred ground, a holding place for divine artifacts, but I know it for what it truly is: a prison. My son has been cooped up there for centuries with no hope of escape, that is, until now. Though he probably doesn't know who you are, you're his only hope of escape. Alban's guards think they've sealed off the only entrance to the temple, but they obviously haven't scoured through every crack and crevice. There's a tunnel just outside the village that worms through the ground and leads straight to the Buried Temple."

"If this is true, then why haven't you freed Mishal yourself?" Cail asked.

"We're a generous and merciful village, but we're nowhere near as courageous as you. None of us have ever attempted to brave the Buried Temple and steal the King's ultimate prisoner from under his nose. If you succeed in doing this, our village will be indebted to you for every day the sun rises."

Just outside of the village was a terrain with tall, thick, emerald blades of grass swaying in the wind. Robust trees were scattered across the land, creating a dark shield from the morning's sunlight. Then, without warning, Edgar halted and pointed a railing finger toward a dark crevice in the ground, which was barely wide enough for Cail to crawl through. "That is your path forward. It's a tunnel that winds and turns, but there are no forks in the road ahead of you. When you reach the Buried Temple, you must move as silently as a snake. If the guards find you, I fear they'll also find this secret passage."

"They won't hear a sound from me," Cail promised with confidence.

"You best be off, then. The best of luck to you, Cail," Edgar said with a sincere smile. Cail nodded and then squeezed through the hole in the ground. It was a tight fit, but Cail managed to slither his entire body through until he slid down a steep slope of moist dirt and mud. He came to an abrupt stop when he slammed into the bottom of the tunnel. Darkness enveloped Cail; all was invisible to him. The ground gave way to his weight, sinking his feet into the dirt. Cail could feel the moisture clinging to his skin, dampening his clothes. The venture through the tunnel was a lonely one. There was nothing to see, nothing to listen to. He had to endure the thoughts pounding against the inner walls of his skull. Cail wondered if the old man was truly Mishal's father. *It could be a trap.* Cail thought. Edgar had sent him into a dark tunnel, which could lead anywhere for all Cail knew.

The ground solidified and Cail's feet no longer sunk into mud. Instead, he could feel solid concrete. Then, as though a hand uncovered a candle's flickering flame, the tunnel became illuminated and the suffocating grasp of darkness loosened its hold. His eyes felt relieved, like a cool breeze brushing against his face during a scorching day in the desert. The walls of the tunnel were rough and jagged, like the surface of a boulder. Cail followed the weaving corridor until he found the first sign of life since his departure from Edgar. The life Cail saw was trapped within impenetrable iron bars. The prisoner sat with shoulders that slumped over his heart, fully displaying his defeated lifelessness.

"Mishal?" Cail whispered, standing next to the bars.

The prisoner's head slowly lifted and dark eyes looked at Cail from beneath a mat of black hair. "How do you know my name?" he responded with a hoarse, raspy voice.

Part of Cail's mind didn't know what to say. Was he supposed to say he heard an ancient tale from a talking amphibian? Or was he supposed to say he had been made a fool by the same girl who had robbed Mishal of his powers? Despite these thoughts, there was only one sentence Cail could utter. "You're the Descendant of Aithnen."

Mishal looked at his feet, which wore stained, torn, leather shoes, and lowered his head once again. "Not anymore, kid. I was bested by the King's daughter. She's a snake. You see the good in her heart, or at least the good she wants you to see. Eventually, she'll break your trust like a frail twig."

"She already has," Cail said, almost subconsciously. He could feel Mishal's affliction and suffering. Or was it his own? There was a blurred cloud in his mind that obscured his feelings and emotions. "I'm one of the Four, and I thought she was as well. Serafine betrayed me to my death, but I was grossly underestimated. I survived her treachery."

"You're the Descendant of Kordon?" Mishal asked, intrigued. Cail nodded in response. "The world has waited a long time for you. Prophecies have been told across generations about The Last Descendant. Darkness has plagued the nations of Neptil for an age and countless people have needlessly suffered, but you're the catalyst that will propel the entire world into an era of peace."

"I will do everything I can to fulfill those prophecies, but first, Serafine must be dealt with. I can't defeat her on my own and I need your help."

"Cail, Serafine has all the powers that the gods granted to me. You must climb this mountain under your own strength," Mishal responded.

"I don't think I can," Cail said. He vividly remembered his tumultuous trek through Aithnen's wilderness. It had claimed much of his strength, energy, and vigor. His past struggles would pale in comparison to the task at hand. Serafine was growing in strength with every passing day and if she managed to acquire Malgor's spirit, she would liken herself to the cruel malice that was Kalil.

"If you don't find a way to stop Serafine, I fear no one will," Mishal said with a hushed voice. "I'll be of no use if I go with you, but I do have something that you'd be interested in." Mishal reached into the pocket of his torn and stained pants and retrieved something Cail least expected to see: an Air Rune. It wasn't just any rune, though. Cail had seen it once before when he saw Serafine cast it over the edge of a cliff and into a rushing river. He had convinced himself that the rune was lost for eternity, buried beneath a rolling current of water. Yet, the rune was now just a few inches from his fingers.

"How?" Cail asked.

"To be honest, by a string of dumb luck, that is, if you don't believe in fate. There's an arena deep within this prison. Once a week, the guards drag me down into that pit of misery and torture me. I'm beaten, whipped, kicked, punched. Every week, I come within an inch of death, and that's when they stop. Serafine can only possess her powers for as long as I'm alive, so everything they've worked for will come unraveled if I were to die.

"Anyways, while I was being beaten to a pulp, one of the guards, I didn't see who, hit me in the back of my head with a rock, or at least that's what I thought it was. The pain was piercing and my head throbbed as though an iron staff had walloped against my skull. I collapsed onto the ground and inches away from my body was this Air Rune. It immediately encapsulated my eyes, but for reasons unbeknownst to me, none of the other guards seemed to notice. Instead, they were bickering and arguing amongst themselves over some trivial matter. I seized the opportunity, snatched the Air Rune and hid it before the guards could notice. I took my finding of the Air Rune as a symbol of fate, a sign that my redemption would soon be coming."

"Serafine will pay for what she's done and you will enjoy the free air once again, that much I can promise you," Cail said. He was determined to ensure that no one would ever suffer on account of Serafine's lies ever again.

"Only Serafine's death can bring about the second coming of the Descendant of Aithnen. Are you prepared to do that?"

"Of course," Cail said with unbreakable confidence. Serafine had been his friend and companion in the past, but those days ended as soon as he learned of her treachery. Now, she was his sworn enemy; threatening his life and the lives of those he cared about the most. She was even putting Laney's life in danger. The thought of Serafine killing Laney stirred Cail's anger and he fumed.

"Since that's the case, I think the time has come for you to take what's rightfully yours," Mishal said, then he extended his arm, freely offering the Air Rune. Cail quickly snatched it away and held it in the palm of his hand. For reasons Cail couldn't explain, this rune felt different than the rest. It carried a heavier weight, testing Cail's strength. White light illuminated from the foreign markings on the stone's surface. Then, the rune sunk into the skin of Cail's palm; his body was absorbing the rune's powers. Howling wind started to swirl around Cail's body and Mishal used his arm to shield himself from the violent gusts. After gradually descending, the rune disappeared into Cail's palm and the vortex of wind slowly died until the air was still once again.

Cail opened his eyes and saw Mishal staring back at him with eyes that were partially filled with amazement and partially filled with horror. "What's wrong?" Cail asked, but Mishal couldn't respond. Then, Cail noticed Mishal was staring at his feet. Cail looked down and saw something that nearly made his heart skip a beat. His feet were no longer touching the ground! In that moment, Cail felt completely weightless. He was entirely unattached from the ground beneath his feet. Instead, his body clung to the air and he felt a sense of unity with the wind. Not only did his body feel weightless, but his mind did as well. Stressful thoughts swam away like frightened fish in the ocean. All of a suddenly, Cail felt as though he was invincible and no force of evil could ever stop him. Slowly, Cail's body descended until his feet were firmly planted on the ground once again. However, the feeling of weightlessness didn't dissipate; it thrived in his mind.

"You can fly!" Mishal exclaimed, still stunned by what he saw.

"It appears I can," Cail responded.

"You've never done that before?"

"Not until now."

"Well, this makes your journey back to Kordon significantly easier. If you're swift, you may yet have a chance of beating Serafine to the Shadow," Mishal said.

"Not without you," Cail responded. "I need to find a way to free you."

"No," Mishal protested. "Right now, no one else knows you're here. The second the guards see my empty cell, they'll know you set me free. If you leave me in my cell and escape this prison unnoticed, the King's army will never suspect anything."

Cail didn't like leaving Mishal behind, but he knew it was probably the best option. "I'll come back for you," Cail promised as he looked into Mishal's eyes.

"I know you will. The lives of the innocent and pure rest in good hands."

Chapter 23: A Hidden Gem

Flying through the open sky was exhilarating. Cail didn't realize how much of a toll Aithnen's fumes had taken on his body until he saw the ground shrinking beneath his feet. Houses and stores turned into grains of sand, the vast forest became no more significant than blades of grass, and mountains were humbled into being rolling hills. From this altitude, the world wasn't so gargantuan, from this height, Cail felt like he was larger than the realm beneath him. As the ground retreated, the skies opened like the towering doors of a castle. The blue sky was the immaculate marble floor of the ballroom, the clouds were the paintings and portraits of the kings and queens of years past, and the beaming sun was the glistening chandelier that ensnared the eyes of all those who gazed upon its beauty. The sky was a castle and Cail was its King.

As Cail ascended, the islands of Kordon came into view and he finally felt at home. He could see Silman directly over his head, he could see the vast island of Cestmir and the Ivory City to the north, and to the east, he could see his home, Elona. Cail so desperately longed to see Laney again, even though he was certain she was still infuriated by his departure. That reunion would have to wait for a later time, though. Stopping Serafine was a much more pressing matter. Cail flew above the island's surface and began his ascension up the side of the mountain. Even though the golden sun was shining its light upon the entire world, the mountain's air was still frigid. Boreal gusts bit Cail's skin and stabbed him like a needle.

Upon arriving at the mountain's entrance, Cail couldn't help but reminisce on his first venture into Darzomil, when he learned of his heroic fate. Of course, he couldn't remember Darzomil and not think of Caldir. Remembering the old wizard brought sadness into Cail's heart. It wasn't fair that Caldir was captured and tormented by Kalil, it wasn't fair that he succumbed to such a malicious force of darkness, it wasn't fair that Caldir was dead. "I should've done something," Cail said to himself. "If I wasn't so weak, I could've saved him."

"There was nothing you could've done." Cail nearly jumped into the air from his fright. The apparition of Caldir was standing next to Cail, wearing a smile of amusement.

"Caldir?" Cail said, unable to believe what he saw.

"Yes, Cail, it's me. I felt your melancholy and I've come to offer comfort."

"That's kind of you," Cail said. "I just wish there was a way to bring you back to the realm of the living. The tasks ahead of me are daunting."

"While that's true, it's not the first challenge you've faced, and it won't be the last. You truly are an exceptional person, Cail. You're capable of far more than I ever anticipated. Darkness has fended off the light of the world for centuries, but you're gradually chipping away at the walls of evil. The dawning of a new age is upon us."

"That sounds wonderful, but I fear that I'm grossly outmatched. Serafine is stronger than me. Her mastery over fire gives her an advantage over me."

"You're much faster and smarter, though," Caldir argued. "Doubt can be a crippling crutch that defeats you before you ever enter the fight. You must be more resilient, Cail. Serafine won't be beaten by her own mind, and you shouldn't be beaten by yours." Cail knew Caldir was right. Serafine's mind was as strong as the rest of her body. In order to be the victor, Cail needed to believe in himself and cling to his confidence.

"Thank you," Cail said with a bright smile. "I still wish there was a way to bring you back. The world needs you just as much as it needs me."

"I wish I could come back, Cail, but my time has passed. My destiny is fulfilled and I accomplished what I was sent to do," Caldir replied.

"Which is?" Cail asked.

"Find the Last Descendant. Now, you must fulfill your destiny as well. Go in the mountain to Darzomil and find Wallen, he will lead you to the Shadow." With those final words, Caldir's ghost slowly faded away until he vanished completely. Cail stood alone, before the entrance to Darzomil, but he didn't feel alone. He felt as though Caldir was still standing by his side, willing to follow him into battle. For the first time, Cail could feel the wizard's strength enter his body and course through his muscles.

Cail entered the side of the mountain and was relieved to discover that the frigid wind hadn't penetrated the tunnel. The mountain was surprisingly warm, like an oven that was baking bread. Everything had remained exactly as Cail remembered. Every groove in the walls, every clang sounding from the miners' hammers, every step Cail took on his way to Darzomil, he remembered. It was as though Cail had left the mountain only days ago.

Darzomil buzzed like a legion of busy bees. Hordes of people swam through the city like stormy waves in the heart of an ocean. Clamor echoed throughout the cave; people engaging in quaint conversations, people bartering in the marketplace, people arguing with their friends and family. Even though the city was full of life and vitality, it was far too assiduous for Cail's liking. He felt much more comfortable living in his peaceful home of Elona.

Cail didn't have the slightest clue regarding where he should start looking for Wallen, and there was no one else in the entire city with whom Cail was familiar. If Cail was going to succeed in finding Wallen, he would have to do so with grit and determination. Just inside the city's limits, there was a marketplace with a large assortment of shops: Jewelries, groceries, antiques, and even an armory. Cail went from one store to the next, asking anyone he could for Wallen's location, but no one knew.

After visiting nearly every shop, Cail had nearly given up hope. Then he heard a woman's grunts coming from a nearby jewelry shop. Cail burst through the doors and saw an elderly woman struggling with a box that looked as though it weighed as much as she did.

"Let me help you with that," Cail said as he grabbed the box from the woman's grasp. She couldn't talk because she was out of breath, so she pointed to an open doorway in the back of the store, signaling for Cail to take the box back there. The box was so heavy that it strained Cail's arms to carry it; he wasn't sure how the woman managed to lift it off the ground. Cail slowly progressed through the store, careful not to bump into any valuables. There were innumerable gems and treasures throughout the store, protected in glass casing. The entire room glistened like crystals in a cave, fully displaying their immaculate beauty. Through the doorway was a storage closet packed from the floor to the ceiling with thousands of trinkets and keepsakes.

As Cail placed the dense box on the ground, the woman said, "Thank you, young man. I don't think I could've carried that box by myself."

"What do you have in there?" Cail asked between deep breaths.

"I'm not entirely sure. A mysterious gentleman dropped it off to me as a donation. It's probably filled with junk, but a few items of interest might pop out. Collecting is my trade. People bring their trash, or what they deem as such, to me and I find the value in what they fail to."

Cail looked more closely at the cluttered horde in the closet. There were plenty of old, dusty books, each the width of his palm. Worn and torn paintings and decorations leaned against the wall, remnants of the past. Untouched boxes were stacked on top of each other, waiting to be sorted through, along with large sacks with grooves and indentations from the mysterious objects they contained. Cail was just happy this wasn't his store; he had no idea where he would begin, how he would organize this mess, how he would separate the valuable collectibles from the junk. Then something caught his eye. A glimmer from beneath a chaotic pile of books ensnared his gaze.

"What's that?" Cail asked, pointing to what he saw.

"You're a curious mind, aren't you?" the woman giggled. She saw what caught Cail's attention and immediately recognized it. The woman retrieved it from the pile, tugging mightily on a handle that was crushed beneath the weight of dozens of heavy books. In her hands she held a massive sword with a seamless blade. The spotless iron shined like the morning sun and the hilt was made of solid bronze. It was the perfect sword, seeming as though it had been crafted only hours ago. "This is an old heirloom of mine. It's clearly endured the test of time."

"Old?" Cail repeated with incredulity. "It looks like it's never fought through a single battle."

"Nor do you, but we both know that's not the case," she said with a grin.

"You know who I am?" Cail asked.

"It'd be a shame if I didn't. You did save all of our lives, after all. Defeating an oppressive tyrant is bound to come with a bit of notoriety, don't you think?" Cail hadn't considered that. He wasn't familiar with anyone in the mountain, but they were very familiar with him. "You're grossly mistaken, Cail. This sword was at the forefront of a terrible battle between two great nations: Kordon and Aithnen. Carnage and bloodshed flooded a vast plane in the Domain of Fire. My great ancestor, Sirith, wielded this sword and used it to carve through the lives of thousands of enemies on that day. It was a day the Aithnenians would crave to forget, but none of them ever could."

"How long ago was this war?" Cail asked.

"Thousands of years ago, when the nations of the world were still young. The leaders and kings were ambitious, hungry for power, craving more land. Charismatic personalities clashed against each other like boulders in a head-on collision. Along with power, the Aithnenians coveted the freedom of Kordon. We're blessed with the open air, cool winds, and golden sunlight. They succumbed to jealousy; it firmly grasped their hearts and manipulated their minds. Aggression became their downfall as they planned their overtake of the Domain in the Skies. The Kordonians were grossly underestimated, though. The strength and unity of the Dragonfolk was unmatched. This blade was just one of many to slay the aggressors."

"What became of the Aithnenians? For how long did we rule over them?"

"Rule over them?" the woman repeated, Cail nodded. "Cail, we're a peaceful nation. Our lives were threatened and we responded accordingly. Tell me, when Kalil imprisoned your loved ones and their lives hung by a thread, how did you react? Did you not become the aggressor?"

Like a bright light flashing before his eyes, Cail instantly remembered his rage, his fury. The hatred and anger he felt toward Kalil spread throughout his body like a wildfire. It was something that was beyond his control. "Yes, I did," Cail said after a moment of silence. "Why are you telling me this?"

"Because I can see into the depth of your eyes. You have the look of someone who is being threatened." The woman looked down at the sword in her hands and then offered it to Cail. "I want you to take it."

Shocked by the propoundment, Cail said, "No, I can't. It belonged to your ancestors. I can't take that away from you."

"My ancestors would be proud that their sword was passed along to the Last Descendant. Take this weapon; you'll need it to fend off the threat that looms overhead." Cail took the sword by its bronze hilt and held it firmly within his grasp. It was strong enough to carve through armor like a knife sliding through bread, but it was light enough to swing like a tree branch. The woman turned around and dug deeper into the pile of books and retrieved a sheath for the sword, she handed it to Cail. He effortlessly slid the sword into its sheath and then strapped it onto his belt.

"I don't know your name, and yet, you graciously give me a gift like this?"

"My name is Adelia," the woman replied with a smile.

"Do you always give elegant presents to strangers?" Cail asked while wearing a sly smile.

"I must admit, you're the first person I've given a sword, but on occasion, I do freely offer my treasures to those who need it the most," Adelia replied. "Now, if you don't mind my asking, what war will be brought to the edge of that old sword?"

"There's no war. Not yet, anyways," Cail answered. "I'm hoping to prevent a war, to stop years of bloodshed. A friend has betrayed me, someone who I trusted, someone who was close to me. Even though I was blind for far too long, my eyes have been uncovered in the nick of time."

"Betrayal is the conception of all conflicts, wouldn't you agree? Nearly every war that was started, nearly every tyrannical regime that was erected, nearly every quarrel amongst kingdoms was instigated by a simple act of betrayal. It's simple, yet so destructive. You're kept in the dark, unaware of the happenings that surround you. Then, within the beat of the heart, the lights illuminate your world, and you see all there is to see. Your traitor is standing just before your face, looking at your stomach. You look down as well, and that's when you see it; the blade that was cast into your stomach, the killing strike. In that moment, a million questions rush through your brain. *Why would they do this? How did they do this? Who else knew about it? Why couldn't I see what they were doing?*

"All these questions are useless, of course. While your mind paralyzes your body, blood is gushing out of the freshly cut wound, pouring like a waterfall of anguish. There's no time for questions, no time to worry about the fine details. All you can do is patch the wound and ensure the traitor feels the same pain."

Adelia's words perfectly embodied how Cail felt when he learned the truth about Serafine. In a world filled with darkness and danger, his collection of allies was thin, and her betrayal only made matters worse. He felt as though shadows were pinning him into a corner. Cail still managed to stand in the light, but it wouldn't take long for the darkness to overcome him.

"I need to find a man named Wallen. He lives somewhere in the city, but I haven't the slightest idea of where to find him."

"Nor do I," Adelia responded. Cail let out a sigh of disappointment. "However, I do know someone who would. In the store neighboring mine, there is a young merchant named Toby. Along with owning and operating his own grocery, Toby is also responsible for Darzomil's annual census. If anyone would know where to find Wallen, it'd be him."

"I don't know how I could ever repay you," Cail said gratefully.

"You can repay me by honoring the sword's past. Use it to defeat those who threaten and betray you, use it to humble those who view themselves as mightier than the rest of the world."

"I will do that," Cail promised, giving a slight bow to Adelia. "I've been blessed with good fortune to have met you, Adelia."

"It's not fortune, my dear, it's destiny. The gods gifted you with a gentle heart, a heart with enough kindness to help a struggling woman. Many of the things that happen to us aren't a result of good fortune, but instead, they're a product of who we are."

As Cail left Adelia's store, he couldn't get her words out of his head, he couldn't stop wondering whether she was right or if she was just full of superstition. He considered the possibility that everything that was happening around him, all the changes in the world, were all predetermined. It seemed like a ludicrous notion. Cail felt as though he was fully in control of his own actions, however, the more he thought about it, the less control he appeared to have. Kalil had forced him into saving his loved ones, forced him into freeing the entire nation from a reign of darkness, and now, Serafine was forcing him to go to the Shadow. And yet, there were plenty of choices he had made under his own volition. Cail had chosen to venture into the forest and assume the responsibilities of the Last Descendant, he had chosen to leave his home and discover a world that was previously hidden from view, and he had chosen to travel with Serafine to Aithnen and unknowingly walked into her trap.

Bearing all that in mind, there was one more question that perplexed Cail: What was the truth? Was he in control of his own actions and his own life? Or was he nothing more than a puppet created by the gods, exercising their will? *I determine who I am and what I do.* Cail thought to himself. He wanted, more than anything, to believe it, but he couldn't. While he told himself that he could do whatever his heart desired, he conceded that he was being forced to the Shadow. *When will I cease to be a slave to the darkness?* That question resonated in his mind. It wasn't the gods who were controlling him, after all, it was the darkness. The forces of oppressive maliciousness and cruel evil were bending him over backwards, tugging him from one edge of the world to the next. As Cail walked toward Toby's shop, Cail said to himself, "I will no longer be a slave to darkness. It will bow to me."

Chapter 24: The Trap

"Toby's Comestibles" was splattered in royal blue paint on a rotting, wooden sign that hung over the shop's door. The name struck Cail as being odd and rough, but he shoved that thought aside and proceeded into the grocery. Dozens of people were crammed in each of the aisles, shoving each other aside to get to the food they needed. Cail was expecting a fistfight to break out at any moment because of everyone's angst and aggression, but, to his pleasant surprise, no conflicts arose. Along the back wall, he saw a counter with a young girl, who was about the same age as Laney, standing behind it. Cail gradually pushed his way to the back of the store, ignoring the angry glares and scolds from those he accidentally bumped into.

"Well, hello there," the girl said with a pleasant smile after Cail arrived at her counter. She was a pleasant looking girl; she had shiny, black hair that was neatly tied into a thick braid, blue eyes encapsulating all who gazed into them, and skin that was pale and without any blemishes.

"I'm looking for a man named Toby," Cail said.

"Who isn't?" the girl scoffed. "He hasn't shown his face all day long, leaving me alone with the chaos you see in the aisles."

"You have absolutely no idea where he is?" Cail asked, hoping for a lead.

"His bedroom is just above the store. The staircase is through that door," the girl said as she pointed to a door made of rusting iron. "However, I checked earlier this morning, but there was no sign of him anywhere."

"I'll go look for myself," Cail said brusquely. He opened the heavy, iron door and ascended the narrow staircase. The walls nearly touched his shoulders and the wooden stairs bent beneath his weight. Another iron door waited at the top of the staircase, but it was slightly cracked open. Cail cautiously pushed it, hoping for no threat to be awaiting his arrival. Instead, he found a quiet living room that was dimly illuminated by a small, flickering candle sitting on a round table in the center of the room. A thick, but also worn, rug was spread across the uneven, wooden floor and Cail could see a layer of dust resting on the old furniture. Everything seemed to be in its rightful place and Cail couldn't find anything out of the ordinary, that is, until he saw a thick, dark spot on the edge of the rug, a spot that appeared to be larger than Cail's head. Cail snatched the candle from the table and shined the light closer to the spot. After closer inspection, Cail noticed that a pool of blood had soaked into the carpet and there was a wide trail of maroon blood leading out of the living room, into the neighboring kitchen and through another cracked door.

Cail quickly followed the trail, but stopped at the door. He absorbed a deep inhalation into his lungs, trying to calm his nerves. The closed door was the last wall between him and whatever darkness awaited him. Cail pressed on the wall and it was leaden, either from its weight or from Cail's fear, but it moved nonetheless. A room filled with darkness revealed itself. There were no windows, so Cail's candle was the only source of illumination. Cail squinted his eyes, but he could only see a small area of the room in front of him. He looked at the floor and began following the trail of blood once again. Pain rushed into his foot when he rammed it into the leg of a bed. Cail cursed under his breath and stood still as he waited for the pain to simmer. Once it had, Cail held the candle closer to the bed and was terrified by what he saw. A young boy, Cail presumed the boy to be Toby, laid on the bed, facing toward the ceiling, with a dagger lodged in his chest. Toby remained as still as a stone and Cail could see the coldness of Toby's body, the coldness of death. Bloodstains seeped out of his chest, onto the bedsheets, and dripped down to the floor.

"Who could've done this?" Cail asked, once he had gathered his breath.

"She was right," said a new voice. Cail spun around and saw a couple dozen men, all of whom were much larger than Cail, standing with torches and pitchforks in their hands. The man at the front of the pack said, "She told us we'd find you here."

"She?" Cail repeated. "Who's she?" From behind the wall of men appeared Serafine, wearing a victorious grin, a smile filled with treachery. She had caught up to Cail, or possibly, he had caught up to her. Either way, they stood only a few steps apart, but she was accompanied by her own militia. "You," Cail said with resentment.

"Hello, Cail," Serafine responded, still with a confident smirk. Then she turned to the men and said, "We can't let this murderer get away, can we?"

"What? No! I didn't do it!" Cail responded, appalled by the accusation.

"Save your excuses for someone who cares," one of the men said as he violently snatched Cail's arm with his muscular grasp. "We know a murderer when we see one." As Cail was being dragged away, he flailed his limbs and jumped around, trying to escape. A club came crashing onto the back of his skull, quickly followed by unmatched burning and pain in his head. Then the room around him immediately went black.

When Cail awoke, he found himself lying on a bed that was as comfortable as a wooden plank. As he sat upright, his head was hit with a new wave of throbbing agony, nearly forcing his body back down to the bed. Fighting through the ache, he observed the room around him and discovered that he had been thrown into a jail cell. The floor was cracked and caved in the middle, a small bowl of water had been left by his bedside for his consumption, but no food, and a pair of rats could be heard scampering inside the walls.

"I hope you're making yourself comfortable. It'll be a long time before you breathe the free air again, if you ever do," said a familiar voice. Cail looked toward the iron bars of his cell and saw Serafine standing just outside with the same malicious grin. He could see the victory in her expression, the look that she knew she had beaten him.

Cail immediately rose from his bed, ignoring the massive headache, and got as close to Serafine as he could. "You killed Toby, didn't you?"

"No one likes a know-it-all," she responded with sarcasm.

"Why did you do it? He was completely innocent and blissfully uninvolved in our quarrel. Why kill him?"

"Because I knew he would be the only one in Darzomil who could lead you to Wallen. Originally, I was going to hide his body, but that would still leave the small window of opportunity for you to find the entrance to the Shadow. So, I decided to use Toby's corpse as a trap and you walked right into it."

Cail couldn't believe that he had fallen prey to Serafine again. He thought everything he had endured had made him wiser and stronger, had opened his narrow sight, but he felt as blind as ever. Serafine got the better of him once again; she precisely calculated Cail's every move and now, she had him trapped in an iron box. Cail didn't want to believe it; he couldn't believe it. There needed to be some other reality where he was the one standing outside Serafine's cell, where he had saved the world. If that reality did exist, it was far away from Cail.

"What are you still doing here?" Cail asked in a defeated tone. "Shouldn't you be heading to the Shadow?"

"Believe me, I will," Serafine responded with a taunting mannerism. "But first, I wanted to come here and soak in the warm bath of my victory."

When Serafine saw that Cail had nothing more to say to her, she proudly walked away on her way to the Shadow. Cail dejectedly sunk onto his bed once again, knowing there was nothing more he could do. Despite being trapped in a cold cell and having failed in his attempt to stop Serafine, Cail felt a strange sense of peace. He allowed his body to remain still and the pains and aches of all his joints drifted away like a thick fog being lifted by the morning sun. The short period of serenity was rudely interrupted by three piercing clangs on the iron bars of Cail's cell. Cail shot off the bed and saw Wallen standing just outside the bars. "I couldn't believe my ears when I heard it, but here you are," Wallen said with hostile words.

"Wallen, you have to believe me. I was set up, I would never do something such as this."

Wallen swiftly rose a thick hand in the air, signaling for Cail to be quiet. "I'm not here to listen to your lies. I've come to take you away to your death."

"What? No! You can't do that. I'm innocent!"

"That's enough, Cail!" Wallen shot back with a thunderous voice. "You were caught red-handed, and now it's time for you to face the consequences." The cell's door unlocked with a solid clang and Wallen walked into the cell with several burly guards following closely behind him. If Cail was to have any opportunity to escape, it would have to wait. He was grossly outnumbered; his efforts would've died before they even began. Wallen nodded his head and a couple of the guards strode toward Cail and briskly snatched his arms. They dragged Cail through the dark, damp corridors of the prison. As Cail passed by the cells, he could hear the prisoners murmuring amongst each other. Even though Cail tried with all his might to avoid eye contact, he couldn't help but catch the paralyzing gaze of some of the inmates. None of them said a word to Cail, but they didn't need to; their eyes did all the talking. They knew exactly where Cail was headed, they knew Cail's future was bleak, they knew of the terror he was about to face. Once outside of the prison, the civilians in the streets of Darzomil greeted Cail with hostility. The gentler souls did nothing except cast Cail a glance of disgust or mutter an unheard obscenity beneath their breath. However, there were several people, mostly men, but also some women, who screamed in Cail's face and spat at his feet. They knew what he had done, or at least, what he had been accused of doing. No one bothered to consider the possibility that Cail was innocent, to consider the possibility that he had been wrongly accused, to consider the possibility that Serafine was the real murderer who needed to be glared at, yelled at, and spat on.

The guards stopped on the edge of the city. "This is as far as our jurisdiction will allow us to go," said the guard who had a firm grasp on Cail's right arm.

"That's alright, gentlemen. I can handle things from here," Wallen said as he took Cail's arm into his muscular hand. The guards swiftly returned to their posts in Darzomil and Wallen and Cail began their trek away from the city. "You can relax now, Cail. I'm not going to hurt you."

"What? What was that all about, then?" Cail asked, shocked by what Wallen had said.

"I know you're innocent and I know Serafine pinned Toby's death on you. You see, I have a lot of leverage in this town, even in my late years. My eyes and ears encapsulate the entire city. Nothing happens in Darzomil that I don't know about."

"How?" Cail asked, amazed by Wallen's knowledge. "How have you managed to keep such a watchful eye over the city?"

"There are plenty of people in Darzomil who have very specific, confidential, and desperate needs; needs that I can meet. In exchange, they help me keep a close dome of surveillance."

"Why? You're not in a position of power, nor are you trying to acquire any leadership in Darzomil. Why go through the effort and trouble?"

"I can see why it's difficult for you to understand. At this stage in your life, you're a wanderer. You travel from one corner of the world to the next without blinking an eye. Neptil is an open field of grass to you. It's enticing to venture from one place to the next when you're young; I would know, I was just like you. I had an adventurous spirit and a heart that urgently craved to see wonders that would amaze my eyes. Believe me, now that you've catalyzed the opening of the world, the blending of nations, you'll witness cities and terrains you could never dream of. Neptil will seem as though it's a painting that could only be conjured by the chaotic meshing of colors.

"However, I'm well beyond the prime of my life. My bones are dry and my muscles are drained of their strength. You see, as much as one loves to travel, eventually there comes a moment in everyone's life where they crave to settle into their home and live out the rest of their days in the place they belong. Darzomil is where I belong, Cail. I'll admit, it's not the most glamorous city in the world, but it's a city I love. I don't keep a close eye on Darzomil because I want to possess power over smaller folk. Instead, I want to tightly surveil the city because I want to keep it safe, I want to preserve what I hold most dear."

"What do you hold most dear?" Cail asked, intrigued.

"Such a fine question," Wallen said with a gentle smile peaking from beneath his white beard. "To tell the truth, I enjoy the simple things: The warm aromas from all the shops, the buzz of the busy marketplace, the clamor of all the civilians. Even though many will find it to be inauthentic, I've developed a strong attachment to the sights and sounds that often go unnoticed. Once your journey ends, you should do the same, Cail."

"Move to Darzomil?" Cail asked, trying his best to the mask the appalment he felt toward the idea of living in the city buried beneath a towering mountain.

"No, my lad. I know your heart belongs somewhere else, and you should discover where that somewhere is. It may be Elona, or it may be a place you least expected to find. Wherever it is, make sure it's a place filled with small things you love, make sure it's filled with things no one could notice but you."

"I'll do that," Cail said with a smile. His first inclination was to believe that Elona was his eternal home, it was the refuge to which he would always return, but then a curious thought crossed his mind. *What if my home isn't a place, but rather, a person?* Cail thought silently. If that was the case, which he certainly thought it was, then there was only one name that came to his mind: Laney. Without a shadow of a doubt in Cail's mind, he knew that when he was with her, their surroundings didn't matter. They could be in Elona, Darzomil, Ijsbrandur, even Aithnen. As long as they were together, the warmth of happiness filled Cail's heart. Now, however, they were a world apart and he needed to do whatever was necessary to find her again.

Darzomil faded from view and Cail and Wallen were soon walking on the rough, rocky terrain of the mountain's colossal cavern. "Where are you taking me?" Cail asked.

"Serafine came here in hopes of finding the Shadow, didn't she?" Wallen asked in return, to which Cail nodded his head. "There's a temple beneath the city that I showed to her several weeks ago. At the time, she didn't know that it was the entrance to a hidden realm, but now that she knows, there's no telling what malevolence she could find there."

"I know what she seeks," Cail said with grim words. "If she finds it, I'm afraid even I won't be able to stop her."

"Serafine can't be too far ahead of you," Wallen said, trying to restore Cail's confidence. "She left Darzomil only a few hours ago." Wallen meant to offer comfort to Cail's worries, but no solace was found in the old man's words. Every second Cail lost to Serafine was another opportunity for her to find what she was looking for.

Wallen led Cail to a narrow staircase that curved along the edge of a steep cliff. Since there was no railing, Cail couldn't help but look down the decline into darkness. The thought of falling to his imminent death dizzied his vision and tossed his stomach. He had to take in a few deep inhalations to stop himself from fainting. The staircase wound down to the temple's entrance and Cail was floored by the glittering treasure that awaited within. Cail was immediately entranced by the jewels and gems; it was blatantly obvious that their value could be tied to no number. Cail reached his hand out to take hold of a nearby gold coin, which was engraved with a vast number of strange markings, but Wallen swiftly slapped the top of Cail's hand.

"You mustn't touch anything in this temple, save for that," Wallen said as he pointed toward the front of the cave. Cail immediately saw the object of interest. Beyond the overflowing mounds of gold, beyond the stone pillars, and beyond the colorful rainbow of jewels, there stood the silver statue of Loni, the mythical protector of Kordon, a majestic falcon with its wings fully extended.

"A falcon?" Cail said as he slowly approached the statue. "So Emey isn't alone?"

"This isn't just any falcon, it's the statue of a fabled beast from an ancient era, but that story must wait for a later time," Wallen said. "For now, all you need to know is that this is your window into the Shadow."

"A realm of darkness, hidden by a statue of silver," Cail whispered to himself. He reached his hand out to touch the falcon's chest, but his wrist was snatched by Wallen's powerful grasp.

"Wait. Before you enter, there's something about the Shadow you must know. I've walked into the Shadow once before, and I never will again. It's not just a dark realm, it's a twisted perversion of the world we know."

Wallen's words didn't soak into Cail's ears as he was much too eager to find Serafine and destroy the threat of her empire. Cail forcefully tugged his arm away from Wallen's grasp and braced his mind for whatever evil awaited him. He extended his arm further and cautiously placed his palm on the cold silver of the falcon's thick chest, sending him into the Shadow.

Chapter 25: The Shadow

Cail closed his eyes and braced his mind and body for the transition into the Shadow, but there seemed to be no difference. He opened his eyes once again and found himself still standing before the statue of Loni. Confused, he turned around and said to Wallen, "Nothing happened and time is running short. Soon, Serafine will be out of my reach!" Cail awaited a response, but none was given to him. Wallen stood a few paces away, blankly staring over Cail's head; he stood as still as the statue Cail had just laid his hand upon.

Cail looked around the temple and noticed something that terrified him: there was no color. The vibrant glittering of the treasure horde had dissipated and the temple was nothing more than a lifeless pile of bleak coins. He scooped up a handful of the coins and brought them within inches of his eyes. Even after tightly squinting his eyes, the coins remained colorless. For a moment, Cail's heart started to race and he hyperventilated, afraid that he was beginning to lose his sight. He was convinced that a mysterious curse was glued to the statue, plaguing all those who laid their hands upon it, spreading blindness like a disease. That didn't explain why Wallen's body was paralyzed, though. Cail looked at Wallen once again. With a pointed finger, Cail pushed into Wallen's thick chest, but it was as solid as stone.

"Welcome to the Shadow, Cail," a familiar voice said. Cail spun around and saw Claeg, the Hidden King, sitting upon a towering pile of coins and jewels, reaching far above his head. For the first time, Cail saw Claeg as someone who was more than an apparition, more than a remnant. Claeg's muscular legs were stout tree trunks, his broad shoulders were an iron fortress, and his pulsating arms were a pair of solid, wooden clubs. Even with all the power Cail possessed over the air, he wasn't convinced he could win a battle against the Hidden King.

"This is the Shadow? But everything is just like the real world," Cail said.

"Of course it is. Isn't your own shadow just like you? The Shadow is a mimicry of the world you know. There is no light here and it is colorless."

"Why is he frozen?" Cail asked, pointing toward Wallen.

"Because time is frozen. You see, Cail, many people who pass away come to the Shadow because they still have unfinished business in the real world. Perhaps they need a loved one to hear one last resolution, or maybe they seek revenge on the one who did them wrong. No matter the reason, those restless souls come here and wait in the Land of Frozen Time for the opportune moment." Cail immediately thought of his mother and instantly craved to see her again. It wasn't beyond the realm of possibility for that to happen. He wasn't very far from the Shadow's version of Elona, so perhaps, after his quarrel with Serafine had been settled, Cail could see his mother once more.

"Serafine. I have to find her," Cail said. "She mustn't be allowed to find Malgor's power."

A perplexed glance fell onto Claeg's face. "She's not here."

"What do you mean she's not here?" Cail asked, frustrated that he couldn't gain any sort of advantage on his adversary. "Serafine framed the murder of an innocent man on me so she could come to the Shadow. She must be here!"

"I've waited right here for your arrival. If Serafine would've beaten you to the Shadow, I surely would've told you."

"Well, there must be another entrance into the Shadow," Cail insisted.

"There is no other way into the Shadow. The only passage to or from this world is through the Statue of Loni. I don't know where Serafine is, but she isn't in the Shadow."

Cail couldn't think of any other place she could possibly be, but he was relieved that good fortune was finally smiling upon him. Even though his mind was still concerned about the sudden disappearance of Serafine, he was relieved that he was no longer trailing behind her furious pace.

"We'll wait for Serafine and ambush her upon arrival," Cail said confidently.

"Cail, do you remember the first time we met? In your dream?" Claeg asked. Cail recalled it vividly in his mind; it was a dismal vision filled with death and suffering. "All the violence, all the demise, all the destruction; it will be the result of Malgor's spirit."

"That's why we need to stop Serafine from finding it," Cail said.

"And when you stop her, what then? Who will be the next person to seek this foul malevolence? Will we not be facing the same amount of death? Malgor's spirit has thrived for far too long and it must be destroyed."

Every corner of Cail's mind was telling him to wait for Serafine and pounce on her when she arrived, however, he knew that if he did that, he would remain vulnerable to the possibility of her escape, something he simply couldn't afford to have happen. If Cail was to ensure Serafine never laid her treacherous hands on Malgor's malignant magic, he would have to destroy it himself.

"Alright, we'll destroy it," Cail said to Claeg. "Where must we go?"

"I'm not entirely certain, but I have a hunch."

"A hunch?" Cail repeated. "Under no circumstance can Serafine be allowed to come within spitting distance of Malgor's spirit. The fate of the world depends on us. If we're going anywhere, we must be certain, without a shadow of a doubt, that it's the right place to go."

"Cail, relax," Claeg said nonchalantly. "I'm confident in my guess and you need to learn to place more trust in me."

"I'm sorry, but my trust has been shaken by the actions of a lot of people. Lately, I've felt as though the only person I can trust is me."

"You can't allow the lies and deceit of a few bad people ruin the faith you have in everyone as a whole. If you close your heart and your mind, you'll be secluded from those who wish to help you."

For a brief moment, Cail felt ashamed of himself. The last opportunity for him to save the world from Serafine's greed and avarice was standing just before him, and he needed only to let it in. He needed to let go of the quarrels he had with Serafine, the Blue Assassins, and anyone else who had ever wronged him and he also needed to accept the helping hand that was extended toward him. "Where do you suggest we go?" Cail asked.

"To the Castle of Taurim. In life, Malgor was greatly attached to the entire city and the castle and he were inseparable. He clung to it with all his strength, hopelessly addicted to its walls, its halls, its winding stairways. Surely, his spirit would've instantly craved to find the castle in the Shadow."

"We have an arduous venture in front of us," Cail said regretfully.

"Yes, *you* do," Claeg corrected Cail. "I'm the master of the Shadow, and you are merely a visitor. I will wait for you on the castle's doorsteps. Until then, you must find your own way." Claeg's body started to fade away like a ghost until he was completely invisible. Cail stood alone in the Shadow. Isolation and solitude enshrouded Cail like a black, stormy cloud. Although he couldn't quite place a finger on why, being alone in the Shadow was much different than being alone back in the real world. Here, the knowing that he was separated from everyone else was a heavy burden that weighed mightily on his heart. The curse of sequestration draped iron chains over Cail's shoulders and cramped his spine.

Despite his ill feeling of loneliness, Cail ventured out of the colorless temple and made his way toward Darzomil. In all his adventures, Cail had witnessed ferocious monstrosities, merciless storms and punishing environments, cities that were entirely abandoned, but none of what he had ever witnessed could prepare him for what he saw in that moment. Darzomil, or at least the Shadow's diminished version of the city, was a city that was frozen in time. Every person wore the same expression they had just before Cail laid his palm on the Statue of Loni. Some people wore an expression of happiness, others of contentment, and others of frustration. No matter the emotion, that was the expression that was permanently plastered on each person's face.

Silence infected the mountain like a poisonous plague. Not only was Cail unable to see color, he was unable to hear anything around him. There was no clamoring of the civilians, no opening and shutting of doors, no crunching of the dirt beneath thousands of feet. It was dizzying and terrifying to feel the pressure of stillness. Cail felt as though his skull was being squeezed. Until he heard the reverberations of his own footsteps, Cail thought he was deaf. As he walked through the city, Cail occasionally stomped his feet and clapped his hand in an attempt to create more of a commotion. In a strange way, noise had become a resource that Cail desperately depended upon. The slightest sounds massaged his ears, they gave him a breath of fresh air after drowning in a lake.

Cail expected to feel the cold, windy air of the mountainside when he left Darzomil, but he was sadly mistaken. There was no movement in the air, no scents of the trees, no moisture in the snow. No temperature could be felt; he didn't feel warm and he didn't feel cold. There was no temperature, no color, no life. Cail looked above his head, into the sky, searching for the sun, but it was nowhere to be found. An empty void hovered over the entire world; it reminded Cail of the ocean of clouds that had covered Aithnen for centuries, stripping the Domain of Fire of their light. Even though he had seen Aithnen during its cursed era, during its period of shadow, he still couldn't fathom how an entire nation could endure the lack of light for centuries on end.

"I need to do what I came here to do and leave this wretched world," Cail said to himself. As he progressed down the side of the mountain, his steps sunk into a thick layer of snow, but the bottom of his pants didn't feel cold or wet. Then, Cail stopped and scooped a small pile of snow into his palm. He could only feel its weight. Normally, the snow on Silman's mountains would be too cold to hold in a bare hand for more than a few seconds, but it didn't faze Cail. He didn't feel anything. "What kind of world has no color, no sound, and no feelings? Who would wish to come to this cruel remnant of reality?"

Cail dropped the snow and continued down the side of the mountain. He tried feeling the rough edges of tree bark, but they were dull, he tried rustling branches that were riddled with leaves, but they were silent, he tried snapping a twig with his hands, but there was no crack, there was nothing. The world surrounding Cail was void of anything that was sensory, it was void of life.

Other than the lack of sensations, the Shadow was an exact reflection of the world Cail had grown to know. Cail stood on the western edge of Silman and saw Elona in the distance. He wondered what he would find if he traveled there. Would everyone there be frozen in time as well? Would there even be anyone at all? Would the feeling of serenity come back to him? The questions to all those answers would need to wait for a later time, a time when Malgor's threat no longer loomed over the rest of the world.

Cail closed his eyes and honed his mind on the matter at hand. After a silent moment of concentration, he felt his feet leave the ground and his body hovered over the drab grass. Then, as effortlessly as Cail had snapped the dry twigs in his hands, Cail shot his body through the air and descended toward Aithnen. To his extreme displeasure, Cail couldn't feel any wind brushing against his skin, not even a faint whisper of air. Even as he fell toward the Domain of Fire, he couldn't wrap his mind around the fact that nearly all sensations and feelings were banished from the Shadow. It was unsettling; Cail felt as though everything around him was nothing more than an illusion. He could see all of Neptil, all the islands were exactly as they had been, all the landscapes and terrains were exactly as he had remembered, but he couldn't experience any part of the world.

Just as Claeg promised, the Hidden King was sitting upon the front steps of Taurim's castle. When he saw Cail land at the bottom of the steps, Claeg stood up and said, "You've mastered the ability to fly?"

"Yes," Cail answered. "Serafine tried to hide the Air Rune from me, but fate founds its way, I suppose."

"It has a tendency to do just that," Claeg said with a grin.

"Claeg, there's something I must know. How did this world come to be? I'm haunted by the lack of sensation. I feel as though I'm already dead."

"That's exactly why very few living people come to this world. The Shadow's conception is a sad story, a tragedy. The story dates to the very first generations of Aithnenians, millennia before you or I were born. In those days, there were no kings and thus, no kingdoms. Tiny villages were spotted throughout the land, with no true authority to tell them what to do. For years, the settlers within each village kept to themselves and enjoyed the company of their own, but legend tells of one village that gave birth to darkness.

"Ilosa was the name of this village and it housed a man who was a master of peace. No one who's alive today knows the name of this man, but his reputation was much more important than his title. He was a strong tutor to more troubled minds, offering his irrefutable wisdom to those who sought it out. Word of his guidance traveled around the nation and soon, families were venturing across Aithnen to ask him to take in afflicted minds. The man agreed and as more people flocked to him, the larger the village of Ilosa grew to be.

"Over time, the man's wisdom and guidance morphed into a dogmatic system of schooling. He expanded his home so he could offer refuge to those who needed it the most. While his acts were gracious and done out of charity, they backfired on him in the worst possible way. He had a very young student by the name of Lidal. Lidal was a troubled boy with an unfortunate childhood that forced him to go crawling to the teacher's doorsteps. All throughout Lidal's stay at the man's house, he was wreaking havoc on the other students. Lidal would start fights, bully and torment the other children, steal their meals and belongings. The teacher had an innate ability to soothe the mind of any person, but for a mysterious reason, Lidal was a challenge he was unprepared for.

"The teacher and the student butted heads, with each side unwilling to give way to the other. It grew blatantly obvious that their relationship wasn't healthy, but no one did anything to relieve the tension. Although, to be fair, no one knew to what extent their conflict would go, no one knew what Lidal was willing to do."

"What did he do?" Cail asked, intrigued by the story.

"He murdered his teacher. In the silence of the night, Lidal crept into the master's bedroom, wielding the sharpest butcher's knife he could find, and killed his teacher in cold blood. Using one hand to stab his victim and using the other hand to cover the teacher's mouth, no screams were heard that night. No one witnessed the gruesome killing, but once the body was discovered, everyone knew who had committed the crime."

"What happened to Lidal?" Cail interrupted.

"No one knows for certain, but many people suspect he was imprisoned somewhere hidden, a place that would keep him hidden from the light of life."

"The gods saw what happened to the teacher and sympathy fell upon their hearts because when they looked at him, they saw all the good and righteous acts he had done, they saw all the damaged lives he had repaired. It was unjust, in the eyes of the gods, to allow this treacherous act to strip such a paramount force of charity from the world. As a way of ensuring the longevity of the teacher's kindness, the gods created a world which was connected to the world you know and mirrored its every crack and crevice. The Shadow, as it was aptly named, served as a realm that would allow the restless spirits to continue to exert their influence on the world you know. At first, the Shadow was an exact replication of Neptil, having all the sensations and feelings you've come to experience, but over time, darker spirits invaded this hidden world. The Shadow, as you see it now, has fallen victim to a number of different forces of darkness, it's beyond saving."

Cail wanted to hold on to faith, just like he held onto his happy memories. He wanted to believe that there was hope and that the Shadow could be saved, but the painful truth was right in front of his eyes; the truth was that Cail could no longer lie to himself and wholeheartedly believe that everything he touched would be saved. He needed to accept that some things were beyond his control, and the Shadow was one of them.

"Why are you here?" Cail asked.

A perplexed expression fell onto Claeg's face, "I'm here to help you defeat Malgor, of course. I thought that was obvious."

"No. I meant why are you *here*, living in the Shadow?"

"Ah, I see. A fine question, indeed," Claeg said, seeing the intent of Cail's inquiry. "I'm here because my life has come to an end, and I must ensure that the same ending comes to King Alban, the corrupt king who killed me. Now, I have a better question: Why are you, Cailean, the Descendant of Kordon, here in the Shadow?"

"I've come to stop Serafine."

Chapter 26: Above the Mist

The castle's doors creaked as they slowly swung open. Malgor's fortress awaited Cail and Claeg. There was no sign that Serafine had arrived already, and, as far as Cail could tell, she didn't appear to be trailing behind. With all that in mind, the upcoming task was simple: Defeat Malgor's spirit, thus ending the threat of Serafine reigning supreme over the entire world.

"What should we expect to find in here?" Cail asked, hoping for guidance.

"Your guess is as good as mine. I've always steered clear of this accursed castle. Malgor isn't the only unspeakable demon who dwells here."

Part of Cail didn't want to take another step into the castle's corridor. He was tempted to turn around and head back to the temple beneath Darzomil, where he would wait for Serafine's arrival to the Shadow. It was much too late, though. Cail had made his decision, albeit by Claeg's aggressive suggestion, to pursue the more daunting challenge of destroying the evil at its source. The same silence that plagued Cail's venture to the castle was painted on the walls, floor, and ceiling of the corridor. None of their steps clapped against the solid marble beneath their feet, the flames on the mounted candles flickered, but there was no crack. Then, as though an avalanche began tumbling down the side of a mountain, a thunderous voice pounded against the corridor's walls.

"Intruders, turn back now." Cail looked all around, searching for the body to which the voice belonged, but he saw no one.

"Where are you hiding, Malgor?" Claeg yelled out.

"You're truly mistaken," the sonorous voice responded. "I'm not hiding. As a matter of fact, I'm all around you. Every brick in the walls, every chandelier hanging from the ceilings, every stainless window, they're all a part of me. I am the castle."

"We're intruders you can't scare away," Claeg shot back. "Your castle is large, but no larger than our courage. We will find you."

Cail and Claeg stood in silence for a moment, waiting for a response, but there was none. "What do we do now?" Cail asked, breaking their silence.

"There's nothing left to do other than find Malgor. We need to search every corner of this castle. You must promise me that no matter what happens, we must stick together. Malgor will undoubtedly try to tear us apart. On our own, we're vulnerable, but he can't defeat us if we remain unified."

"I promise," Cail responded. Claeg nodded and they started their venture into the depths of the castle.

At first, it was hard to believe that a dark entity could synonymously encapsulate a fortress like the castle, but as they delved deeper into its halls,

Cail started to feel it was true. No matter how quiet and empty each room was, he still felt as though he was being watched, he felt as though every time he turned around, he would find a monster standing behind him. They searched through dozens of bedrooms, along with every closet, but all they found was dusty sheets and forgotten antiques. The kitchen and dining room provided no clues either, only empty cupboards and pantries that offered no food or water to the pair of scavengers. Afterwards, they made their way to the main ballroom, which instantly brought dread upon Cail's heart. For reasons he couldn't explain, he felt certain that dark spirits were hovering around them like a frozen wind, but he couldn't see them. Cail didn't want to display any sign of fear or weakness to Claeg, so he started searching behind the tall drapes covering the windows.

After a moment of investigating the room, Claeg said, "We've searched the entire castle that's above ground. I think it's time to make our way to the dungeons." Claeg pointed to a wooden door that was beneath a spiral staircase.

"Claeg, wait," Cail said. He could no longer stop his fears from suffocating his mind. "Do you feel as though we're being watched? I can't see anyone else with us, but I feel as though someone is attached to my hip, someone who wants to hurt me. I can feel their cold breath trickling down my neck, I can feel their piercing glare cutting into my body like a knife."

"You can't let Malgor control your emotions," Claeg said, putting his hands on Cail's shoulders. "Remember, he wants to separate us, he wants to deter us from completing our objective. We must hone our minds and focus on our goal. The quicker we find Malgor, the quicker we can leave this accursed castle."

In the blink of an eye, the entire room went dark. Cail could see absolutely nothing in front of him and he nearly stumbled from the shock of losing sight of everything. Worst of all, he no longer felt Claeg's hands on his shoulders, in fact, he couldn't feel Claeg's presence at all. Panic and terror consumed Cail's mind and he started to hyperventilate. He didn't know where he was, what was happening, or what he could do to escape this encompassing darkness; he could only wait for it to pass. After an excruciatingly long moment, it did finally pass. Cail found himself in the ballroom once again and everything had returned to exactly as it had been, except for one thing: Claeg was gone. Cail frantically looked all around the vast ballroom, but the Hidden King was nowhere to be found. "Claeg!" Cail screamed, but there was no response. Cail yelled his name time and time again, but it was useless. Cail was all alone.

Cail was so ridden by fear, he collapsed onto the floor. He immediately regretted the decision to come to this castle. The forces of darkness and ghastly spirits seemed too powerful to overcome, the task seemed too tall. *If only I would've trusted my instincts and waited in the temple,* Cail thought to himself. *I would've defeated Serafine and Claeg would be safe.*

"Cail, rise out of your self-pity," a familiar voice said. Cail looked and saw Lydia standing over him. At first, he couldn't believe his eyes, but the deceased fortune teller stood before him, nonetheless.

"Lydia, what are you doing here?" Cail asked, bewildered.

"I've been searching for you, of course. Why else do you think I would come to this dreadful place?" Lydia responded matter-of-factly.

"You need to get out of here," Cail said, his voice still ridden with terror. "Malgor has already taken Claeg, and he will surely find me before much longer. You must leave while you still can."

"Snap out of your stupor, you fool!" Lydia shot back. Cail was so shocked by her outburst that he completely forgot about his consternation. "Nothing is going to happen to me because I'm not the one Malgor wants, you are. Why are you so frightened by the dark spirits that dwell within these walls? Aren't you the Last Descendant who braved the battle against Kalil's Seven Servants? Aren't you the same boy who stood victorious over your ancestor, Tarvaris? If you weren't too cowardly to conquer those feats, why are you so terrified now?"

Cail opened his mouth to argue with her, but he knew she was right. After crossing paths with the depravities he had faced in the past, there was nothing he couldn't confront. He only needed the courage to do so. "You're right, Lydia. I don't know why I became so petrified; I suppose I just lost control of my emotions in the heat of the moment."

"It happens to the best of us," Lydia said with a smile. Then she turned and pointed to the door leading to the dungeons. With a creak that sent a frigid chill down Cail's spine, the door slowly swung open. Nothing could be seen through the door; there was only the absence of light. "You must tread carefully, Cail. Malgor is waiting for you, anxiously anticipating that you'll fall prey to his trap."

"I can't do this alone, I need you to come with me," Cail said, subconsciously allowing his fear to creep into his head once again.

"We're all stronger than our minds care to admit," Lydia said, trying to reassure Cail. "You can conquer this ancient force of malice, but to do so, you mustn't allow him to beat you from within. Malgor will try, with all his might, to crawl into your mind and control your thoughts. You can't give in, Cail."

As much as Cail wanted to run away from the door, he found himself walking closer to it. The darkness grew larger and the light of the ballroom faded away. In a matter of seconds, he was completely encompassed by blinding darkness and the last source of light disappeared as the door slammed shut behind him. Cail wanted to turn around, beat on the door, and scream at the top of his lungs, begging for Lydia to open it, but he knew it would be no use. He had but one path to take, down into the dungeons.

Cail took his first step, but his sight, or lack thereof, betrayed him and he tripped over the edge of a step. His body tumbled down the stone staircase. Over and over again, his bones slammed against solid concrete, with each impact sending an agonizing wave of pain through his limbs. Cail abruptly halted at the bottom of the staircase and lied still. He clenched his fist, trying to endure the overpowering pain of his fall. The soreness slowly subsided and Cail pushed himself up to his feet, letting out a loud groan in the process.

The room around Cail was still engulfed in darkness, but a sliver of light could be seen through the cracks of a wooden door that was in front of him. It wasn't the dull, colorless light that was all too familiar in the Shadow, though. To Cail's pleasant surprise, this was not that light; he saw the light of a yellow fire. Not only did he see vibrant light, he also heard jubilant chatter that faintly echoed through the cracks of the door. Cail blasted through the door and found an entire dining hall, filled with a couple hundred exultant faces, enjoying their warm meals and pleasant company. Immediately, everyone looked at Cail and then either rose their glasses in recognition of Cail's arrival, or happily shouted his name. The warm welcome bewildered Cail; he couldn't believe what he was seeing. He had gone from a world void of color, sound, and life to a room that was more joyful than any he had ever remembered.

That was when he remembered this dining room, he remembered all the people contained within, he remembered the exact day that this festive occasion had taken place: the day he had been crowned the Lord of Elona. All the sights and sounds from that day rushed through his mind like a river, his emotions swirled in his head like the winds of a blizzard. Cail felt the pride and honor of carrying the torch for his family's name, a name with responsibilities and expectations that he would meet. He felt the anxiety of having the entire village focus on him, of having hundreds of eyes turn to him in search of leadership. Above all, he felt the uncertainty of a new era in his own life.

"Cail!" someone yelled from across the room. Cail's heart nearly skipped a beat when he saw it was Laney waving to him from the table that she and Kadir sat at. They both signaled their hands, inviting Cail to sit with them. After a moment of hesitation, Cail made his way across the dining hall and sat in between his two closest friends.

"Where in the world have you been?" Kadir asked once Cail had joined them. "If you don't get something to eat soon, all the good food will be gone!"

Cail remained speechless. He had no idea how he had gotten to where he was, he had no idea how it was possible to be next to his best friends, and, most importantly, he had no idea whether he was still sane.

"Hello? Cail?" Laney said, waving her hand right in front of Cail's face.

"I don't understand what's going on," Cail said softly.

"I'm sure that becoming the Lord of Elona is an intimidating change, but you're a strong person," Laney said, offering her confidence to Cail. "You'll adjust to your new responsibilities." Cail appreciated Laney's comforting sentiments, but he was still too baffled by his surroundings to say anything.

"I just wish we would've been on the stage with you," Kadir said.

Cail looked at Kadir with a glance of intrigue. He vividly remembered Laney and Kadir sitting on the stage with him and his father during the ceremony. "What did you say?" Cail asked.

"I just meant that since we're your closest friends, it would've been nice for us to be on the stage with you to show our support," Kadir responded, blissfully unaware of Cail's suspicions.

Although Kadir had no knowledge of his egregious error, his words had revealed the truth to Cail, they painted a clear picture. "This isn't real," Cail said with a hushed voice. Then Cail shot up from his chair and yelled, "Malgor! Reveal yourself! I don't know how you've extracted this memory from my mind, but I know this is nothing more than one of your tricks." Immediately, all the sounds and clamor of the dining hall fell silent, the warm, inviting aromas of the freshly cooked food dissipated, and the vibrant colors turned gray. Everyone who was engaged in thoughtful conversation froze within the blink of an eye.

"Your grueling battles against your enemies have worn you down, haven't they?" Malgor's voice echoed through the hall, "I can offer you an escape; it's right here, in the Shadow. This was one of the most peaceful times in your life. You lived a comfortable life with your friends and your father, you knew nothing of the Four Descendants, or of any of the evils in the world outside of Elona, you only knew the serenity of your home."

Malgor's words soothed Cail's mind. For the first time in years, he remembered how it felt to be lost in a life filled with bliss. He saw himself standing on the coast of Elona, with Emey standing right beside him, gazing at the vast ocean of clouds that stretched all the way to the horizon. There were no other islands, no other nations, no other paths to take. Elona was the entire world, and Cail felt perfectly content in knowing that. "How can you promise to take me back to my home?" Cail asked, intrigued by Malgor's offer.

"I can do many things, Cail, just about anything you could possibly dream of. Not only can I take you to your home, but I can also leave you in that state of happiness and joy for the rest of eternity. Your mind will be lost in that felicity for as long as you desire."

Cail's mind was in a constant battle against itself. He knew what was the right thing to do: continue to battle through his adversaries and cast aside all the shadows in the world. However, his body was growing weary of persevering on his own, and he truly was all alone. Cail didn't have Laney or Kadir, he didn't have his father, he didn't have Caldir, he didn't have Serafine, he didn't have anyone. Surely, Cail was convinced, there was a limit to what he could endure. He couldn't deny that the thought of giving up the fight was an alluring temptation. Cail felt as though there were broad, leather straps wrung around his chest, pulling him back toward an empty chasm of darkness. All he needed to do was lift his feet, allow the pressure to take him, forget the struggles he knew all too well.

As Cail was engulfed in the tossing and turning of his own thoughts, a black mist descended upon the floor of the diner. It slithered across the floor like a venomous viper. Inch by inch, the mist moved closer to Cail. Malgor had a firm grasp on Cail's mind, which paralyzed him, and soon, Malgor would have his body. Cail would be his faithful and unquestioning servant, dutifully obeying every one of Malgor's commands. Through Cail, Malgor would unleash an unstoppable force of malice. The black mist wrapped around Cail's ankles and slowly crept up his legs. Then, from beneath Malgor's dark voice, Cail heard the faint whispers of someone he knew, someone who had always offered a helping hand of guidance, someone Cail had not heard from in far too long: his father. Cecil's voice was desperately trying to break through the iron barriers that Malgor had built in Cail's mind. Even though Cail couldn't distinctly make out the words, just hearing his father's voice brought him closer to the light. Vitality poured into Cail's mind once again and broke down Malgor's walls.

Cail looked down at his feet and saw the black mist that was progressively consuming him, trying to claim his body. He instantly sprung into the air, freeing himself from the darkness that clung to him so tightly. While hovering in the air, Cail was appalled by what he saw beneath him. The diner was now an empty chamber; there were no more tables, no more chairs, no more people. Everything that Cail had felt, seen, and experienced in this room was a lie, it was nothing more than an illusion. Now, the entire floor was engulfed beneath a layer of black smog, threatening like a shark swimming in the ocean.

"How long will you hide in your cowardice, Malgor?" Cail yelled out, trying to find his hidden enemy. Responding promptly, the creak of a door flooded the entire chamber and Cail spun around to find a new opening through which he could fly.

"Through this door, you'll find the cave in which I dwell. Come face me, Cailean. Don't shy away from this final challenge."

Chapter 27: Facing the Demon

Cail was uncertain of what he would find in the depths of the castle. He followed a narrow staircase through a short opening in a stone wall, which he had to crawl through. The cave was riddled with boulders, creating a vast labyrinth of stone. Cail crept into the arena, where he would be locked into battle with his malicious foe. Silence was draped over the entire cave like a blanket covering a bed. Cail cautiously stepped on the jagged floor of the dungeon, wanting to remain hidden for as long as Malgor was. No sounds reverberated through the air except for the racing pounds of Cail's anxious heart. He moved as silently as a cool breeze, but he still felt as though he was being closely followed by a legion of shadows. Cail quickly spun around; nothing except still boulders stood behind him. Thoughts of paranoia and anxiety pulsated through his mind, beating in perfect harmony with his racing heart. Breaths grew shorter and his muscles compressed, tightening his body. Cail had become convinced that the outcome he feared the most was inevitable; Malgor would find him. In this moment of hopelessness, Lydia's words rang through Cail's head once more. "Don't let Malgor beat you from within," she had said to him. The fortune teller was right. Malgor's spirit wasn't inside Cail's mind any longer, but the fear of him was. Like a fisherman who casts a fish back into a lake, so too did Cail rid his own mind of Malgor's intimidation. The demon no longer possessed any power over Cail's thoughts.

Heavy breaths hissed from somewhere just beyond the boulders; Cail was close. It was only a matter of time before he would face the villain who was diligently trying to crawl into his mind. As Cail progressed, the breathing grew louder, like the chattering of an approaching crowd. After approaching a break in the wall of boulders, Cail knew that the beast awaited on the other side of the wall. Cail hid behind the last boulder, preparing his mind, trying to muster whatever amount of courage he could find. After a moment of pause, Cail placed his hand on the hilt of his sword and quietly unsheathed it.

Then he heard a voice that he knew all too well and it instantly brought dread into Cail's heart: Serafine's voice. "The Spirit of Malgor. It's finally mine."

Cail knew he had only seconds to spare before the entire world would be in grave danger. No matter what he decided to do, Cail needed to keep Serafine away from Malgor at all costs. He peeked his head around and saw Serafine standing in the middle of an arena filled with sand. Just in front of her was a black mound, rising no higher than her waist. She was blocking Cail's view, so he couldn't quite make out what the mound was made of. A window of opportunity laid just before him; Serafine had her back turned toward Cail and she didn't have a clue that he was standing right behind her. Cail wanted to find a way to stop her and spare her life, but the threat of Malgor's prowess loomed too largely. If she did manage to harness his spirit, or if he managed to take control of her, there was no telling what damage would be done. It wasn't in Cail's nature to aggressively take a life with no sign of mercy. He tried to imagine what it would be like, to have his life taken away without even seeing the one who had murdered him. *Would she have this same hesitation, though?* Cail thought to himself. The question didn't even need to present itself, for he already knew the answer. When it came to accomplishing her goal of attaining more power, it had become all too apparent that there was no one to which she would show mercy, no one who she would not cast aside. Then a strange thought sparked in Cail's mind, something he had never thought of until that point: Everything that Serafine had done since Cail first met her would never have happened if it wasn't for him. He was the one who had saved her when she was imprisoned in the Servant's Tower. If he wouldn't have found her, she would, in all likelihood, have been dead already and Mishal would be the Descendant of Aithnen once again.

While these thoughts pulsated through Cail's mind, precious seconds were ticking away. The time for action was quickly approaching and if Cail didn't make a choice soon, it would be made for him. With his sword at the ready, Cail sprinted as swiftly as he could toward Serafine. Cail expected Serafine to hear him approaching, to jump away from her attacker, but she did no such thing. She was trapped in a trance and her body remained frozen like a glacier. Before Cail could react, before he could fully comprehend what he was about to do, he saw the sword slide into her back. Serafine didn't scream or yell, she only let out a soft gasp, as though she knew exactly what had happened and she had accepted the finality of it. The blade stole the air from her lungs and drained her muscles of all her strength. Serafine's body fell limp and the sword remained in Cail's hand as Serafine fell to the ground, landing on her back.

"Cail," she said, looking at her killer. Even saying something as simple as his name was excruciatingly painful. Cail didn't say anything in response, he couldn't. Words were flooding through his mind, but his tongue was corked. Serafine said, "I'm sorry."

"After all you've done, after all the people you've hurt and planned to hurt, all you have to say is you're sorry?" Cail shot back, still fiercely bitter.

"I know," Serafine said. "I truly wasn't trying to harm all the lives that I did, it's just…. It's just—"

"It's just what?" Cail yelled, trying to get her explanation.

"It's just easy to lose control," Serafine answered. Each of her breaths grew shorter as her seconds were dripping away. "At first it was the little things. I took more money from my people, then I took their homes. Before I could come to my senses, I was here trying to consume this ancient evil."

"I don't believe you," Cail said, fuming with rage. For the first time, he saw through her lies in the moment she said them. He wasn't going to allow her to victimize herself. Even though the fatal wound through her back was dealt by Cail's sword, they were self-inflicted.

"It doesn't matter," Serafine said after a loud grunt of pain. "You've done your damage to me, which, I must admit, was a long time coming. Now, you must fend off Malgor's spirit. He's so hungry for freedom."

"How do I stop him?" Cail asked, but Serafine's eyes slowly slid shut. Cail yelled out again, "Serafine! How do I stop Malgor?" Serafine remained perfectly still as her final breath hissed from her mouth. Her life had passed away.

"Very well done, Cail. Delivering the killing strike is no simple matter," Malgor's voice resonated through the cave, although he couldn't see the demon. "Serafine was a traitor to you, although you could only see her as your friend. Surely, it must have been so difficult to stab your friend in the back, much like she did to you."

"Enough!" Cail yelled out in frustration. "Show yourself, Malgor!"

"Open your eyes, Cail. I'm just before you," Malgor responded with a sinister chuckle. Cail took a closer look at the black mound in front of him. It wasn't a mound after all; it was the body of a black dragon. A thick armor composed of reflective, black scales covered the dragon's body, ivory claws, each as sharp as Cail's sword, were firmly attached to its hands and feet, and black wings, which were nearly as long as the dragon's massive body, laid in resting position. The dragon appeared to be trapped in a deep sleep. Malgor's voice echoed once again. "Until you wish for my body to awaken, I'm completely harmless. Come closer and lay your hand on my scales."

Cail cautiously inched closer to the dragon, keeping his sword at the ready. Instead of placing his hand on the scales, he swung his sword with all the strength he could muster, but it panged off the dragon's armor. The sword shot out of Cail's hand and flew to the other side of the arena. Malgor's scales created an impenetrable barrier through which no weapon could pierce. After a moment of pause, Cail slowly shifted his hand closer to the dragon's back, terrified that at any moment, the beast could awaken and tear him apart with his claws and teeth. Cail's fingers touched the scales and they were warm, like a window that had spent an entire afternoon soaking in the sunlight. The warmth slithered from his fingertips into his hand and up his arm. Then Cail suddenly realized that he couldn't pull his arm away. He vigorously tugged on his arm with his free hand, but it was no use; a mysterious magic clung to Cail's skin. The dragon's warmth soothed Cail's anxiety and his fierce desire to remove contact from the scales dissipated. Cail felt a rush of energy and strength; not only in his arm, but in his entire body. He felt as though he possessed the brawn of a dozen men, the speed to outrun any foe, the wits to trick the wisest souls. Violent winds circled around Cail and Malgor, gusts that were faster than Cail had ever experienced before. His feet slowly lifted off the ground until he was hovering over a layer of sand that was swirling with the wind. Gradually, the gusts slowed to a halt and Cail's feet descended until he was standing on solid ground once again. The dragon's warmth rushed out of his body and his hand was free to remove from Malgor's scales. Cail didn't want to, though. The strength he had just possessed was beyond anything he had ever experienced before. As Cail returned to his former self, he felt somehow diminished, as though he had been robbed of his own vitality.

After Cail had removed his hand from the dragon's scales, the beast awoke. The dragon's black eyelids opened, revealing eyes as bright and yellow as the burning sun. As Malgor rose to his feet, the ground rumbled and shook. The dragon proudly towered over Cail, fully displaying all of his strength and prowess. The demon had been awakened.

"You've experienced the full strength I have to offer," Malgor said. His voice rumbled like thunder and his tongue cracked like lightning. "I can give it to you, all of my power, all of my prowess, all of the essence of my life. You crave it, don't you?"

"Yes," Cail said, the temptation had dragged him into a mindless trance. Then his consciousness tried to fight back. "I mean, no. No! Your massaging words won't work on me. I won't fall prey to your trap."

"There's no trap, Cail," the dragon said, slyly trying to convince Cail of what he said. "Look at Serafine. She was a traitor and a liar. Her punishment was a necessary form of justice. Do you honestly believe she's the only one of her kind? I can tell you, with absolute certainty, that the world is plagued with people just like her: liars, thieves, murderers. Neptil is a realm filled with darkness, Cail. With my help, you can bring swift righteousness to all the nations. You only need to submit yourself to me."

Malgor's promise was appeasing to Cail. Just in the course of the last couple of years, Cail had witnessed such foul evil: Kalil and his Seven Servants, the Blue Assassins, and now, Serafine. Though he wished not to admit it, he feared that he was barely scratching the surface of darkness. Like an ocean that rises from the floods of a hurricane, so too were forces of maliciousness rising from every corner of Neptil to challenge Cail's light, to challenge his hope. Cail's list of allies was growing no longer and he was quickly becoming outnumbered. Perhaps saying 'yes' to Malgor was the right thing to do, after all. The black dragon clearly knew more about the rest of the world than Cail did. Malgor knew where to find the darkest corners and the brightest fields. Harnessing the power of a dragon as powerful as Malgor would certainly help scare away those with evil in their hearts.

Cail was on the verge of accepting Malgor's offer until someone else popped into his mind, someone he had completely forgotten about. "If I'm going give myself to you, there's one question you must answer," Cail said after a moment of silence. "Where is Claeg?"

A crooked grin crept onto the dragon's face, revealing his blades of teeth. "I'm glad you asked, Cail. He's the first one you will force your justice upon, after all, he must answer for his crimes."

"Crimes?" Cail repeated. "What crimes?"

"His wicked crimes of lying and deceit, of course," Malgor answered. "He betrayed his king and the laws of his homeland, all in the name of acquiring more power. For that, Claeg must be severely punished."

"No, you're wrong!" Cail shot back. "Claeg was trying to overcome the corruption that had strangled the innocent lives of Aithnen for centuries. King Alban is the one who needs to pay."

"King Alban will answer to his lies when the moment comes, but Claeg is just as guilty as his king, is he not? Is the Hidden King not a liar as well?" Cail could think of no retort to Malgor's accusation. As much as he wanted to defend Claeg's actions, he couldn't. Malgor was right; Claeg did deceive many who had trusted him, he did abandon the laws of his own country, and he did attempt to overthrow his own king. The evidence slapped Cail in the face, and he wanted nothing more than to throw it all away, to pretend that Claeg had done nothing wrong. After Malgor saw that Cail had nothing more to say, the demon said, "The time has come for you to choose."

The dragon stomped his foot and the ground began to rumble. Just in front of Cail, the sand started to move upward, creating a small dome. Slowly, the sand rolled off the dome, revealing a head, Claeg's head. Somehow, Malgor had trapped Claeg beneath the sand arena, but managed to keep the Hidden King alive. Claeg's head continued to rise until the rest of his body ascended above the ground's surface. The Hidden King had a dirty, torn rag muffling his voice and his arms and legs were bound by chained links, which were tied to a tall, iron rod. Pity instantly fell upon Cail's heart as he saw a man who wore the exhaustion of torture; the dragon had undoubtedly dealt an unimaginable amount of pain and agony to him.

"Take your sword, Cail," Malgor commanded. Without resistance, Cail obeyed the orders and strode over to where his sword had landed, the sword that had failed to pierce through the dragon's armor. Cail wanted to force himself to stop, but he couldn't; he was a puppet and Malgor firmly held his strings. After Cail had returned to his original spot, Malgor said, "The time has come. Claeg must be punished in the same way Serafine was, he must pay for his lies, everyone must pay for their lies."

Without a will of his own, Cail's fingers gripped his sword more tightly, strangling the hilt. Claeg could see that Cail had lost all control over his own body and he started to scream, but only mumbles could be heard through the rag wrapped around his mouth. Cail felt as though a brutish hand was strangling every joint of his body, powerfully exerting its will upon him. Then the hands let go of him and Cail collapsed to the ground, exhausted from the fight for his own will. "What are you doing to me?" Cail asked between breaths.

"I'm showing the vulnerabilities you have without me. You're weak, Cail. I can twist and turn your body in any direction I want and there's absolutely nothing you can do to stop me. That is, unless, you accept my offer and smite the criminal who stands before you. If you do that, then you will possess the same advantage I have over you. Your enemies and deceivers will be bent like you are now."

Cail remained on his hands and knees with his head faced toward the ground, still trying to catch his breath. He could feel the towering dragon standing over him, watching his every move. As he remained humbled before this mighty beast, Cail feared that all hope was lost. He was trapped in the depths of the Shadow, far away from anyone who could help him. If Cail was going to overcome this final challenge, he would need to find the strength to do so from within. He lifted his head up slowly, and saw the chest of the dragon, holding firmly in place like an iron shield. Then Cail's sharp eyes caught something he couldn't have possibly seen from a distance: a scar, no wider than the blade he held in his own hand. For the first time, Cail could see clearly and his thoughts were untangled. The dragon was exactly where Cail needed him to be. Carelessness had led the beast astray.

"Do you think it's wise to stand here?" Cail asked with confidence. "To stand over me like the master of a puppet."

"That's all you'll ever be, Cail," the dragon growled. "You're nothing more than my little puppet."

"I'm about to cut the strings," Cail said. Then, in a movement so swift it was nearly invisible, Cail thrust the sword into the scar and it slid seamlessly through the dragon's chest as though the original wound had never fully healed. Malgor let out a deafening roar of pain. The dragon tried to pull away from the sword, but it was firmly lodged in the beast's chest. Black smog sprayed out of the wound, the same smog that had once tried to take Cail's body. The mist dissipated, though. It held no more power, no more prowess. The dragon cringed and crumbled beneath the excruciating torment dealt by Cail's blade. After several roars and cries of agony, the mighty beast collapsed to the ground, sending a cloud of sand into the air, and lied as still as the boulders that surrounded the arena. The spirit of Malgor was slain.

Not without a cost, though. Cail's muscles were strained and worn, like rubber that had been stretched too far for much too long. He dropped to his knees and allowed his body to fall limp. Even with his entire frame at complete rest, his muscles, bones, and limbs throbbed with ache and pain. He could feel his arms pulsating to the slowed beating of his heart, his legs starving for a day of rest. However, the largest toll was paid in his mind. Even though Cail had slain the menacing dragon, it had successfully slithered into his head and bent his thoughts. This was a wound for which Cail wasn't prepared, a new exhaustion that anchored his entire body, his will to keep fighting.

After a few quiet moments of resting in his soreness, Cail heard muffled yells. He had forgotten all about Claeg being trapped in chains. Cail quickly tugged his sword from the dragon's chest and slashed at Claeg's bonds, cleanly breaking the iron chains. Once free, Claeg quickly removed the rag from his mouth and threw it aside.

"For a second, I thought you had given in," Claeg said.

"I thought so as well," Cail said, wanting to forget the feeling of losing control of his own body. He looked toward the corpse of the dragon, laying lifelessly in the sand, and then to Serafine. Throughout his journey through Aithnen and the Shadow, he had faced some of the toughest challenges in his entire life and he was dealt wounds that would always leave their mark on him, but he had persevered. Cail rose above the cloud of darkness that engulfed him.

"You did it, Cail. The world is safe from Malgor's malice," Claeg said, putting a comforting hand on Cail's shoulder.

"Not yet," Cail said. The response planted an intrigued expression on Claeg's face. "King Alban still lives. As long as the breath of life still thrives in him, the world isn't safe. He must pay for what he's done. His corruption has survived for far too long."

Chapter 28: The Hidden King

Once Cail and Claeg had arrived at the foot of Silman's mountain in the Shadow, Cail said to Claeg, "Wait. There's something I must do first. I'll meet you in the temple." Claeg nodded and Cail flew to the east, toward Elona.

The village's houses and shops looked the same, but everything was silent and lifeless. Cail felt as though he had opened the casket of his own home. He couldn't stand the sight of it, of his home being stripped of its vitality. Though his heart was saddened by the listlessness of his home, he found refuge in knowing that the real Elona was safe and sound.

"Cail?" a voice asked, a voice that Cail immediately recognized.

"Mom!" Cail yelled as he spun around and saw his mother standing behind him with a perplexed look. Bliss instantly filled his heart. Ilona was as beautiful, if not more so, as Cail remembered. Glistening eyes soothed the burdens of a troubled heart with a gentle gaze, dark hair flowed down her head and onto her shoulders like a thin layer of water streaming over a boulder, her skin looked as pure as a cloud, seamless and without blemish.

"What are you doing here?" she asked.

"Aren't you happy to see me?" Cail responded.

"Of course I am, but it's not safe for you to be here," Ilona answered. "You need to leave, immediately."

"If it's so dangerous, then why are you here?" Cail asked.

"Until now, I didn't know. The gods commanded that I go to the Shadow and wait in Elona; that's all I was told. None of that is important, though. There are legions of dark spirits in this world, hostile spirits. I'm terrified for my own life."

"I've already killed Malgor, though. We're safe now."

"You think he's the worst of them? There are spirits much more foul and despicable than him." Ilona grabbed her son by the shoulders and tried to shake sense into his mind. "I promise I'll find you in the real world, but you must promise to leave right now!"

Cail obeyed his mother's commands and met Claeg in the temple beneath Darzomil, and, to Cail's surprise, Wallen was still in the temple, frozen in time. The pair stood before the statue of Loni, the lone bridge between Neptil and the Shadow.

"No one, save for Wallen, will have even noticed your disappearance, and yet, you saved every single life on the face of Neptil. Without you, the entire world would've been forced to bow before the union of Serafine and Malgor, but you have slain Aithnen's forces of evil. Once King Alban is removed from his throne, the Domain of Fire can begin to rebuild its foundation, a foundation of hope and peace."

"We better get started, then," Cail said with a confident grin that showed he had regained his strength and valor. He stepped forward toward the statue, but Claeg remained still. "Aren't you coming with me?"

"I'm sorry, Cail, but my place is here," Claeg said.

"What? Why?" Cail asked, perplexed.

Claeg let out a deep sigh, sadness was painted on his face. "You're about to do what I could not. I spent the entirety of my adult life trying to take down that foul leader, if you'd be generous enough to call him that. My identity completely revolved around my efforts to dismantle the pillars of his sovereignty, but, in the end, I failed."

"That still doesn't explain why you can't come with me now," Cail argued. "This is the opportunity you've waited for your entire life."

"But I'm not alive anymore, am I?" Claeg shot back. Cail was taken back by the sharpness of his words, the anger that was spewing from his mouth. "Every spirit that remains in the Shadow does so for a very specific reason. Malgor remained in the Shadow so he could rise again and unleash his terror upon the world. Like all the other spirits, I'm also here for an intended purpose: to guide you through the Shadow. I showed you all the lies and deceits of Serafine, I showed you the ancient horrors of Malgor, I led you to the malicious demon, and now, I've finally led you back to your home. Once you leave, I will destroy the bridge between our worlds and move on to my eternity."

"I see," Cail said. Those were the only words that came to mind. "I wish you could witness the salvation of Aithnen."

"As do I," Claeg responded. "However, I can rest in peace knowing that the fate of the Domain of Fire rests in your hands. You carry more influence than you can possibly imagine, Cail. The entire world had been locked in a solitary void for centuries, no, millennia, until you came along. You're a catalyst, Cail. As you expand your horizons, hopeful hearts will flock to you. Hope is contagious, after all. If someone simply catches the faintest scent of opportunity, it's only a matter of time before the entire world believes in it."

Cail didn't see the truth in what Claeg had said. Even though he had freed his own nation of Kordon and prevented a catastrophic evil from rising in Aithnen, he was still all alone with no one to lean on for guidance. He hoped Claeg was right, though. Cail wasn't sure how much more he could endure without any help.

"There was one thing Malgor said to me that I simply can't get out of my head," Cail said. "He asked if I truly thought Serafine was the only one of her kind, meaning that there are more people like her in the world. I can't help but wonder if that's true, if there truly are more people who are so hungry for power that they'd sacrifice the people closest to them to attain it? If that is the case, am I the catalyst, or are they?"

"Optimism and hope will always prevail over evil. Millennia have passed since there's been a force of light strong enough to stand up to the world's malevolence. As word of your deeds spread across the land, people will rally behind you and, one by one, the strongholds of darkness and evil will fall." Cail still remained skeptical, mostly because of his lingering feelings of loneliness, but Claeg's words of confidence and support lifted Cail's spirits.

"So, this truly is where we part ways?" Cail said, wishing it weren't so.

"I'm afraid it is," Claeg answered. Then he extended his hand, and Cail shook it.

"I couldn't have done this without you, Claeg," Cail said.

"And the world would be doomed without you," Claeg responded with a bright smile. "Now, you must return to the land of the living. There's still much for you to do. Leave the Shadow and never come back. The Hidden King commands it."

Cail removed his hand from Claeg's grasp and faced the statue. He closed his eyes and slowly inched his open palm toward Loni's proud chest. As soon as Cail felt the cold silver touch his hand, he opened eyes. Cail nearly wept tears of joy when he saw the assortment of colors in the shrine. He could see gold coins, gems of ruby, emerald, and sapphire, silver plaques and statues. At long last, he had escaped the bland lifelessness of the Shadow. Cail quickly dropped to his knees and scooped up a handful of gold coins. Instead of keeping the coins for himself, he threw them as hard as he could toward the wall of the temple. He was overjoyed when he heard the coins' jingle echo into his ears.

"What in Neptil do you think you're doing?" a voice said. It wasn't Claeg's voice, but Wallen's. Cail truly had returned to his home.

"Wallen! I did it, I truly did it!" Cail shouted with words of jubilation.

"What are you talking about?" Wallen asked, confused. "You were gone for no more than a couple seconds."

"Yes, I know. Believe me, Wallen, we have nothing more to worry about."

"And Serafine? What became of her?" Wallen asked.

"My hand was forced," Cail responded. "If there was a way I could've brought her back, I would've, but I was running out of time and options."

"Sad as that may be, the important thing is that the deed is done and we are all safe," Wallen said with a heavy heart. He was saddened by Serafine's corruption, by her mind's obsession with gaining power.

"We're almost safe," Cail said. "I need to return to Aithnen and take down King Alban. He's as treacherous as Serafine was and he will find another way to threaten the safety of the free world. Once he is out of power, the rest of the world will finally be safe again."

"Agreed, but you'll go nowhere until you've received your proper amount of rest. The battle against Serafine and Malgor will have surely taxed your body and strength."

"Aren't I still a wanted criminal, though?" Cail reminded Wallen.

"Ah, yes. We have Serafine to thank for that, unfortunately," Wallen said as he scratched his beard. "No matter, though. I should be able to pull plenty of strings for you to safely rest in the city."

Cail heard rhythmic creaks of a wooden chair. He opened his eyes and found himself laying in a wide bed. The room around Cail was tightly cramped. A small, wooden nightstand sat next to the bed, a thick, wooly rug, splattered with a large assortment of colors, rested beneath the bed's legs, and the creaking was coming from the rocking chair in which Wallen sat. He was far too overweight for that little of a chair, but Cail didn't want to show any sign of impudence. Cail sat upright on the comfortable mattress and was relieved to discover that all of his body's aches and pains had dissolved. He felt renewed.

"Surely, you remember my home, don't you?" Wallen said after he had given Cail a moment to come to his senses.

"Yes. I remember it very well," Cail answered after a deep yawn. "You gave me the first Air Rune, you helped me become who I am today."

"That's a very generous compliment," Wallen said with a chuckle. "However, I must confess, I was withholding another rune from you, Cail, a rune possessing powers that I felt you weren't ready for at the time."

"I think that was a wise choice," Cail admitted.

"Quite so. Regardless, a few months ago, I entrusted Serafine with the Air Rune so she could pass it on to you when the right time came. Of course, this was before I learned of her treachery and betrayal. She played me for a fool. I assume she never gave it to you?"

"No, she didn't, but it fell into my hands anyways," Cail said with a grin.

Wallen let out a deep sigh of relief. "Thank the heavens for that. I must ask, though. How did you come to find it?"

"Fate always has a way of finding its way in the end," Cail responded. "Mishal, the true Descendant of Aithnen, snatched the Air Rune from King Alban's grasp and passed it along to me when I found him."

"Wait just a minute. You mean to say that Serafine wasn't even one of the Four Descendants? She was an imposter?" Cail nodded his head in response and then continued to tell Wallen all that he had discovered. As Cail progressed through his recollections, Wallen's eyes widened and he occasionally shook his head in disbelief. After Cail had finished, Wallen said, "My word. Serafine's deceit truly did know no bounds. It appears she posed more of a threat to the world than any of us had realized. If it wasn't for you,

Cail, I believe Serafine's empire truly would've come to fruition. Stopping her plans saved the world."

"I'd have to agree, but there's still more to do. My return to the Domain of Fire is imminent. King Alban needs to be stripped of all his power and Mishal must resume as the Descendant of Aithnen."

"Before you go, there's one last thing I must ask you," Wallen said, placing his hand up to stop Cail from darting off. He paused for a second, thinking over his words, and then asked, "The Shadow, what was it like?"

The question hit Cail like a crashing wave; he was completely unprepared for it. At first, Cail was haunted by the lack of extremities in the world; there were no colors, no sounds, no scents, no tastes, nothing. Experiencing a numb world was a torment he could never have dreamt in his worst nightmares. It was unlike anything he had ever experienced and the Shadow left a hefty scar in his mind. Cail felt as though a dagger had pierced into his stomach and twisted his skin. No matter how long he allowed the wound to heal, every time it was touched, the pain would come back, burdening him like a ghost. Cail cast the agonizing memories out of his mind; he knew that if he didn't, the wounds would be slashed open once again. He said to Wallen, "No one needs to worry about the Shadow ever again. The portal to that wretched world has been decimated."

"You still didn't answer my question," Wallen said.

"That's all I'll say about the Shadow," Cail snapped back, adamant to forget the afflictions of his venture. Wallen was unsatisfied with Cail's stubbornness, but he respected Cail's wishes, nonetheless.

"What's your plan moving forward?" Wallen asked, changing the subject.

"Simplicity," Cail said with an arrogant grin. "I'm going to fly down to Aithnen, march into Kye's castle, and rip King Alban from his tainted throne."

"Are you sure you don't want to try something a little more… subtle? Alban does have an army of his own, you know." Cail pondered carefully over Wallen's suggestion. He hadn't considered that he would be outnumbered by thousands of armored soldiers.

"I should find Mishal. He'll know what to do," Cail said, having made his final decision. "I want to thank you, Wallen, for giving me the first Air Rune and for helping me find the Shadow. If it wasn't for you, I would probably still be locked in the dreadful cells of Darzomil."

"No thanks are necessary," Wallen said with a bright smile. "I'm simply happy to have had the opportunity to play a role in the dynamic fate of the world. Now, I believe my role is complete."

After a warm meal of freshly cooked soup that filled his starving belly, Cail left from Wallen's home and made his way through Darzomil. The sights and sounds of a living city nearly brought tears of joy to Cail's eyes. After being trapped in a world void of any feelings or senses, experiencing any source of life was a miracle in itself. At first, he was afraid that many people would still view him as the humbled criminal that Serafine had made him out to be, but, to his pleasant surprise, no one spoke a word to him. *Wallen must have a lot of pull in this town.* Cail thought silently as he observed the blissfully ignorant faces of all the people who walked past him.

He felt someone, who was walking much too close to Cail, bump into his sword, which was still in its sheath, attached to his belt. Cail's mind instantly jumped to the memory of him thrusting the blade into the heart of the black dragon. The demon's scar pricked his mind like a rose's thorn. He remembered the shape of it, the width of it; the scar had the same width as the blade of his sword. "No. It couldn't be," Cail said to himself, but he needed to know for sure. Weaving through the intricate streets of the city, Cail sprinted toward the jewelry he had visited, where the sword had been gifted to him.

Upon his arrival, the old woman wore a beaming smile as she saw who entered through her doors. "Young Cailean! You've returned once again. I've heard rumor that you were caught in an unfortunate misunderstanding."

"Ah, yes," Cail said, wanting to forget about the fiasco. "Thankfully, a friend was able to sort the situation out."

"It's good to have those, friends. You never know when you'll need to fall back on them, or when they'll need you to fall back on. Now, I suspect you didn't come here to speak of your friends. What can I help you with?"

Cail drew the sword from his belt and held it out, with his hand firmly wrapped around the hilt. "You told me that this sword had seen a terrible war between the Kordonians and Aithnenians. Did it ever kill anyone… of importance?" Cail asked, choosing his words wisely.

"I assume you mean to ask whether it killed any kings?" she asked, Cail nodded his head in response. "Yes. It pierced the life of one king, a malicious one at that."

"Malgor?" Cail asked, impudently interrupting the storekeeper.

"How do you know that name?" she asked.

"You wouldn't believe me if I told you," Cail responded.

"Try me," she shot back.

Cail let out a sigh, not wanting to relive the brutal memories, but decided that since she had gifted him with the sword in the first place, the least he could do is be forthright with her. "After Malgor was killed, his spirit endured in a hidden realm called the Shadow. He tried to revive himself and rise again, but this sword put a stop to that. I came here to find out if this was the same blade that had taken his life."

"Yes, it is," the woman said. Then she reached her hand out and gently took the sword from Cail's grasp. "It appears that this is a weapon of destiny. Coincidence can't explain the fact that this blade is solely responsible for the demise of one of the most malevolent forces in the history of the world. The sword I hold in my hands was crafted with the direct intention of protecting Neptil, which is why you must take it. This sword is your tool of protection."

Chapter 29: Uprising

Laney and Kadir remained in their cell in the dungeons of Kye's castle for what seemed like an eternity. Hunger railed their bodies, dehydration discolored their skin and dried their breaths. Laney no longer possessed the will to move, and Kadir seldom did. They both sat against the cold walls of stone, waiting for anyone to give them a sliver of nourishment.

"I don't know how much longer I can endure this," Laney said to Kadir. Her voice was hoarse from her scratchy throat.

"I know, but what are we supposed to do?" Kadir responded. Laney had no answer. "We're trapped behind iron bars, with no hope of escape, Serafine is on her way to unleash her fury upon the rest of the world, and there's no telling where Cail is right now. He could be dead for all we know."

"That's not true!" Serafine barked at Kadir. "Cail's still alive, I can feel it. He's too strong and valiant to be defeated so easily. We would've known by now." She firmly believed every word that came out of her mouth. Even though Kadir had surrendered the hope of finding a way out of their confinement, Laney would not. She clung to her faith in Cail.

A deep tremor echoed through the ceiling above them. Laney and Kadir looked at each other; they both had the same question in their minds. "What was that?" They sat in silence, anxiously listening for another sound. After an excruciatingly long moment, another tremor resonated above their heads, this one louder than the first. It sounded like a giant beast, much larger than Emey, was vigorously stomping its feet on the floor. The tremors pounded like the sonorous booms of a drum leading a legion of soldiers into battle. Every quake grew louder than the last until Laney and Kadir could feel the ground vibrating beneath their feet. Then a deafening blast sounded from above, this one so powerful that it rustled grains of dirt from the ceiling. For a split second, there was anchoring silence, but that quickly ended when the deafening roar of a crowd echoed throughout the Castle of Kye. Laney and Kadir said nothing to each other as they listened to the racket above them. The crowd repeated an indiscernible chant time and time again, chants of anger and aggression.

"The castle is under attack," Laney said, looking at Kadir.

"Attack?" Kadir repeated, bewildered. "Are you sure?"

His question was met with thousands of footsteps beating on the floor of the castle like a horde of wild beasts stampeding through the wilderness, the clangs of iron swords clashing against each other, and the yells, grunts, and screams of a vicious battle. The ceiling pounded time and time again, sending reverberations through the iron bars of the jail cells and down into the floor.

Then, on the other side of their bars, Laney saw a crack in the ceiling. With every pound, the crack expanded and slid across the ceiling like a deadly serpent. Realizing that she had only seconds to spare, Laney snatched Kadir by his arm and they darted into the far corner of their cell where they covered their heads and braced themselves for the imminent impact. The thunderous pounds continued, nearly in a sonorous rhythm, but Laney didn't dare to look up. Then a deafening crack exploded and the ear-piercing claps of falling rocks and boulders filled their ears. Laney screamed, terrified of being crushed beneath a wall of rubble and dust. The freefall only lasted for a few seconds, then the clamor of the battle resumed. Laney slowly lifted her head from her chest and was pleased to see that the dungeons weren't quite so dark, but then she saw something she couldn't believe. A massive boulder, nearly as tall as Laney, had rolled through the bars of their cell and stopped only a few paces away, creating an opportunity for escape. There was but one path to take, though. Boulders blocked off all the corridors leading away from their cell and their only option was to climb a ramp created by the rubble, ascending into the battle.

"Come on! We have to get out of here!" Laney said without hesitation.

"Are you crazy?" Kadir shot back, grabbing her by the arm. "We have no weapons and no means to defend ourselves. Imminent death awaits us at the top of that incline."

"And if we stay here, guards will come and ensure that we remain imprisoned. We've been begging, praying for an opportunity to leave, and this is it. You can stay if you want, but I'm leaving." Kadir cursed beneath his breath, knowing that there was nothing he could say to change Laney's stubborn mind. Laney led the way up the ramp; it was a steep climb. They used the jagged boulders as their stepping stones. Their feet slipped on the loose dirt, but they still managed to ascend through the hole in the ceiling. At the top of the ramp was the remains of a ballroom. The towering curtains were engulfed in flames, stone statues were fractured and thrown to the ground, the corpses of the King's soldiers were piled on the marble floor with rivers of crimson blood flowing from every body.

Laney heard the yells of the battle coming from the far end of the ballroom. A horde of several thousand men were trying to push through a single door, presumably to chase after the remainder of the King's army. She noticed something odd about these men, though. They weren't soldiers; they didn't wear iron armor and they didn't possess the sharpest blades. The men attacking the castle were commoners: family men, blacksmiths, merchants, tailors, men of all trades in the city. That's when Laney realized the truth: This wasn't just an attack on the castle, this was a rebellion, an uprising. Laney didn't know what the King had done to push the civilians to this outrage, all she knew was that there was no stopping them; they wouldn't rest until they had claimed the castle.

"They've come to conquer the crown," Laney whispered. Kadir remained silent. He was either terrified or amazed, Laney couldn't tell.

"Laney! Kadir!" a voice shouted from behind. They both spun around and saw Cail sprinting toward them. Laney's heart jumped; she wanted Cail to take her into his arms, she wanted to feel his warmth, but she knew this wasn't the time for that. It would have to wait. As Cail approached, he asked, "What in the name of Neptil are you two doing here?"

Laney's tongue froze and her mind was jumbled, so Kadir said, "To make a long story short, King Alban imprisoned us and we had a stroke of good fortune that allowed us to escape."

"The details of your story can wait. You both need to get out of here," Cail said with urgency. "The whole city has gone mad and the streets are filled with chaos. It's not safe for either of you here. I need you to flee to the east, where you'll find an ocean. Wait there and I'll find you when the dust has settled."

"Come with us, Cail. You must come with us!" Laney said, not wanting to depart from him again. "Like you said, the city's not safe."

"I'm sorry, Laney. I can't leave King Alban's fate to chance. He's far too dangerous. I must ensure that his era comes to an end today. Kadir, please keep her safe." With that, Cail darted off toward the battle. Laney took a step to chase after him, but Kadir held her back. She struggled against Kadir's strength for a moment, but realized it was no use. Cail was gone.

"Come on, Laney. If the city truly is a madhouse, we need to leave as quickly as we can." Though Laney didn't want to admit it, Kadir was right.

Outside the castle, Kye was unlike anything Laney or Kadir had ever witnessed. Entire blocks of the city were engulfed in flames, screams of terror and agony exploded through the air, and angry mobs marched through the streets. The city truly was as chaotic as Cail had said. Laney and Kadir sprinted through the streets as swiftly as they could, trying to pass by unnoticed. Fires heated the air, making sweat roll down their foreheads, shops were broken into and looted by those who were now living above the law, and helpless women and children cowered into their homes and dark alleys, praying to find refuge from the merciless violence. Laney could see the fear in the eyes of the innocent; they had no way to defend themselves, no place else to hide, their fate was sealed. She wanted to reach out to them and offer them a helping hand, offer them words of hope, but she didn't know what words would give them comfort. Laney could do nothing but shamefully look away.

Kadir didn't say a word during their entire venture through the city. He kept a straight face, not wanting to display any signs of weakness in front of Laney, but horror was in his eyes. Never before had he witnessed such atrocities as were prevalent around them in that moment. Seeing a city burn itself to the ground was beyond what he could bear. In that moment, there was only one thing he wanted to do: get out.

After they had escaped to the outer border of Kye, Laney turned around and looked at the chaotic city behind them. "Those poor people," she said with a soft voice. Her words were ridden with pity, feeling sorry for the innocent victims of this rebellion. "They have no hope of safety; they're trapped in a container of bedlam and havoc."

"Laney, we can't go back into Kye, there's nothing we can do for them. A rescue mission would be suicide," Kadir said, trying to convince Laney.

"Cail's still in the castle, though," Laney said with a worried tone of voice. "He'll come to us, won't he?"

Kadir could hear the anxiety in her words. Trying to soothe her mind, he said, "Of course. If Cail could singlehandedly take down Kalil and Tarvaris, there's nothing he can't handle. However, right now, we need to focus on traveling to the east. I'm anxious to see the ocean."

Laney agreed and they began their venture away from Kye. It didn't take long for them to realize that the farther they walked from the city, the less of a grip fear had on their minds. The air was cooler, the sun was brighter, and the grass was more radiant. They walked upon a dirt path that wove through emerald plains. This peaceful world was a far cry from the turmoil they had just escaped. An hour of silence passed as they continued their journey toward the ocean. Then Laney heard the gentle crashing of waves. It was the most soothing sound she had ever heard. A few minutes later, the ocean came into view. A gargantuan body of water rested on the horizon, a turquoise world of water.

"Wow," Laney said. At first, that was the only word that came to her mind. She had seen a lake before, but never a body of water that stretched from one edge of the horizon to the other. Laney felt tiny, as though she was nothing more than a grain of dirt and the ocean was the entire world. The size of this mammoth was beyond anything Laney could comprehend, and she didn't even know how far the ocean extended, she didn't know where it ended, if at all.

"Amazing, isn't it?" Kadir said, admiring the world that laid before him.

Laney took her first step onto the sandy beach and she nearly stumbled when her feet sunk into the ground. She quickly ripped her worn shoes off her feet and let her tired toes soak in the grains of sand. The beach healed her body and mind. Vitality was absorbed into Laney's body like water soaking into a plant's roots. She took another step toward the ocean, fully embracing the relaxation and comfort the beach offered to her. Laney stopped on the edge of wet sand and waited for the next wave to come crashing in. As the cold water gently slid onto her feet, she felt a strange sensation of her memories being suppressed. All the hunger from her empty stomach, all the thirst from her dried throat, all the aches and pains from her beaten bones, all of it drifted away like the wave receding back into the body of water. The ocean had taken all her troubles away, drowning them beneath its immensity.

"Cail needs to come here," Laney said softly, her mind still enveloped in the healing magic of the ocean. "He needs to step into the ocean."

"It's beautiful, I'll grant you, but the faster we can get out of Aithnen, the better. No ocean is worth the trouble that Aithnen has put us through."

"This ocean is," Laney asserted. "What I'm feeling now, it's unlike anything I've ever experienced before. You're right, ever since our arrival to Aithnen, we've endured so much harm and turmoil, but the ocean has taken it all away. I feel the same way as I did when I was a child and my mother assured me that she would never let harm fall upon me. I can feel her tight, warm arms around me once again. The ocean gives me that same comfort. It makes me feel like I'm back in my home, surrounded by the safety of Elona." In that moment, Laney missed Elona more than she ever had before. She felt as though a part of her life was missing, like she was incomplete.

Before walking back to the grass, Kadir said, "Once Cail does what he has to do, I'm sure it'll only be a matter of time before we're able to go home."

Cail wanted to be the first one to King Alban, to be the one to slay Aithnen's corrupt ruler, but he was too late; the rebellious mob beat him to it. His disappointment didn't linger for long, though. After word of the King's demise reached the streets, the entire city was in jubilation. The men who barged through the castle's doors returned to their families and delivered the good news: Kye was free. Cail did nothing except for stand in the middle of Kye's market, observing the passing faces. Cail saw a group of children playing in the middle of street, not having a care for what was happening around them, he saw a middle-aged man who took his wife into his arms, affectionately comforting his emotion-ridden partner, and he saw two brothers, not much older than Cail, talking and laughing with each other. No one talked to Cail, or even acknowledged him, but no one needed to; he was perfectly content with seeing hope contaminate the entire city. Happiness spread throughout the streets like an aroma, tightly clinging to every person it touched.

A part of Cail's mind still felt uneasy, though. It was a small thought, but also a nagging one. He played all the recent events through his mind, all the way from when he and Serafine had left Cestmir to travel to Aithnen. After all that had happened, after all he had endured, after all he had accomplished, he still felt as though there was something he was missing, something blatantly obvious that was staring him in the face, or standing right behind him.

"Cail!" a voice called out from behind. Cail spun around and saw Mishal standing just a few paces away from him with the brightest smile Cail had ever seen. Mishal still had the same black hair and pale skin, but the energy of life had been restored to his eyes and his step had a new bounce. "You did it! You truly did it! Serafine and her father no longer hold Aithnen by the neck, and it's all thanks to you!"

"I can't take all the credit," Cail said with a slight grin. "Granted, I defeated Serafine all on my own, but I had nothing to do with what you see around you."

"You mean you didn't lead the charge into the castle?" Mishal asked.

Cail shook his and said, "No. By the time I returned from the Shadow, the civilians had already broken down the castle's door and defeated their king. The death of King Alban came too swiftly for it to be dealt by my hands."

"Believe me, Cail, King Alban's death was anything but swift," Mishal insisted, undoubtedly referring to the fact that he had spent centuries imprisoned in the Buried Temple. Cail couldn't imagine what Mishal had to go through. He was a guardian chosen by the gods, and then he was reduced to rubble by someone who he protected with all his might. Surely, there was no treachery greater than that. "None of that matters now, though. You defeated Serafine, which has given the people of Aithnen the Descendant they deserve."

"I'm glad I could help," Cail said as he clapped his hand on Mishal's thick shoulder. Changing the subject, he asked, "What will become of the Domain of Fire? What's your next step?"

"To be perfectly honest, I haven't thought that far ahead yet. I've been fully enveloped in this nation's victory over evil," Mishal responded. Cail certainly understood what he meant. After Cail had defeated Kalil, there were no thoughts about the future; he only cared about living in the moment, experiencing every second of happiness he could cling to.

"Will you assume leadership over your people?" Cail asked.

"Only for a short while," Mishal answered, Cail was surprised by his response considering that he had just escaped from years of imprisonment. "As much as I would love to assume the responsibility of serving my people, someone with my... abilities can't be given too much power."

"A fair point," Cail admitted.

"With that being said, appointing another king would lead us down the same path from which we just left. Instead, I believe the next leader should come from the people who took this nation by storm. The civilians have reclaimed the power, and I fully intend to make sure they keep it." Mishal's suggestion was such a novice idea that Cail wished he would've thought of it. "What about you, Cail? What's the next adventure for the Descendant of Kordon?"

"Honestly, I would rather not have any adventures for a while. I'm happy I could guide Aithnen to an era of liberation, but it nearly claimed my life. My home is calling my name."

"Then that is where you must go," Mishal said, respecting Cail's wishes.

"However, first, I must make my way east, toward the sea."

Mishal shot a glance of disgust and disdain at the notion, as though Cail had just insulted his ancient ancestors. "What madness would drive you there?"

"My friends, who were also imprisoned by King Alban, managed to escape from the dungeons and they fled to the sea until I could find them. What's your quarrel with that place?"

"It's not with the sea, but with what lies beneath the water's surface. Ever since the dawn of time, Fontana has ruled all the seas of Neptil, hiding in their realm of waves. When the nations were young, there were no such things as enemies. If one nation fell into a period of struggle or suffering, then the others would come to their aid. The entire world was an unbreakable community. That is, until Lord Balavan assumed his reign over Fontana. Balavan came from a long line of lords who had ruled over the seas for millennia, ever since Fontana's beginning. The Fontanians adulate and revere their Lord; they believe the Lord of Fontana is a provider and leader who has no equal, and therefore, there is no one who can question his authority, even those who live outside of the seas.

"For reasons that are beyond my understanding, Lord Balavan resented all Aithnenians. He made no efforts to hide his hate for us, openly insulting and mocking our royalty. While King Alban grew increasingly agitated with Balavan's antics, Alban didn't see any signs of aggression from the Fontanians. However, he didn't anticipate what they would do to his son."

"His son?" Cail repeated. "King Alban had a son?"

"Yes. I'm not surprised that you didn't know. It was something that neither he, the Queen, nor Serafine ever talked about. The pain ran deep into their minds. Tragedies do that, you know. Our worst memories are the ones we cling to the longest; they're an adhesive that follows us against our will. I would give anything to forget about the centuries I spent being imprisoned in the Buried Temple, the torture and suffering my body had to endure, all the nights I spent wallowing in my pain, but I'm afraid that those nightmarish memories will be planted in my mind forever. Surely, you have a moment you would love to forget, but see it play it through your mind time and time again, don't you?"

A moment exploded into Cail's mind. It wasn't the grueling battle against Kalil, it wasn't his days of imprisonment by the hands of the Blue Assassins, it wasn't any of the lies Serafine had thrown in his face, and it wasn't his trek through the merciless wilderness of Aithnen. No, none of those moments could eclipse the nightmare that recited itself over and over in his mind. Cail saw the empty void of the Shadow. He vividly remembered the absence of vibrancy, he remembered the blandness of the world around him. It was something he simply could not forget. Without a sense of individuality, the Shadow seemed empty. Cail also remembered the silence that filled the air; it still pricked his ears. No matter how hard he stomped his feet, no matter what he hit, there was no noise. Why did he care so much about the noise, though? Perhaps it was because noise is a sign that someone is interacting with the world around them. It showed that the world was reacting to what Cail did and thus, the objects and beings around him were acknowledging his presence. In that moment, Cail realized that that was what truly frightened him about the Shadow. It didn't just take away all the colors of life, and it didn't just take away all the sounds, it also stole your existence.

"Yes, I know exactly what you mean," Cail responded, not wanting to say anything more about his past nightmare's.

Continuing on, Mishal said, "So, the King never spoke of his son, understandably so. I resent King Alban for what he did to me, but I pity his son, Arsim. The boy had a kind and innocent soul, not wanting to hurt anyone at all. I wonder what kind of man he would've grown into, with his father and sister turning into the monsters they were. Would Arsim have fallen into that trend, or would he have rebelled against his corrupt family and defiantly stood up for what's right? I suppose we'll never know. Anyways, the boy didn't deserve the cruel treatment he was dealt.

"Now, I don't know what grudge Balavan held against Alban, but our King didn't take Fontana's threat very seriously. You see, the Aithnenians are blessed with prolonged life, and the Fontanians live a life that's no longer than any of the other races of Neptil. Alban saw this as a clear advantage since the life of a Fontanian is nothing but a blink of the eye to Aithnenians. In King Alban's mind, Lord Balavan would live a short life and then a new Lord would rise, a new leader who wouldn't audaciously insult the other nations of Neptil."

"King Alban truly believed that foolishness?" Cail asked incredulously.

"Wishful thinking, I suppose," Mishal chuckled. "When we wish for deceit to pass to truth, all that's needed is for us to tell ourselves the lie over and over again. Eventually, our foolish minds will believe anything we want it to.

"Getting back to the story, rumors were circulating around Kye of strange disappearances near the ocean. There was no pattern to the stories; men, women, and children were vanishing with no sign of where they went. King Alban suspected that the Fontanians were at the heart of these disappearances, but he needed to be certain. One day, the King led some of his finest soldiers to the east to investigate the beaches. Alban's company was followed, though. Arsim had a very curious mind for being as young as he was, so he couldn't help but follow his father to the ocean. Little did young Arsim know, he was walking right into Balavan's trap. King Alban and his soldiers searched through the sand, but found nothing except footprints of previous visitors. While they were distracted, Lord Balavan took advantage of his golden opportunity. Arsim either heard or saw something in the ocean and became entranced by it. In a hypnotic state, the young boy mindlessly started to walk into the water, hopelessly unaware of the imminent danger that awaited him. King Alban didn't see his son until the last possible second, when the boy's head descended beneath the ocean's waves. In distraught, the King sprinted into the water, desperately chasing after his only true heir, but it was no use; the son of the city of Kye was lost to the accursed sea. Lord Balavan had won the battle.

"Arsim held a promising future of a charming prince, but all that was swept away by Balavan's atrocious act. For years, King Alban stewed in his anger and hatred of the Fontanians. A fierce campaign against the nation of Fontana was ignited and it didn't take long for the entire nation of Aithnen to loathe the Domain of Water. King Alban vowed to himself, and to all his civilians, that the unforgivable sins of the Fontanians wouldn't go unpunished and that Lord Balavan would pay for what he did, but that promise was never fulfilled."

"Why not?" Cail asked. After all King Alban and Serafine did to him to try to end his life, he didn't think he could possibly feel pity for them, but he did. The story truly was a horrible tragedy.

"There's no possible way King Alban could've fulfilled his promise, not without fooling Lord Balavan into leaving the sea and stepping onto Aithnen's land, which would've been nigh impossible in itself. For good reason, the Fontanians view themselves as the superior race of the world. They're brilliant strategists and ruthless warriors. If they have a weakness, I don't know of it."

"Why would he need to summon Lord Balavan out of the ocean? Why couldn't he just go to Fontana instead?"

"Because no one has *gone* there, Cail," Mishal responded, unable to believe that Cail was this ignorant about Fontana. "The only ones who know where Fontana is are the ones who have lived there their entire lives. All we know is that Fontana is hidden somewhere in the ocean."

"I don't understand," Cail said. The story didn't fit together. He felt as though he was missing the heart of the puzzle. "Why would Lord Balavan do such a horrible thing? What grudge does he hold against King Alban?"

"It's hard to say," Mishal responded. "For reasons I'll never understand, King Alban didn't trust me with inside knowledge of any of his relationships. If he did do something to upset Lord Balavan, it was hidden from my view. Obviously, I don't care about King Alban's broken heart, not after what he did to me, but I was truly saddened for Arsim. The boy was an innocent soul who had never hurt anyone in his entire life. For the Fontanians to take a child away from his nation, his home, and his family, that's simply unspeakable."

"Normally, I would say you're right, but I can't see any difference between me and Balavan; he killed Arsim and I killed Serafine."

"That's completely different," Mishal argued. "Serafine betrayed you and threatened the innocent lives of the entire world, she was even willing to sacrifice her own people for the sake of acquiring power. You did what was needed; you slaughtered the demon."

Cail reminisced on the first time he ever met Serafine, when he had saved her from the suffocating grasp of Kalil's Servants. It seemed an eternity ago and so much had changed since that moment. He wondered about all the events that had transpired, what had morphed Serafine into the malicious foe that she was, what Cail could've done to avoid this fiasco. Part of him wished that he never would've found her in the tower, he wished she would've been left to suffer at the hands of Kalil's Servants. That was when a thought illuminated his mind like an explosion in the dead of the night. He thought of the fact that Serafine had stripped Mishal of his powers granted to him by the gods; this fact shined a new light on who Serafine was. Cail realized that Serafine had been a treacherous threat the entire time he knew her. Serafine didn't change who she was, she just ran out of ways to hide it.

"Do you think Arsim still lives?" Cail asked.

"I suppose it's not outside the realm of possibility," Mishal responded. "Arsim was just a young boy when he was abducted and he certainly *could* be alive. However, a better question is whether the Fontanians saw it necessary to keep him alive?"

"If there's a chance that he's still alive, we need to rescue him," Cail said.

"And how do you propose we do that?" Mishal scoffed at Cail's determination. "First of all, we don't even know whether or not the young prince is still alive, and secondly, even if we did know that he lives, we would have no way of rescuing him. There isn't a single person in all of Neptil who knows how to find the Domain of the Seas."

"You've just escaped from centuries of imprisonment," Cail reminded Mishal, standing firm in his argument. "If there was sliver of a chance that you could be rescued, wouldn't you want that risk to be taken?"

"Yes, but there's no window of opportunity that rests before us," Mishal said, trying to convince Cail. "We both come from damaged nations, starved and parched by an era of totalitarianism. Instead of trying to right the tragedies of the past, let's focus on the future. Together, we can usher in a new era of peace and prosperity. People have suffered for far too long by the hands of selfishness. Will you be a part of the first alliance in centuries?" Mishal asked as he extended his hand toward Cail.

Without hesitation, Cail shook Mishal's hand with his. "Of course. You're right, Mishal. It's time to give our people ease of mind. War and corruption has plagued our beautiful nations for far too long. I'm happy to call you my ally."

Cail left the market and progressed eastward through Kye. The sights and sounds around him were those of a broken city. Houses were beaten and burned to the ground, windows were shattered to tiny shards and specks, and the streets were flooded with the blood and debris of the rebellious battle. The uprising had taken its toll on Kye. The people of the city told a different narrative, though. Despite their homes being torn apart and burned to ashes, he could see the optimism in their eyes. In that moment, Cail realized that hope truly was contagious. He forgot all about the darkness and negativity in the world. Kalil, the Blue Assassins, King Alban, Serafine, Malgor, none of them mattered when he saw the happiness of everyone around him. Cail realized he had been so wrapped up in the fears and worries of malice that he lost sight of the pure and beautiful aspects of life. It was easy to do, to become engulfed by darkness. Negativity and malevolence are like a river. When Cail was focused on the evil in the world, he was swimming with the current, easily flowing with the water. Turning his attention toward happiness and jubilance was the true challenge; it was the swim against the current. It consumed all his attention and demanded all his strength, but it was worth the fight, seeing all the smiling faces was definitely worth the fight.

Mishal was right, Cail realized. He needed to stop focusing on the horrors of the past. Cail felt pity for Arsim. A tragedy of that magnitude should never happen to a child, but there was nothing anyone could do to save his life. That story needed to remain in the past. Now, he needed to turn his attention to the present. Kordon was in the process of rebuilding from an era of decay, and it was time for Aithnen to begin their resurrection. If both of the nations could restore themselves to their fullest potentials, then an alliance could spell the end of all evil.

Chapter 30: Confessions by the Sea

A cool breeze swept off the ocean's surface and brushed against Laney's smooth skin. Hours had passed, but she remained in the sea, her feet submerged beneath the gentle waves. Though she knew their departure was inevitable, she wanted to keep the ocean with her. The salty air tickled her nostrils, the massaging waves soothed her weary muscles, and the playful wind flipped her hair this way and that. The ocean was a place she never wanted to leave, it was a place she wanted to call her home. Then there were whispers, faint whispers hissing from the deeper waters. There was only one voice, hoarse and quiet. Laney could feel it reaching out to her, guiding her into the water. The voice was reciting its words; perhaps a verse? No, it was singing to her.

> "Another step, another step,
> The water will hold your hand.
> Another step, another step,
> Guided by the sand."

The song was a merry tune, despite the raspy voice. Laney couldn't help but let out a soft giggle. She felt giddy, as though she had morphed into a small child and she had just been freely given a large bowl of vibrant, delicious candy. With every repetition of the song, the whispers grew louder until they were easily distinguishable. Laney slowly lifted her foot and stepped forward, her leg pushing against the momentum of the waves. She wanted to keep pressing forward, but a strong hand snatched her shoulder. Laney immediately halted and turned; the hand belonged to Cail, who was wearing an expression of concern on his face. "It's time to come out of the water," he said. Laney twisted her head back toward the ocean, toward the voice, but the whispers were gone. Everything was gone. The feelings of giddiness, the sensations of happiness, the connection to the ocean, all of it evaporated into the wind.

"I-I don't know what happened," Laney stuttered. "What vile sorcery lives in these waters?"

"A force that's not to be taken lightly. Let's make our way back to land," Cail said, offering a hand of guidance. Laney looked down at her feet, but she couldn't see them; she couldn't even see her legs. The water was all the way past her hips. Only seconds ago, or so it seemed, the ocean's waves barely covered the tops of her feet. Somehow, she had become hypnotized by the whispers; her mind was nothing more than a puppet on strings. Laney laid her hand in Cail's palm and she instantly felt his firm fingers tighten into a rooted grasp, much like a tree that clings to the grass. She felt safe once again; the warmth of Cail's skin comforted her troubled mind.

Once they reached the edge of the ocean, Cail stepped onto the dry beach, but Laney didn't. She felt an urge to remain in the water. The waves were hands and fingers clawing at her ankles, pulling her away from the land. For a moment, she remained still, as though she was a stone statue. Then, Cail looked into her eyes and said, "Laney, please. Won't you follow me?"

Laney paused for a moment longer. She couldn't hold on to the land, but she could grasp Cail's words. "Always," she said. Laney took her final step onto the beach and the water peeled off her skin like a leech. When Laney first walked into the ocean, she thought it was trying to help her, she thought it was trying to comfort and replenish her body. However, it wasn't until she removed herself from the water that she realized it was trying to claim her life. "Cail, please tell me. What was trying to lure me to my death?"

"It's something we're not going to discuss at this particular time," Cail said. He knew exactly what it was. The same force of enmity that took Arsim from King Alban was also trying to lure Laney away from Cail. Somehow, though Cail couldn't understand how, this mysterious entity already knew about Cail and his close connection with Laney. It couldn't be Lord Balavan, though. His life had surely passed by now. Perhaps it was the new Lord of Fontana? In the present, it was impossible to know for certain. Concerned about Laney's well-being, Cail asked, "Are you okay?"

"Yes, I'm fine," Laney answered. "My mind's just a little shaken. I honestly don't know what happened, Cail. One moment I was standing on the edge of the water, enjoying the tender waves that were brushing against my toes, and before I could blink, I was waist-deep in the ocean. It was as though you woke me from a forgotten dream."

"Everything will be okay," Cail said with a soft voice, trying to comfort Laney's mind. Emotions rushed through her head and she flung her body into Cail's arms. She wrapped her arms around Cail's torso as tightly as she could, nearly squeezing all the air out of Cail's lungs. The warmth of her embrace with Cail was the only thing that ran through her mind in that moment.

"Where's Kadir? Why didn't he stop me?" Laney asked.

"He's sitting in the grass," Cail said. He removed himself from Laney's suffocating hug and pointed in the opposite direction of the ocean. Just as Cail had said, Kadir was sitting in the plains, blissfully toying with emerald blades of grass. "You can't blame him for not protecting you and you can't blame yourself for falling prey to the ocean. The two of you didn't know of the threat that dwells here; I only learned about it just before I arrived. Aithnen has had a history of people disappearing on this beach."

"You've learned so much about this nation in such a short amount of time," Laney said.

"I haven't only learned, Laney, I've seen. My eyes have witnessed a lot of the turmoil in Aithnen. In a time long past, this was a very proud nation filled with elegant cities and honorable folk. However, evil dampened the spirits of all those who made life beautiful. Aithnen is wounded, much like Kordon was when Kalil was laid to waste. We've experienced what the Aithnenians are about to endure. If we offer them our guidance, they can walk down an easier road."

Laney snatched Cail's hands again and looked deep into his eyes. "Cail, it's time for you to come home. You're the Lord of Elona, the Descendant of Kordon, not the protector of the entire world. You did what needed to be done, you humbled a corrupt king and defeated his deceitful daughter. It's not fair to expect the fate of Aithnen to remain in your hands."

"Perhaps you're right," Cail admitted, bringing relief to Laney's ears. His entire body was sore and weary from his arduous venture. Starvation gnawed at his stomach and drowsiness continually clawed his eyes. Even though Aithnen was in a fragile state and the nation's future stood upon the edge of a knife, perhaps returning to Elona was the right thing to do. The thought of enjoying the warmth of his own bed seemed beyond the realm of possibilities, but it would soon become reality. "I wish you wouldn't have come here. You and Kadir could've died."

"I know. I'm sorry," Laney said, embarrassed by her brash decision.

"So, why did you?" Cail asked.

Laney froze. A part of her mind wanted to scream the truth; it wanted to pour out her feelings and emotions like a river. Fear snatched her tongue, though. There were millions of things to be afraid of. She was afraid of how Cail would view her after she told him the truth, she was afraid of the possibility of rejection, she was afraid of how their relationship would drastically change if Cail didn't share the same feelings Laney felt toward him. Another fear gripped her mind more tightly than all those, though. It was the fear of letting a golden opportunity slip through her fingers. There seemed to be no better time than the present to say what she had fiercely desired to say for years. Still, the words remained on the tip of her tongue.

"Kadir and I were worried about you," Laney said, trying to hide her disappointment toward her cowardice. "Once the ocean of clouds cleared, we saw an opportunity to try to help you, but we were in too far over our heads."

"Yes, you were," Cail said. Laney could tell he was suspicious of her. She looked down at her feet, not wanting Cail to see the truth. "You're acting very… strange. Are you sure you're okay?"

"Yes, Cail. I swear I'll be fine," Laney lied, wearing a masked smile.

"Well, in that case, we'd better be off," Cail said. Then he turned around and started his walk toward Kadir. Laney's mind raced and her breathing began to accelerate. The windows of opportunity were closing and there was no telling when they would open again. The current of the winds of change would come to a halt and she would be imprisoned in regret. If Cail took just a few more steps, her opportune moment would be lost forever.

"Cail, wait!" Laney blurted out. She truly didn't mean to; it was her heart making the decision for her. Cail slowly turned around and faced Laney once again, waiting for her to speak. As Laney approached Cail, she shakily said, "I do have something to say." The next words were, by far, the most difficult. Losing a tooth would've been less grueling and agonizing than confessing her true feelings, her feelings that had been kept a secret for so long. This confession was the only thought on her mind since she and Kadir left Elona; it was the primary motive for their departure. As she stood there, embarrassing herself with her inability to piece together a single strand of words, she continued to try to convince herself that the reward would be worth the risk, that it was perfectly safe to tell the truth.

"Yes?" Cail said, growing slightly impatient.

"I love you," Laney finally let out. A small tear trickled from her eye, thanks to the swelling gravity of her anxiety.

"I'm sorry?" Cail responded, unable to believe what he had heard.

"When I saw the clouds beneath Kordon dissipate, all I could think about was finding you. I knew I wouldn't survive on my own, so I asked Kadir to come with me. At first, he adamantly refused to leave Elona; he thought a rescue mission would be foolish, which, admittedly, it was. It didn't matter in my eyes, though. If there was a chance that I could save you from this nation's wickedness, I knew I had to take it. There was no choice to be made, not in my mind. Just a few moments ago, you asked why we came to Aithnen. Kadir came because he was trying to be a good friend and help me when I needed him the most. However, I came for an entirely different reason. My venture to Aithnen was centered around the fact that I love you."

Cail didn't say a word, he couldn't. His mind was frozen and his tongue was tied. With every silent second, Laney's anxiety swirled like a storm cloud. She had just poured her heart out to him and fully professed her feelings and he wouldn't utter a single word. Rejection seemed imminent at that point. Her heart sank like an anchor falling to the depths of the dark ocean. She wanted to profess her feelings to Cail all over again, praying that that would produce a different result.

Finally, Cail opened his mouth and asked, "You truly love me?" Laney nodded her head, unable to say anything else. Cail remained frozen in shock, as though his mind was torn by what to say, what to do.

"Aren't you going to say something?" Laney asked, on the verge of tears.

"No," Cail swiftly answered, then he took her hands into his and kissed her lips. The world was a thin cloud drifting in the wind. Warmth hovered around them, as though the sunlight of a summer morning was shining upon them. In that moment, they were in a nation that was riddled with pain, suffering, and grief, but that was nothing more than a forgotten memory. All that mattered was the touching of their lips, the unity of their minds, the creation of a memory that would last a lifetime. Cail had no idea how long the kiss had lasted; it could've been only a minute, or it could've been an eternity. He removed his lips from Laney's and they leaned toward one another, their foreheads meeting with a gentle touch. Everything was synchronized: their heartbeats, their thoughts, their emotions. Racing, thunderous drums were beating inside their chests, pounding to a frantic rhythm. The same thoughts were plastered in each of their minds: *This can't be real. Surely, this is a dream and I'm on the cusp of waking to bleak reality.* It was no dream, though. The moment they had both dreamed of for so long had finally come and they were fully alive in it.

"You've no idea how long I've waited for this moment," Laney said, fully immersed in the most beautiful and elegant moment she had ever experienced.

A blissful smile was on Cail's face, but it slowly faded. For a reason that was hidden from Laney's view, Cail was sad. "You fully and openly confessed your deepest secret to me, and now, I have a confession of my own: I'm a coward."

"You're nothing of the sort!" Laney interjected.

"Please, let me finish," Cail said and Laney nodded her head in agreement. He continued, saying, "After I defeated Kalil and Tarvaris, after you were forced into a state of unconsciousness, I brought you back to Elona, I carried you home. Every day, you slept in my house. I felt so powerless when I saw you lying motionless. There was nothing I could do to wake you up, nothing I could do to go back to the battle and prevent the curse from falling upon you, nothing I could do to force my words through your ears. The only thing I could do was watch over you and count the days that had passed. Laney, I loved you long before you were afflicted by the curse, long before my adventure through the undiscovered islands of Kordon, long before I ever became the Last Descendant. All throughout our lives, I had opportunities spring up time and time again, chances to uncover the love I have for you, but instead, I clung to my cowardice. Until the day I left to investigate the Blue Assassins, I sat by your bedside every single day. For months, I was repeatedly given a bitter reminder of my inability to be forthright with you. It should've served as a valuable lesson. I had convinced myself that if the gods blessed me with a second chance at life, then I would immediately unsheathe my love like a stainless sword.

"The defining moment arrived in Cestmir. There was a choice for me to make: Either spill out the truth, or follow Serafine to Aithnen. Instead of allowing love to take control of the reins of my life, I chose to run. That's why I'm a coward, Laney. I avoided love, and it nearly cost my life."

Laney could see the weight of a heavy burden on Cail's mind. The feeling of guilt, whether justified or not, is enough to make the strongest and bravest of men to crumble before the faintest of foes. Undoubtedly, Cail was crumbling before Laney, but fortunately, she was no foe.

"Cail, you've faced challenges that most people wouldn't find in their worst nightmares. Calling yourself a coward is absolutely ludicrous," Laney said, affectionately hugging Cail in an attempt to push away his sadness. "Everyone has courage in a unique way. Your courage is one that can face the dark forces of malice that threaten our world, Kadir's courage allows him to go to the ends of the world for his friends, and my courage allows me to unabashedly offer my love to you. We all have different walls we can break through, and we also need to lean on others to break down sturdy barriers."

Cail couldn't hold off the happiness that was trying to flood into his heart once again. The girl that he had always dreamed of being with had risked her own life to travel to a foreign nation to find him, to tell him that she loved him. He realized that clinging to his sadness would only push her away. There was a closed door separating Cail from Laney, a door that only he had the key to. Laney was tapping on the door, trying to enter. A bronze key was resting in Cail's palm, motionless and heavy. Sadness and anxiety wrapped heavy chains around his wrists, constricting his movement. The chains tugged on his arms, anchoring his muscles. Every knock on the door grew fainter, telling Cail that he only had a limited amount of time to make his decision. He couldn't allow the chains to stand in the way of love any longer. Cail ripped the chains from his wrist and forcefully threw them to the ground; a loud clang echoed in his mind from the impact. His body was free and he inserted the key into the door's keyhole. Cail twisted the key and the door unlocked with a loud click. The door swung open and Laney entered his heart. Cail could feel the weight of his guilt lift off his shoulders and evaporate into the air, much like smoke ascending from a fire. He felt as though he could fly, and he didn't realize that he was.

"Cail! You're floating!" Laney exclaimed, amazed by Cail's new ability.

Cail looked down at his feet and saw that they were hovering inches above the sand. "It appears I am," Cail said with a soft chuckle. "I've yet to master control over my flying."

"Since when have you been able to do that?" Laney asked.

"To make a long story short, Serafine was hiding an Air Rune from me. It found its way into my hands, though."

Laney scowled at the sound of Serafine's name. "If I'd known what kind of demon that girl would turn into, I never would've let her anywhere near you."

"I know you wouldn't have," Cail said with a smile. "It truly is sad what she did, not just to me, but to everyone around her. She led me to believe she was one of the Four Descendants, she lured you, Kadir, and Mishal into wrongful imprisonment, and I'm certain she deceived countless others. There was no limit to what she was willing to do, no end to her deceit."

"There's no possibility of her survival, is there?" Laney asked.

"No," Cail assured her. "Her corpse will rot in a world far away from here. We're safe now, Laney."

"That's good," Laney said, forcing a faint smile. "I'm angry. Not at Serafine, but at myself. Serafine was just trying to acquire more power, but what was I doing? What were we doing? From the moment we met her, she lied through her teeth to us about who she was and what she wanted to do."

"There was nothing any of us could've done, Laney. Her tracks were covered very well. Even after I came to Aithnen and met her father, I still didn't see how intricate her web of lies was. At times, it seemed like she could control people's minds."

"Yes. I suppose that's what frightens me the most. If we couldn't see the most obvious fabrications, what else were we blind to? What else was Serafine hiding from our view?"

"It doesn't matter anymore," Cail said, wanting to move on from the subject. "Serafine is dead, Aithnen is safe, and now, it's time for us to go home."

Chapter 31: A Day of Rest

The journey back to Elona was an arduous one, at least it was until Emey found the trio traveling toward the Bodaway Volcano. Laney and Kadir rode on the falcon's back and Cail followed closely behind. Upon their arrival back to their island in the sky, the entire village was in an uproar. A massive crowd was harassing them, cramping their personal space, asking a broad assortment of questions about their venture. None of the three friends gave away any answers, though; they were far too exhausted. As soon as Cail walked through the door of his house, he saw his father sitting at the kitchen table, fiddling with a small contraption that he commonly used in the garden. Cail looked into his father's eyes and saw a million questions, but Cecil also looked into his son's eyes and saw the weariness of a soldier. Though they said nothing to each other, they understood one another. Cail would rest and then they would discuss the ramifications of what had happened since Cail left. Cail trudged through the kitchen, up the stairs, and into his bedroom where he finally collapsed onto his warm, inviting mattress. He surrendered to the immense gravity that was pulling on his eyelids and he drifted into sleep.

Cail didn't have a dream, he didn't have a nightmare, and he didn't have a vision; exhaustion lured his mind into an empty, black void. No thoughts stirred in his head, no conflicts awoke his anxiety. His mind rested and Cail was locked into a state of restoration. In the same way that a tree absorbs the spring's sunlight after a harsh, cruel winter, so too did Cail soak in his sleep, forgetting all about the pain and suffering he had endured. The extended period of rest remained uninterrupted through the rest of the day and into the night. Cail's body didn't move an inch, he didn't speak a word in his sleep. If it wasn't for the faint whispers of his own breath, one could have mistaken him for a corpse.

When Cail finally awoke, the next morning had come and he was greeted by a soothing aroma of potted flowers that were sitting on the sill of his window. At first, he remained perfectly still, lying flat on his back, fully embracing the opportunity he had to heal his body. The dangers of Aithnen had pursued him for such a long time that he couldn't remember the last time he had slowed the world around him to a halt. Cail closed his eyes again and focused on the breath in his lungs. He pushed it out and brought it back in, like a weight being tugged on a rope. The fresh air softened his chest and opened his throat.

Finally having the strength to move his body according to his own will, Cail sat upright on his bed and looked around the room. Only a couple of months had passed since his most recent venture began, but it seemed as though an eternity had passed since Cail had slept in the comfort of his own home. Cecil had left his son's bedroom untouched. Everything was exactly where Cail had left it. A pile of wrinkled, smelly clothes was thrown into the corner next to his closet, his father's hunting dagger, which Cecil gifted to his son, sat on his broad, oak dresser, and on Cail's nightstand sat the painting of Cail's family, when Cail was an infant and his mother hadn't yet passed from the land of the living. Cail took the framed painting into his hands and stared into his mother's eyes. Part of Cail's mind wanted to go back to the Shadow again to see her, but that was impossible now that Claeg had destroyed the only portal between the real world and the Shadow. Ilona promised her son that she would find him, although Cail had no way of knowing when that would happen.

After staring at the painting for several minutes, he returned it to its rightful place and then slid off the bed and onto his feet. Cail's knees buckled, but he caught his footing before tumbling to the ground. He looked toward the dresser and noticed something leaning against it that had never been in his bedroom before: his sword. The morning sunlight nearly blinded Cail when it reflected off the seamless blade. Cail wrapped his fingers around the hilt of the blade. The battle against Malgor instantly flashed through his mind, he saw the entire scene in the blink of an eye. Paralysis gripped his entire body, just as it had when Malgor was trying to manipulate Cail's movements. He dropped to his knees, crippled by the memories of his past horror. The recollections cramped his muscles and bit into his bones. Cail had fallen to the floor, with sweat rolling down his forehead, and the sword landed on the ground, right in front of Cail's face. The black scales, the crimson eyes, the ivory fangs; the entire nightmare was fully displayed in his mind. Cail slowly moved his right hand toward the hilt of the sword, his arm straining against his body's paralysis. Once he felt the cold iron, victory flashed in his mind; he saw the sword being thrust into Malgor's chest once again. Strength rushed through his body and he finally possessed enough vigor to push himself up to his feet. Deep breaths were needed to stop from passing out. Somehow, the petrifying fear of the Beast of Taurim had laid an egg in Cail's mind.

Cecil burst through Cail's door, wearing an expression of deep concern for his son. "Are you alright? It sounded like you ran straight into a brick wall."

"I'm fine, dad," Cail responded, trying to hide the pain he'd just endured. "I'm just recuperating from the journey."

"Well, why don't you come down to the kitchen and tell me about it? I've got a warm, fresh kettle of tea waiting on the stove."

"I'll be down in a minute," Cail said. Cecil nodded and headed out the bedroom door. Cail sat back down on his bed for a moment. He needed to meditate on something comforting, anything that would distract his mind from the Shadow. He knew that that fiendish world would leave a mark on his mind, but he had no idea he would continue to feel its reverberations. Cail did have a memory that could overcome that darkness, though. It was a memory that would never cease to bring happiness into his heart; it was the moment he had kissed Laney. The rest of the world had vanished and Laney's touch absorbed all of his thoughts. Her lips were as smooth as velvet, her hair brushed against his face like a gentle splash of water, and her skin was a seamless stream. Since their monumental moment of affection, they had not discussed it at all, mostly because they were accompanied by Kadir throughout the remainder of their venture back to Elona. Thinking about Laney restored Cail's vitality, so he proceeded down the stairs and into the kitchen.

"You took long enough!" Cecil said with a hearty chuckle.

"Sorry about that. I'm just so exhausted," Cail said as he poured himself a cup of tea. He sat down in the chair opposite his father and told him everything that had happened: being captured by the Blue Assassins, following Serafine to Kye, venturing into the hostile wilderness of Aithnen, and braving the Shadow where he laid waste to Serafine and Malgor, thus saving the world from an evil Empress. Cecil didn't speak throughout Cail's entire tale, he didn't even move his face or change expressions.

After Cail had concluded, Cecil rubbed his chin and said, "So, Serafine was just using you as a stepping stone and none of us had the wits to see it."

"She was adept at deception," Cail admitted.

"Being adept is one thing, Cail, but hiding the truth from everyone she encountered, that's an entirely different matter. Serafine was truly gifted in the art of lying. Her betrayal, had her plan come to fruition, would've blindsided the entire world. Not a single person questioned who she was or what her motives were. She was completely invisible to all of us, Cail. With that said, we're very fortunate you acted so promptly."

"I need to go," Cail said after taking his last sip of cooled tea. "There's something I need to talk to Laney about."

"You better get to it, then," Cecil said, smiling at his son.

Cail darted out the kitchen door and found an exuberant morning outside his home. He squatted down and brushed his fingers against the emerald blades of grass. Dew droplets spread onto his fingertips and he inhaled the revitalizing aroma of life. Only a few paces away, Cail saw a bed of flowers that his father had planted. The vibrant assortment pleased his eyes and Cail couldn't stop himself from walking over and smelling their soothing scent. Gently using his index finger and his thumb, he picked a flower with sapphire petals and placed it behind his ear, saving the flower until he could gift it to Laney. The moment he left his yard, villagers relentlessly approached him, asking him where he had gone, telling him they were happy to have him home, asking him whether he would be leaving soon. Cail tried to answer, but he was bombarded with questions so swiftly that he didn't have a chance to say a word. Once he arrived in Laney's front yard, he was finally left alone by the rest of the village. Cail walked up the short dirt path leading to her home and lifted his hand to knock on the door, but his arrival was anticipated. The wooden door swung open and Laney was standing in the doorway with a smile as bright as the sun.

"Elona's biggest celebrity comes knocking on my door," Laney said jokingly.

Cail took the sapphire flower from behind his ear and offered it to Laney. "I wanted to give this to you."

"I adore flowers!" Laney squealed as she snatched it from Cail's grasp. "It'll fit in perfectly with the others I have in my room. Won't you come?" Cail nodded and then he followed her up the stairs to her bedroom. He sat on the edge of Laney's mattress, which felt like a soft bed of leaves, while Laney placed her new flower into a glass vase filled with water and five other flowers, each a different color. Once she was satisfied with the positioning of all the flowers, she sat on her bed next to Cail.

"Did you get enough rest?" Cail asked.

"I slept like I never had before," Laney answered with a smile. Though she looked happy, Cail could see that something was still troubling her mind, something she was trying to hide from Cail's view.

"What's wrong, Laney?" Cail asked, partially wishing he hadn't.

She remained silent for another moment, blankly staring at her feet, then she said, "When I woke up this morning, I was thrilled beyond words to be home once again. Elona is our home, Cail; nothing will ever change that. Despite my appreciation of our return, I can't help but remember where we've just returned from. I can't forget the wretched dungeons Kadir and I were imprisoned in for weeks; we were both afraid that it would bring our demise."

"What did they do to you?"

"Nothing, and that's what was so agonizing. They didn't speak to us, they didn't look at us, they gave us absolutely no food and scarce amounts of water, just enough to keep us alive. It felt like we were ghosts, like we were no longer a part of the natural world. We might as well have been invisible. If you're wondering whether they beat and punished us, they didn't. Had they done so, I think it would've killed us."

"As long as we're together, your life will be threatened. I think we should keep our relationship a secret," Cail said, wanting to protect Laney's life.

She gasped, as though Cail had lied or insulted her. "How could you say that? We've cared about each other our entire lives and now that we've finally mustered up the courage to tell each other, you want to hide it?"

"Laney, I don't want us to hide it, but it's what we must do," Cail argued. "Surely, there will be others like Kalil and Serafine, others who will try to spread their darkness and acquire more power. Once the time comes for them to face me, they'll do everything they can to hurt me in any possible way. You're the one way they can bring me to my knees."

"And you think I don't know that?" Laney shot back. "As soon as you became the Last Descendant, I knew that my life would be at risk if I ever told you the truth, but that's a risk I'm willing to take. Love isn't meant to be hidden behind closed doors, Cail; it's a flower that can only blossom and flourish if it's exposed in the sunlight. If we hide the connection that we have, then years will fly by and regret will boil in our minds."

"You need to be keep safe, though," Cail pleaded, trying to convince Laney.

"And I will be because I have you to protect me," Laney said with a smile. She gently placed her smooth hand on Cail's arm, trying to comfort him. Cail didn't like the thought of her life being put at risk, especially considering all the times her life had been threatened already, but he did love her with all his heart. If she was willing lay down her life to be with Cail, he would simply have to do whatever it took to keep her safe. Laney removed her hand from Cail's arm and rested it on the side of his cheek. They stared into each other's eyes, just like they did when they kissed for the very first time. Cail slowly leaned his head toward Laney's. He could feel her warm breath pulsating in and out of her mouth, moving like the waves in the ocean. They were just inches apart when footsteps faintly clapped from the stairway; someone was approaching. Cail let out a sigh of disappointment and Laney returned to her original sitting position on the bed.

Kadir burst through the door and shouted, "There's the love birds!" Cail and Laney's eyes shot wide open, shocked by what Kadir had deduced. "Yes, I know the truth. Often times, eyes say much more than words. I could see the way you two were looking at each other during our journey back home."

Cail's cheeks turned as red as a rose from embarrassment. Laney said, "We're sorry for not telling you. We didn't want to make you feel awkward."

"That's alright. All hidden truths come to see the light of day eventually, don't they? Regardless, that's not why I'm here," Kadir said. Cail and Laney cast him a glance of intrigue. "Cail, you've been summoned."

"Summoned?" Cail repeated. "By who?"

"The Court of Elders," Kadir responded. "I don't know what they want, but I do know it must be important. The Elders usually keep to themselves and seldom do anything to draw the watchful eyes of the village."

"And if I decide not to go?" Cail asked.

"Why wouldn't you want to? All they want to do is talk to you," Kadir said.

"We've only just returned to Elona. I want to enjoy a day of rest."

"Cail, I think you should go and listen to what they have to say," Laney said, injecting herself into the conversation. "The Elders still have a lot of pull in this town. Ignoring the Court entirely could agitate them. Although none of them can hurt you physically, they can still influence the village's view of who you are and what you've done. You need to pick your battles wisely." Kadir nodded his head, agreeing with Laney's advice.

"Very well," Cail said after pondering over his thoughts for a moment. "Where am I supposed to meet them?"

"Under the shadow of the Ole Greene," Kadir answered, referring to the towering oak tree that stood in the center of the village. "Also, they told me that they want to speak with you and no one else. You're to go there alone."

Chapter 32: The Iron Fortress

"Come sit with us, Cail. Today is a lovely day," said an older gentleman, one of the five Elders. They were all sitting in a soft bed of grass, covered by the tree's shadow. A circle was formed by the Elders with one spot open for Cail to sit in. It truly was a beautiful day in Elona. A gentle breeze rustled the emerald blades of grass and whistled in Cail's ears, the sky was cloudless and blue, and the sun watched the entire island like a father standing over his child. Cail sat in the spot saved for him and completed the circle. He looked at all the Elders that sat next to him, some of whom he knew and some he didn't; there were three men and two women. The members of the Court of Elders were aptly named; all of them were old, much older than Cail's father. The man who had originally invited Cail to sit with them was a short, thin man with a bald head and he wore glasses with the thickest lenses Cail had ever seen. Cail had met him a few times previously, but couldn't remember his name. He was a pleasantly kind man who lived a solitary life in his home. After giving Cail a chance to settle into the circle, the man said with a wide smile, "To start things off, the Court of Elders would like to formally welcome you back to Elona. My name is Edgar and I'm the overseer of our esteemed company."

"Thank you. That's very kind," Cail responded with a matching smile. "I was gone for longer than I had anticipated, but I had unforeseen... complications arise. I've returned as quickly as I could."

"Yes. I spoke with your father a short while ago. He informed us of your adventure. It's unfortunate that such depravities spawned from Aithnen."

"That's true, but all is well now. The powers that Serafine stole from the Descendant of Aithnen have been restored to its rightful owner and the corrupt King of Kye was humbled by his own civilians." Edgar's smile slowly faded. He let out a quiet sigh and gently rubbed his forehead, as though he had a nagging headache. Cail noticed that the other four Elders were anxiously looking around at each other. Cail asked, "What's wrong?"

"While we're very happy to hear that order has been restored to the Domain of Fire, we've had some preliminary discussions and there's a major concern we feel must be addressed," Edgar answered. A couple of the Elders nodded in agreement with him. He continued, "In a matter of just a few weeks, the Blue Assassins, who hailed from Aithnen, assumed complete control over Cestmir and nearly killed you in the process, and Serafine, the heiress of the most powerful kingdom in Aithnen was well on her way to being responsible for one of the most terrorizing empires this world was has ever seen."

"I understand that," Cail replied. "We were able to overcome those obstacles, though. What's your point?"

"Our point is that Kordon is in a vulnerable state right now. Just about any hostile force can attack our islands and there's little to nothing we can do about it. The Elders have unanimously agreed that we need to take stronger actions to defend ourselves."

"That's a fair argument," Cail admitted. "We have plenty of time, though. Kordon is in an era of peace and the threats of Aithnen have been diminished."

"For how long, though?" Edgar retorted. "While it's true that the storm has settled in the Domain of Fire, we don't know how long we have until the next force of malevolence spawns and tries to conquer our land."

"So, what do you propose be done?" Cail asked.

Edgar remained silent for a moment, as though he was preparing himself for what he was about to say. The rest of the Elders resumed the anxious expressions on their faces. After a moment of silence, with a quiet voice, Edgar said, "We want to revive the Iron Fortress."

"What?" Cail shouted in disapproval, appalled by the very thought. "Ijsbrandur was Kalil's adopted home. For hundreds of years, that accursed island was the source of our nation's anguish. The fortress is plagued with evil."

"Cail, please. Listen to us. Kalil's actions were absolutely unforgivable, but he did leave us with a fortress that could be our salvation. It's nearly impenetrable. The Iron Fortress would be the perfect location to breed an army that's strong enough to protect our nation. Right now, the only army in Kordon is the Red Pumas, but they're too few in number to be reliably counted upon. The time has come for us to take the fate of our nation into our own hands."

As much as Cail hated to admit it, Edgar was right. If another attack was to come to Kordon's front doors, he wasn't confident that he could fight it off alone. Cail wanted to believe that Aithnen was no longer a threat to the rest of the world, he wanted to believe that the alliance between Aithnen and Kordon would be honored, he wanted to believe that Kordon was safe from harm, but that would mean placing a monumental amount of trust in Mishal, someone who Cail had met only days ago. There was no telling if, or when, Mishal would turn on Cail just like Serafine did. Placing trust in Aithnen simply wasn't a feasible solution at that point in time.

"Don't you think we should speak with Beda before deciding on something as important as this?" Cail asked.

"While you were gone, we took the liberty of doing that ourselves. She agreed with us. The Red Pumas will always fight to the bitter end for Kordon, she said, but their resources are limited. If we're to be successful in defending ourselves, then a new army must be born. We must bring the Iron Fortress back from the dead."

"So, I assume you want me to open the fortress's front doors?" Cail asked.

"Actually, we have something else in mind, something that can only be accomplished by you. Have you ever heard the tale of the Western Skies?" Cail shook his head. "It's an ancient story of Kordon. The legend has been passed down through the generations of this village's Elders, but we feel the time is right for you to learn it as well.

"As you already know, all the islands of Kordon were connected by giant wooden bridges that stretched across the skies. Today, Ijsbrandur is the farthest one can travel by foot, but according to this legend, there are islands far beyond that can be reached through the air. In the ancient days of Kordon's past, long before Kalil ever rose to power, the Western Skies was a territory in Kordon to the west of Ijsbrandur that was disconnected from our network of islands."

"The Western Skies; is that where Conrian is located?" Cail asked, referring to the Kingdom of Light.

"No. Conrian is far beyond the reach of those with the ability to fly. That's another story for a later time, though. The islands in the Western Skies were plentiful and abundant with riches and strength. Three of the islands in particular separated themselves from all the rest: Arion, Jurdia, and Xarax. All of these islands were home to vast cities that would easily put Cestmir to shame; they were all unique, though.

"Arion was an entire island of ruby. Everything was as red as the blood that runs through our veins. The city was as radiant as the sun. Arion was one of the earliest strongholds of Kordon. Some claimed that it was the very first city created by the gods. If you manage to find the Ruby City, respect is demanded. The civilians are a proud community who pay heed to all their ancient traditions, young and old. I imagine that they'll offer a slight amount of leniency to an outsider, but you'd do well to learn their acts of respect.

"Jurdia is a hidden gem, in every sense of the word. The surface of the island shows no signs of significance. A thick forest circles around the outskirts of the island and inside the wood there is a vast lake. In the center of the body of water, there's a small mass of land, not much larger than the circle we sit in, with an opening to a cave. This cave descends deep into the darkness and leads to the Sapphire City, which is aptly named. Jurdia is a dark city, but also a powerful one. Some of Neptil's fiercest warriors live within that cave, which is why it needs to be your first destination. If we could snag just a portion of their army to defend the Iron Fortress, then our region of Kordon would certainly be safe from all harm."

"I will make it my highest priority, then," Cail responded. "What about Xarax? What's significant about that city?"

"Ah, yes. The Steel City," Edgar said His eyes were glazed, as though he was envisioning a memory of the past. "I doubt we'll find much help from that island. The civilians are a reserved bunch, wanting to remain in an uninterrupted state of isolation. I'm sure there are plenty of capable soldiers who could help defend Ijsbrandur, but we'd be hard pressed to lure them our way. I believe Arion and Jurdia would be willing to aid us, though."

"That'd be great. I will always fight to protect our lands, but even with the powers blessed to me by the gods, I'm only one man and there's a limit to the dangers I can overcome."

"It's settled!" Edgar exclaimed, clapping his hands on his knees. "You better get to it then, Cail."

"Now?" Cail asked.

"Yes, now. At the moment, Kordon is a soldier who has been stripped of all his armor and weapons. We need protection, Cail. If we don't take the proper precautions, we will continue to leave ourselves suspect to hostile attackers. Malicious enemies like Kalil, Serafine, and Malgor will continue to come to our islands, hoping to take full advantage of a defenseless nation."

"That's true, Edgar, but I still feel that this is something that can wait until I've fully rested my body."

"We insist that you start on this mission right away!" Edgar said, growing agitated by Cail's lack of cooperation.

"I will argue with you no more," Cail said calmly. His mind was made and there was no changing it. "You have my word that I will see this mission to its completion, but I will do it in my own time. Until then, you'll simply have to wait." With that said, Cail rose to feet and left the circle, beginning a walk back to his home.

He was content to be back in Elona. In a way, it made him feel as though none of the bad things had ever happened to him; they faded like a foul odor being swept away by a gust of wind. That was how he knew he was exactly where he needed to be. Elona was a place that could constantly offer him a pair of comforting arms wrapped around his shoulders, like a father protecting his son. One good thing about Cail's adventures was that he was always reminded of how special Elona was when he returned. Laney, Kadir, and his father, Cecil, would always be there with him. In Elona, Cail was never alone.

About The Author

Clinton Mathew is a mathematician turned author. As a 2016 graduate of Purdue University, Clint focused his studies in the fields of Mathematics and Computer Science. Shortly after graduating from Purdue, Clint started the process of writing his first book, The Last Descendant: The Air Runes. Throughout his entire childhood, Clint had an affinity for the genres of Fantasy and Science Fiction. Some of his largest inspirations are The Lord of the Rings, Harry Potter, The Legend of Zelda, and Star Wars. Having lots of exposure to different forms of storytelling helped conceive a passion for writing in Clint's heart.

Clint's published works include The Last Descendant: The Air Runes and The Last Descendant: The Hidden King.

Clinton Mathew is a native of Van Wert, Ohio. Shortly after graduating from high school, he moved to Fort Wayne, Indiana to pursue his bachelor's degree. While living in Fort Wayne, Clint met his lovely wife, Lindsay, who he married on October 14th, 2017. The two reside in Fort Wayne to this day.

More short stories, poems, blog articles, and podcasts can be found on his website (link is listed below). To stay up to date on all his recent works, be sure to follow his social media accounts.

Website: www.cmathewbooks.net
Twitter & Instagram: @cmathewbooks

www.ingramcontent.com/pod-product-compliance
Lightning Source LLC
Chambersburg PA
CBHW072225170626
46813CB00003B/1100